THE AGE OF BLOOD AND MAGIC

THE AGE OF BLOOD AND MAGIC

HANNAH MATHEWSON

HARPER
Voyager

Harper*Voyager*
An imprint of
HarperCollins*Publishers* Ltd
1 London Bridge Street
London SE1 9GF

www.harpercollins.co.uk

HarperCollins*Publishers*
Macken House,
39/40 Mayor Street Upper,
Dublin 1, D01 C9W8
Ireland

First published by HarperCollins*Publishers* Ltd 2026
1

Designed by Nancy Singer

A catalogue record for this book is available from the British Library.

ISBN: 978-0-00-877894-1 (HB)
ISBN: 978-0-00-877895-8 (TPB)

Printed and bound in the UK using 100% renewable electricity by CPI Group (UK) Ltd

FSC
www.fsc.org
MIX
Paper | Supporting responsible forestry
FSC® C013604

For my siblings, Sam and Ellie.
This is a love story.

Dramatis Personae

VALENTINA MADDOCK, *an heiress*

CHARLOTTE MCNAMARA, *Valentina's friend*

OSCAR MADDOCK, *Valentina's father*

DR. CLAUDIA CABOT, *Mythos Head Magician and acting CEO. Valentina's mother.*

JUDE MADDOCK, *a socialite and art collector. Valentina's half brother.*

FRAN, *house manager at Fable*

MARIO, *head of security at Fable*

HUNTER CORCORAN, *Mythos Chief Financial Officer*

ROMAN ASTOR, *an arsonist and friend of Jude's*

ATHENA VAN THIEL, *an English aristocrat*

GRAHAM CRAIN, *Athena's fiancé*

ERIC BURTON-SHAW, *a pharmaceutical magnate*

NICOLA BURTON-SHAW, *Eric's second wife*

ZAZIE REYNOLDS, *a* Fuel *heiress*

MARIAH OF HOUSE GOTHENBURG, *a vampire*

RANDOLPH OF HOUSE GOTHENBURG, *a vampire*

LUCAS SAYLE, *a vampire*

Prologue

One hundred years ago, humanity mastered magic, but we were the ones who owned it.

The age of magic rose with a hazy dawn, summer fermenting into autumn, air sharp as champagne bubbles bursting on the tongue. Martin Maddock, an entrepreneur and outdoorsman, went into the woods with his five-year-old son, Fergus. Neither was seen again until the first frost, when the shape of the man tore from the tree line, alone.

The witch had his son.

And Martin had the secret to harnessing magic for human use.

He couldn't or wouldn't tell the police much else. In Rachel Maddock's interviews with the press—and later in her memoir—she recounted the search for her husband and son, then just her son, in calm language and exhaustive detail. The Maddocks had means, and Rachel had used them all. Manpower and dog power, eye-watering rewards and national media campaigns. Fergus was gone for a year before Rachel released her grip on the woods, her white-knuckled fingers pried one by one from the search by grieving family and resigned experts. No evidence could be found that the boy had ever stepped foot past the tree line, let alone met a witch there.

But it had happened, irrefutably, as five weeks after his reappearance, Martin patented his method for the human use of magic. Two months after that, he registered the company name Mythos. Somewhere between his divorce and his ex-wife's civil suit, Martin cast his first successful spell, and conjured into being an empire that would have compelled Caesar to kneel.

Like all empires, it had its dissenters. For the first decade, the fae folk and witches, goblins and djinn tried to take magic back. They clawed their way out of mountain streams and mossy groves, separated from shadows, appeared in mirrors and the backs of spoons by the dozens. They broke locks on warehouse doors, cursed contracts as they changed hands, sent shipments to the ocean floor, their efforts scattered and imprecise, their enemy not a man but human progress; progress fortified by the wills and wallets of investors from Philadelphia to Shanghai, by hunger. The locks were replaced, the contracts rewritten, the shipments rerouted—the money endless when the promised returns would raise a new breed of titan. The real magic was that a transatlantic telegraph could spread the news worldwide in twenty-four hours; that between one sunrise and the next, a man could forge a whole new world. No witch could do that, and so they lost.

But Martin would never lose again. Mythos launched its first line of spells the same year he welcomed the only child of his second marriage: my grandfather, Rufus Maddock. The magic worked through a user interface, named the *Moth* for the moonstone pendant worn by clients and the fluttering shadow within the stone. An object, to cage the otherworldly within something one could see and feel. In the seventies, it was redesigned as a wristwatch. Then later, an ethereal orb, roughly the size of a grapefruit, that hovered near the client's shoulder. Clean and aesthetic. Soothingly conquerable. If you could use a microwave oven, video cassette recorder, smartphone, or VR headset, then the Moth promised you could use magic.

And that was its only purpose: to make the frightening familiar. But by the time the products were entrenched, the interface was too. For why would anyone give up a visible marker that they had spent tens, sometimes hundreds, of thousands on power? That they commanded a force and enjoyed a luxury that gave money itself a new meaning? We made the Moth even prettier and put it in our logo.

We signed twelve-figure contracts to summon plastic from the oceans, others to keep planes in the air. We were granted unprecedented exemption from anti-trust laws; no other company was able to replicate Martin's results, and Mythos's impact was simply too valuable to temper with regulation.

We are the world's first trillionaires, and nobody has seen a witch in nearly eighty years.

Vampires, though. Humanity's new to exploiting vampires.

1

My father had been in a coma for nineteen hours when I arrived at Fable.

As I stepped out of the car, the sun-bright flare of the spell still fading from its bodywork, I thought about when travelling by magic was still kind of gauche. There were videos of my grandfather, Rufus, athletic and silver-haired, popping into being with a suitcase at his feet and a rabid audience of journalists bellowing for his attention. *Swift* was the most groundbreaking spell to come out of the company yet. But the society pages were more taken with the retired Martin Maddock's comment to a paparazzo as he left the opera the following night.

"He looked like a fucking hitchhiker," Martin said of his son.

And it was true. In one stroke, Grandpa both won a Nobel Prize and made travelling anywhere in the world in literally a split-second look cheap.

So now *Swift* wasn't Moth-managed; it was built into our cars, and all discretion was lost. Which was all well and good for Grandpa; he'd been a quiet, sedate man, with none of my flair for the dramatic, so he'd probably never decided he needed to stage an ambush.

Charlotte alighted from the SUV behind me. "Wow. I saw this place in *Architectural Digest* once, but I didn't realise it was so . . . gigantic."

I knew the article; I'd cut the photos out of the magazine and put them in my journal when I was nine, so I could look at them whenever I was homesick for the place I felt I most belonged. But the pictures didn't do it justice. In the mellow grey of an overcast dusk, birds playing their sleepy tunes from the surrounding forest, Fable looked like a slumbering giant. Ivy softened its sharp, unembellished edges, the flat roof, and the endless, uniform arches of the loggias that wrapped around both floors. Its vast rooms encircled a courtyard, then met another block just the same at one corner, which then met a third, like a figure eight with an extra bulb. The jagged waves of each wing were almost brutalist, the featureless grey marble of the entire structure even more so. Yet mottled as it was with ivy and surrounded on all sides by the forest, blue in the evening light, it hardly looked like a house at all. It looked ancient, geological, placed here not by machinery and magic but by the weather and the shaking of the earth.

On Friday night, forty of the world's wealthiest and most important people would arrive here and willingly be trapped for the duration of the weekend.

Light spilled from beneath the central arch as the door opened, revealing the silhouette of someone without a Moth. A lot of Mythos products worked like medicine or drugs: you took one, it worked, it wore off. Moths were used for permanent spells, the truly life-enhancing stuff—*Upskill* for skill enhancements; *Polish* for aesthetic ones; *Shield* to repel a bullet or a grabbing hand; others for magically enhanced acoustics, tastebuds, sleep. Access to those kinds of spells were profoundly exclusive and cost tens of thousands at a minimum. Meaning anyone at Fable without a Moth was staff.

As we got closer, someone's potent disapproval fogged up my awareness. An ice-blonde pixie cut caught the light. Fran, then. My father's live-in house manager.

"Valentina. We weren't expecting you." The words were almost lost under the crunch of gravel as we crossed the drive, but I could still detect the monotone she used whenever she spoke to me.

"No shit," Charlotte muttered.

A housekeeper hovered behind Fran in the entrance hall. She was young. I studied her as she took my coat, catching a flash of her sympathy for me. Fran hired these people to be anonymous, to flit through these rooms without needs or notice. I'd slipped one of them some cash and my phone number, told them to spy on Jude whenever he came by. I was only here because they'd done me one better and told me of my father's condition—but had it been this girl? I couldn't remember. I smiled at her, just in case, and turned to Fran.

"Where is he?"

Fran's sun-weathered face was a picture of serenity, a lid battened down tight over a cocktail of indignation and despair. Up close, I could tell she especially hated me today. *Empathy* allowed me to read only her feelings, not her thoughts, but I imagined she was thinking of her job, and Fable, and Jude. Of robbery and injustice. All of it needed a villain, and through my father's front door I had conveniently sauntered.

That was fine. I didn't like Fran either.

"They only released him from the hospital a few hours ago. We set him up in his bedroom." She gestured towards the stairs, the motion reminiscent of tai chi, her fingers pressed together. "I'll take you to him."

"No need," I said, ignoring her air of permission and sweeping past, Charlotte behind me. Of course Fran followed too. I could hear her oversized linen ensemble—grey today, like the stone of Fable—whispering as she walked.

Charlotte's hand found my back and pressed comfort into it. "Okay?" I only nodded. "Your dad's house is a bit much, isn't it?"

She was trying to keep it light, but I felt my mouth twist unpleasantly. It wasn't a *bit much,* actually. I suspected it intimidated her, this totem of my family, with its high, bare ceilings and too-wide corridors. It was as unlike a house inside as it was out. The size, the simplicity, the endless planes of unembellished stone gave the impression of a natural, if strangely quadrate, cavern someone had filled with curated modern lighting and art-as-furniture. But that was the wonder of it. No other house existed like Fable because no one except the Maddocks could use such staggering amounts of magic to carve one. *Logistically* they could—the construction spell *Edifice* was a thriving pillar of Mythos's business—but the wealth required to do so was obscene. And, anyway, it wouldn't be polite. This house represented who the Maddocks were, to scale. Magic belonged to no one if not to us, and the rest of the world enjoyed it at our discretion.

"I happen to love it," I responded.

"Oh." She put her hand on my arm and squeezed, then let me go.

The house staff were making up rooms for the weekend's guests, and a gentle chorus of linens and quiet feet emanated, always from unseen corners or adjacent halls, as if they were no more than negative space at the edges of my awareness.

We turned a final corner. A heavy gloom had descended over the east-facing corridor, dark falling faster here. A marigold arch of light burned across the marble floor, coming from my father's open bedroom door. I stopped. But there was already no turning back—my father's stroke had happened, and even the Maddocks couldn't change that. My throat tightened with a pressure close to bursting.

Before Charlotte could coax me to move, a shadow—softened at the edges by the glow of a Moth—appeared in the lit archway. A moment later, the slight figure of Claudia Cabot emerged into the corridor.

I pressed the tightness down. This was an ambush, and Mythos's Head Magician could not be allowed to see me emotional.

My own Moth cast its moon-tinged light as it hovered, motionless, above my right shoulder. Yet several seconds passed, my mother hugging her arms around herself and staring blankly out the window, before she turned and noticed us.

"Teeny," she said with a sigh. Though the collapse of her shoulders might have passed for regret, *Empathy* told me otherwise.

No one ought to know what their mother feels about them, how easy she is to please, how often you fail at it anyway. How you've branded her with every cross word and sullen silence. And the love—the way you anchored tethers to her bones with your existence, only to rattle and pull on them for the rest of her days.

All of which was an indignity to Claudia Cabot, who wasn't a mother until Oscar Maddock asked her to be. I knew because she had told me, and it was better for both of us if I didn't dwell on it.

What I felt from her now as I came down the corridor was a wall raised in defence.

"How could you?" I began.

She raised her hands as if to placate me and spoke in her usual quiet, edgeless tone, little more than a whisper. "I was about to call you this very second, actually."

"The only right time to call me was yesterday. Why didn't you?"

I knew, of course. My parents divorced before I was born, and if the winner had been decided, nobody had told my mother. I was her favourite battleground, every scrap of preference I showed a prize to be won. But she couldn't compete with a coma.

I also knew what she would say instead.

"Your big assignment. The deadline was today, wasn't it? I decided it could wait." I caught a pang of her anticipatory hurt, like an animal shrinking from an expected blow. "I'm sorry if that was wrong."

She didn't ask how I'd found out. She probably had spies among the Fable staff too.

"What if he'd died?" I braced to hear that I was being dramatic. Instead, her emotions turned pitying. As she took my hand, my stomach dropped. "It's—it's bad, isn't it?"

"It is, Teeny. I'm sorry."

I was still breathtakingly in denial at that point, so the apology didn't register for what it was. I lowered my voice to exclude Charlotte and Fran, who hovered a little way down the corridor. "What's going to happen with—"

I cut myself off as the glow of another Moth fell over my mother's face. Hunter Corcoran stood in the bedroom doorway.

Mythos's Chief Financial Officer was a relic of my grandpa's time, and godfather to both Daddy and Jude. Me, he had never cared to get to know. He must have been nearing eighty, but with *Polish* he'd redesigned himself as a forty-five-year-old (a bit much, most sensible people would say; a healthy sixty would have been far more chic), one with Old Hollywood good looks I knew for a fact he had never possessed. He gave me a flat, compassionless look to go with his flat, compassionless feelings towards me, showed no sign of noticing Charlotte, and turned to Mum.

"I don't know how this nurse has a job," he said, with no concern for whether said nurse could hear him. "Rock formations have moved quicker. Claudia, you ought to get Oz a better one."

As far as I could tell, Hunter's only trick was telling people, unsolicited, what they ought to do. That, and commanding a salary he was not worth. But he'd been at Grandpa's side through the boom of the *Swift* launch and the company's growth in the decades following, and Daddy was nostalgic about Hunter giving him his first cigar, so here he was, still in the job.

Mum said something in reply, but that was the moment I glanced past Hunter into Daddy's room and put a visual to the beeping of a machine, the hiss of air from another as it pushed and pulled. A hospital bed had been swapped in for the low, sleek bed frame that belonged there. Gone was the expanse of taupe silk and the rows of pillows, replaced by the paraphernalia of sickness; and at the centre, comatose, my beloved father.

I sidestepped Hunter and went to his bedside, reality sharpening and contracting until it didn't feel like reality at all. I looked down on a scene that was wrong in impossible ways. Daddy had a distinctive smile; it stretched mercilessly wide, his cheeks dimpling with concentric creases as if from constant use. If you looked him up, you would see a thousand pictures of that smile. The first would be the infamous *TIME* magazine cover. Pictured off-centre to accommodate his Moth, he's squeezing his eyes closed as he's spattered with fake blood. It's in his brows and his lashes, flying through the air around him, spraying across his skin as if an arterial calamity is occurring just out of shot; and he's grinning through it, in on the joke. The second picture you'd see would be the reference image: he had been talking at an event on a university campus when an anti-capitalist protestor stormed the stage and doused him with a gallon of pig's blood. Hardly any of it had stuck to him—he had *Spotless* running, of course, and so the blood slid off his clothes and hair and skin to pool on the floor. Except that the protestor had caught him smiling, and *Spotless* didn't work on teeth—it made it impossible to chew effectively. There Daddy stood, teeth bloodied like a vampire's, impervious to the grizzly insult, laughing like a mouthful of gore was the best joke he'd ever heard. And those creases. You wanted to put your fingers in the creases of his cheeks to feel how deep they went.

Now the skin of those same cheeks, pulled down by gravity, had sunken away from his mouth. A tube had been forced down his throat and strapped to his face. I wanted to rip it out—such a thing had no business touching him. His Moth hovered above his pillow. I tried to imagine him laughing at *this*—the heir of magic lying in a coma as all the power in the world floated, impotent, beside his ear—and couldn't.

A hand landed on my shoulder. "I'm so sorry, Teeny, but they don't think he's going to wake up."

I laughed at that. I had seen him four days ago for our weekly lunch. Just yesterday, I'd sent him an article about a new kind of recreational submarine on the market and we'd messaged about it. So this couldn't be that serious. A lock of Daddy's chestnut hair had been displaced, and I twisted the curl around my finger as I swept it from his brow. Flawless; he was always completely flawless. "Don't be ridiculous."

Fable tended to echo, but the silence that followed was weighty enough to smother it. I looked around; Charlotte was still in the hallway, out of sight, but in here five faces were turned towards me and the bed. Mum, whose pity had intensified so that I could hardly stand to meet her eyes and feel it. The nurse (her name was Natasha, though I only learned that later from the news articles) looked as if she wanted to speak but felt she would rather catch fire, which I should have known boded ill. Fran was gazing at my father's comatose form with the expression of a bereaved acolyte. Hunter's expression showed very little of anything, and as his gaze was focused on Daddy and not me, there was nothing to sense in his feelings either.

And in a far corner of the room, cloaked in the shadows like the reaper waiting to collect: Jude. They'd called *him,* of course—I had the sickening thought of Jude by Daddy's side in the hospital while I was sat in an applied statistics lecture, forgotten. His silver-blue Moth illuminated one side of his sharp-boned, pale face as he leant against the wall, head tilted back so that his eyelids fell heavily. But they were open and fixed on our father. It was hard for me to pity him, but I could see the cruelty of fate when it struck a blow; Jude had only this one parent left.

But he'd had most of him. Weekday mornings, every holiday and vacation, instead of one in two, the larger share of his love. My sympathy was short-lived.

"He'll pull through," I said. "He'll have to stop working but surely he'll still pull through."

I directed the remark mainly at the nurse, whose wish for her own death intensified.

"If he were to wake up," she said with a professional calm that belied her feelings, "it's almost certain he would be severely brain-damaged. And I'm afraid even that is incredibly unlikely."

"He can recover from brain damage," I returned haltingly, less certain now. Surely Oscar Maddock could recover from anything. I slipped my hand into his—it was warm—as my panic caught up to correct me. Unable to look at the ghastly hospital tableau in front of me and keep my sanity, I let my gaze track upwards to the cluster of framed photographs hanging above the bed. Photographs of me, and Jude, and Grandpa, and Aunt Georgia. And at the centre of the cluster, the largest photograph was of Daddy wearing that infamous smile. In it, he was sat astride an elephant, one of the troupe he'd had illegally imported for his forty-fifth birthday party. It was four months after Aunt Georgia died, and he'd decided it was time to restore some joy to his life with four hundred of his closest friends. The infringement made international news and inspired a spiralling cycle of media discourse that lasted for weeks, on animal welfare, the excesses of the super-rich, the reality of who was really punished with a fine. Protestors camped out at his gates; petitions were signed; politicians proposed crackdowns and new bills. I'd been twelve years old at the time and terrified that my father would go to prison.

Of course, nothing ever came of it. Not only that, but all that furore happened entirely beyond the world he occupied. It passed over him like a fleeting mist. "Honey, if it's a bad day to be me," he said at the time, "then no one's told me yet."

Nobody ever did. He was entirely, spectacularly untouchable.

Until now.

"So, what does that mean?" I asked. I heard the staccato tone Mum said I used when I was emotional, the syllables wobbling imperiously. "We simply give up? Pull the plug and shrug it off?"

Glances ricocheted around me, some landing beyond my sight.

"Nobody is thinking of that just yet," said Hunter. His emphasis got a little nastier every syllable, but he could think what he liked about me. I was *checking*, not *hinting*.

Because Oscar Maddock could not die. Not now, when all he had to do was be well for a little longer. The stunning cruelty of it—the universe laughing at us.

I glanced again at Jude, and my thoughts of fate faded as I catalogued the changes. He had taken out his earrings, and his bleach-blonde hair, forever in his eyes, was now sensibly combed back. In place of his typical high-fashion, monk-chic layers was black Hugo Boss.

The suit was suspicious; the absence of a liquor smell and a lingerie model on his arm bone-chilling. Jude hadn't just come to his father's sickbed in grief; he had come as a sober and appropriate successor.

"Can we all talk in the hall?" I said.

"Yes, let's," said Mum, taking my arm.

Jude didn't follow. Instead, he pulled up a chair to Daddy's bedside. Fran stood next to him, one hand on his shoulder in a way that would have made me shudder but that Jude clearly didn't mind.

Outside the room, I found that Charlotte had moved to the very end of the hall. The echoing susurrations of our conversation would still reach that far, but the words themselves wouldn't. Hunter still gave her a flat look, before he turned back to me, his feelings stirred with the type of ire you reserve for a child who should know better.

"Weren't you told to keep this quiet?" he said.

"No, Hunter, I wasn't *told* anything. I had to find out an hour ago from a housekeeper, and Charlotte was with me."

Since I hadn't found out from an alert on my phone, I knew that Oscar Maddock's coma was not public knowledge. But it would have taken a stronger woman than me to return to my table in the university library, calmly pack up my things, and tell Charlotte a lie. She'd heard my voice rising, rising, then breaking on a sob and had come to find me in an alcove beyond the anthropology section.

As for bringing her: she'd insisted. Certain as I was that there'd be sparse comfort here from the likes of Mum and Fran, I'd been unable to leave her behind.

"She'll sign an NDA," I said as Hunter drew breath to needle me some more. "The contract's already on its way." I paused, hoping someone would jump in with what I was so obviously waiting to hear. "What's happening? Do we need to convene the board?"

"The board already had an emergency meeting," said Hunter. I would have been sick from dread had I not surmised from the sudden tightness in his jaw that the result was bad for him and thus good for me. "Claudia's interim CEO."

I only nodded like I thought that was sensible, but since noticing that Jude had come to rumble, the wheels were turning. This was a boon. Of course she should take the helm at a moment like this: the company's Head Magician, the true architect of their breathtaking next chapter. She should get to turn the page herself.

But she wasn't the blood of Martin Maddock. She had been married to his grandson for eighteen months, more than twenty-three years ago. And Martin had been so certain that the magic he'd been given would answer only to a Maddock that he'd invented the *blood rule*. Written into Mythos's bylaws, the *blood rule* stated that only a blood descendant of Martin Maddock could helm the company. If Mum signed a contract to be installed as the permanent CEO, no one knew what would happen to the magic our empire was built upon. Perhaps nothing, but that was the power of Martin's singular and unknowable achievement: Who were the Maddocks to rebuild the world and then risk its most essential resource?

Which meant there were only two choices for the board: me or Jude.

"*Interim*," repeated Hunter, lest either of us had forgotten. His singular feeling, before turning to my mother, was the wish to level any satisfaction I might be experiencing with a psychic wrecking ball. "The board were clear that'll change if the soft launch this weekend isn't a stellar success."

So Mum had just this weekend—the most important in the company's history—to prove herself or be replaced.

"In the meantime, she's also still Head Magician," Hunter went on, his tone arch, the comment evidently belonging to an extant argument. "So responsible for some clarity on how much faster—"

"I'm at a loss for what, exactly, you don't already understand," Mum cut in. "The product can't fix this. It could preserve him in the state he's in now, and maybe that's something, but it's not healing magic. It can't undo the damage the stroke did to his brain, and as of yet, neither can medicine."

"Keep him like this?" My voice didn't sound like my own. I didn't want my father to die, but neither did I want him breathing through a machine for more years than he'd smiled. "As a body in a bed—*forever?* You would be trapping him in his worst nightmare."

"You've changed your tune fast," said Hunter. He gave me a long stare, his mouth moving in this masticating tic he had. Hunter could chew air like it was cud. "I suppose you remembered there's an empire up for grabs, didn't you?"

This was what Jude had realised before I did: the dynasty had no named successor. I guess that was what happened when you thought you'd live forever.

"That's not what I'm saying," I bit out, trying to hold back tears. I didn't want to launch into this battle, not so soon after learning I was probably losing my father forever. The ghoulishness of it was overwhelming me. The problem was, I was constitutionally incapable of letting Jude win, so if he was making moves, then so was I.

Hunter sniffed. "Good, because we all know who Oz would want."

"Well, that's too bad," said Mum with no attempt to hide her derision. "If Jude hadn't been on a bender in Bali—"

"He was on a bender in Bali?"

"He got here half an hour before you did," said Mum, and it was like the sun came out, burning away the spectre of Jude at Daddy's hospital bed as if it were mist. "Completely unreachable. If he'd been here, then maybe he could have made his case to the board, but really. We agreed nearly unanimously that naming a successor could wait and I would be best to bridge the gap. Through the announcement at least." Hunter made a noise she pretended not to hear. "Jude is just too immature."

It was with a collective certainty that we turned to see Jude was in the doorway, listening to himself being insulted. Since Mum had always hated him with shameless abandon, he had the dignity now to ignore her. Instead, he was looking down the hall at Charlotte, because he was a pig and she was shimmying out of her jumper to reveal her tank top. Once liberated from the garment, she looked up and met his gaze in the unflinching, self-possessed way she did everything. Something like interest darkened her eyes.

Certain that this was a situation I wanted to know nothing about, I looked away.

"I assume we're cancelling the soft launch?" Jude said as he dragged his eyes away from her.

"No." Mum made a gesture of hers, a sort of *Hamlet to Yorick's skull* raise of the hand that meant *Oh, come on* in any number of tones. "It's far too late for that."

Even Hunter was forced to agree. "We're already going to take a hit when news of Oz's stroke breaks. Delaying the launch would kill us."

Jude went to rake the hair back from his face, but of course it was already perfectly in place—the hair of the future CEO he wanted us to see. "Well, call off the party, at least."

Words I never thought I'd hear him say.

"Well—" began Hunter.

"That would be as bad as postponing the launch entirely," I cut in, mainly because the idea was Jude's. "Our biggest clients already planned their schedules around being here. If Mum's CEO for the sake of this product announcement, let her announce it as planned, at the party. This isn't the type of thing you drop on social media."

Mum was nodding at every point. "Cancelling is out of the question."

Conveniently, I was right, and so it was decided that the party to announce the new product that weekend would go ahead. But perhaps we all knew that Claudia Cabot was also the last woman to shy away from claiming her moment; to let the misfortunes of a faithless ex-husband hamper her success.

And so my mother ascended to the role of CEO the same way she had been promoted to Head Magician: with a Maddock in a hospital bed.

It was gone midnight local time when Mum and I retreated to her home, an hour later and three thousand miles away.

But the night was far from over. In the five minutes it had taken to drop Charlotte back at college and say goodbye, Mum had sat in the car and answered email after email, message after message, her face ghostly in the phone-screen light, thumbs flying across the keyboard without ever seeming to pause. We arrived not at a sleepy home, but at a CEO's crisis control hub. Half a dozen people folded Mum into their ongoing conversation as soon as she stepped out of the car.

"Where are we?" was her greeting.

"Julian's ready for you in the sitting room," said some assistant as she handed Mum a tablet and ushered her towards the house. "I have a selection of pull quotes. We just need to approve a couple for the social media team . . ."

I climbed out after her. Light pulsed as the car vanished, and then Mum was gone too, carried off within a swarm of staff. She had said we'd have a drink, decompress. I considered calling the driver back and going home, crawling into the centre of my bed and crying until my head hurt, until I'd spent too much energy to feel this overwhelmed and stricken. But I couldn't. Jude was mobilising, and the sooner Mum and I talked, the better position I would be in.

If she was busy, I would make some calls.

My childhood address was a grand red brick Victorian set on three acres, with a vegetable patch and an unloved tree house rotting at the end of the garden. I had done the bulk of my growing up here, but it was the first time in a while that I was coming directly from Fable, and so the old corridors felt shrunken once more, and the creaking of the floorboards underfoot sounded to my ears like decay.

There must have been two dozen people inside, all talking at once. The dining room was full of Mythos's legal and press teams making calls to arrange embargoes on the new product announcement. *Monday,* I heard again and again. We would announce to a select group of clients at the party this weekend; then the world would hear on Monday.

In the hall, I passed a tall, authoritative woman talking to someone I recognised from the PR department.

"Given the situation, the new strategy is Claudia," she was saying with a perpetual, vigorous nod, the way you exaggerate an action for a child until they copy you. "Claudia's the story."

The PR guy frowned. "I'm sorry, who even are you?"

If anyone tried to offer their condolences about Daddy, or in fact talk to me at all, I would scream, so I kept my head down and avoided making eye contact. At the doorway to the sitting room, I picked out Mum, surrounded by people waiting for her attention. The assistant who'd snagged her from me in the driveway did not appear to have stopped talking.

". . . and then we'll schedule the photoshoot for tomorrow and make sure we see a finished piece for approval before Friday, because you'll want to focus on the party."

"And when will it run?" replied Mum as she caught my eye. *TIME magazine,* she mouthed to me. She rolled her eyes, but the smile that broke free was goofy and untamed. With difficulty, I smiled back. She should have this; I was happy for her. I would try not to resent that it had come at Daddy's expense.

I got a glass of water from the kitchen and escaped to my old bedroom, a time capsule of tennis trophies and heavy metal posters, the story of an angry and competitive teenager. A collage of photographs of me with celebrities ringed the vanity mirror; another on the wardrobe door was of cutouts of clothes I'd seen in *Vogue*, things to choose from when the next formal or gala came around.

Whenever Daddy looked in here, he'd ask questions about why I hadn't made my clean, cream-toned space at Fable my own like this one. He couldn't understand that I *had*, that my room at Fable was everything and this was a junk drawer, a scrapbook. It was the place I kept the mess of myself.

It was nearly two hours before I heard someone downstairs rounding everyone up to leave. Sick nerves bloomed to meet the sudden quiet. It was time to talk.

The staff had swept their pizza boxes and plastic cups away with them, leaving only the familiar smudges around my mother's house. She liked solitude, and so the housekeeper came only twice a week. Dropped flower petals lay dying for days. Sticky crescents of juice dried on the kitchen table. One of the crystal bowls out of which she ate yogurt and granola before dawn every day was cloudy because she'd accidentally put it through the dishwasher, but it remained in rotation like she hadn't even noticed.

All my life I had been obsessed with cataloguing these chips and scuffs and yellowed pages, the pilling on a cashmere jumper she wouldn't toss out because she liked it. The patina on my mother's life. To me, it was a tapestry of damage taken and, worse, a resigned shrug at damage still to come. All of it unbearable, when for two weekends a month I could exist in another life, one of flawless perfection. But I was glad of the contrast. When I looked at the decade-old dent in the cushion of Mum's sitting room couch, the velvet loose and sagging over the collapsed filling—"comfortable," she called it; "used," I called it—my conviction about what I wanted had something to cling to.

"You must be exhausted," I said as she dropped down on the couch, right into the dent shaped like her, and curled her bare feet under her body. I took the orange she had fetched for me and went to the mahogany-framed nook enclosing the wet bar.

Mum gave a laugh that turned into a sigh. "I haven't had the time for exhaustion." And then, eyes full of mischief, "You should have seen

Hunter's face when the board voted to make me CEO. I almost feel sorry for him. Any other week in the history of the company, I'm sure it would have been him."

I dropped sugar cubes into lowballs and peeled strips from the orange. "So, Monday?" I looked over when there was no response. She was worrying a thread that had come loose in her sleeve and staring inward. "Mum? I heard we're announcing on Monday. I thought the party was the soft launch, and then marketing would strategise from that . . ."

I trailed off when it became obvious she wasn't listening.

"I'll need to let Ansgar know what's happened before Friday," she said to no one.

Only in my enduring silence did she finally remember I was there. I'd expected to take some psychic abuse in this conversation. Temporary spells couldn't be uninstalled or toggled off—you had to wait for them to wear off on their own—and I'd opened the Moth app before being alone with her to see that my current dose of *Empathy* had over an hour left. The spell drew a blank as she turned and blinked at me—meaning her feelings were elsewhere, not about me—then hit me with a rush of well-worn irritation as she saw my expression: sullen, sour, disapproving.

"Oh please, Valentina," she said with a sigh. "He's coming, alright? We can't exclude him and we don't have to. The problem's in your head."

Despite my best efforts, Ansgar was the guest of honour this weekend and Mum's invaluable partner in the development of the new product. His collaboration had won him a share of the company and a seat on the board. He was also a vampire, and I had made it clearer than clear I'd prefer not to welcome him at Fable, or be near him, or remember he existed at all.

It would be my first time seeing a vampire in the flesh. They couldn't be captured with anything but the naked eye; not on film or in digital photography, or even in a reflective surface. The closest things were images they *weren't* in, like the recent viral surveillance footage of *no one* leaving an office building at night, pedestrians passing like normal as a *Swift* car at the curb popped open a door all by itself. One couple cast a glance back like they were wondering if they recognised this conspicuously wealthy not-there person. Another man did a little side step just after the car door closed, as if he was avoiding a driver or bodyguard who also wasn't there. That was the worst part: those people in the footage had no idea they'd just passed a vampire.

Other than that, the closest you'd come was the rare facial composite in the local news, police pleas for caution after a body had been found, but always with the same three caveats no one needed because everyone remembered them: the stop, drop, and roll of vampire know-how.

The first: that by the time you know there's a vampire in town, they're already some other town's problem. The more careful they are to cover their tracks, the longer they can stay put and continue to feed on a community. So if you've found the exsanguinated corpse of the girl who left the bar with that mysterious passer-through, he knows as well as you the jig is up.

The second: you better not be homeless, or travelling, or new to town. The less likely you are to be missed, the less conspicuous your sudden disappearance.

And third, always delivered as a reassurance: vampires are rare. It's much more likely your sister's roommate fell afoul of a statistically more dangerous monster: the living man. A boyfriend or a blind date. Put another way, the police will almost never assume vampire.

Move in the right circles—and I did—and you might hear it whispered that law enforcement's lack of interest in vampires was by design. Because what were they, really, if not the oldest of old money? Even the vagrant, penniless vampire could enjoy the protections of the noble vampire houses if it stopped humanity turning as one towards the problem of their only natural predators.

We could talk about such things, bond over the open secret of it all, because among us—the wealthy—vampires were something else entirely. They bought houses we had built, banked with institutions we had founded, owned stock and seats on boards and politicians. And yet their lives so rarely brushed up against human ones. When they deigned to infect their superior society with our own, it was only ever on their terms and unapologetically to their benefit. Which, when you stared reality in the face, was how we all wanted to live. They were an aspirational class, possessed of the only thing we couldn't yet buy: immortal life. To be touched by the opaque desires of a vampire, the way Mum had been by this collaboration, was to be elevated momentarily above the rest of the lesser beings.

So hosting Ansgar this weekend was an incalculable honour, and naturally, the excitement amongst our soon-to-be guests was febrile. I was the anomaly. My insides did wet, unhappy things at the thought of being trapped with Ansgar and his entourage all weekend. It meant little to me that noble vampires were too well-mannered to accept an invitation then terrorise their fellow guests. For the love of all that was holy, they lived on *human blood*. Sorry that made me uneasy! It baffled me that *I* was always the one explaining myself.

"Monday," I pressed, in lieu of treading the Ansgar topic again.

"Right. Yes." She shook her head as if to clear it. "It just felt like the way to go about it. I mean, the spell works. I didn't spend a decade writing and rewriting code, killing myself to get the software to tell me the programme works, just to pussyfoot around announcing it. I just—" She threw up her hands. It made her look so young, so impassioned, like an adolescent fighting for her right to date some barely human, piece-of-garbage boy her parents rightfully hated. When she found the words, there was an audible lump in her throat. "I just worked so *fucking hard*. If I don't believe in this, why should anybody?"

Her need for validation was like the hands of a thousand children pawing at my clothes.

"You're right," I told her, and the hands rested. I swallowed hard as I arranged my next words. "It's just that Hunter said the board will replace you if this launch weekend isn't a resounding success. And . . . on the business side, the question of client uptake is more complicated. A soft launch is about . . . positioning it right—"

"I know."

"—pricing it right. It's about making sure we're squeezing the absolute maximum out of what we have."

"What *I have*," she said, and the pronoun felt pointed, "everybody wants. *Everybody*. I guarantee you, Teeny, we're hosting forty guests this weekend and we're taking forty pre-orders for the spell. By the time Monday comes around, the board will be falling over themselves to sign off on taking pre-orders wide. We'll be in production and shipping out the first doses by the following Saturday."

And she would be on the cover of *TIME*. It was hard not to see where she was coming from. For a decade, all she'd wanted was to succeed at this one thing and tell the world about it. If I'd been handed the reins to launch it as I saw fit—with the focus on the magnitude of my achievement—I'd be doing the same thing.

Yet my stomach churned to think of how much was riding on this weekend. If we announced the product with poor pre-orders from the soft launch, tech journalists were sure to sniff it out. The sales projections would take a hit; the rest of the client base would turn lukewarm—some would even hold off on purchasing the spell, afraid Mythos hadn't met the moment, that the latest offering wasn't "it." And all of this would be unfolding against the backdrop of Oscar Maddock's stroke and a change in leadership.

This product was the central pillar of Mythos's entire strategy for the coming decade. If it failed, so did everything the Maddock dynasty had been building for a century.

"Five days?" I turned to face her. The spoon I was holding dropped sugar and bitters onto the carpet, which wouldn't be cleaned for days. "If we'll be in production by next Saturday—is that how long the upload will take once the board signs off?"

Appreciation and pride swelled within her. She was glad I'd asked. "It's the most complex spell in the history of magic." She meant the history of human magic—of the company—not that I'd have made the distinction either at the time. "The coding's nearly three hundred pages long. That's a hundred more than *Fuel*."

Magic in the hands of humans was a two-stage process. First it was programmed in a language Martin Maddock had invented to focus and instruct his power. These days, spells were completed and spells failed at the say-so of Mythos's patented AI software without the need to ever test on a person, just like how a computer programme will glitch or run smoothly. Only when we were almost ready to deliver the product to clients or ship it to stores (depending on the price bracket) was the spell programme uploaded to the production lab hardware for manufacturing to begin, and it was imbued into tonics and vapours and what have you.

If five days sounded like a long time for a programme to upload, consider that we were literally making magic. When I was little, Daddy had explained it to me like a witch brewing a potion—she stirred the mixture in a cauldron over a flame for as long as it took for the colour to change. Mythos used the same process, improved and streamlined. A day or two was typical for upgrades or new strains. *Fuel* had infamously taken four and a half days, but five would be the record.

Restless, Mum leapt up and came to the wet bar, where she leant against the wood to watch me muddling the drinks. She folded her thin arms across her chest, the sharp corners of her shoulders and elbows forming a square. Most days, she wore a uniform of tailored black trousers and a black turtleneck. Everything about her appearance—the washed-out grey of her eyes, the fraying inch that needed trimming off her pin-straight, mousy hair—was unselfconscious, unobtrusive. There were fine lines drying into her face—lines less serious, intellectual Moth users would never tolerate. As soon as she'd let me, I'd used *Polish* to colour my eyes violet. I'd made my hair black. I'd leant into my jaggedness by adding an extra four inches of height. And I was adamant that I would never look older than thirty.

"Your friend Charlotte seems nice." I pictured Charlotte hearing herself described as *nice* and managed a smile. She tried to leave people awed and clutching her business card. That she'd shown restraint on her solemn trip to Fable was the sign of a true friend. "Is she on your programme?"

"Computer science. She was the only person at a departmental mixer who didn't pitch me her product upon introduction."

"Good for her."

We were talking around it, but the space at the edges was getting smaller. Now a silence fell, and I wondered if this was it. But Mum wasn't ready. I knew the absent way the fingers of one hand tapped her elbow, the way her teeth worried her lower lip. I could have told her Charlotte was studying circus skills and she'd have forgotten ten minutes from now, because even when she wished to be, she could never be distracted from her current goal.

That night, it was world domination.

"This is what Oscar would have thought was right," she said at last. "It sends a strong message to have me handle the soft launch this weekend, and . . . What, Teeny?"

I shook my head. I didn't want to cry. "You're talking about him in the past tense."

The perfect square of her folded arms relaxed, and I sensed the mangled panic of someone wishing to extricate their foot from their mouth. A moment later, her hand rested on my arm. "I'm sorry. I forgot that you only just found out."

"How does that change anything? He's not dead."

"No. But." She took the glass I offered her. "Thank you."

"To you," I said, mustering a smile and raising my glass. "Congratulations, Mum. No one could deserve it more."

She lit up with gratification, then burnt out as quick as a flare. "I struggle, sometimes, to see your father from your point of view. The fact is, I often forget that you've forgiven him."

Someone else might have mistaken it for an apology, but to me it was an accusation—a familiar one. I suppose I had to pay somehow for all the emotion I'd been leaking over my dying father.

"He was a shitty husband to you, but he's a good father."

"Anyone can be a good father two weekends a month," she said, following me back to the couch. "And of course let's not forget that he's also the reason you've had to explain to every friend you've ever had that your half brother is also your cousin."

"I didn't say he was perfect," I snapped.

The hard lines of her face softened, but a defensive rush of irritation rose in her feelings. *Don't be dramatic now, Teeny*. I took the hand she offered me, squeezed perfunctorily, and let go. "You're right. It's not the time."

But maybe it was the time. My hurt was real and yet it felt like a performance, because if she was doing away with tact while my father lay on his deathbed, then I could too.

"The company needs to come to me," I said in a rush.

Mum took a pull of her old fashioned and stared towards the window as her throat worked.

"I know," she said at last, shoulders dropping. "If Jude takes it, he'll make my life a misery."

I mean, sure. That would have been the angle to go with if this was about her.

"The nerve of Hunter to postulate like that about Jude inheriting," she added.

There was no need to belabour the injustice of the idea. I was the older heir, by two months and twenty-six days. I was the child my mother had consented to have so that the Maddock dynasty could continue—only to learn her sister was to give her husband another before the season changed. But Jude was the lovechild, the childhood cancer survivor, the motherless son. He was my father's favourite.

"I feel badly about it, Teeny," she went on. "I know you saw your future in the lab, but I think this could be a good thing. You could take us back to the way the company was always meant to be run. Your grandfather was a magician. His father was a magician. And then I suppose the gene skipped a generation—not to mention Jude—because Martin Maddock's grandson, the heir of magic, is squatting on the spoils without the slightest interest in the thing the whole empire rests upon." I was usually good at shutting out her casual criticisms of Daddy, but now was not the time. She caught the look I gave her and felt chastened. "All I'm saying is we have a chance to put magic back in the hands of people who value discovery. Imagine it."

The knot in my stomach pulled painfully tight. I resisted the impulse to stammer a correction, because she was describing the woman she had intended for me to become: learned and curious. A scientist.

A Cabot. I had been raised not with predictions of fame, or power, but the quieter kind of betterment: the pursuit of knowledge. I was my mother's little "future world-leading expert."

Except that I wasn't. I never had been. I had the grades—easy enough with every available magical enhancement, a roster of specialist tutors, and wilful parenting—and three-quarters of a master's degree in artificial intelligence, chosen as a foundation for joining my mother's team in my father's company.

But I was not a Cabot, and I didn't want to be her daughter. I wanted to be Oscar Maddock's.

My mother was a genius, and a leader—and an ordinary woman full of resentments and covered in scars. I needed to be more. Impervious to harm, like my father, the man who laughed with pig's blood in his teeth. Who wanted to ride an elephant at his birthday party, so did. Thanks to Martin Maddock, he had been born into power so insulating that pain, suffering, uncertainty glanced off him like blood off magic. Even the truly bad days—the death of his second wife, his son's leukaemia, the cruel irony of how it almost killed me too—struck and hurt but failed to leave even a scuff mark once the pain faded. The only thing that had ever harmed him was this stroke, and as undignified as that was, when my mother's project was complete, I would be protected from that too.

If I became my mother, I would still be capable of being used. If I became my father, I would be untouchable.

And I'd had a plan. With a master's degree in a computing-related field, I could join the lab as a trainee. From there, I would complete the foundation year, take a job as a junior magician, and work my way up to running my own research and development team, preferably within five years—I mean, what was the point of being a Maddock if it couldn't get me ahead at my own family's company? It was there that I'd develop a spell for an industry not yet revolutionised by magic: I had telecommunications in mind, possibly information too; the next smartphone, the next paradigm shift. With my own technology, I would get the jump on every other player in the sector and launch my own company, contracting out to Mythos for the magical components. Once I'd made my own billions and proven myself a leader—while Jude partied and spent his trust fund—I would be the only plausible choice to take over from Daddy when he retired. And of course he would have retired, because surely he wouldn't have wanted to run the company forever.

It was the long way round, but I would have done it. I'd have applied my intellect, committed my years. I had Cabot genes in me yet—but I would abandon them in a heartbeat. The plan was only ever a means to an end, and that end was power. It wasn't that I didn't understand the value in building something from scratch, but I wasn't chasing my mother's glory. I didn't want to *strive*. Oscar Maddock never had, and his true heir shouldn't either. Inheriting his power by virtue of being born to it wasn't only quicker and easier; it was the difference between a true titan and a pretender. It was everything.

"I just spoke to my lawyers," I told her, shifting so we were face-to-face on the couch, my legs folded beneath me. "They think I should move to settle the estate as soon as possible. Fast and aggressive. They said if someone comes out on top—wins Fable, that is—there's a good chance the board will follow suit. The blood rule only states that the CEO has to be *a* Maddock, not the first of their generation, which unfortunately means they're free to choose either of us, but they might be swayed by the image of a singular Maddock heir."

"Winner takes all," Mum said on a breath.

Winner takes all. I was dizzy from the pace of the past few hours, still spinning from grief—the air felt thin and ached in my lungs—but this had to happen, and it had to start now. *Fast and aggressive.* Jude had probably already spoken to a lawyer, because in what world would he and I ever settle this ourselves? It probably occurred to him before he even arrived at Fable.

Fable. For Jude, his childhood home. For me, a monument to the version of myself that felt just out of reach, even now.

"I know what you're thinking," said Mum, perhaps reading my hopelessness, "but Jude is only alive to contest your inheritance because of your stem cells. That might be an incredibly valuable chip to you, Teeny."

It'd better be. I'd been waiting on the universe to settle the debt since I was seven. Karma owed me a fat check.

"I also strongly suspect Georgia's prenup was more favourable than mine, so you could argue that she and Jude received preferential treatment—the board might be inclined to rebalance in your favour. But Jude will be counselled that he's starting on the back foot, so you need to be ready for a fight. This doesn't have to go their way."

"*Their* way?"

She blinked. "His. Jude's."

But she had been thinking of her dead sister, of how she could finally make this even by taking it out on Jude.

"The feeling among the board," she went on, "was that I would helm the company for the next year. That would give them a chance to take your measure—yours and his—and give you both time to present your case, as it were." She was talking quickly, like someone might stumble upon the planning of our coup at any moment. "We just need a way to position you as the better choice."

My heart jumped into my throat as we reached the crux of it, the thing I wanted from her.

"I kind of already had something in mind," I said. "I was thinking . . . Hunter's job. Not right away," I added in a rush, "but I thought when I graduate in a few months I could start training up for it. If I'm CFO this time next year, I'd be the natural choice. I've interned with Daddy for four summers and I keep up with everything that's happening on the business side." This last admission triggered a rush of scepticism from Mum. She hadn't raised me to be concerned with business. Thinkers and innovators like her *tolerated* the commodification of their genius. But as I started to lose her, an outrageous piece of manipulation spilled from my lips. "I'll train as a magician in the evenings." I could sense this piqued her interest, so I kept going. "I want to lead Mythos with a focus on magic, not the bottom line. Fresh ideas, innovation. More basic research and experimentation."

I thought I'd taken it too far with the buzzword bingo, but Mum's eyes were widening in interest. Her feelings telegraphed more excitement than she let on.

"I could finally run my lab without the opinions of people who don't know the first thing about magic." She glanced at me guiltily for that added swipe at Daddy, but I had her, so I controlled my expression. "Real freedom to create what I want."

She wasn't asking; it was an unqualified demand. I could feel her scrutiny lapping at me.

"Yes," I said.

It wasn't all a lie, not strictly. Maybe somewhere down the line I'd make the changes Mum wanted to see. The only thing that mattered was getting her support *now*.

Still, I swept from the couch and went to the window, where I held my cold glass to my brow, my cheek—was I red? The guilt and shame and deception felt like they were burning on my skin—and collected myself with my back to her.

She wanted to see Jude lose, but only if she thought it was her wish and not mine. To my mother, he was not just a threat to the work but the antagonist she'd made him in the wake of Daddy and Aunt Georgia's betrayal. To me, he was the usurper who had to be unseated for me to reclaim my father. If she realised what he represented for me—the life I wanted, the person I was determined to be; not the striving intellectual she had raised me to be, but an oligarch; not a Cabot, but a Maddock—she would snatch it all away.

But she didn't need to know, not while our goals aligned. She could find out later.

When the Maddock empire was mine.

She watched me as I returned to the couch, unblinking and radiating hope.

"All eyes will be on the both of you this weekend. The clients' and the board's," she said, her voice rich with whiskey and omen. "Everyone will know of Oz's condition by then. We'll downplay the severity, temper the rumours, but people will talk. This might be your only chance to get them all in the same place, so you'll have to make the most of it.

Your youth is your main flaw, so the key is to appear mature. Confident. Focus on being the host your father would have been—you're good at being charming." Thank you, *Empathy*. "They're looking for a leader, not an expert, so leave selling the tonic to me."

At this, a flash of possessiveness. She would let me play at being a miniature CEO if it benefited her, but she drew the line at me dimming her light.

"But make sure people know you'll be training as a magician," she hurried on. "I'll emphasise that the product is a triumph of magic and lay the groundwork for the promise of shifting Mythos's focus to greater experimentation, more discovery." Her eyes and emotions were alight with fervour when she looked at me. "Do you think you can do that?"

"I can," I said, squeezing her hand. I was dizzy all over again, this time with anticipation. "Is that a yes?"

She smiled, but a tightness remained at the corners of her mouth. "It's a yes."

So it was decided: Claudia Cabot's first act as interim CEO would be to launch her masterpiece into the world. Her second would be to tell Hunter Corcoran he'd be retiring in six months.

2

The party began at seven p.m. on Friday and wouldn't break up until Monday morning after breakfast. Forty guests—Mythos's top-spending clients—would fill the rooms of Fable and allow us to convince them that taking their money was our deepest privilege.

One might assume that magic sold itself. It didn't. It was something we had rescued from the forest floor, where it had lain in rot, grown lichen, fed mushrooms, and been home to spiders. You could blast the mulch and earth from its surface, polish it to a blue-and-white shine, but people would still remember that in its nature was ugliness and filth. "Crude magic"—that was the name we'd given to the thing we had taken, the raw material Mythos had refined.

The branding was meticulously constructed to reflect that refinement, to make people forget the filth and fungus. That weekend, the messaging was clear: we were as far from the forest floor as it was possible to get. This was the aspirational pinnacle. This was completion. And if you detected a flicker of the unsavoury? Look away.

The sunset drenched Fable in gold like a blessing as I stood on the balcony above the ballroom and watched the guests arriving. It was a room so vast it defied any sensible purpose—unless you counted inspiring awe, in which case Fable's architects hadn't been messing around. It stretched the full length and height of one of the intersections of the house, from the southeast corner of the first quad to the northwest corner of the second. A towering archway at one end led from the entrance hall. Down the centre were a series of rectangular infinity pools carved into the floor, extravagantly dangerous in their design, the still black water shot through with intermittent patterns of light. In each corner, a staircase wound up to the balcony, which traced the outline of the room.

There was an ache in my chest as I took in this marble palace. I had coveted Fable my whole life, wanted it to be my home instead of Jude's; my address, not just my father's. I had assembled a legal team. I was ready to set the battle over the estate in motion. For the price of a man whom I had clung to like a raft in a storm for twenty-three years, it might soon be mine.

How shamefully cold I must have been, to want it still.

In the entrance hall, visible from my vantage point, new arrivals were surrendering their devices. They had already committed to remaining here for the entire weekend with an unprecedented agreement: that they would be barred from accessing the new product for the next ten years should they wish to leave. For three days, the announcement would be contained to Fable, a privileged secret between the chosen few, before—pre-orders allowing—we released the news to the world on Monday and the spell went into production.

The arriving guests turned *Shield* off in the Moth app—the centimetre-wide protective force field of trademarked Mythos Blue momentarily visible as they toggled off the spell—dropped their phones and tablets into baskets, took the proffered champagne, and swept into the ballroom to the delicate strains of a string quartet, their Moths bobbing at their shoulders. So much space did peculiar things to sound; under the music, phantasmal snatches of conversation still reached me high above.

. . . terribly charismatic . . . but I barely remember . . .

. . . like animals to them . . . lesser beings . . .

. . . when they feed, they . . .

I clutched my hands around the soft flesh in the crooks of my elbows and leant heavily on the solid marble of the balustrade, the thought of being *fed on* triggering a cascade of reactions that made me want to absorb the stone's cool indifference.

Because I had been fed on. Not by a vampire, but by a needle and a tube; by a whole team of adult medical professionals who had agreed, with my mother's consent, to treat me like a human blood bag so that Jude could live. I knew the pain of being used, the helplessness, the terrifying weakness of having your life drained from you.

I was still trying to breathe through the memories when Charlotte appeared at my side. She was dressed in red, bold as a flower bursting defiantly from the stone. Her mahogany hair spilled over one shoulder like a lovely accident. She held herself as if a dress draped her body like that every day (she'd probably taken a seminar on projecting confidence), but she couldn't quite pass for one of us, and not just because of the lack of a Moth. Half-moons of purple still showed under her makeup, telling the story of a scholarship student who delivered pizzas in the evenings. Whatever time she had left was spent trying to get her embryonic tech startup off the ground.

Stood this close to all the money and power in the universe, anyone would be invisible in its glow. The best of friends were the ones who were discreet about it. Charlotte McNamara hadn't lacked the ambition of the rest of the computing department when she chose not to pitch me her company on first introduction, only their short-sightedness. She was, in fact, perpetually engaged in a dance I'd never learned, known as *the hustle*. I was forever certain I could capture the lead before the next turn, that I hadn't yet been permanently outdone. But she had good stories about bad men and the mouth of a sailor for the odd paparazzo who appeared on campus looking to catch the Mythos heiress worse for wear at a party. It was the most I could hope for as the foundation of a friendship.

She had insisted on coming with me to my father's sickbed on Tuesday. This morning, a last-minute invitation to the weekend had materialised from higher up—a sweetener to the NDA that asked her to forget what she knew of Oscar Maddock's coma, I assumed. Somehow, being with me when I got the call had metamorphosised into a ball gown and a golden ticket, and what had seemed like kindness now looked like a trick I'd blinked and missed.

Charlotte took me in where I was glued to the balustrade like I was afraid of falling. "What's the matter with you?"

"Vampires."

A feral curiosity—not strictly about me but about my reply, enough that I could feel around the edges—rose as she went to the railing and looked down hungrily. "They're here?"

"Not yet, I don't think." My voice was one tremble away from breaking into a sob. "Didn't they always sleep in little crypts in old movies? Why can't we go back to that?"

"I think a German film director made that up. And I thought you were cool about this."

"Why?"

"Because I remember you saying 'imagine if one of them slaughtered Jude,' and I said, 'Don't worry, I'm sure he'll be fine,' and you told me I'd misread your tone."

"Excuse me for trying to put a positive spin on an unpleasant situation."

Her brows pulled together. "You also said there's no danger."

"There isn't," I muttered. "That's not the point."

We had never gotten into the details of my stem cell donation. Anyone with an internet connection could read about how Jude Maddock survived childhood leukaemia; how my mind had made monsters of the ordeal and given them teeth was obscure and harder to explain.

"I know a girl who knows a girl whose dad found a body washed up when the river at the end of his property burst its banks. It was some local guy they thought left town." She pointed two splayed fingers at her jugular. "Two big holes in the neck. Nobody went out past sunset for like a year, but they decided in the end it was a passer-through."

"I'm begging you to stop." A cold sweat tried to coat my neck. *Spotless* scrubbed me back up before it could settle.

"Why doesn't that happen more often? Why don't we hear about more vampire attacks on the news? Where are the bodies?"

"Riverbeds, evidently. Buried in the woods. Incinerators, pizza ovens, I don't know. Where would *you* hide a body?"

Charlotte replied without hesitation. "The Slavic studies section of the library—I already told you. They only have a single student this year, and he looks like he'd snatch a body up for his collection sooner than tell anyone."

Moved by compulsion, I chanced a glance down at the guests, searching despite myself for the presence of vampires.

I found Jude instead, in conversation with Hunter but hardly listening. It seemed he was still trying to cosplay as someone worth taking seriously. Usually, he turned up to parties like he'd been dragged from something more debauched, hair well-handled and bow-tie self-consciously unslung. But tonight he was in an inconspicuous black tuxedo, classically tailored. The jewellery was still stripped away, and he looked *sober.*

Well, the night was young.

At first, I thought he was watching me, and I fixed my face into an appropriate sneer. But *Empathy* delivers a person's feelings to you with crystal clarity when your eyes meet, and Jude's were fuzzy at the edges. I looked to the side to find Charlotte staring back at him, the two of them strung together by some shared knowledge, and I understood.

"Oh my *god,*" I groaned, earning her attention. "*He* invited you."

Charlotte's feelings flashed with defiance. "Well, *you* certainly didn't."

"Only because this is a client event," I said haltingly. Of course, that hadn't stopped Jude doing whatever he wanted. He might have been trying his hardest to take the future of the company seriously, but he couldn't resist a petty swipe. "He's targeted you. He thinks he can rattle me by *stealing you away.*"

I rolled my eyes as I said it, like the idea was ludicrous. Charlotte quirked a brow.

"Okay, Paranoid Penny. Or maybe it's not about you at all?"

I angled away, but I still caught the tendrils of her sympathy as I said tightly, "It's what he does."

It wasn't even that Jude turned people against me—he just threw his money around to make them dance and revealed them as the barnacles they'd always been. The barnacles I preferred to pretend they weren't.

But even as I recoiled at the idea, my mind was turning over the potential plays, his and mine. Jude could still be trying to lay bare the transactional underbelly of another of my friendships . . . but what if I did it first? Yes, he had gotten her here, but that meant nothing—Charlotte wouldn't pass on a three-day lock-in with the kinds of people who could change her life if the offer had come from Satan himself. And now, maybe, I had a Trojan horse.

I drew breath to speak but couldn't decide on the words.

"What?" said Charlotte, wary.

"Is anything going to happen between you two?" I said, aware the answer might have me begging for silence.

"Traditionally, I think we were going to see where the weekend took us," she said slowly, but the binds of conspiracy were bleeding into her emotions: intimacy, intrigue, danger. She knew what I was thinking before I even had to say it. "But maybe if the opportunity arises, I could find out what he has planned to win over Mythos's board?"

"Only if the opportunity arises," I repeated archly.

Charlotte was smart, and our friendship was what it was; I didn't need Jude to make me lonelier by proving it. So I didn't have to spell out the deal: play the spy and cement her friendship with the future CEO of Mythos. Possibly the most valuable friendship a person could ever hope to make.

And who knew? Perhaps one day, she and I would have been equals.

"I'll keep an eye on him, get him to open up," she said with a wicked grin. "I don't think it'll be that hard." She gestured to herself—the spill of her hair, dark eyes lined with kohl, dress wrapping her hourglass figure. "Trust me, his motivations for inviting me were magnitudes less sophisticated than you imagine."

By some trick of a draught and an echo, the front door closed with a fatal, resounding *thump*. Charlotte and I looked down on the ballroom. Full dark had fallen, as if the heavens had snuffed out the last candle while I was looking the other way. A lull dominoed through the guests, beginning at the archway. Charlotte craned over the railing. "I think it's time for your exposure therapy," she said, "because the vampires are here."

While the woman I wanted to be was delighted to have vampires to show off to her guests, the girl I was would be deep-breathing the way her therapist taught her for the entire weekend. As I dragged myself to the railing and looked down, my awareness of the pair of strangers entering the ballroom came from deep in my flesh.

They were unremarkable to look at, she a girl of nineteen or twenty, he a man of middle age. She wore her auburn hair in the glamorous, silken waves of a 1940s starlet, and her slight figure was draped in a champagne-coloured gown. Her lips were painted dark red and stood out against her skin like a lighthouse.

The man was tall and square, with a stiff posture and sickly complexion. His face was almost comically mean, with a villainous arched brow and an unhappy mouth. He held her hand in the crook of his arm as they stopped near the entrance, their uninterested faces staring down the human guests as they converged on them in an obsequious mass.

"I don't think that man is Ansgar," I said to Charlotte. I scanned the ballroom for the vampire Mum had described—tall, dark, and handsome, thirty at most in appearance—but he was nowhere to be seen. "He's their Maker. That's like their . . . king? Their patriarch? I'm not sure."

"So, they're royalty?" said Charlotte.

"They're members of House Gothenburg, one of the noble houses—basically, very old, very wealthy clans who all stem from the same Maker. Like a family, I suppose. I don't think House Gothenburg ranks all that highly among the six."

"Based on what?"

"Wealth. Age. Gothenburg, Montreal, and Cuzco were all founded in the last millennium"—*Millennium*, mouthed Charlotte—"Avignon, Lahore, and Thebes in the one before that. Thebes being the oldest and the most insular."

"*BCE*," said a voice from behind us. I'd been so loath to take my eyes off the vampires that I hadn't noticed the glow of his Moth.

Roman Astor emerged from the passage behind us. He was a friend of Jude's: strawberry blond, with pink-toned skin and—I was certain—born heavily freckled, though the latter he'd done away with through the magic of *Polish*. The result was an incongruous porcelain finish that made me want to reach out and smudge him with my thumb. His exhausting and unrelenting hunger for attention was so fierce that his life had quite literally gone up in flames after he started a series of fires on Yale's campus in his first year. Jude had already been on academic probation when he aided in one of them, and his resulting expulsion caused a bad atmosphere that Christmas when he refused to let Daddy buy him a free pass to return. Yet Jude and Roman's friendship endured, and Roman had escaped Daddy's ire; deep down, Daddy quite liked a hell-raiser.

"Gosh, we really must have been handing out invitations like they were candy," I said. "Or are you a plus-one?"

"I'm sure you'd have been given one too if you had any friends," he said, self-satisfaction blooming. He turned to Charlotte, and the onslaught of his need receded. "You must be Valentina's emotional-support poor person."

"Roman—"

"You and I should start a club. We can swap stories about how low we can grovel and how high we can jump."

Sometimes, you had to laugh at someone's bad jokes to win power over them; the thrill of pleasing you made them crave it again. The opposite was true of Roman Astor. Better to deny him the thing he needed from me: a reaction, any reaction at all. He didn't need me to be pleased; he needed only to feel that he marked people as he went. That he wasn't a ghost. The more untouchable I was, the harder he would try, and the more completely I would own him.

And I had always enjoyed taking Jude's things.

Blessedly, Charlotte took my cue. We looked at each other without expression until, flustered, Roman moved off to regroup, or perhaps build his confidence back up with more fruitful prey.

"A favourite client?" said Charlotte, deadpan.

"He's Roman Astor, and he's not a client."

"He has a Moth."

"He's not a client *this weekend*. He's a friend of Jude's. They were kicked out of Yale together."

Charlotte clicked her fingers. "The arsonist."

"Hence his lack of money. His parents cut him off after they had to bribe the university to not press charges. He's been financed by Jude's purse strings ever since, which is another way of saying the Maddock purse strings."

Charlotte snorted. "Not having money really means a totally different thing where you come from, doesn't it? You don't think Jude's going to spring for . . ."

Mythos's latest product was guaranteed to have an eyewatering price tag. "He can't possibly be that generous. I'm sure Roman's just here for the free booze." Charlotte's attention had slipped from the conversation. She narrowed her eyes at me, her feelings swirling with grisly fascination.

"What?"

"Did you do something different?" She waved her fingers in front of her face. "You look . . . mean."

I beamed and felt her flinch internally. "That is the sweetest thing you've ever said to me."

I'd commissioned the spell by appointment at the lab on Wednesday, the morning after Mum and I hatched our plan. It had arrived in a lacquered white box with the Mythos logo on the lid. When I pressed it, the logo had emitted a pulse of blue light and split down the middle, the petals folding up and out. Nestled in a velvet lining was a single white tube—a spell applicator; inside was a brush with which the user stroked the bespoke magic onto their face—and a letter of instruction containing a simple line drawing of a face. Certain areas were highlighted in blue: her cheekbones, brows, nose, and a dot at each corner of her mouth.

"This is rather extensive," the technician at my appointment had said. "Are you sure you wouldn't like to split it into several spells and see the changes gradually?"

But there hadn't been time for that; the race between Jude and I began tonight, and I was determined to get off to a stellar start. *Focus on being the host your father would have been,* Mum had said, and I had taken that to heart. When the world found out that I was training to replace Hunter Corcoran as Mythos's CFO, the guests would think back on the party and remember me one of two ways. First, that I was young and grieving. Too sensitive, too easily bruised, perhaps a little too inward-gazing, like my mother.

Or that I reminded them of my father; that I was powerful, resilient. Untouchable.

If the board wanted to see a leader, what better tactic than to literally model myself after the greatest leader I knew?

The alterations were not drastic. My brows were only a little flatter, my cheekbones only a little less sharp. The nose was more masculine, less delicate. Altogether, I was not as pretty as half a dozen previous spells over the years had made me. But when I'd stood before the mirror and forced a grin, joy had followed. No, not as pretty, but more like my father. My smile was like his now, a grin that was wolfish and dazzling.

A grin I had coveted my whole life.

Next, my stylist had cut my hair above my shoulders with a comb and a razor, all one length, the edge sharp and perfect. I had chosen a dress in a mature midnight blue, the silhouette structured and broad-shouldered. I was crafting the shell of the Maddock heir, piece by hard and shiny piece.

"Valentina!"

The squawk echoed so shrilly in the vast ballroom that all other conversation stuttered, but my internal scream was louder. Cutting across the floor below was Athena van Thiel, one arm flailing in greeting, her Moth and her fiancé tearing after her.

"Just kill me," I muttered as I descended the stairs, leaving Charlotte to her own devices. Athena, her fiancé, and I met in the middle of the floor, our feelings a commingling of discomfort on my part, searing white panic on his, and good-natured delight from Athena, who kissed the air above my cheeks and complimented my gown in confounding obliviousness.

The van Thiels were old English money and aristocracy, and Athena and I had gone to high school together; though, last we'd seen of each other, our relationship had soured significantly. She was dressed in a silver slip of a dress that hung low at the back and looked wont to fall right from her shoulders. A smear of black makeup was bleeding around her eyes—a shade of blue that was more electric than was natural—and the suggestion of dark roots peeked from beneath her curly, platinum-blonde hair. After adjustments, we were both tall and fine-boned, but what was elegant on me gave Athena a kind of designer necrosis.

"What an occasion!" she said, blinking hugely as if she was trying to dislodge a stray eyelash. I didn't think that much of it; it was always possible Athena was on drugs. "I *died* when I got the invite. Although, Vee, you mustn't let me get as messy as last time. That charity gala, do you remember?"

She fell to cackling at her own antics, and I used the opportunity to pillage her emotions with *Empathy*. There was a sense of camaraderie—a relic from our school days, and me holding back her hair at the aforementioned gala—and a gnawing anticipation I took to be about the weekend and my closeness to it. Everything else was faint and benign; no misery, no animosity, no defensiveness. Odd, given how recently her betrothed had declared his love for me.

"Graham," I said in greeting to the bland, new-money Adonis at her side. "You look . . . tall." He was, I would estimate, around six feet, six inches, having gained an inch or two since our last encounter.

"Valentina. A pleasure as always," he lied as a tension that hurt my molars and a violence that threatened to break them pulsed through his feelings. "I'm from tall stock. My father was six foot two by the age of fifteen."

Which was just the type of "achievement" a deeply self-conscious man such as Graham would insist we all take seriously.

Athena put a hand on his arm the way she might draw your attention to a new bespoke dining table and said, "He visited the lab and went up again about a month ago."

I couldn't read Graham's feelings about Athena, but how I'd have loved to; judging from his expression, they were brutal.

"I wonder, where does one stop?" I asked him. "Do you think you'll ever go another inch or two higher? Is it difficult for you when you meet taller men?"

Graham considered his options through a miasma of furious, impotent chagrin and settled on the funniest thing he could possibly have come out with. "There *aren't* many men taller than me."

"No, no," I cooed. "Of course there aren't."

Graham Crain had been born to a relatively modest background that he seemed to believe had been dealt him by mistake and which had been causing him masculine embarrassment probably his entire life. Several months earlier—his confidence no doubt buoyed by his technically perfect physical form and by having ensnared Athena with a diamond she'd paid for herself—Graham must have gotten into his head that the van Thiel billions were less than he deserved. He broke off the engagement and told me very confidently that *I* was where he belonged. When I informed him that was unlikely, Athena took him back, but the interlude had been sordid enough that I hadn't heard from her since.

Now Graham projected a baffled anger not far removed from how he'd felt when claiming to love me, and Athena was all sweetness and enthusiasm. Was this some sort of power play on her part? And how could she disguise what she felt about our shared past, not only in her manner, but in her emotions? Far from helping me work out how to behave, *Empathy* had only put me on the back foot.

"Oh, gosh, but how's Oscar?" she said, clutching my wrist.

"Doing better," I lied brightly.

There'd been no way around Daddy's absence but a version of the truth: Oscar Maddock had had a stroke and was unable to participate in the soft launch while he recuperated. We had let the guests know Mum would be running the event in his stead. The news that she'd been installed as interim CEO—that Oscar Maddock would never return to work—would come next week once the guests' pre-orders had been secured.

Athena squeezed my arm with more sympathy than she felt, the top note of her feelings being impatience for what was to come. "Is he awake? Can he talk?"

"He's getting a lot of sleep." My voice shook. "But improving every day."

"Brilliant news," said Graham, eyes tracking above my head as he searched for an escape. "He really should have been here for this."

"Oh, but what a moment!" Athena's clutch on my arm got tighter, anticipation spiking as she brought the topic back to the most important thing. She leaned closer. "You *must* tell me: Is it ready? Is there a waiting list?"

Of course there was. Mythos had pulled out all the stops to enhance exclusivity.

"My mother will be making the announcement before dinner," I said. "Please, enjoy yourselves. It's all to come."

I was moving away before I finished speaking, unsettled but determined to maintain my sense of control. Over the next half hour, I restored my confidence by unleashing *Empathy* on guest after guest, crafting the impression of a powerful and competent leader one feeling at a time. Some saw power in effusive charisma; others were better brought under my thrall by pretending to be bored by them. An Italian duke was impressed by a staid and humourless heiress, a tech magnate by flirting. I listened to eulogies about my father, answered questions cryptically, luxuriated in the molasses of their want—dirty, feral, uncontained.

All the while, the presence of the vampires was a bright spot in my awareness. After the first time I missed someone's question because I was certain I felt cold breath on the nape of my neck, I took pains to keep them in my field of vision—though that was almost as bad. It was like trying to enjoy the view as a mountain lion crept closer, my nervous system warning that an emergency needed to be addressed. They didn't circulate or try to make conversation. They just stood in the centre of the room, their attention only lightly grazing the fawning guests who were scrambling to introduce themselves and be impressive. If I didn't know any better, I'd have said the vampires didn't want to be here at all.

At last, we were ushered from the ballroom for dinner. Down the hall, the dining room had been set up with a horseshoe-shaped table.

The surface was mirrored, the gold and silver and crystal doubled, the room an infinite chasm within its glass. Tall arrangements of roses ringed the table, enclosing us, making the gathering feel intimate.

I sat down in the centre of the horseshoe, next to the empty space reserved for my mother. The House Gothenburg vampires, mercifully, had been seated towards the end of the left-hand flank. I searched for Jude too and found him next to Roman. He had been relegated to a corner, not that he seemed to mind. With him in it, the chair became a throne. The way he slouched, one arm thrown over the back, was the picture of entitled arrogance. He looked up, head turning and finding me like he already knew I was watching him, his deep-set eyes two dark hollows in his sharp-boned face. Daddy had the heinous habit of calling us his *twins. The twins, my twins,* he would say as he introduced us, as though anyone we met didn't already know what we were, what he'd done to my mother.

I often wondered if Jude had picked up his most famous habit as a distraction. When he was mentioned in the press, Jude Maddock was the dynasty heir who bought boats just so he could sink them. Sailboats, speedboats, yachts. A houseboat once, when he was feeling folksy; I'd read he'd walked by it one day and given the couple living there a fortune just to scuttle it and go about his day. He had spent hundreds of millions, racked up misdemeanour charges in fifteen countries, become a meme at the Venice Film Festival one year. When people thought of Jude Maddock, they didn't think of leukaemia. But as far as the press was concerned, *I* had done nothing more interesting than saving his life, so every mention of me led back to Jude. It led back to DNA, *special bonds,* how woven together the lives of two children might be if they were both siblings on their father's side and cousins on their mothers'.

But at least only Daddy ever called us his twins.

Applause was breaking out at the far end of the horseshoe, nearest the door, and the strings fell silent. I rose to my feet as my mother came along the table. She was shorter than everyone there, only visible in snatches, but I caught glimpses of her outfit; it was the uniform—black turtleneck, black slacks—as if she was too serious to dress up for the occasion.

It didn't seem to dampen the crowd's veneration. As she took her place beside me, the applause swelled. She met my eyes, and a rush of her feelings—crushing, imperfect, beautiful—swept over me before she turned to the guests, a saleswoman's smile she'd pulled from god knew where gracing her face as she waited for them to fall silent and take their seats.

"Welcome to Fable," she began. "Thank you for being our honoured guests on what I promise will be a truly thrilling weekend."

Emphasis on the word *thrilling,* so low and heavy I felt the hairs on my neck stand on end. Even talking to a room of forty people, she still sounded like she was whispering. Before that night, I would have described her as soft-spoken, but now it was obvious that her canorous tone was meant for this.

"By now, you will all have surrendered your devices for the weekend. This is not because we don't trust *you* not to share what's revealed over the next three days. But our would-be rivals, bless them"—she paused for a spatter of laughter—"have tried all sorts of things in the name of corporate espionage over the years, including remote bugging. We understand we've asked you to make a sacrifice. We understand, too, the peculiarity of asking that you don't leave the grounds again for the next three days. But I promise you . . . I'm about to make it worth it."

The cavernous stone room did strange things to the guests' breathless chuckles, both amplifying and transforming them. They sounded, I realised, like dying animals. The bounty of an entire hunt, gasping for life. I imagined thrashing horns and snapped legs in the shadows thrown by the candlelight.

"I want to start with a word for our dear friend Oscar. Only a few days ago our family was dealt a horrendous blow."

She reached down for my hand, and I slid it into hers and held tight. I didn't need to take my eyes off her to know the person who slammed their glass down too hard was Jude.

"For those of you who don't know, Oscar's condition is stable, but the stroke was severe. At this stage, we can only hope and pray that he improves. Oscar's children and I can't thank you enough for your kind words and the gifts you've sent him. If he knew what an outpouring of love he'd inspired, I know his heart would be so full. Thank you." She raised her glass to lead a toast, which was echoed with a sombre weight. "Knowing Oz as I have these past twenty-five years, I know that what we both wanted more than anything was this moment. He wouldn't want Mythos's latest creation kept from you a single second longer on his account."

The energy in the room changed. The marble walls pressed closer. The gathering's focus was a heat, all concentrated on the woman next to me, who smiled coyly. She held the silence for a nearly insulting interlude—an indulgent, cavorting display of power. But her audience were fish on a hook, already nine-tenths drowned in air, not even struggling.

She leant forward and clutched the back of her chair with both hands. "I think by now you all know why you're here. In this room are some of the most prosperous people on the planet. You have wealth. You have power. Attention. Respect. Prestige. *Envy*—perhaps you don't like to admit it to yourself, but I know the envy you inspire feels nourishing. You're only human, after all. But I know the question that haunts the back of your mind, because it haunts mine too: What is it all for?"

The silence was profound. Just for a moment, I closed my eyes to sink into it, and I could have believed I was completely alone.

"You've come further than anyone else. You have everything that a person can possibly obtain. Everything a person can want. But are you *satisfied?* Do you even know what would satisfy you? What you're chasing?"

The guests shifted in their seats, eyeing one another as her tone sharpened into something accusatory and disappointed. Her hands slipped from the back of the chair as she straightened. Taking her time again, she let her gaze linger on one guest, then another. Her mouth was a serious line, but electricity crackled behind her eyes as she turned to face the front of the room. "Because we do. Allow Mythos to offer you your completion."

Mario, Fable's head of security, was suddenly at the edge of the table, trying to get Mum's attention. I was halfway out of my seat to intercept him before Hunter finally decided to be of some use and pulled him into a corner.

None of the guests noticed, because it was at that same moment that a banner dropped from the ceiling behind the head of the table. From somewhere, spotlights burst into being to illuminate blue silk, unspooling prettily. As it unfurled, it revealed first the Mythos logo in white, then below it the name of the tonic.

The silk hadn't struck the floor before they were on their feet. I rose too, the scrape of my chair a whisper beneath the clattering of applause, loud enough to be from five hundred people. I put my back to the banner and watched them. Wide-eyed. Breathless. A little afraid. It was hard to control a product announcement when the leaks inevitably began months beforehand, but who would have dared to truly believe it? The holy grail of magic; of *life*. The pinnacle of Mythos's empire.

Immortality.

The sting of tears hit my eyes. Shivers rocked me. I knew Mum's whole speech and its thesis had been devised on the marketing floor of Mythos's New York headquarters, but good marketing was effective because it struck something true. This one struck my bones, and the rightness vibrated through my entire being. I was trying to get closer to something, to the person I would turn into once I had enough—*was* enough. Everything was going to be easy once I had it, once I was complete. The idea was that with enough money and power it could never be stripped away. In fact, nothing could be taken from me or done to me at all. I could never be robbed, abused, ignored, cheated, misunderstood, left out of the joke, caught unprepared, or dressed inappropriately for the occasion. I wouldn't need love or anyone to protect me. I wouldn't long for anything it wasn't in my power to give myself. My efforts would stop feeling effortful. My thoughts would never be dark.

In the dining room of Fable, on the first night of that fateful weekend, I suddenly understood when it would be enough. The only thing that would satisfy was everything, for eternity.

"Immortality," Mum began, and the applause receded with startling eagerness. "Immortality has been the foremost desire of humankind for millennia. We have never ceased seeking it, be it the pursuit of the philosopher's stone or the hunt for the fountain of youth. Martin Maddock himself worked for long years on finding the key to eternal life, and sadly failed. Every Maddock and every magician in their labs has turned their sights to it at some point. It wasn't until a decade ago—a few years after I took on the role of Head Magician—that the solution finally revealed itself. Immortals have always walked among us, have they not? What if there was a way to harness the desirable component in the vampire's curse, to separate it from the vampire's essential nature and make it safe and beneficial for humans?

"The answer has lain this whole time with vampire venom: the elixir that has induced immortality in the bitten for millennia. Unfettered access to venom has allowed me to isolate the active component and, with patented Mythos technology, harness it in a tonic. This is a standout achievement in the company's history and makes *Immortality* unique among our products as the first spell we've developed with the aid of outside magic."

This was the reason security around *Immortality* was on another level. If Mum could refine a component of vampire venom to produce immortal life, then in theory, so could somebody else. Granted, they didn't have access to the proprietary tech she'd used to do it, and Mythos had patented the compound, but we weren't taking any chances. A security detail would deliver each and every dose to clients, who would swallow it under supervision.

"For that, we owe a debt of thanks to the noble vampire house of Gothenburg, who assisted with the project," said Mum, extending an arm towards our vampire guests. "Please give them a hand."

Another standing ovation, this one uncomfortably short; the Gothenburg vampires' reactions saw to that. While the man continued to stare into space—he did not seem to notice the room had broken into applause—the girl curled a lip in blatant distaste. The impact was a round of clapping that wrapped up in an expedient six seconds.

Mum cleared her throat. "I also owe a debt of gratitude to my team, Dr. Owen Chandler and Dr. Jonathan Yang."

More applause as she indicated two men standing against a wall. They smiled and bowed their heads and shared in her moment. I had met Owen Chandler and Jonathan Yang many times, but I hadn't recognised either. Dr. Chandler, formerly round-bellied and a little stooped, had gotten unrealistically fit. He was strong and broad, square-shouldered where he'd been sloped. Dr. Yang had back the full head of hair he must have been without for a decade, and he was tall now. Not Graham Crain tall, at least not yet, but six feet and change.

As their heads bobbed in acknowledgement of their acclaim, their new Moths moved with them. There was no way Owen and Jonathan were making the kind of money Moth owners had, nor did Mythos ever hand out the products to its employees. Their bonuses for pulling this off must have been astronomical.

The magicians made a quiet exit as the attention moved back to my mother. "Our *Immortality* tonic will successfully harness the most covetous quality of vampirism—permanent stasis—and deliver it to you with a one-time purchase. You will, of course, remain living. *Immortality* clients can continue to have children, enjoy sunlight without sickening. You will develop no aversion to water or silver." Her mouth curved slyly, and she dared to direct her next words to our House Gothenburg guests. "I understand the impact of garlic and religious totems are myths? So no problems there." A chuckle ran up and down the table. "And of course, you will still be able to use the full range of Mythos's other products as we continue to find new ways to fill your lives with magic.

"*Immortality* works. A single dose, and you will live forever, never ageing, never getting sick, never slowing down. A vastly limited number of injuries will be a danger to your life, and you'll be given the full information on what these are. And should you ever decide you wish to move on"—she gave an airy shrug—"*Immortality* can be uninstalled in a matter of hours to trigger a completely painless, dignified departure.

"It's now a matter of time before we deliver it to our first clients. To you." She smiled her new smile again and picked up her glass. Most of the guests reached for theirs too, the anticipation of toasting our shared victory too much to bear. "Starting this weekend, you are invited to place your orders with me personally. I'll be waiting to answer your questions and share all the necessary details, but we're here to celebrate as well. Tomorrow, you're invited to join a hunt in the woodland to the east of the house, followed by a masquerade party in the evening. On Sunday, there'll be games in the garden, and a very special buffet lunch. We'll close out the weekend with a candlelit ball on Sunday night, before we say our goodbyes after breakfast on Monday. Your every pleasure is ours to satisfy while you're here; please don't hesitate to ask the staff for anything. But for now, I would like to invite you to join me in a toast."

A tinkling filled the room, just like the noise magic made in old movies, as we raised our glasses.

"To the first night of the rest of our lives."

3

Servers swarmed into the dining room with the first-course plates as Mum took her seat and kissed my cheek.

"You were brilliant," I said. "You *are* brilliant."

I sensed her delight. It blossomed like a time lapse of a peony and rotted just as fast. Her eyes were on my face, narrowing as they grazed my brow, my cheekbones. As she reached up to brush my cheek, I felt her mourning, like the ache of an old injury.

I always knew she would hate it if I looked more like Daddy. It's why I'd held off until now.

"Lovely," she said anyway.

Silver-rimmed plates of steak tartare appeared in front of us. The tension in the room had snapped; conversation and crockery formed a humming bass note for the four-piece band who struck up in the corner. Hundreds of flecks of light danced off crystal. My eyelid reacted with a flurry of spasms.

Mum glanced up from her plate as I poked at it. "Are you alright?"

It had been happening since Daddy's stroke—a stress symptom, the internet believed—but I didn't get a chance to answer.

"Claudia."

Before she could take one bite, she rose from her chair to greet the man who was approaching. Eric Burton-Shaw was a pharmaceutical magnate and the second-richest person on the planet. Despite being in his eighties, his alterations gave him the look of a sixty-something who still rose with the sun, climbed mountains, and took his vitamins through an IV.

He was lithe and tall, with a full head of gunmetal grey hair, and a stern, narrow face with a long nose. His eyes were ice blue and piercing. I didn't know what he looked like without magic, but this quietly powerful, self-assured exterior was a fascinating study in how people saw themselves. Because the man beneath was a bona fide sweetheart, a total marshmallow. He was chuckling as he fondly embraced Mum and then me.

"Astonishing, Claudia. You clever, clever thing."

"Oh no," Mum said with a wave of her hand, her tone at once bashful and audibly hungry to hear more. The trials of genius.

Eric clutched us each by one hand and kissed them, drawing a smile from my mother and the full force of my new grin from me. The latter caught him by surprise, though his expression didn't waver. I sensed a mix of recognition and curiosity, and a rising to a challenge that warmed me to the core. If one of the most powerful men in the world was challenged by me, I must have been doing something right.

He dragged his eyes back to my mother. "I can't tell you how delighted I am. I, ah . . ." He cleared his throat. "I've been given a rather unfavourable diagnosis, you see."

"Oh, Eric." Mum clutched his arm.

"Can you imagine?" he said, laughing despite it all. "Just as I'm starting to get my second wind after losing Amelia."

We followed his gaze to his new wife, a freshly Mothed redhead named Nicola. Amelia, to whom Eric had been married longer than Nicola had been living, had succumbed to a stroke three years ago, and Eric had finally moved on. I watched Nicola poke at her steak with a stunned expression. Immortal life, courtesy of an eighty-five-year-old man she'd snagged only a few months ago. She looked like she couldn't believe her luck; but good or bad, it was hard to say.

"I hate to press," said Eric, "but time is really of the essence. My doctor says . . . well, he's talking in months rather than years."

"Say no more, Eric," Mum said. "If I remember, your slot to place your pre-order is tomorrow afternoon? You and I will talk then. But I promise you," she continued, practically glowing, a saint about to heal a beloved child, "you won't be disappointed."

Eric's eyes grew glassy in a way that turned them to blue diamonds. "Astonishing," he said again softly. "You're a miracle, Claudia. Thank you, truly. I would say you'll be remembered, but it doesn't seem appropriate on this occasion. What you will have, Claudia, is so much more. Now, I must eat something to soak up all this champagne."

He moved away. We had half turned back to our dinners when Hunter suddenly appeared in the space where Eric had been.

"Give me strength," muttered Mum. Then, louder: "Yes, Hunter?"

We'd both been avoiding Hunter as if he carried something contagious. As soon as the launch was over, Mum would break the news of his retirement to him. She already had a brand-new bon voyage Patek Philippe watch wrapped and waiting. Until then, the less we interacted with him the better.

He came forward, and my pleasure at Eric's reaction withered and died under the force of Hunter's apathy. I saw him notice my new face, but inside him was a tundra, and I was just another ripple of wind through the gorse.

"Someone's arrived," he said, nodding towards Mario, our head of security, who was hovering behind him.

Mum looked around the room, one long-fingered hand holding Yorick's invisible skull. "This is everyone. I was assured the guest list was entirely checked off."

"He's not *on* the guest list," said Hunter. There was intrigue in his manner, some angle of this he was enjoying. "You'd better come."

I was the first to move. The summons might not have been for me, but I wasn't about to let Hunter exclude me, as I was sure he wished to. Mum followed, sighing a curse. Fran—who had been hovering tight-lipped outside the dining room—fell into step with our party.

As we walked, Mario, usually a hulking presence at our backs, slipped between Mum and me. "Ma'am." His tone was deferential, conciliatory, which was unusual for Mario, whom Daddy kept around largely because he found it amusing how much Mario brazenly resented his job and all of us. "We've checked, but he's not on the guest list. He flashed an invitation at us and . . . he wasn't visible on the security cameras. His vehicle had left him there before we realised he'd gotten out of the car."

The cameras covering every inch of the drive? I began to say, but we were coming into the entrance hall—our footsteps echoing against the distant ceilings—and a handful of security guards had come into view. They flickered, or seemed to. It was an illusion made not with magic but with the dim light thrown from the corners of the sepulchrous foyer and the way the guards twitched from foot to foot, shadows dancing at their heels. I wondered why they'd covered the door so heavily, and then realised: they had come in from the garden, out of the way of the unexpected guest on the threshold.

"Or he's a vampire," Mario finished.

A chill shuddered through me, sending my hairs on end in a wave. My feet wouldn't take another step, yet the open door drew closer anyway as my awareness narrowed. I tasted iron.

Fran stepped beside my mother. Her voice sounded distant beneath the rush in my ears, like I was underwater. "Is he House Gothenburg?"

"I don't think so. I've certainly never seen him before."

One of the guards moved aside, and there he was. The vampire was dressed in a wine-coloured suit of flawless tailoring. He held himself with his hands clasped behind his back, pulling his shoulders straight, his weight on one leg like a Regency gentleman, an Austen hero. Like he hadn't sent Fable's professional heavies scrambling out of his reach, back beyond the threshold where no vampire could follow without an invitation.

"What kind of operation are you running that your people behave like this?" said Mum.

"Dr. Cabot," Mario protested, "none of my staff had ever met a vampire before tonight. We were prepared to receive two, and two arrived. This man is a stranger claiming to have an invitation when he's not on the guest list. I *told* my people to step out of his way."

I was unprepared for this too. My chest filled with a grasping panic, fluttering like the wings of a trapped bird. Vampires with whom Mythos had allied—who'd worked alongside my mother for years—were one thing. But *strange* vampires trying to trick their way inside? I was going to simply expire. There wasn't enough oxygen to sustain me in this whole air hangar of a foyer.

"Dr. Cabot," the newcomer called across the foyer, and my rib cage tightened in my chest as if a scream of mortal terror had echoed through the woods.

For a moment, Mum considered her next move, her fingers tapping out a rhythm against her thigh. She glanced at me, and her eyes were drawn down to the white-knuckled grip of my fingers around the insides of my elbows, a compulsion of mine—I hadn't realised I'd done it. When our eyes met again, I shook my head minutely. She must not let him in. I couldn't have explained then what I knew to be true, even to myself: that this was an omen. This was the part in the fairy tale where the fatal mistake was made; the deal that couldn't be undone.

But we had conquered fairy tales. The only power left in the story was us.

So my mother crossed the entrance hall, Hunter, Fran, Mario, and me behind her. The cluster of jittery guards parted as we approached. Ten feet from the door and nothing was before us but the gaping entryway, the balmy night—vital with the scent of cypress and lavender—and the vampire.

His mouth was fixed in an effortless sort of smile, as if his lips just fell that way, and he drew breath like someone who knew he'd already captured his audience.

"Dr. Cabot, my name is Lucas Sayle." Not just any vampire—a Midwestern vampire. "And there seems to be some confusion regarding my invitation."

He dipped a long-fingered hand into his breast pocket and withdrew a rectangular card, which he offered over the threshold. For a moment, nobody moved to take it. At last Mum signalled Mario.

With undisguised hesitation, he approached the door, one hand across his body as if to retrieve his weapon from under his tuxedo jacket. He stopped just short of arm's reach and held a hand out for the card.

Lucas Sayle, the invitation still raised, didn't move.

"I'm sorry," he said through a congenial smile. "I would come closer if I could."

Every breath drawn from the throats of those watching eddied through the foyer. Mario shuffled closer by inches, until he could close his fingertips around the edge of the card and snatch it away.

Mum took the proffered invitation, on which the name *Lucas Sayle* had been handwritten in ink—the personal touch courtesy of a Mythos intern, no doubt.

"Is this genuine?" she said to no one in particular. A woman with a tablet and a handheld scanner—the event planner—rushed forward.

I glanced back at the doorway. If the vampire took any offence to the scrutiny, none showed in his expression. He had rearranged himself as he was before, hands clasped behind his back, his face patient and open. Without warning, he looked over at me. I jumped, my shoulders convulsing in an attempt to curl around my chest. But his glance was my own doing, I realised; I had moved closer, angling instinctively to get a read on him. There was nothing—his feelings were a void. He was a dark corridor, the end unseen, and the longer I looked, the more convinced I became that something sinister crouched in the shadows.

But no. I couldn't sense his feelings because *Empathy* read *human* emotions, and this was a vampire. He was closed to me.

"It's right here," said the event planner as the scanner beeped. She scrolled on the tablet. "It looks like Oscar sent out a bunch of last-minute invites. There are . . . maybe a dozen here."

Mum gestured in irritation. "Why weren't they on the guest list?"

"It might be because they don't have names attached in the system. Someone must have printed the invites, wrote the guests' names in and sent them, but forgot to record who they went out to on the record. They wouldn't have shown up."

"Well, where *are* all these people?"

This last part she addressed half to the event planner and half to Lucas Sayle, who gave a shrug. "My invitation arrived on Monday, that's all I know. I'm not aware of anyone else who got one."

Monday: the day of my father's stroke. He'd invited a dozen extra people, told no one, and then slipped into a coma. But who were they all? And why had only one of them shown up?

"This only says Lucas Sayle," said Hunter, who had claimed the invitation and was frowning at the name.

"That's right," said the vampire.

"Then which house do you belong to?" Lucas shook his head. "You're not affiliated?"

"Many of us aren't."

Mum's brow creased thoughtfully. "Then how do you know Oscar?"

"I'm sorry," said Sayle, shaking his head again. "I don't."

Silent seconds drifted one after the other into the night, but he offered nothing more. I joined the others in a huddle, our voices a susurrating obbligato to the distant strings still playing in the dining room.

"What on earth was Oz playing at?" said Mum. "The guest list was approved by two dozen people. Who did he even want who isn't here already?"

"If Oscar invited him, then of course we have to respect his wishes," said Fran, whom no one had asked. I felt a pang of pity for the event planner, who had to contend with Fran's territorial nonsense all weekend. Fran's eyes landed on me, and I sensed her spite, sour and corrosive. "This is *his* house."

I couldn't let her casually undermine me, even to herself, but with the vampire's presence burning into my back, I could barely think. "How do we even know my father sent those invitations?" I shot back, petulant.

The event planner turned her tablet towards me. "If an invite is the particular request of someone, we mark it in the system." She scrolled down the list of unidentified invitees, each with my father's name next to the empty field. What had he been doing?

I wasn't the only one who couldn't guess. A vacuous quiet stretched, no answers forthcoming, Hunter and Mum and I darting glances at each other like one of us might twitch a hand towards their trigger. If this launch went off the rails, Hunter would claim interim CEO on Monday, and Mum knew it, but neither of them seemed to know which course of action sabotaged whom. For my part, if I argued against letting Lucas Sayle in, I left myself open to being overruled, and that would be the death of the last scrap of control I was clinging to with bleeding fingers.

"It doesn't mean we have to honour the invite," I said instead. "It's up to Mum now."

To my relief, no one contradicted me. The only response was a tidal wave of acid from Fran, a murky, indignant stab of contention from Hunter, and a satisfied preening from my mother. I hoped it would be enough to win her to my side, but those hopes were dashed when she said ponderously, "For his faults, Oz always knew what was best for the company. He must have had a good reason for sending the invitation."

Daddy's not here, I wanted to argue. If there was a single silver lining to that, let it be no more vampires in the house. My gaze—and my hopes—abandoned Mum and swung to Hunter; surely he would have something contrary to say to that, and I could sigh and gripe then admit the sense of it.

Shockingly, the antique waste of space let me down.

"He already *has* Oz's invitation," said Hunter, "so why can't he come in?"

Mum broke the huddle and put this question to the vampire.

"I'm guessing Oscar Maddock doesn't send his own mail," replied Lucas Sayle. "He was probably never even in the same room as that invitation. The spirit of a bit of magic matters just as much as the rule, and a piece of card from the desk of some assistant doesn't make something an invitation into Oscar's house just because his name's on it. If I had to guess, I'd say that's why I'm still out here."

"The others had the same issue crossing the threshold," said Fran. "When I invited them inside, it didn't work. We had to fetch Jude."

Mum wrinkled her nose at the mention of his name and turned to me instead.

"Teeny," she said. "Would you please invite our guest in?"

I grasped her wrist and squeezed hard. She flinched; her only emotional response was frustration, weary and decades old, grating like sandpaper against an oozing sore. As usual, my reservations about welcoming him in were a me problem. Wasn't it always a me problem, after all, my neuroses and my trauma wounds, my inability to just *be fine* when it mattered to her most?

If only she knew I would choose any other death. How slowly did a person die in the arms of a vampire? Did they make their victims feel safe even as they drained their life away? My grip tightened on her wrist as I used her to steady myself. It *was* a me problem—an old and well-worn neurosis about bleeding—but surely it was sensible not to let strange vampires in.

"We can turn him away," I said, not even a whisper—whispers could travel in halls of stone—but a breath tracing the shape of the words.

I sensed contention, a feeling like struggling out of bonds. I knew the argument she wanted to make, because I could hear it knocking at the back of my mind too: *But Oscar invited him*. For better or worse, Lucas Sayle's presence here was Daddy's wish. She could scorn his heedlessness, his arrogance, his lack of interest in the magic that had bought him the world.

But she had never learned the strength to fail him.

"It's not like he's going to hurt anyone, Teeny." She tugged her arm free of my grip. "Now let him in."

She was right, of course. Whoever a vampire's victims were—friendless men from small towns who washed up on riverbanks—they weren't among us, the highest ranks of human society; the supplicants who fawned and bowed and welcomed them into our homes, these old-money creatures possessed of the only thing we lacked. In my head, I didn't believe Lucas Sayle was any different.

In my scar tissue, I ached with warning.

But that was the weakness I was trying to exorcise. My father would never have allowed himself to feel this way, and if the woman I was trying to be had skittered into a corner with the shadows, I would simply have to pretend.

As I stood before the door, I couldn't have been more aware of him if his lips hovered an inch from my neck. It felt as if they did. In a voice that wasn't my own, I said: "You're welcome to come in."

Sayle's expression didn't change, nor did he move. He only looked up, eyes travelling the length of the doorframe, all the way up to where it carved through the stone high above him.

"I can't," he said, gaze coming to rest on me. It wasn't an accusation; it was a verdict. With his next words he brought the gavel down. "It seems this home isn't yours to open to me."

A ringing silence was broken by a tiny, thoughtful, "Well."

Mum.

It shouldn't have pleased her, all things considered. Fable, not my *home*, just an occasional residence where I darkened the halls as an outsider. Aside from the knife newly planted in my gut, it was a heavy point against my hopes of inheriting. And yet, there it was in her feelings, a satisfaction just enough about me that I could sense it, like the passing scent of a half-imagined cologne. Because I was hers, not Daddy's. Magic confirmed it.

"But—"

"I suppose someone better fetch Jude," she went on.

Jude.

"Wait!"

The cavernous entrance hall elevated my cry to a thunderclap. I winced. A dozen shadowed faces stared at me, immobile, as I swam in their squeamish anticipation. "Wait," I said again, affecting a tone of composure, as if I could strike through any impressions of hysteria and start over. I turned my back on them all, stood squarely before the open door, and looked Lucas Sayle directly in the eye. "Please come in."

I bargained with the universe to feel the touch of magic; some benediction from the monument that represented everything I wanted. But Fable remained a boulder in the forest, and the vampire's patient, open face contained something different now: apathy. He said nothing this time, only slid his gaze past my shoulder to the crowd behind me.

Very quietly, I heard Mum say: "Get Jude."

Lightheaded, I peeled away. I imagined wisps of vicarious shame drifting across the hall. Putting my back to everyone, I focused instead on a still, shadowed corner. My eye twitched until it was almost painful.

It was not long before Jude sauntered into the entrance hall, led by Mario. A glass of purplish wine dangled from one pale hand like it was an extension of his arm. Fran spoke close to his ear, a motherly, possessive arm wrapping around his back. Their two bleached heads bent close together was unsettling in a way I couldn't pin down.

When Jude pulled away, he scowled first at Mum, then the vampire. He looked about to refuse—and why wouldn't he? If it caused his aunt a single moment of grief, that was as good a reason as any. Then he noticed me.

With *Empathy*, I could read him more thoroughly than some twin telepathy might allow, and still nothing was clear. What Jude felt for me was a tangled and ugly loathing, transmuted from so many other things. I could sense the shells of them at the very edges, husks sucked dry to feed something he could tolerate better; something he had hardened into armour.

As Jude started to understand, new emotions—pillowy and sweet—numbed his animus. The downward curve of his arrogant mouth softened.

He'd been summoned because Fable wasn't mine.

"Somebody film this for my lawyers." He said it like a threat, or a promise, his eyes on me as he approached the doorway.

Mum made a disgusted sound at the back of her throat. "They can't," she said. "The cameras inside the house have been turned off for the weekend and we've taken everyone's devices."

"Small mercies," I muttered as Jude—a useless amoeba of a person—looked to Hunter to solve this for him.

"All of you," said Hunter, stepping forward and gesturing to the assembled staff, "pay attention, because you're getting subpoenaed as witnesses."

There were grumbles of complaint from the onlookers, but they all obediently fixed their attention on the doorway, and the vampire, whose mild affability had sharpened to interest.

It was unbearable. I couldn't stand there and watch Jude enjoying himself as he pulled ahead of me, so I stalked toward the stairs to escape. But Mum was suddenly at my side, fingers tight around my arm. I was trapped, forced to listen as Jude did what I could not.

"Welcome to Fable, Mr. Sayle. Please come in."

4

"He has to know Oz." Mum's eyes were sharp with interest as she watched Lucas Sayle, who was across the foyer introducing himself to Jude. "If he really got a random, last-minute invitation from a complete stranger, why show up?"

It was an excellent question, one I hoped someone else would take it upon themselves to answer. Jude, for example, in whom the vampire seemed to have already made a friend. Jude was . . . I doubted "affable" was in his repertoire, but he was attentive. Genuine. Probably because Sayle was flirting with him. The way his hand rested brazenly on Jude's arm couldn't be interpreted any other way.

And it wouldn't do. I couldn't let Jude succeed where I was failing. Once in my lifetime was enough; a second time this evening and I may as well kill myself. So when Mum asked if I wanted her to introduce me to the vampire, I pictured my father's audacious grin—held it in my mind like a talisman of strength—and said yes.

"Mr. Sayle, meet my daughter, Valentina Maddock. She's going to be looking after you this weekend."

I couldn't control the wide-eyed horror as it leapt onto my face. The top note of Mum's feelings, by comparison, was effervescent with the discovery of this idea: that she could palm this confusing complication off on me. We'd had some rough times, she and I, but this moment would get some serious airtime in my therapist's office.

Helpless to do anything but, I took the hand the vampire offered and shook. It was a normal hand: cool, but only the way a person's is when they've come in from bad weather, with ordinary skin and ordinary tendons that flexed as he gripped my fingers. His eyes—the blue-grey of rainwater—were round and wide, and didn't crease away when he smiled, which he did with his teeth; normal teeth, white and even. His hair was a sandy brown, combed neatly away from his face. I tried to guess his age, and placed him at younger than thirty.

No, that wasn't right: younger than thirty when he'd died.

"Call me Luc," he said as Mum left us alone. "I'm sorry I upset you."

I plastered on a smile. "Upset me?"

"The mortifying threshold thing. It's a finicky rule." But hadn't he just said the spirit of a piece of magic mattered just as much as the rule? "You look more like your father than I thought."

I let my smile turn hard. "But you said you didn't know my father."

"I meant from pictures," Luc said. "You smile just like him."

I knew what liars felt like when they were combing through their own words for mistakes. I knew the momentary freefall of a comment that felt like a harpoon, the single missed beat of their heart before their feet landed under them and they could think again. While it sounds like a poor attempt to catch him out, with *Empathy* it had worked for me time and time again.

The trouble was, I could sense nothing from him. For a moment, panic got the better of me. I felt my father's smile slip. My breathing was shallow and serrated—had been since the moment I realised a vampire was at the door—but I was never more aware of it than the moment Luc noticed it too. He watched the rise and fall of my chest and the rush of air from between my lips with naked interest.

By some blessing, it was at that moment the event planner appeared at my side. "We have a room for you, Mr. Sayle," she said, indicating a quaking man carrying what must have been Luc's weekend bag. Another member of the staff who had never come across a vampire before.

"Thank you." Luc turned to follow him—the man tried to straighten but only seemed to collapse in on himself even further—then turned back to me. "Where should I find you?"

"We're in the middle of dinner. I don't know if—"

He cut me off. "Then I'll join you."

My father would have refused him just for daring to presume, but right then I didn't have the composure to summon his strength.

"Fine," I said. "Excuse me."

I needed to get away from him—from *everyone*—so I could collect myself. But as I started across the entrance hall, I was intercepted yet again.

"Well, well," Jude drawled. "This isn't your home, after all. As if anybody but you were in doubt."

"Oh, perish," I hissed. "I couldn't care less what a bit of crude magic believes—it's not yours either. It's Daddy's, and if the worst should happen, I'm taking it for my own."

The clouds parted, and Jude's demons fell away. A single, clear feeling struck me: hatred, so blindingly hot I swear I felt a bead of sweat slide between my shoulder blades. I didn't care. Dividing the company and the house equally would make sense on paper, but absolutely nothing about Jude and me had ever once been that fair. If I got Mythos and Fable, and Jude got to be alive, *that* would be fair.

"Unfortunately for you, petal, my father is still alive."

His tongue rolled slowly over the pet name. The full honorific was *precious petal,* historically delivered under the breath when no adults were listening. It began when we were very little, on a misty night at a villa overlooking Rio de Janeiro. Jude had told me the lights of the city—diffuse and spectral in the mist—were will-o'-the-wisps, put there by the faeries to lure us away to be eaten. I had cried as he'd taunted me—baby, scaredy cat, *precious petal precious petal precious petal*—until Grandpa had someone call the city to turn the power off and on again at his command to prove Jude was lying.

I'd clawed a chunk of his cheek off by then. Absent of *Polish,* he still had a scar. Now "petal" was our chosen term of endearment for each other, if a term of endearment could be fired off to make you grind your teeth. When it was family, it absolutely could.

"Hunter knows what you and that witch you call a mother are up to, by the way," he went on. "That she's going to try and make him retire so you can be CFO and look like the perfect little heir. How predictably vicious of you both."

We had wanted to catch him unawares and without a countermove. This would put a wrench in things. "How did he find out?" I said through gritted teeth.

Jude's brows jumped up his forehead, and a breath like a laugh burst out of him. "Oh, petal," he said almost sweetly. "You made that too easy."

He threw a look over his shoulder and found Hunter, lurking in the shadows of the main staircase. Jude nodded a confirmation—one I had handed him—and the older man's face contorted into a sneer at once triumphant and full of rage. As Jude turned back to me with an ugly, satisfied grin, I hissed my frustration. *Of course* Hunter was expecting to suffer under Mum's rule, and of course he was paranoid enough to suspect a full-blown ousting. But now I had given everything away and he could plan exactly how to counter, and there went another point to Jude.

So this was how the battle lines had been drawn. Mum and me, Jude and Hunter. All Jude would have had to do for the CFO's support was promise he could keep his job. Now I had to be on alert not only for Jude's potential moves—as idiotic as they were bound to be—but Hunter's marginally more intelligent ones. And if the launch didn't go to plan and Hunter replaced Mum, he would almost certainly pull our own move on us, placing Jude in his old role so he could ascend to CEO when the time came.

But I'd be damned if Jude would see that idea get to me. "Whatever," I said on a sigh. "Hunter's really got his work cut out if *you're* the horse he's backing, and I wouldn't want it to be too easy. *I* want to feel like I've earned what I have." I patted him on the arm and smiled sweetly as inspiration struck. "You can have Charlotte as well. I know how you have to buy people's affection."

I'd expected a flare of fury, but instead his feelings lulled with something unsettlingly like concurrence, the edges festering like an infected wound, hot and painful.

"You know if I can buy her, she wasn't yours either, right?" he said slowly, like it was his thirtieth attempt at explaining calculus to a toddler. "You have chronically atrocious taste in people. In fact, the only person you have in your corner is that witch. Except it's really *her* corner, isn't it? We both know what she's up to."

I rubbed the bridge of my nose in exaggerated impatience. "Go ahead. Spew your nonsense, then get out of my way."

"Hunter doesn't respect her, so she's replacing him with someone she knows will crawl at her feet. Someone useful to her. She probably made you think it was your idea."

"It *was* my idea, you cerebral vacuum," I snapped before I could think better of it. Satisfaction bloomed in Jude's feelings; rage whited out mine. Rising to the bait was an obvious error, but the word "useful" knocked loose something that had begun to rattle when I'd shaken hands with a vampire.

"And I suppose you'll tell yourself it was your idea that you take care of the vampire all weekend, but I heard her hand down the order. Clever Auntie Claudia's good at that, isn't she?" He leaned closer. "Making people her tools."

He had aimed to wind me, and to my chagrin it worked. All the air rushed from my lungs. Like puppeting a doll, I arranged my face into a grin, the trembling fingers of my will pushing my cheeks into shape. Jude's snide triumph melted along with his smile, and I wondered if he was seeing Daddy or a hyena, feral with rage. Either would do if it unsettled him.

"If I were you, petal, I would worry about myself," I said as I stepped around him. "And what I planned to do once the only person who loved me died, and I was no longer anything to anybody."

I only caught flickers of his desolation as I fled, and they weren't enough to steady me. His words commingled with the vampire's cold attention, and together they became images of blood. Pooling in the crook of my elbow, the dip of my clavicle, turning my stomach and soaking my mind. Pain didn't scare me—I remembered so little of the pain. Nobody ever understood that the memory that had permanently marked me was blood; that mine was needed, that it would fix Jude when no one else's would, and so they were taking it.

They moved on to bone marrow when they couldn't harvest stem cells from my blood, and that's what nearly killed me. Staphylococcus on a needle, a one-in-a-million string of oversights that saw infection bloom undetected until it was almost too late. Unlike the blood donation, I was anaesthetized for the procedure. When the fever and sickness came and my hip swelled up, I was too young to understand it was because of something that had happened in my sleep.

But I understood blood; the tube, sickeningly warm against the flesh of my arm. My father, so frequently absent when I needed comfort and incapable of explaining why I didn't have a choice. And my mother, who had told me a thousand times that Jude was dying, hadn't she, did I want him to die, what else was she supposed to do?

Nothing, of course. She did exactly what she was supposed to. All except understand that two things could be true at the same time: that I was saving another child's life and that I was scared.

And another two: she was right to consent to the transplant; that she had done so in exchange for the Head Magician job was a wound that could never fully heal.

I was stumbling as I made it to my room. I took a cartridge of *Calm* from the drawer and snapped the thumb-sized stick close to my face, closing my eyes as the blue powder burst free. By the time the spell took effect, the powder had vanished, leaving no trace. Above my shoulder, my Moth pulsed in recognition of the upload. The jagged edge of a panic attack receded. I went into the bathroom, where I locked the door, knelt on the floor with my forehead pressed to the cool stone edge of the counter, and drew in lungfuls of air.

I didn't want to be anyone's tool, let alone Mum's. But once I was CEO, I wouldn't have to be. I could fire her and install a new Head Magician if that's what I needed to feel safe. And none of her recriminations could hurt me, because I would need nothing from anybody. As CEO and with *Immortality*, I would be complete.

Jude knew the words that would slide right between my ribs. But they were just words, and letting him undermine my determination was not an option. I could hold it together because I had to, and that was all there was to it.

I hauled myself to my feet. My knees were putty, and I leant heavily on the counter as I looked up, expecting to see a pale version of my face in the mirror.

But I wasn't pale. I was flushed. The memory of the vampire, inches away, watching me breathe like the needs of my mortal body fascinated him, was a tight knot aching in my stomach, but I couldn't stop replaying it. I was like a child waking in the night and seeing creeping hands and looming figures behind my eyelids, compulsively replaying the thought of something crawling closer.

He couldn't hurt me, I told myself. No vampire would dare touch me inside the walls of my own home. And Fable *was* mine by right; I didn't give a damn what a bit of crude magic believed. I pressed both palms to the wall, to the flawless, ageless stone. Only with magic could marble remain perfectly undamaged. Perfectly untouched. Here, in this monument to my name, I could be who I needed to be.

At the very least, I could fake it long enough to get through the weekend.

By the time I returned to the dining room, I had affected a mask of ease. My smile was back in place. There was no sign of our newest guest, but another place had been set beside my own. The steak tartare was gone, and a stuffed, roasted quail on a bed of wilted greens was waiting for me. Most of the other little birds were halfway devoured, the guests dabbing grease from their mouths or prying meat from bone. I made a single cut into the breast of the quail. The knife punctured the crispy skin, then met resistance as metal scraped bone. My heart seized like it had expected something other than a bead of juice and tender white meat beneath. I put my knife and fork down.

I hadn't been hungry anyway.

My gaze was drawn through the flickering candlelight toward the Gothenburgs. They had also been served dinner; the male vampire's quail was untouched, but the girl was shredding hers with her bare fingers. A neat heap of white-meat mulch studded with pulverised quail skin was growing next to the carcass. Her long red nails gleamed with grease.

I leant close to Mum. "Where's Ansgar?"

She only briefly glanced across the table before continuing to saw at her bird. "They didn't say."

"Who are they?"

"Mariah and Randolph. I met them both during the production process. They brought their—I can't remember the minutiae of their hierarchies—their *underlings* to the lab to donate venom for testing."

Venom donation. I didn't care to wonder what that entailed. "They couldn't just give you their own venom?"

"I suppose not. They're both important. I don't think they rank directly under Ansgar but they're possibly the next rung below that. Or Mariah is at least." She lowered her voice. "She's been warmer when we've met in the past. Randolph is always unpleasant, but neither of them seems to care how obvious it is that they don't want to be here."

After several years of working towards the creation of the tonic, for neither Ansgar nor any of his seconds to show up struck me as odd. Not even the representatives they *had* sent were in the mood to celebrate. Mariah was decimating the pointless offering with her elbows on the table and an air of concentrated frustration, as if she just needed to finish the task and then she could leave. Randolph, the recipient of a stream of chatter coming from the heiress on his right, was slumped low in his chair and staring into his wineglass with abject apathy, as if he was completely unaware his talkative dinner companion was there.

A prickle along my neck drew my attention to the arched entranceway, as the third vampire joined us. Luc's motions were loose and patient as he made his way around the table towards me, but as he came closer, I saw the pulsing of the tendons in his neck as he swallowed, the tightness in his jaw. It was performative ease, and I hoped my efforts weren't showing as much as his.

As he took his seat, his sleeve brushed mine, and I suppressed the urge to flinch. Had the air taken on a chill, or was my imagination already consumed by the thought of him closing the space between us, pressing cold fingers under my chin, exposing my throat so he could taste me?

I followed his gaze to the apparent cause of his tension: the Gothenburg vampires. Randolph had sat upright and was eyeing Luc with disbelief. Beside him, Mariah had ceased mutilating her quail and gone still. After a moment, the three of them locked in some kind of standoff, Mariah reached for her companion's wrist, and he bent his head close to her like a supplicant. She whispered something, her lips so close to his ear that they brushed the shell, but her eyes never left Luc. The stream of her words went on for a minute, maybe more, punctuated occasionally by a nod or shake of the head from the second vampire. Whatever they agreed at last made Randolph sit back in his chair and resume staring into his wine. Mariah, done with her grisly busywork, wiped her hands on her napkin, pushed the plate away from her, and called a server to top up her untouched wine.

With the Gothenburgs' attention elsewhere, Luc's posture loosened, and he seemed to forget about them. Another pointless dinner plate was placed in front of him. I had wondered if he might actually eat it, having been so insistent on joining us, but though he unfolded his napkin and placed it across his lap, he paid no attention to the food. Nor did he touch the wine that was poured for him. Whatever had occurred between the three vampires had quickly passed, but there was no ignoring what it meant:

They knew each other.

"Friends of yours?" I chanced to say, heart in my throat. I was no longer merely sitting with a vampire—I was starting conversation.

"Who?"

"Our House Gothenburg guests." I tipped my chin toward them. "You know them."

"By reputation only," he said with a look that dared me to argue.

Unable to hold his gaze without my vision darkening at the edges, I turned away. Mariah had obtained a full bottle from one of the waiters and was holding it above her head, topping up her own wineglass with a thin, high stream that appeared to enthral her. She didn't stop, even as the wine overflowed the rim of the glass. News that another vampire had joined us seeped along the table—if I had to guess, from Jude to Roman, to anybody who would listen to Roman talk—and Luc had become the focus of a raft of stolen glances, which he ignored.

As if from nowhere, his voice sounded again too close to my ear, giving me a mortal fright as he said, "You'll get used to me. I'm sure of it."

But there was little chance of that. My hands shook. The room spun. I tried to hide it with a sip of wine, but I could feel myself floating away. I was leaving my body, retreating to a safe place somewhere above. The room was growing quieter as I tuned everything out. That was good; it was the only way I would survive this.

Then Luc spoke again and I came slamming back down.

"Chicago," he said into the silent dining room. At some point in my fugue, a dozen conversations had been whittled to just one. "Originally."

"I mean," amended Eric Burton-Shaw, "which noble house do you belong to?"

Luc said again what he'd told us at the door: that he was unaffiliated with the houses.

"Until you introduced yourself, I was under the impression all vampires belonged to a house," Mum said.

"You're not familiar with our culling ritual then, Dr. Cabot," Mariah called from down the table. She was still pouring the wine, which had long overflowed her glass and was spilling onto the mirrored table in a widening pool. Rivulets of crimson crawled towards the edges and dripped onto the marble, where two servers were on their knees with wads of dish towels. I glanced around at the other guests to confirm: yes, we were all pretending we didn't see it.

"Culling?" said Eric mildly. "You excommunicate members of your houses?"

"Excommunicate?" Mariah gave a chuckle. "No, dear, we slaughter them."

Out of respect, fear, or possibly a combination of both, every person in the dining room managed to withhold a reaction. Only the steady *drip, drip* of wine on stone answered her.

"Your own kin?" said Eric at last, going for casual but nonetheless delivered with a considerable squeak. Out of the corner of my eye, I saw Mum fidgeting like she couldn't decide whether to divert the topic of conversation. But before she did, Mariah was launching into an explanation.

"Every forty-two years in House Gothenburg, but all the houses do it. The Maker and the Ancestors—" She twirled one delicate wrist as she considered. "Ancestors are those the Maker sired themselves; their heirs, I suppose. They meet in a ritual ceremony at the end of every cycle and they decide which of the many spidering lineages below them needs to go. It's dreadfully dramatic, everybody arguing their case. Usually a member or two will have been exceedingly silly and drawn the Maker's ire. Sometimes it's completely on the Maker's whim—they hold the final decision, you see. But it's not just the offending individuals and below; it's the entire lineage, usually up to the first descendant—that is, those below the Ancestor. Sometimes only up to the second if the first is very loved. Gosh, sometimes the Ancestor too if they're *not*! It's never happened in Gothenburg, but House Cuzco had *ten* Ancestors at one point—they currently have six. Take Randolph and me for example. If one of my dears, or one of his, had been especially naughty, we might be on the chopping block. Even a descendant many generations removed from us. I'm the sire of five generations." She made scissors with one hand and snipped violently at the air, making the man next to her—and me—jump. "But we always cut near the top."

Athena cleared her throat before venturing a question. "What does this have to do with vampires like Mr. Sayle? Those without—"

"Oh, yes, yes! I've gotten completely off track, haven't I?" Discovering she'd poured out the last dregs of the wine, Mariah abandoned the bottle, letting it clunk onto its side and roll towards the edge of the table. One of the towel-bearing servers below her saw it coming and snatched it before it came down on him. "Back to the point—sometimes someone might escape. They're hunted, of course. We catch most of them eventually, but often during their time out there in the wild"—here she looked across to Luc, and the candlelight danced in her eyes like specks of glee—"they propagate. They can't help themselves; they're lonely, of course. Some even start raising their own little armies, because they think that will keep them safe. It only ever gets them discovered."

Several heads swivelled as their owners glanced from Mariah to Luc and back again. I realised, with a pang of distaste, that Mariah had captured her audience not with horror but with entertainment. The sparkle of intrigue and excitement shone in more than one pair of eyes. Because we weren't really talking about cold-blooded murder. Murder was done to one human being by another.

Graham was the oaf unafraid to say what everyone was thinking. He waved his grease-streaked knife at Luc. "So, you would hunt . . ."

"Oh, good heavens, no!" Mariah drew the "no" out like the misunderstanding was perfectly ridiculous and not a reasonable conclusion to draw on the heels of having ritualistic vampire slaughter laid out for us. "No, we have no complaint with common vampires—the strays, if you will. Catching our own exiles is diversion enough."

Diversion. These killings were sport for them. I glanced at Randolph, still staring into his wine like the boredom was bone-deep, and reminded myself that neither he, nor Mariah, nor the composed and elegant being to my right were human.

"How brutal," Mum said mildly. The servers had begun to collect our main-course plates—Luc's untouched, mine with a single cut, many abandoned at the start of Mariah's tale.

Mariah, far from offended by my mother's comment, smiled like this was a seduction, Mum a doting suitor she had wound round her finger. "We have no choice. We don't die, but we can't continue to grow in numbers exponentially, can we?" She tilted her head, eyes softening, as if Mum was now a child Mariah was tasked with teaching. "Do you think we would all be enjoying dinner together like old friends if vampires multiplied like humans do? We would be at such odds, don't you think? Us leaping out of every dark alley to slake our thirst, you holing up in your homes after dark just to make it tricky for us. Not to mention, our resources are plenty, but they're not infinite." Her eyes suddenly widened, and she let out a cackling laugh, one delicate hand bobbing in front of her mouth in a nod to etiquette. "Oh gosh, what am I saying? You'll know for yourself soon enough, won't you?" It took her another moment to calm herself, by which point tears had gathered along her lash lines. She gave a sigh and gestured in a way that included every one of us in what she said next. "You can of course come up with your own system, but feel free to borrow ours."

A couple of guests started to laugh, but trailed off when they realised they were the only ones who'd taken this as a joke. I felt, rather than saw, Mum cringe beside me as the mood curdled. It was Luc who rescued us.

"I'd take her first suggestion if I were you. Leaping out of dark alleys is hell on the lumbar spine."

If you think a vampire-attack joke from an actual vampire would not improve the atmosphere, you've forgotten that we aren't the victim class. The laughter was thirsty and grateful.

And that was not the limit of Luc's charms. He played the picture of ease as the guests peppered him with questions. He was our unknown quantity. Our enigmatic stranger. How did he make his money? (Real estate.) Where did he summer? (Buenos Aires, but it was winter, technically; vampires travelled with the dark.) Who did he know? (He preferred to keep to himself.)

"Then I suppose it's a stupid question to ask why I've never heard of you," I said for only him to hear.

He replied in a voice pitched even lower, like a fingertip barely grazing my skin. "Or why you're hearing of me now."

"Two truths and a lie!" interrupted a shout, and fists drummed approvingly along the table.

"Alright, two truths and a lie," he said, and as I watched him, a chill spread through me. It was the moment I noticed—the uncanny valley, the bodily recognition, all of a sudden—that the thing by my side was crucially different.

Put simply, it was how little he moved.

As he'd agreed to the game, I'd had the impression of him quieting the room with a raise of his hands, or a nod; some movement or gesture that confirmed that the coaxing could stop, that he was about to speak.

But he hadn't. The room had fallen silent for Luc to speak, and he had done nothing outwardly to force it. His hands were laced in his lap, where they had been since he'd taken his seat. His posture also remained the same. I wondered, shudderingly, if he had even turned or leant in when he'd spoken to me a moment before. I'd thought that he had, but now I questioned whether I'd truly seen him gesture at all since I saw him at the door.

Whether I'd seen anything human in him at all.

Vampires varied from us in much the same way as witches and fae folk; where humans had a life force we could understand in terms of electromagnetic pulses, witches and the like had a life force of magic. The crucial difference between other magical races and vampires, however, was that vampires had once been human. At their death, they were afflicted with a curse that permanently altered their nature, from human to magic. We had almost everything in common, so it was easy to imagine while talking to Luc that he was something like a serial killer, or a dangerous psychopath, or just a man in an alley with a gun and a hankering for your purse.

But the danger of him was something far stranger. He had an innate magic—a glamour of some kind—that helped him craft the human man we needed to see; that his *victims* needed to see. Did he wield it consciously? Was his boyishly handsome face the one he'd worn in life, or was that a manipulation too?

Worst of all: Would I be aware of it if he dipped his head, brought his lips close to my skin?

"The first truth," Luc was saying, and I dared not take my eyes off him in case I stopped noticing the magic, "is that I share a birthday with Martin Maddock."

"Oh, so do I!" cried a movie mogul. Luc acknowledged her with a smile, but was there hostility in it? A disdaining edge the woman couldn't see because she didn't know to look? Perhaps I was the one seeing something that wasn't there.

"Second: I spent time in prison."

"What for?" someone called.

"Gang-related offences," said Luc.

A chorus of mirth rustled along the table. *Not any old vampire! One that might have been a killer in life too!*

"And third: I'm an art collector. The jewel of my collection is an Eva Hesse."

In his corner, Jude deigned to look up from his drink, and I think the vampire's gaze met his.

Because the jewel of *Jude's* collection was a Hesse. I didn't know what it looked like or where it lived, because I'd never asked and I didn't care. But my father had gone with him to view it before the auction, had listened fondly as his son had waxed lyrical about post-something and whatever ugly plastic the sculpture was made from, about Eva Hesse and her genius. Then my father repeated it all to me, as if by bridging the gap he could create some proxy for sibling bonding. It was one of Daddy's far-fetched tactics; I'd learned more about Jude this way than I ever cared to know.

Jude was looking at the vampire now with nascent interest, which I feared was the point. Somebody always wanted something from you when you were a Maddock.

The third was a lie.

"The second must be a lie," someone said, and all along the table, the guests agreed.

"You're correct, of course," said Luc.

Delighted and charmed, they all cheered. Luc turned to me with a smile. He had dimples when he smiled, I realised, boyish and cheerful. Though I trembled with the instinct to flee, I made myself take him in. I catalogued his eyes, his normal teeth, the twist of his shoulders, seeking gaps in the glamour—seeking *hope,* that I might be able to keep my eyes on the monster.

But I had already lost sight of it. There was nothing. He was normal, handsome, disarmingly magnetic.

"I must be a very bad liar," he said, and he winked.

Or he didn't. I've never been sure.

5

My most recent dose of *Empathy* had completely worn off by the time dinner was over. As the guests were ushered back towards the ballroom, I slipped away and sought the sanctuary of my room once again.

When you're trying to be someone, your sharpest tool is knowing in real time how you're perceived and adjusting accordingly. I'd been using *Empathy* since I was fourteen or fifteen, when it occurred to me I might be attracting a life like my mother's instead of my father's by appearing as if I belonged there. Did people see a girl who was studious and serious because it was what her ambition required, or did they think I was naturally my mother's daughter, a born magician? Was my self-conception at odds with where the world had neatly slotted me? Without looking at all, had they seen Jude in the space next to my father and so placed me beside my mother? How symmetrical. How pleasingly balanced.

How intolerable.

Empathy had its drawbacks, of course—the warning leaflet Mythos had been forced to include in the box enumerated them. *This product has been linked to increased anxiety. If you are struggling with self-esteem, see a therapist. We strongly advise that you disclose your use of the spell to others.* The same way cotton buds told you not to use them for their main utility: sticking them in your ears.

It was a cartridge here and there, only around the people I was most eager to impress. Celebrities, for example. The board of Mythos. Daddy's friends. My current chain usage was a case of exceptional circumstances.

I would ease off again when I could afford to: when I had been crowned my father's heir. But until then, I couldn't fathom giving up the way it made me feel. It was like I was stepping into someone's private, interior life while they were smiling and shaking my hand. *Empathy* defied boundaries, defied decency, and people *didn't even know* they were being violated. I didn't have to announce myself at the door, didn't need to ask for their consent. There was nothing they could do to stop me, and that was the purest rush of power I knew.

There was a fresh box of the spells in the drawer beside my bed. I ripped the plastic off and took out one of the glossy white cartridges, along with another cartridge of *Calm*, to make my usual cocktail.

The *Calm* came first; I snapped it in front of my face and let the blue powder dust my skin, where it swiftly vanished. The fluttering tightness that had begun building in my stomach as I came upstairs mellowed. My muscles softened. A feeling of wellness descended.

If I had had my phone, I would have opened the Moth app and checked the "time remaining" bar. *Calm* burned faster the more acute one's panic. The maximum for temporary spells was around four hours; when I used it this way, I averaged about thirty minutes.

Because *Empathy* was not a powder or an applicator spell. Nor was it a tonic, a friendly little vial of sweet-tasting liquid you knocked down in one. The cartridges were thick discs, like small, white hockey pucks, with a fingerprint-sized dent on the rim.

I sat on my bed and placed my finger over the button. It felt counterintuitive to sprint towards the thing that scared me, but I'd learned it was best not to let the anticipation fester. Even with the *Calm*, the best I could do was dissociate, suck in a breath, and let it out slowly as I pressed down.

The needle burst from the cartridge and pierced the pad of my finger, always sharper than I anticipated and yet always a twisted rush, a pulse of adrenaline before I crumbled. You never saw the needle of a cartridge spell, nor the pinprick wound, which healed before a single drop of blood could fall; it was the only reason I could force myself to use them. I discarded the disc and gave in to the compulsion to wrap my hands around the soft insides of my elbows to protect them. Shudders of nauseous unease ran through me. They would have been much worse if not for *Calm*.

As I waited for the nausea to recede, I tried to recall if the leaflet said anything about eye twitches, the fluttering kind I usually associated with too little sleep but had plagued my right eye since Wednesday morning. At first, I thought it was a symptom of having cried myself to sleep. But not only had it persisted, the twitching grew worse when I focused on it. Was it possible it wasn't the stress and grief? Maybe it was a side effect of absorbing others' emotions.

After a minute or so, I felt like myself again. I let out a single note of dry laughter; now the only thing left to remind me how it had felt to bleed was a house full of vampires. I took my own advice—not to let the anticipation fester—and made my way downstairs.

In the interval dinner had provided, the ballroom, once stone, had become flesh. Mauvy purple lighting pulsed with the beat of the music, each thump throwing shadows into the crevices under the balconies, the ballroom expanding and contracting like the bellowing of a colossal lung. The air was warm and close. Bespoke cocktails in gemstone hues—ruby, sapphire, onyx black—were stacked atop a mirrored table, their crystal glasses winking with a million tiny lights. At other stations were miniature desserts, a champagne tower, bowls full of party magic—*Dancing Shoes, Good Time, Attract,* the latter of which heightened one's sexual appeal and was also popular as a confidence booster. The death-trap pools lining the centre of the ballroom had been covered, and on stages above them dancers, acrobats, and contortionists writhed in the twilight gloom.

Dark and loud and ideal for someone pretending she wasn't feeling vulnerable and terrorised, so I made a lap through the guests. It helped, in a small way, to imagine I was my father when I felt the least like him; anxious where he was entertained, shaken where he was solid. I paid special attention to members of the board, fielded their questions about Luc with the air of someone who invited mysterious vampires into her house on the daily, for the love of it. Fingers crossed he'd already had dinner! We thought we'd put him in *your* room, hope you don't mind!

All the while, I scanned for the offending vampire himself, and picked out Charlotte instead. She had ingratiated herself with a group including Hunter and a couple of other guests. She smothered a yawn, champagne dangling forgotten in one hand, an intensity to her as she put on her most charming self in the face of exhaustion. I plucked a spell from a bowl and went over to her.

"Catch," I said, tossing the cuboid cartridge—a vapour spell—as she turned around. She caught it awkwardly and turned it over until she found the product name on the side: *Revitalise*.

"Is this the good shit? These things are, like, two grand a pop." She'd probably only handled the less potent budget line. Holding the spell under her face, she pressed the logo on the cartridge and inhaled the blue vapour that rose from inside. It was like watching someone jolt themselves awake. She sucked in a breath, blinking hard.

"Holy fuck." Her eyes were wide. "I feel fantastic."

"They're good, aren't they?"

"No, seriously. I can't remember the last time I wasn't tired. I had no idea . . ." She looked at the spent cartridge in the palm of her hand. "These must be, like, ten times more powerful than the hundred-dollar boxes."

"I don't know exactly," I said. "But that'll wear off in a few hours. They're in the bowl over there. Just be warned, if you do more than two or three back-to-back, either have another ready or be lying down, because you'll pass out where you're standing the second it wears off."

Meanwhile, talk amongst the group had turned to the price tag for the tonic. "I assume no less than forty-five, fifty, correct?" said a Saudi prince.

"*Million?*" said Charlotte. All heads turned her way as if she'd smashed a glass. Into the silence, she said, "Forty-five to fifty million?"

Hunter didn't know what to do with her incredulity, so he ignored her and turned back to the prince. "There's a pricing structure that will reward purchasing multiple doses. For families. You'll want to enjoy your immortal lives together, of course."

"And how do you decide who gets to?" Charlotte said. Her tone was cool, but her face did several involuntary things to undermine her. "I suppose it can't be everyone, right? Humanity would buckle under the population growth."

She was met with silence. Hunter looked at me as if Charlotte were my fault, which in a way she was. I turned to her to answer, and to my horror, my hand almost came up to cup Yorick's imaginary skull: *Oh, come on, be serious.* The product was priced according to what Mythos believed people would pay, as with anything. I could not fathom what Charlotte had learned that she hadn't expected.

"That's part of it," Hunter said, recovering before I found my words. "We don't need regulators swooping down on us to point out the problem with two billion people suddenly becoming immortal. But even if they didn't, do we want our immortal lives to be bought so *cheaply*? Wouldn't we dishonour every person who had acquired everything other than completion—who were one tonic away—by handing it out to the masses?"

It was annoying to witness Hunter be right. The guests were nodding their profound agreement. Completion was priceless; if Mythos was forced to put a figure to it, the company would get as close as it could.

Charlotte's steady gaze locked on mine, her expression opaque, her emotions probing. I felt like a curio in an antiques shop, something she was turning over in her hands as she examined me. Then her feelings withdrew, disappointed, like she had decided to leave me on the shelf.

"Of course." She flashed Hunter a smile. "You wouldn't want to dishonour your clients, would you? Excuse me."

Charlotte slipped between two bodies and started away. I followed and caught her wrist before she could disappear.

"Hey," I said. Her primary emotion as she turned to me was relief, and she watched me expectantly as I tried to parse what it meant. When I gave up, I said, "Have you talked to Jude yet?"

The relief was strangled and withered in an instant. A bright burst of something multifaceted—half a dozen prickly things I had no time to grasp on to—replaced it and was likewise quickly smothered.

"No," she said before I could pursue it. She shook her head like she was shedding the spent husks of the feelings. "I tried—a couple of times actually—but that vampire has totally annexed him."

"Which vampire?" I said, but I already knew. Only one had taken a targeted interest in Jude.

She nodded over my shoulder. "They're over there."

At first, I couldn't find them, but then a roaming spotlight swept the negative space in the shadow of a staircase and briefly illuminated Luc and Jude with its violet glow. They stood inches from each other, heads bent close as if they were conspiring. As the spotlight circled again, I saw something akin to interest painted on Jude's face as he listened to Luc talk. I'd seen him look at a speedboat that way, an hour before it found itself at the bottom of Venice's Grand Canal. If Luc's goal with the Eva Hesse gambit had been to hook Jude's attention, he had it, and Jude was too stupid to notice he'd been lured in or question why.

"If you can peel the vampire off him, I'll slip in," Charlotte said at my shoulder. My whole body grumbled a complaint, muscles tensing as if preparing to fight me. My aversion must have been obvious, because Charlotte sighed in impatience. "Oh, come on, Vee. Since when has a vampire ever been a threat to anyone in this room?"

"Right," I said without feeling, but Charlotte had already drifted away to find a spot from which to pounce.

It wasn't the task of prizing him off Jude that propelled me over there. It was the certainty that Daddy wouldn't be afraid; that I had no choice but to fake it until I wasn't either. So I swiped another glass of champagne from a passing server—which made about eight fewer than I needed to get through this night—forced down my sickening dread, and went to interrupt them.

Sure enough, they were talking about art. Neither acknowledged me, so I cut across Luc to say: "So you were in a gang?"

I didn't know everything my new face did, but I trusted the look I gave him was sufficiently arch.

He ignored it. "Actually, no. If you remember, that was the lie."

"Is that so?" He nodded, determined not to drop the act. To Jude, I said: "Be elsewhere a moment, won't you, petal?"

Jude turned to me while taking a gulp of champagne, like I wasn't another person at all but a thing to look at during a lull in conversation. A film of alcohol dulled his gaze, but inside he raged with superiority. "No."

If I had known a single thing about art—or if I had been able to use *Empathy* on him—perhaps I could have probed at Luc's act until it fell apart. As it stood, I was helpless. Jude's delighted sense of power grew the longer he watched me fume, but if he thought I would say "please," he could dive head first off the balcony.

"I was sorry to hear your father is sick," said Luc, a little to me but mostly to Jude. "How is he?"

"As good as dead," said Jude flatly. One had to know him very well to hear the lie in his tone, and I did, but it didn't make his words any less of a gut punch. That he would say that about Daddy and not care that I'd heard. "He won't wake up."

"My condolences. Does that mean Dr. Cabot's new position is for the long term?"

"Why do you want to know?" I said at the same time as Jude slurred, "Not if I have anything to say about it."

I hadn't noticed just how drunk he was. His words were soft, like someone had filed off the corners. "Just because he doesn't have a will, *she* thinks she can swoop in and take everything— *Ouch*."

I dug my fingers into his elbow, but despite his protest, I doubt he really felt it. "You need to go to bed."

He shook me off his sleeve. "Oh, fine. Play your little games. It's not like I care."

He walked away—not towards bed but to the bar. I fortified myself with a swig of champagne and turned to Luc.

"You know that I know you lied, don't you?"

He smiled impishly. "But that was the game."

I didn't return the smile, loathe to play nice with this interloper.

"I can't prove you've been studying up on how to ingratiate yourself with Oscar Maddock's son. But if you have, you've wasted your time. What he said was true: there isn't a will. Whatever you believe he's about to be worth to you is yet to be decided."

The vampire looked over his shoulder, and I followed his gaze to where Charlotte had successfully intercepted Jude. He stood with his arm flung around her as he talked into her ear, looking a lot like he was going to make this easy for her.

"So the other part's true as well?" said Luc. "You'll challenge him for everything?"

"I don't see how that's any of your business."

He shrugged. "I was under the impression you and your brother were close."

I wasn't Jude; I wasn't drunk or easily bought or so convinced of my own importance that I wouldn't question a stranger's attempts to flatter me. So I heard the intention behind his line of questioning; I just didn't know what it meant.

I chose deflection. "Isn't it funny how literally everyone chooses to refer to him as my brother and not my cousin? Both are true."

Luc was ponderously silent. Then he nodded—or appeared to, at least, that predatory magic doing its work. I didn't want to think about the ways he was monstrous, and yet I was afraid to stop, in case I mistook him for an ordinary man.

"And here I was thinking your animosity towards him was *your* grief manifesting."

"Ha."

Nearby was a table crowded with fishbowls full of spells: applicators, needles, tonics. We both watched Athena van Thiel pluck a vial of *Dancing Shoes* from a bowl, uncork it, and throw it back. Her Moth pulsed once as the spell uploaded. She gave a tinkling laugh as it hit her: the feeling that dancing might be the most joyous thing in the world, the sudden surety in her own limbs and their grace. She spun as she moved towards the dance floor, each move confident and striking. She would dance like a pro for the next hour.

"Here's something I've always wanted to know," said the vampire as he took an applicator of *Attract* out of a bowl and popped the lid off, revealing a brush designed to be swiped onto the eyelids. "This Mythos-branded stuff only works on the living, so forgive me if this is a stupid question, but what makes the difference between a bit of magic like this and one like that, say?" He gestured to the tiny vials of liquid *Dancing Shoes*. "How does someone work out which style of spell will work?"

"You don't—use our spells? Like, ever?"

"I have a *Swift*-enabled car and a *Fuel*-powered house." He gestured again at the buffet of magic. "But this stuff is for living humans. It doesn't work on me any more than it would on . . . a cat. Or a faerie, I imagine." He frowned. "You didn't know that?"

So I had never tried to give a cat *Dancing Shoes*! That Mythos magic didn't work on faeries or vampires was news, but I didn't want Luc to see how disquieting it was that he had outpaced me at my own family's company, so I sidled past the question.

"To tell the truth, the delivery method makes no difference. It's about creating a sense of authenticity. The designs are supposed to emulate the way a witch's spells might work. Potions and"—I hesitated—who knew how witch magic *actually* worked?—then made a gesture for *and all the rest*—"objects transforming in a puff of smoke, that sort of thing. We *could* administer all our spells with the push of a button, but it wouldn't be very magical, would it?"

"And someone in your lab knows so much about witch's magic?"

I laughed. "Of course not. I said how a witch's spells *might* work. Hypothetically. It's not like anyone's going to correct us, is it?"

"But if the idea is authenticity, why do this?" He turned the applicator over in his hand. "It's so understated. Why not make bubbling potions and enchanted jewellery and stuff?"

"Because our customers don't *actually* want crude magic, nor do they want to be reminded of real crude magic, which is dangerous. Marketing Mythos products as the next evolution of tech makes them safer, more reliable, more accessible, while still being wondrous and valuable at the same time. It's a delicate balancing act."

"So is it magic, or is it tech?" he said sceptically.

"It's both."

The decision to market Mythos's products this way had been an early stroke of genius. Whilst people were familiar with the existence of witches and the like, ninety-nine in a hundred rightfully had no interest in dealing with one, the promise of magic be damned. Like the mob, or religion, they offered powerful solutions at steep and unknowable prices. Magic was a cautionary tale, a roll of the dice. It was a trick even when it was real. Tech, on the other hand, could be trusted.

"And the Moth." Luc eyed the orb floating over my right shoulder. "That doesn't do anything either, right? If my understanding's correct, you only acquire one with purchases of a certain price."

I smiled in such a way that he knew I'd heard the cynicism. "Yes, the decision was made to hold it back for permanent spells. High-end products. But the Moth is functional, I can assure you."

"Functional isn't the same as necessary."

"It was *necessary* to assuage customers' fears of a paradigm-shifting product."

Early focus groups had suggested that people were accepting of magic performed on an object, but magic performed on the body unsettled them. They needed to better understand the process by which a powder could erase bad memories or a tonic could improve focus, or else they equated it to potentially harmful junk science. It made them think of snake oil. Lies and unintended consequences. Witchcraft.

Enter the Moth. It was a widget, a visible buffer against the discomfort of the unknown that clients could imagine functioned like any other bit of wireless tech. And it did—it synced to the client and took instructions from the spells they installed via an app—but it didn't *have* to. Magic could act on a person just fine without it. As for the fact a client only acquired one with the purchase of Mythos's high-end, permanent products, if it was good enough for the rich, it was good enough for everyone else. By the time the company launched its first affordable lines of temporary spells, the sense of safety the Moth provided had trickled down.

"So the purpose of the Moth is manufactured," said Luc, "and the purpose of the powders and needles and potions—"

"We call them *tonics*."

"—is manufactured. All to project a manufactured sense of authenticity, but not too much authenticity."

I recognised his tone. I had heard it countless times from idealistic and uneducated people who believed framing a product in any way at all was tantamount to trickery. Like it wasn't a skill, or a feat of staggering creativity and insight. "People want magic to be magic—they just don't want it to be witch magic or fae magic. The Mythos branding sanitises something frightening without damaging the allure."

"Let me point out that the fear of real magic is a Mythos product too," he said with a sharp smile. "Wasn't the term '*crude magic*' invented by your marketing team?"

"*Invented?*" I said, my voice high and staccato. A nearby heiress did a double take at me and lost the thread of her conversation. "We put a name to something that terrorised people for centuries. You know they used to drown innocent women they believed were witches? They used to leave children out in the woods because they were afraid they were changelings. Mythos didn't just deliver safe magic; we delivered *safety*. We put an end to fear by putting that power in the hands of humans—"

I had drawn breath to continue when the entire trajectory of the exchange took shape before me. This vampire had arrived for some unknown reason, lied about knowing the Gothenburgs, tried to seduce Jude, coaxed me to lay out the cornerstones of Mythos's entire marketing strategy—and was now looking at me with the gloating superiority of someone who had me right where he wanted me. Had he been pressing my buttons on purpose, waiting for something privileged to slip? I combed back through everything I'd said, stomach sinking at the thought of having misstepped.

Luc's expression shifted. His shoulders fell. "I'm sorry," he said. "I had a rule before coming here and I've already broken it."

"Which was?"

"To not be self-righteous. Or provocative. Or truculent." He smiled wryly. "Or generally myself. I've been told I need to have the last word."

"You should have said. Welcome to the Maddock residence, you'll fit right in."

It was only then I noticed he was empty-handed. "Wouldn't you like something? A cocktail?"

"No."

I opened my mouth to speak, but I didn't know what to do with that; he hadn't said he *didn't* drink.

"It's alright," he said. He started leading us to a couch in the corner under a balcony. "You can ask your questions."

I sat and tucked my free hand into the crook of the opposite elbow protectively. "Tell me about being in a gang."

"Not those questions."

I shook my head. "I don't need to know."

"Yes, you do."

"Oh?"

"Perhaps not. But you need some cure for the speed your heart is beating before it bursts right out of your chest."

It was a bluff. He couldn't know that, could he? I *was* afraid, exhaustingly so, but it was a fear of bleeding, not of monsters. It was a fear that made the fleeting jab of a needle an ordeal every day. One that plucked up doctor's visits, minor injuries, every period I'd ever had, and wove them into a lengthening tapestry of phobia. I had gotten a tattoo when I was fifteen. It had happened after a school friend read something of my family history and came to me all sympathetic-eyed and righteous, saying things about consent and medical emancipation and children's rights that disturbed the silt I had chosen to let lie. The tattoo—a tiger across my hip—was my best adolescent attempt at taking control, but all the pills and alcohol with which I sedated myself were not enough to blot out the images behind my eyelids: blood seeping through my skin, flowing in rivulets down my leg, turning into a tidal wave that would drown me.

In the hierarchy of things that sent shudders of dread through me, then, yes, vampires were worse than all of the above. But that didn't make them special. It wasn't a fear of the unknown. It was the fear, specifically, of another thing that needed my blood to live; that could and would take it against my will.

No, hearing the details of Luc's existence wouldn't cure my racing heart, as he thought it would. Vampirism demystified would only make me faint.

I raised my champagne glass. "This is my cure. How did you end up involved?"

"Sorry?"

"In a gang," I pressed, aching to change the subject. "I'm having a hard time imagining you as a hardened criminal."

"It was a lifetime ago. And how does anybody end up involved?" He paused, and I feared this wasn't a rhetorical question; that I was supposed to know. "I had a criminal record and no money. I didn't have a lot of options."

"Alright, but how did you get a criminal record in the first place?"

He smiled like he'd caught me out, but I wasn't sure how. "I smashed a glass in the face of a grown man who spat on me when I was seventeen. He was wealthy and connected and he wanted me tried as an adult, so I was. I served six months."

I could hear it now: the combative person he was trying not to be, daring me to form an opinion, make a judgement, tell him who he was. I relaxed a little further after having cracked the first line of code, with or without *Empathy*.

"Why did he spit on you?" I asked, my tone carefully neutral.

"My father had stolen from him," he said. "We had money when I was a kid, but he went to prison for embezzlement when I was eleven. Six years later, I was working in a private members' club. I'd bled and sweated my way into college and I'd gotten a scholarship, but it wouldn't cover everything, so I was working two jobs around school to save some money. Of course, college never happened, in the end."

"So you joined a gang in prison?"

"I finished high school in prison and I kept my head down. It wasn't until I was out that I realised all the choices I'd still been working towards had evaporated. I washed dishes for a while but . . ." He met my eyes, assessing, and when he came to some conclusion said, "Anyway. It was a very long time ago."

"And how did you—"

But that was the alcohol speaking. I stopped myself.

"Become a vampire?" Luc finished. "Are we going to dance around this all weekend?"

"It was a slip," I rushed out. "Truly, I don't want to talk about it."

A long quiet descended before he said, tentatively, "If it helps, I don't think vampires are much of a threat to you, and I don't just mean because of your class. You're too vigilant. You were the most distrustful of me from the second I turned up, and there's so much adrenaline in you that your heart hasn't stopped beating like there's a hummingbird in your chest." He smiled, his teeth blue in the low light. "I won't distress you with the details, but . . . the more trusting, the more easy-going someone is, the easier things are. No vampire I know would bother with the likes of you."

He hadn't been bluffing about sensing my heartbeat. That was distressing. At some point, his arm had stretched along the back of the couch. A few inches closer, and it would be *around* me. His head was bent towards me, close enough that I could smell a smoky cologne.

He lived on human blood. He cornered victims, overpowered them, and tore their skin with his teeth. Or—and my gorge rose as I pictured it, because I instantly knew it to be true—did he meet his victims like this, in bars and at parties? Did they trust him enough that he could get them alone, and then devour them before they even knew their mistake? Helplessly, my gaze flickered to his mouth, and I wondered what it would be like to meet this man in the dark with his honest, open face. Would I know him for a vampire?

"I just . . . Excuse me a moment." My voice broke on the words, but I offered no more before I broke away for the bar. I would take just a moment—three minutes max—to stop picturing bleeding holes in my skin, to numb my fear with something stronger than champagne.

"Whiskey," I told the barman.

I was pouring it down my throat, thinking decisively of nothing but the burn, when someone patted me vigorously on the back.

"Good girl," said a female voice. "We don't want you to lose your nerve, now, do we?"

I coughed as I put the empty glass down. Zazie Reynolds was standing next to me. She was an impeccably sturdy person; tall, wheat blonde, with country-bred good looks. Somewhere in our acquaintance I had developed the notion that she was into foxhunting and that she knocked back a raw egg at breakfast every day. The former I knew to be a fabrication, though she sailed, rowed, and played on a polo team. I had no evidence either way for the egg thing.

The Reynolds family were Mythos's single largest client—the world's first energy providers to switch to *Fuel*—and Zazie was heir to most of the wealth we had helped them make. She was also a Crowther on her mother's side—as in Rachel Crowther, married name Maddock, the mother of my great-grandfather's first, lost child. The shape of the boy was an inculpatory hole that had prevented us from ever being friends. But in that moment, Zazie's fervour to engage with me was like a tidal wave, so heady that I planted my feet as though it might sweep me away. She wanted closeness, inclusion; she wanted to impress me.

"Lose my nerve to do what?" I said.

Zazie gave me a confidential look. "Oh, come on. You and the vampire."

I meant to correct her, but the emotion pouring off her was an on-her-knees cocktail of social desperation and awe. Zazie Reynolds had never been so impressed by me as when she believed I was going to—what? Sleep with Luc? Let him feed on me? The latter caused a fresh wave of vertigo.

Athena appeared between us, flush and breathless from dancing. "Oh my *god,* Valentina. I can't believe you're flirting with that—" She mouthed the word *vampire,* the same way she probably mouthed *abortion* and *cocaine.* Her face was frozen somewhere between outrage and barely contained laughter, and her primary feeling was the nauseous hollowing out of jealousy. Mixed with the same awe and eagerness to please as Zazie, her emotion seemed not to be jealousy over Luc, but over my daring.

I chanced to turn towards the party and was met with a barrage of similar feelings from dozens of other guests, all looking at me: awe, admiration, thrill-laced vicariousness. Unhinged and grotesque. Pure poison.

And it was delicious. Transforming. As I breathed it in, it mingled with the alcohol and fear and undid something inside me. Imagine it: that you steal into a person's impression of you and find not yourself but the person you were trying to be—daring, audacious, afraid of nothing. My heart rate slowed. My hands uncurled, leaving crescents in my palms where my nails had dug in from anxiety, forgotten now. As I crossed the ballroom, the tension ebbed from my limbs, replaced with a sense of power that grew with every person who looked my way and told me—unwittingly—that I was everything they wished they could be.

When I returned to the vampire, I was changed. I took a seat on the couch, closer than before, no goal in my mind but more of this feeling. Everything I knew I should have been rooting out—how he came by an invitation, how he was acquainted with House Gothenburg—felt insignificant now, a distraction.

Luc noticed the change. He hesitated. Or perhaps his magic only wanted me to *believe* he hesitated. I no longer cared. He looked across the ballroom and back at me, as if trying to solve the puzzle of who I'd become since minutes earlier and why.

"I thought I'd scared you off," he said.

"To tell the truth, you had. For a moment." I didn't need to elaborate, but the words tumbled from my champagne-loosened tongue. "I'm inordinately afraid of the thought of my own blood," I said in a rush. "I can't fathom the way everyone around me seems to uncomplicatedly exalt you when all I feel is terror."

He was unreadable as he watched me. I held my aching breath in my lungs as he shook his head, just once. "I don't think you do."

"Excuse me?"

"I don't think you're afraid. Or at least, you're not *only* afraid." He was labouring over his words like they were hard candy dissolving on his tongue; like he could sense we'd turned a corner and he was afraid to follow. I saw the moment he reached a decision, heard the unhesitant commitment to this path in the gravel of his voice as he said, "I think you're curious."

The accusation thrilled and horrified me, and I looked over my shoulder as though I hoped our audience had heard it too. A flickering of emotions, like the blinking wings of dozens of butterflies, reached me as people snatched glances of us. Their captivated wonder may as well have been applause. It was vulgar, but really the vulgarity was all theirs. They might guess—but they would never know—that they had made me a dangerous seductress by thinking it first.

And I was loathe to disappoint them. I leaned closer, like I wasn't turned inside out by the idea of getting within range of his teeth. "Careful, or I might think you're flirting."

His face split into a grin, dimpled and earnest, handsome in an uncannily human way. It devoured the last of my conviction to see through the glamour to the threat of him, which was a risk of a different kind. "Do you mind it?"

"I'm a little surprised you're capable of viewing a human that way," I said.

"Of course I can." The edges of his grin blurred into something more intimate. He had wanted this; had wanted me to ask about what he was, how he lived. And I was helpless not to. I'd broken some seal, reached some volume of alcohol or hubris that made the terrors of earlier into burning curiosities.

"Do you bite your human lovers?" I said, my voice a trembling breath.

He looked at me steadily as he said, "If they ask me to."

I shuddered, the thought running cold fingers across my skin. "Why on earth would they want that?"

"I think you know." Somehow while we were talking, he'd gotten closer, so that the space between us could be crossed with a kiss. "Some people only feel truly alive when they confront death."

Breathless, I weighed this in my mind. "People throw themselves out of planes. It's the same thing, I suppose."

"Have you ever thrown yourself out of a plane? Do you want to?" I shook my head no to both questions. His gaze moved down to my throat and back, just once. My thrumming, bone-deep awareness of him as he did became a mark of my steel; a glorious, exhilarating testament to my own daring. "Then I don't think it's the same."

Because where was death in skydiving? It had its risks (all mitigated to the highest possible degree) but no one was falling through air a thousand feet from the earth, *on purpose,* because they were attuned to their own mortality. They did not leap thinking they might die. It was no closer to what Luc described than crossing the road or eating raw eggs. But to lay your flesh under the maw of a monster, to feed them with your own precious life. Was that living?

I was too aware of my own skin, too hot in my gown. I leant away from Luc's attention to seek strength in magic again, but the *Empathy* was wearing off. It grabbed at threads of primary feelings—fear, shock, excitement—but I couldn't attribute them to anyone, or read them any deeper. This realization had the same effect on my drunkenness as stepping into a gust of cool air. All my armour was down—no magic, no inhibitions. I needed another spell.

Or a stronger thrill.

We don't make reckless decisions all at once. An alley veers right and you decide to go down it; a door swings wide, an opportunity is created. The rush is in reaching the boundary and finding it's crumbled—you've grown bolder. By the time the moment of decision is before you, stepping off the edge is the easiest thing in the world.

So I didn't invite Luc up to my room. I just told him I was going there and asked a server to make sure he knew where he could find me.

I practically ran. Gooseflesh erupted on my skin and the hairs on my neck stood on end, but fear was only one face of the shifting thing inside me, and it would be worth it for the next burst of heady gratification, and the next. There was no other plan, no end goal, but a single hard boundary I already knew I wouldn't cross: blood. I wasn't looking to confront death tonight.

A thunderous boom stalled my flight through the halls of Fable, accompanied by a flash of ghostly light. My heart tried to burst from my rib cage. But it was only fireworks. They strobed through the tall, arched windows in white and Mythos Blue and made a cathedral of the cavernous hallway, the ceilings—once bare—painted intricately with light and shadow. Every step of my heels on the marble was met with a thunder that seemed to come not from a sky full of fireworks but from inside me.

They ended just as I reached my room. The door clicked shut behind me, and I was plunged into a quiet dark; the only sound was my stilted breath, the only illumination the glow of my Moth and the tint of *Edifice* emanating from the marble—a blue moonlight shine, barely there.

As I waited for Luc, I paced the centre of the room, thrilling with anticipation, horror, power, panic. I did this; I stuck fingers in my deepest wounds and probed them as if it didn't cause me agony. Whenever I truly saw myself—broken, phobic, structurally unsound; wont to unravel at the slightest knock to the weakest joints, like the mere suggestion of bloodlust—I countered with any reckless impulse I could grasp for and let it carry me right to the edge. I leant in, never away. Privately, I thought of this as "going felon," because it let me believe there was one person in the world who got it.

Felon. Little felon. Daddy had spoken that name a thousand ways.

"Whoa there, felon!" Laughing, as he snatched me from the edge of the dock before my tiny, jelly-sandalled feet carried me into the water.

"Alright, little felon." Softly, when he came home to learn I'd split Jude's lip open, and I'd burst into tears at the sight of my father and folded myself into his arms.

"Morning, felon." With a grin and a cup of coffee for me, perched on the edge of the bathtub I had slept in wearing last night's dress and my own vomit in my hair.

But always with an edge of pride. I imagined it as a moniker reserved for when he saw himself in me—powerful, exempt from consequences.

Untouchable.

Now, cocooned in the shadowed calm of my room, there was space to change my mind, to abandon this false fearlessness that had begun with *Empathy* and gorged itself on every bad decision since. But once the feeling took hold, I never knew how to stop. Because maybe if I kept probing the silt of my fears and my weaknesses, one of these times I would turn up someone other than myself. Someone more like my father, who laughed at a threat, who wouldn't feel it even when it struck her. Someone I could keep being even once the thrill wore off, instead of a mask I wouldn't recognise later, cracked down the middle and bloodied underneath.

Because that was the problem with shaking the bars of the life I felt myself living, the one where I was breakable: I always came away having bruised myself against them.

Or at least, I usually did. Seconds turned to minutes that threaded one after another onto a lengthening coil of time, and Luc didn't come. I'd had too much alcohol to feel the sting of rejection, but the disappointment thrashed within me like a living thing. I couldn't come this far and stop without getting a fix; without hurting myself to find out if *this* Valentina would feel it, or if at last I'd emerge as someone stronger.

I would have to backtrack to the last viable avenue: the ballroom, the feral awe of the guests. My last dose of *Empathy* had been wearing off when I came upstairs, so I went to the drawer beside my bed and ransacked the box of *Empathy* cartridges, fingers searching. There was a single cartridge left; if only that had struck me as strange at the time. But there was no chance for it to register, because as I tossed the empty box onto the bed, a soft knock sounded at my bedroom door.

My stomach flipped. The heady thrill of recklessness hit me anew. I couldn't give myself time to think about it, so I fumbled for the button on the cartridge and pressed down . . .

And thought of blood. Dizziness rushed up so fast it was all I could do to collapse onto the bed and not the floor. *Calm*. I had forgotten to take *Calm*, and now I was seven years old and a tube was taking blood from the soft crease of my elbow. It ran the length of my arm but escaped over the side of the treatment couch before I could catch it in my fingers—I always remembered that. But what happened next was new. All of a sudden there was no tube, only fingers; cool fingers, the nails blue as they raked softly, reverently, from my wrist up to the vulnerable notch of my elbow. Gooseflesh erupted underneath their caress. I watched them, paralysed, unable to look up, to trace the length of the wrist, the forearm, to find their owner or look into the face of living death. And so I couldn't be prepared when those fingers found what they sought and were replaced by fangs as the vampire dipped their head to my skin. Their jaw yawned wide, teeth serpentine, the colour of bone; mouth salival and red—

I shoved my hands around the crooks of my elbows and squeezed. I was an idiot for thinking I could do this. If I let Luc touch me, I would have a heart attack.

And then I would be exactly who I had sworn not to be. This wasn't defeat; somewhere in the open drawer was another box and the spell I needed. As I felt around for it, a second knock sounded at the door—and a dripping. Once; a long moment later, a second time.

When at last I extracted the stick of *Calm* and snapped it, the relief was enough that a sob escaped me. The blood panic was muffled; the nausea receded. If I'd thought of it, I might have taken a second one. But I was dopey, my thoughts like ribbons streaming from a rising balloon, impossible to cling to. My only impulse was to forge onwards. I rose from the bed, unsteady at first, and opened the door.

He was staring down the hall towards the party, indecision writ large on his face, as though the echoes of the music were calling him to safety. As he turned to look at me, the expression transformed into one of concern.

"You're bleeding," he said.

That sounded correct; hadn't I been a child on a gurney, a tool full of life-giving blood, only a moment ago? But that had been a memory. Luc was confused. "No, I—"

He stepped around me into the room.

"Here." He pointed at the floor. A drop of scarlet. A few feet on, another. "It's your finger."

I looked down. He was right; a trail of wet red crawled down my finger from the tip, which was welling again. As I watched, another droplet hit the floor.

"Oh."

Calm had wrapped cotton wool around my terror, but my alarm was a fire tearing through it. Blood. That was my blood on the marble. Finding the sharpest tooth of my terror and thrusting my hand under it had been the goal, but now it was coming upon me too fast. I would be ripped to shreds.

"What happened?" said Luc. "Do you need—"

Out of time, I crossed the space between us and kissed him, my head filling with intoxicating thoughts of my own daring. The cool of his mouth was a pleasant shock. Luc's lips parted just briefly, his hands found my waist, and then he was pulling away. But I was already remembering this: the time I kissed a vampire.

"You seem a little—"

He cut off as I lost the last of my mind and brought my bleeding finger to his mouth. Blood painted his lower lip, an image I knew I was imprinting on my own bad dreams. But in the moment, nothing mattered but how far I could take this, how close to the fear I could creep, like a child in a game of chicken. This was who I wanted to be: above shame or reproach, above risk. Untouchable. Laughing from the shoulders of an illegal elephant.

Luc hesitated only a moment. Then he wrapped my hand in his own and drew my finger into his mouth. His tongue fluttered over the needle wound, and my eyes fell closed. I was flush to the edge now, about to take another leap or scramble backwards—and in only one direction would I find completion.

He freed my finger and I opened my eyes. Luc was licking the blood from his lip, a crease forming between his brows. He glowered at the wound, my hand clutched now in both of his, then spat my blood out onto the marble. Somewhere in my mind, I yelped in disgust, but my sluggish mouth gave only a curious hum.

"What cut you?" he said.

"I wasn't *cut*." That seemed important to my mental state. "It was a needle spell. Only . . ." Needle spells *healed*. If I'd been in my right mind, I would have realised that sooner. "It's not supposed to be bleeding."

"Where?"

I wandered back through my room until I found the empty cartridge on the floor and handed it to him. An ominous disquiet was punching through my borrowed calm before Luc shook his head and said: "I don't think this was a spell."

I laughed. "That's not possible. It was a Mythos *Empathy* cartridge—what else could it be?"

"It tastes like fae magic," he said, drawing his lip into his mouth as if he was remembering the blood. When he looked up at me, his face was grave. "It tastes like a curse."

6

A *curse*. Crude magic.

I didn't hear much after that. Luc talked on while I sat doubled over in a chair, nausea rising and one hand hanging down outside my field of vision. That was adequate until something hit the marble with a minute splash.

I was still bleeding, and the *Calm* had nearly burned off, along with all my reckless courage. I was the same old Valentina, and like all the times before, I was bleeding.

"The drawer. By my bed," I slurred. "I need more *Calm*."

"I don't think that's a good idea. Someone's tampered with this." He was still turning the *Empathy* cartridge over in his fingers. "They could have done it to any of the others. Look, there's a dent. I need something sharp."

"I'm going to pass out."

But Luc wasn't listening. I lifted my head enough to watch him cross to the desk, where he tore through the drawers until he found a pair of scissors. With them, he pried open the cartridge—it popped along the seam where the flat met the edge with little effort—then stepped back as something ethereal and gold spilled onto the floor, dispersing like mist.

Mythos magic was always blue.

"Mythos magic is blue," I said aloud, in the hope he would correct me.

"This is something else," he said instead, his thumb brushing his lower lip as if to catch the last of my blood there. "It tastes a little . . . artificial, maybe, but that could be the effect of the cartridge. The colour, though. This gold . . . Valentina?"

I had folded my head over my knees again and let out a whine. I could not believe I had put my *bleeding finger* in a *vampire's mouth*. The thought made the world tilt sideways.

"I need a bandage," I said, gesturing wildly in the direction of the bathroom. When Luc knelt beside me a moment later, I thrust my finger at him. But he wasn't holding a bandage. Instead, he flicked open an old-fashioned silver lighter, his face grave.

"What are you—"

"A hunch," he said, stilling my trembling hand in his and igniting the flame. "Hold still. I'm not going to hurt you."

He brought the lighter close to my skin and peered at the minuscule wound. I stared over his shoulder; I was anxious to know what he was looking for, but if I caught sight of the wound, I would faint. For a moment, nothing happened. Then a glint of light, as if reflecting off fresh, welling blood. I squeezed my eyes closed, and that light burned the backs of my eyelids. Too bright. Too burnished.

Luc snapped the lighter closed and sat back on his haunches, his expression tense and distant, his gaze on the middle distance. "It's the Gilded Grip," he said, almost to himself.

The name of the curse was familiar—it turned the veins gold, but slowly, I thought. I wasn't sure. I didn't even know where I was pulling the details from, so I wrenched my attention back to the most important matter.

"Where would he even find something like this?"

Luc had produced a bandage—he must have dashed to the bathroom while I sat with my head hanging down after all—and looked up from dressing the tiny wound in surprise. "Where would *who* find something like this?"

I made a sound at the back of my throat. If Luc didn't already know, what did he think was happening here? "*Jude*."

Luc was slow to reply, his face pinched as if in concentration. "You think your brother planted faerie magic to curse you?"

Faerie magic. I shuddered in horror but pushed the detail aside.

"Of course he did. The only question is, *what the fuck?*" I said, swaying to my feet. I was still dizzy but gaining vitality at an alarming rate as anger coursed through my system. By the time I reached the door, I was practically gliding. "I'm going to disembowel him. Right now, in front of everyone."

I was reaching for the doorknob when Luc's arm shot out in front of me and his hand splayed against the door, holding it shut. I sucked in a breath. His sudden presence at my back—like a predator sprung from hiding—flooded me with a bone-deep reminder of the nightmare I had tempted; of his mouth on my mouth, my blood on his tongue.

"Or," he said, his voice a gentle breath against my ear, "you tread more carefully. If he's done this . . ." Luc sighed and dropped his hand from the door to run it over his face. "If he's done this, he wants you dead."

Well, of course he wants me dead was the reply on my lips, but I wouldn't have meant it. Not *literally*; not the way I realised, with a twisting in my stomach, that Luc did. My hand, still reaching for the doorknob, dropped to my side; the other—my finger pulsing horribly as it bled beneath the bandage—swelled with my awareness. The only question I could muster, expressed as a pitiful gasp from my suddenly weakened lungs, was, "What?"

Something hard underlaid the sympathy in Luc's expression, and I wondered if I was glimpsing the monster beneath the mask again. "In the light of a flame," he said heavily, nodding to my finger, "you have veins of gold stretching from the puncture wound. They'll be invisible in any light other than firelight, but you can check for yourself once the bleeding stops. Over the next three days, they'll spread until they reach your heart." He sighed, his breath shuddering as if it was resisting the confession. "The curse takes full effect by turning the victim's heart to solid gold."

Despite not finding any of this amusing, I laughed. "So it'll kill me."

"There's an antidote," Luc said quickly.

The words came down like a rock breaking through ice. There *was* an antidote. He came alert at the sudden look of revelation in my eyes. "That's where he got it," I said, my memory of why I recognised the words *Gilded Grip* crashing over me along with my relief. "My dad has a whole collection of crude magic artefacts. Illegal stuff. He has the Gilded Grip *and* the antidote in there. It's in his office."

Without another word, I swept out of the room, Luc on my heels. Music still drifted from the ballroom, but the upper floor of Fable was dim and deserted. The lights were set low, just enough to guide the guests back to their rooms. The vampire stayed at my elbow as I led us through the halls, as if he feared I would faint from the horror of it all. But I was doing a great job of distracting myself from the poison in my veins—*crude magic, good god*—by directing all my feelings towards Jude.

This was not, as Luc had characterised it, an attempt on my life. What he couldn't understand—what no one would have understood—was that if Jude had resorted to murdering me, I had won. Even if he got away with it, took the company and the house, reaped the goodwill and sympathy of suffering yet another family tragedy, I would still have won. Because this wasn't really about taking the kingdom; it wasn't even about how the world saw us from the outside—Cabot or Maddock, victim or victor. It was about Daddy. It was about which of us could be worthy of him, and if there was a single thing he had wanted in life that wasn't his to snap his fingers and claim, it was for Jude and me to lay down our weapons. Neither of us could give him that, but we could fight this thing fair. We could refrain from the one sin that would have broken his heart and turned him away from us forever. Even if Daddy had shut his eyes for the last time before the blow was dealt, Jude would always know. He'd have poisoned the banquet before he ever sat down to feast.

So no, this wasn't murder. It was a power play, an attempt to rattle me. Still, it was more horrid than anything he'd done to me in the past. We were in uncharted territory now, more vicious and brutal than anything that had come before.

And I refused to be the less vicious, the less brutal. As Luc and I arrived at the expansive corner room, I was already plotting ways to get back at Jude. Something else from the collection, perhaps. Didn't one of the curses cause food to spoil in the victim's mouth? Maybe Jude would like to eat through a tube for the rest of his years.

When I turned up the lights, Daddy's bloodied face loomed down at me. The print of his *TIME* magazine cover was thrice as tall as he was, stretching nearly to the ceiling and abstracted by the reflections of light on the immaculate glass that held it in place. Before the framed print stood a vast desk of brilliant copper, and before that, two long, sand-coloured couches on a sand-coloured rug.

"Is it always unlocked?" Luc said. He stood by the open door, the tips of his fingers pressed to the pale wood.

It shouldn't have been, not with Fable full of guests. That was the kind of carelessness that made Jude a bad choice to inherit. Although—

"My mother's set up in here," I said. The evidence marred the office like pilling on a sweater or water stains left to dry into wood; a two-year-old laptop, open but powered down on the couch, a scuffed leather handbag on the marble coffee table. A pile of papers she'd stacked on the *floor—give me strength—right next to* the desk. The current CEO was no pillar of conscientiousness either. "She's egregiously sloppy. It was probably open when he got here."

Luc nodded absently. He was taking in the office like a detective gathering first impressions of a crime scene. "Where?" he said.

I went to the wall where a giant cabinet rested. It was made of a dark wood blackened further with age, its screen doors carved with an intricate pattern of cranes and lilies. It might have looked out of place in the contemporary office if it weren't so obviously expensive. Inside was a collection of crude magic treasures Daddy had inherited from *his* father, who had inherited them from his. Priceless and questionably sourced relics of a different age of magic. The collection was one step removed from a secret; first, because it was bursting with black market goods stolen several times over for their rarity and criminalised to high heaven for their unique and unknowable danger. And second, because there was something suboptimal—from a marketing perspective—about three generations of Maddock men harbouring a fascination with what they had warned us all against and had themselves pushed so fiercely to regulate. Still, Daddy loved to brag. He also loved to invite his friends to bask in the audacious glow of his power; to make their days with treats only he could offer. With the promise of silence, the collection had become the type of secret told to only one person at a time.

The cabinet wasn't locked, but it gave a sigh like a seal had been broken as the lights—a modern addition to the piece—came on inside. Some of my father's crude magic treasures rested behind glass. An impossibly fine and decoratively carved pipe was propped upright, a stain of blood red around the bowl seeping along the whorls and rivulets in the wood. A string of beads that looked to be human bone and probably were was arranged like a coiled snake on a velvet cushion; I tried not to look at it too long, because I knew from experience that if I did, it would appear to move, and a singular dread would take hold of me as if it were whispering nightmares in my ears. It was not the most sentient-seeming object in the cabinet—that title belonged to a hand mirror, plain but reflecting the light at improbable angles. My eyes wanted to go to it like it was a friend who'd just walked into the room. A label alongside read DO NOT MAKE EYE CONTACT IN GLASS.

There were no curses on display. These were in a drawer beneath, its contents indicated in antique cursive, black ink fading as the paper darkened within the brass label holder.

The drawer was lined with velvet. More labels were pinned to the fabric, and above each, a bottle. There were two dozen or so, all of intricately cut glass and embossed gold, the contents rainbow-hued and glowing or shimmering with iridescence. As lovely as jewels; as dangerous as loaded weapons.

I didn't need to search hard for the label that read GILDED GRIP; above it was nothing but an empty dent where a bottle should have been. But a second treasure was also missing. The label below read GILDED GRIP, REVERSAL.

There was something else too; as I opened the drawer, a rectangle of black card escaped and floated to the floor, from where Luc picked it up and turned it over. His jaw tightened as he scanned the gold embossed lettering I had only glimpsed. He let out the forceful breath of someone deeply inconvenienced as he handed it to me. The note was short, the instruction simple.

WANT THE ANTIDOTE? TELL NO ONE.

It was so pathetic that I didn't even have it in me to be mad. The ploy was obvious, and juvenile: he meant to manipulate me into giving up the fight, and he thought by throwing in my silence as part of the bargain he could just . . . get away with it.

"He really is an idiot if he thinks I'll play this game with him." I tore the note in half then in half again. "I could probably have him charged with attempted murder, right? I mean, it's obviously extortion, but also assault with a deadly weapon, at the least. Either way, he's going to fucking jail."

It hadn't been how I wanted to win this: Jude making a predictably stupid play and throwing everything away. I had polished myself to a shine to outdo him, painstakingly, over years. I had obsessed over who I needed to be to cancel out Daddy's preference for him, and he had gone and done it all by himself.

But as it turned out, earning my victory on my own merits didn't matter that much to me, because the effervescent lightness of seeing my dreams come true was ballooning inside me.

Luc notched the first, tiny puncture in it when he spoke, reminding me he was still there. "I don't think you should be so sure this was him."

My head snapped up, a wry smile already splitting my mouth. But Luc appeared to be serious. The look in his eyes begged to get through to me.

I folded my arms. "And why do you think you know anything about it?"

Luc gave half a shrug. "I've met your brother," he said, "and I don't think he's capable of this."

"You spoke to him for thirty minutes at most!" I heard myself going up an octave and took a breath. "Look, I actually don't know why you're still here. We both know you didn't come to my room to witness me get cursed."

"Yeah, well." He looked at his watch, like he did in fact have somewhere better to be. "It would kind of ruin my weekend if this killed you."

"I'm flattered," I deadpanned. "But wherever Jude's single brain cell thought to stash the antidote, he'll be handing it over in front of the police twenty minutes from now. I literally can't imagine who you think has cooked this lunacy up if not him."

"That's a worthwhile question. You think the door was open, so potentially anyone." He cast his gaze over the shelves of crude magic artefacts, brow furrowed. "But most of this shit is . . . egregiously illegal, so I assume not a lot of people know it's here? Are there cameras inside the house?"

I sighed. He wasn't going to drop this in a hurry. "Yes, but they're turned off."

Luc tilted his head. "Why?"

"When you invite people to partake in a little debauchery," I said slowly, "it's polite not to film them at it. It tends to give people the impression you're looking to blackmail them."

He was about to say something in response when, behind him, the open cabinet beeped politely, like a housekeeper clearing their throat. Luc closed it, and a low hum started up from inside, the cabinet restoring its internal environment.

"Look at this," he said after seeking out and finding a control panel on the side.

I had a nemesis to vanquish, anything else was boring to me, but I dragged myself over to the cabinet. Luc was looking at an LED screen displaying the measurements of humidity and temperature, both ticking back towards optimal now that the cabinet was closed.

"They're the environmental controls," I said. "To conserve the collection. It's all very old."

"I know, but look." Luc scrolled through a list of readings in red below the current conditions. "There's a history of abnormal readings. This one is just now, when we opened it."

He had scrolled down to where the last three measurements were shown, each accompanied by a date and time, the most recent being minutes ago. The top reading on the screen was from several weeks ago, suggesting the cabinet had been opened then too. But there was another reading between them, one recorded at 11:39 p.m., about an hour and a half ago.

"Okay . . ." I was losing my already scant interest.

"We can narrow it down to anyone who could plausibly have been in here at eleven thirty-nine," said Luc. "Which would be easier if there were any cameras, but . . . Where are you going?"

"To narrow it all the way down," I called over my shoulder as I swept towards the door. "I'm going to find Jude."

Luc had shut the office door behind us. I swung it open and suffered the fright of my life to find myself nose to nose with Charlotte. I yelped; she yelped. I clutched my chest; she danced backward like a boxer evading a blow and nearly lost her balance.

"*What* are you doing?" I demanded.

"I . . ." She gulped, trying to catch the breath that shock had stolen, and pointed down the corridor. "My room is next door. I was on my way there when I heard voices. You nearly gave me a heart attack. What—"

I had pulled her into the office by the wrist. Luc's wide-eyed expression—which pointedly indicated the torn-up threat I was still clutching in one hand—asked what on earth I thought I was doing. Charlotte's asked the same, but in a way that made clear she already had an idea: an attractive vampire, a little privacy. If that cartridge had actually been *Empathy*, I would have been drinking her feelings down as if she were water and I'd been lost in the desert. The absence was uncomfortable.

But Charlotte was just who I needed. She was the perfect witness to prove to Luc—and anyone else who needed to know of Jude's underhanded tactics, like the board, or a jury—that it was no mystery who had planted a faerie curse where I would accidentally activate it.

"You've stuck close to Jude all evening, right?" I asked as I planted her in front of Luc and me.

She didn't answer right away but narrowed her eyes at me and then Luc as though she was trying to work out our angle. "Yeah," she said with a shrug. "Like you and I planned."

I turned to face Luc. I wanted to see the moment all the smug doubt was wiped from his innocent-looking face. "And did he disappear for a little while around eleven thirty-nine? Maybe head upstairs alone for twenty minutes?"

Charlotte laughed bashfully. "Um. Not alone, no."

"What?" I saw her then as if for the first time, with her hair mussed and her lipstick entirely rubbed off. "Oh my— *Gross*, Charlotte!"

"Oh, please," she said with a sigh, running her hands through her hair to smooth it. "So I had a little fun while I was trying to get him to trust me. It worked, by the way."

"It—it did?" Had Jude made my victory that easy? An honest-to-god threat to my life and, to top it off, he'd spilled all his dastardly plans to the first pretty girl who asked?

But Luc cut in before she could reply. "So you were with him at eleven thirty-nine?" he pressed. "In his room?"

Charlotte thought this over for a long moment. "Yeah."

"But it could have been a little later than that," I corrected her.

She shook her head slowly. "I don't think so. We went upstairs just before eleven thirty, I'm almost sure. But if it matters that much, you can check with the housekeeper—Fran? We passed her just outside his room."

"And he didn't leave at all?" asked Luc as I struggled to follow the thread of the conversation through the mounting clatter of discordant chimes sounding at the back of my mind.

"Not until ten minutes ago. He said he was going to sit with your dad." Charlotte's eyes bored into mine, and she frowned. "Are you good? Why do you even need to know?"

I half lifted the scraps of the note as if to show her, and that's when it barrelled into me all at once. The facts arranged themselves like the turning of a lock, tumblers thumping heavily into place, sobering me like ice water splashed on my face.

Not Jude. And the directive to tell no one—the instruction I had almost broken so casually by bringing Charlotte in here—that was real. Someone in this house wanted my heart to turn to gold, and I didn't know who, or why. They had injected me with a curse—crude magic, *faerie* magic—and it was swimming through my veins, infecting me with its malevolent poison. What else might such unknowable, ancient evil inflict on me? Eternal slumber? Unnatural age? Might my eyes turn to gemstones and my fingers to knives? I held my hands before my eyes, inspecting them. I felt for the beat of my heart, the movement of my toes. I touched trembling fingers to my face and felt only its new contours.

"Vee?"

Charlotte's last question still hung in the air between us, but I couldn't answer it. Like the damsel in a fairy tale, I had been bound to silence on pain of unnatural suffering.

"You can't tell anyone about this," I said weakly. "Please."

She looked at me like she wanted to argue, to make me confess all my troubles so she could help me put them right. But I wordlessly begged her not to. At last, her shoulders fell a little as she gave in. "Couldn't if I wanted to," she said. "Are you sure you don't need—"

"I'm fine. Can you leave us?" I said, my voice mechanical and flat.

Charlotte shot a scrutinising look at Luc but left, pulling the door closed behind her. It shut with an echo that left a profound silence in its wake. Luc was looking at his watch again; now that my priorities had been rinsed clean of any obsession with Jude, I finally understood why.

"Three days?" I said in a whisper that nonetheless carried within that chasm of stone. He nodded. "I left the ballroom around midnight. It's now . . . early Saturday morning. If I don't get that antidote, then around midnight on Monday, going into Tuesday, my heart will turn to gold. And I'll die."

This was lunacy after all: a girl being killed at the launch of eternal life. The promise of immortality dangled in front of another Maddock it couldn't save. The tonic wouldn't be uploaded for manufacturing until

Monday, and then it would take nearly five days, Mum had said. Even if I ran to her now and she dashed straight to the lab to begin the upload, it wouldn't be complete in time to save me.

Luc said nothing, which I suppose was better than *I told you so.* His gaze tracked down to the torn pieces of card I was still clutching. I shuffled them around like there was any use in putting the note back together.

"What even is this?" I said. "It's not a real demand! You don't curse someone just to force them not to tell anyone you cursed them. That doesn't make any sense."

"It's just the start," said Luc. "They had to make sure you didn't immediately run to the police, but maybe whatever they really want from you, a note in a cabinet wasn't going to cut it. Maybe the timing has to be right, or they have to line the circumstances up just so. The hard part's done. Until you get that antidote, there's no end to how they can manipulate you."

The feeling of power that had driven me into a vampire's arms not long ago felt like a dream that had dissipated with the dawn, its memory as fragile as mist. *Manipulate me.* I was being controlled with the tacit promise of my future being restored. I was being reduced to a pawn. A tool.

I couldn't let this play out that way. Whatever they wanted from me, the Valentina Maddock who was her father's rightful heir would not give it.

"No," I said aloud, the word like a blade coming down. I brandished the pieces of card at Luc. "I'm not going to be manipulated. I'll find them and get the antidote back myself."

A tension I hadn't noticed him carrying ebbed from his shoulders. "Okay. Good."

"If nobody's left this party, that means neither has the antidote. It's here somewhere, at Fable."

"And whoever has it must have already known it was here," added Luc. "They went for the only curse in this collection that puts you on the clock but also has a fix. Plus, there's the note. This was planned."

He'd worked that out already, when he'd been three steps ahead of me and I was wasting time blaming Jude. "It must narrow it down, right?"

"Hunter knows," I said immediately. He'd probably known about the collection back when it still belonged to Grandpa. "Jude's promised him he can keep his job if he wins the company, but Mum and I were planning on removing him long before that so that *I* could take over as CFO, and he figured it out."

Luc tilted his head to one side, his expression sceptical. "If the deal is *let Hunter Corcoran keep his job in exchange for the antidote,* he'd be telling on himself. He couldn't hope to get away with it. Who else knows?"

"Fran, the house manager. Wait, let me write this down." I took a sheet from the stack of papers Mum had left *on the floor* and turned it over, then found a pen amongst the confetti of things she'd already strewn across Daddy's desk. *Hunter—to keep his job,* I wrote as the first bullet point. *Fran,* I added underneath.

"Would she do something like this?" asked Luc.

I snorted. "Would *Fran* curse me to die? That's her idea of a good time. Plus, she's obsessed with Jude and she knows I'll fire her if I inherit Fable."

"Your friend just said she and Jude ran into her outside his room. Where's that?"

I looked up at him, the realisation pounding in my chest. "It's right next to mine."

Luc frowned. "So she's near your room just before eleven thirty—who knows why—*then* comes and steals the Gilded Grip all the way across the house at eleven thirty-nine, only to have to double back to your room to plant it?"

He was right, it didn't make sense—yet—but I scrawled down the details anyway.

"Roman Astor," I said aloud as I added him next. After Hunter, Roman was the second-most-frequent guest at Fable, given that Jude carried him around like a security blanket. Daddy liked him—he liked most people—and that was enough of a reason to suspect he'd shown off and let Roman see the collection. Roman stood to benefit from Jude's good fortune—which was my bad fortune—almost as much as Jude did. For all I knew, he might have hoped to be married to him one day and call himself a Maddock; unfortunately, I'd never paid enough attention to their relationship to understand what they were. That would have to change.

"What about your mother?" asked Luc. Delicately, he rotated a half-empty mug of coffee left to scum over on the coffee table, sans coaster. The woman had clearly done what she always did in the space she was working and asked the housekeeping staff not to enter. "She's using the room; she had the most access to the curses."

I shook my head. "But she's on my side."

Luc looked up. "Your side of what?"

"The *succession battle,*" I said as if he had asked me what year it was. "If I don't become CEO, then Jude does, and he almost certainly fires her on day one."

"Alright." There was a hard edge of amusement in his expression. "And if this is about something else?"

"I—"

The possibility this was not, after everything, still about Jude hadn't crossed my mind. Could it be that someone at this party had another grievance against me, one dire enough that they'd decided to threaten my life? Or worse: that they might puppeteer me for the realisation of some obscure, pedestrian goal in which I had no part yet. The manipulation of the markets; the fixing of an auction; the fall from grace of a treasured enemy. I sunk—put-upon and weary—into the high-backed chair from which Daddy oversaw his kingdom.

I did not have the fucking time to get swept up in someone's lesser aspirations.

"My mother still wouldn't do this," I told Luc, even as I added her name under Roman's, in the interest of being thorough. "I don't mean that she loves me too much—though she probably does. I mean that this product is everything to her. Its success is her completion. Nothing would compel her to sow this kind of chaos, this weekend of all weekends."

"Then is there anyone else who might have been shown the contents of that cabinet?"

My pen hovered over the page as I drew a blank. The collection was illegal; there was no way Daddy talked about it freely with acquaintances and colleagues. But he also liked to show off, especially after a few drinks. Anyone who'd been a guest at Fable and had the pleasure of meeting four-drink Oscar—self-worth at its peak, full of stories, ready to be your best friend—might have been shown one of his favourite treasures.

I tucked the notes into the pocket of my dress and made for the door. "Come on."

"Where are we going?" said Luc, catching up.

"To make sure every last person who could have done this is on my list."

We arrived back at the ballroom via the west balcony, where the softly pulsing lights did not reach. Opposite, on the east side, a dark-drenched couple were pressed against the wall, limbs wound round each other, but on this balcony, Luc and I were alone. Below, the party showed no signs of slowing down—no doubt most guests would enjoy our hospitality until the dawn, then refresh themselves with *Revitalise*.

"They've got to be here," I said over the music. "If you were going to do this, you'd be back in the thick of the crowd as quickly as possible, right? Everyone's drunk enough that no one could say you were definitely missing."

"It makes sense," said Luc, leaning on the railing and nodding to the bar. "And there's Hunter Corcoran."

"Roman too." He was doing shots with a member of the bar staff—or at least *near* a member of the bar staff. She had the look of yet another person who didn't have the energy for Roman Astor, simultaneously both bored and harassed. "And there's my mother."

It injured me deeply to even think of her doing this, so deeply I wanted her to look up and meet my eye, like I could find the truth of her love for me there. But she was absorbed in conversation with some members of the board. If anyone couldn't sneak away for ten minutes, it was the host of the party and the mastermind behind *Immortality*.

But as I cast my gaze over the assembled guests, I saw the roster of potential suspects blossom. Athena was dancing, either still under the thrall of the *Dancing Shoes* I'd seen her take or on to a second one. "Athena and Graham have been guests here before," I said to Luc. I searched the ballroom for Graham, who'd scented out the other alpha types and was deep in some whiskey-drenched dominance ritual on some couches in one corner. "Graham golfs with my father. They've come to a couple of dinner parties."

In broad strokes, I explained to him the Graham Situation. Athena had consented to their engagement for love, Graham for money, but either way I was a threat to it, which gave them both a petty reason to murder me. Extort me, though? Might Graham think there was yet a way he could secure the even bigger bag he thought he deserved, *and* avenge himself against me for having the feminine audacity to visibly gag, just a little, when he tried to tell me he loved me? If it involved a second black card, with the details of an anonymous bank account in the Cayman Islands, I could picture him imagining he'd get away with it.

"Eric Burton-Shaw and his first wife have also definitely been guests before," I said, pointing Eric and Nicola out for Luc. "That's his second wife. She's never been here before."

If sweet old Eric had motive, I didn't know what it was. He raised a hand in greeting when he spotted me staring at him, and I raised one back.

"What about the blonde woman?" said Luc. "The one you were talking to earlier at the bar."

"Zazie Reynolds," I said. "Her family and ours have this decennial tradition where they throw their weight behind some book or documentary or lawsuit, and we try to suppress it."

Luc's face twisted in confusion. "What?"

"She's a Crowther, on her mother's side. Martin Maddock's first wife was a Crowther." Luc shook his head, still nonplussed. Aggrieved, I forced out, "They had a son? He went missing."

"Of course. Fergus, wasn't it?" Luc said, the light of recognition in his eyes. And something mean, like maybe he'd just wanted to make me say it.

Daddy had hosted the Crowthers, including Zazie, at Fable on one occasion a couple of years earlier. That particular parley had been a success, and they'd dropped whatever attack they'd been mounting against us, so the possibility of Daddy showing off the collection as part of a victory lap was on the table. And if holding fast to the idea that our whole empire was built on the back of some deplorable betrayal of which they conveniently had no proof wasn't motive for cursing someone, I didn't know what was.

"Can you see her?" said Luc, scanning the crowd.

I couldn't. We walked the length of the balcony and descended to the ground floor, then climbed the opposite stairs to the parallel balcony, peering into every corner and shadow, but Zazie wasn't there.

"If this was her, not coming back to the ballroom seems a risky move," said Luc. "It's conspicuous. She could have gone to bed. Or found somewhere more private." He tipped his chin to the pair who were grinding ever harder against each other in the dark, neither of whom was Zazie.

He was right: hotfooting it straight back to the ballroom was the obvious move, but I added Zazie to my mental list regardless.

"Hunter, Fran, Roman, and Graham," I said, counting them off on my fingers. "They're the ones who want something obvious."

Luc's attention was on the western balcony. "And what about House Gothenburg?" he said.

A chill already raising the hairs on the nape of my neck, I followed his gaze. Mariah was leaning on one hand against the marble railing, auburn hair red-black in the darkness, skin the colour of bone—watching us from the very spot where we'd stood a moment earlier. As if she'd been stalking us. She broke into a slow smile, but shadows filled her eyes sockets, and there was no telling whether her expression was for Luc or for me.

I shuddered to think it was the latter. Worse, the thought of a vampire having done this brought back a wave of the blood-soaked horror my indignation had pushed out. My finger pulsed with the memory of the needle, like teeth, puncturing my skin. I pressed my hand against the fabric of my dress as if I could protect it.

"The other one's not here either," said Luc, scanning the ballroom floor. He was right—wherever Randolph had got to, he was no longer trailing in Mariah's wake like a shadow.

"They've never been to the house before tonight," I said, recalling that Jude had been summoned to let them in, as he had Luc. "But I supposed they're . . ."

"Vampires," supplied Luc when I trailed off. "They have a . . . diminished sense of your value. It would be nothing to them to hurt you if it served their own ends."

What was unspoken hung in the air between us, where I left it; I did not want to think again of feeding my own blood to this being I kept mistaking for a man. Instead, I added the Gothenburg vampires' names to the list, aware—though remotely—that they were outliers among the suspects in a crucial way.

"What is it?" said Luc after a long moment passed and I was still frowning down at the party.

Some part of me had understood the truth at once, back in my room, but I had refused to look it in the eye. Now it blinked at me, and in the glassy black of its pupil, I saw the blood drain from my own face.

House Gothenburg would not only have needed to know about the curse collection. There was other information they couldn't have had either.

"*Empathy,*" I said on a breath. "Whoever planted the curse knew that I'd use that cartridge. It wasn't in the *Calm* or the *Revitalise*—they put it in an *Empathy* cartridge because they knew I'd use it this weekend and find the note."

"Alright," said Luc. "Then who on this list could have known?"

I knew the answer I wanted to give—*no one, and that's the point*—but it was a lie. Anyone who knew the signs could put it together. The way my eyes unfocused when I was looking at someone's feelings instead of their face. The way I stood, my whole body turned to a person—I'd read in a self-help book that it made them feel heard—but it was because it made their emotions clearer. Someone had turned my own trick against me, had taken this thing I always thought was power and turned it into weakness.

My distress was soul-deep. It must have shown on my face, because a crease appeared in Luc's brow before he said, "What are you thinking?"

The gold lettering of the instruction—TELL NO ONE—burned white in my awareness. "Something reckless," I murmured.

I wouldn't dance on strings like a marionette doll. I couldn't. I was getting the antidote back, and I would do it without giving an inch to the person who thought they could wrest power from a Maddock.

"*I'm* not allowed to tell anyone," I said, ignoring the way my heart beat in my throat. "The note didn't say anything about you."

I gave it fifteen minutes before returning to the office, my stomach a nest of snakes the entire wait. They thrashed harder as I turned the final corner and, sure enough, Luc was there, and not alone—the stone walls sung a chorus of echoes, coming from the office.

"What's going on?" I said from the doorway, as if I'd just been passing by.

Mario was there, as planned; I'd told Luc to ask for the head of security. He was standing in front of the open, complaining cabinet, murmuring into his headset as he stared down at the drawer of curses.

Fran's presence was *not* planned. She twisted her upper body to look me up and down before turning back to Luc. "I'm sorry, but I still don't quite understand what you were doing in here in the first place," she said in that obsequious tone, as if the mistake must be hers and she didn't wish him frog-marched from the building.

"I was looking for"—he shot me a glance over Fran's shoulder, and if his discomfort was part of the performance, then he was a generational talent—"a different room. But when I came this way I heard the alarm, and the door was open." He gave a self-deprecating laugh. "I'm sorry for being where I shouldn't have, but when I saw the cabinet was ajar, and then the empty spaces where the bottles should have been . . ."

He raised his hands in a shrug, but Fran wasn't charmed.

"The contents of that cabinet are—"

"Illegal," finished Luc. Fran stiffened, as did Mario, who was probably percolating on what kind of threats you could make to keep a vampire quiet, and whether he would delegate the task. "Personally, I couldn't care less. But it occurred to me, it's probably going to be bad for Oscar Maddock or"—he made a gesture in my direction—"his inheritors if and when these very illegal, very dangerous bottles turn up and they're traced back here. Not to mention, if it ends up in someone's drink and the antidote's nowhere to be seen, you guys have a problem."

He was only supposed to insist that the curse was dangerous, maybe point out that he knew about these things, being something other than human himself. But some light cover-up work was also in Mario's purview—working conditions for the staff, for example, or a protestor who definitely stepped right into the head of Daddy's golf club as he swung—so it was an effective touch.

"And how do we know *you* didn't take the bottles, Mr. Sayle?" said Fran.

Luc's smile was affable and patient. "I guess you don't. But why would I tell you they were missing?"

"Maybe because this cabinet was last opened less than twenty minutes ago," said Mario. He didn't mention how he knew—the control panel—but kept his eyes on Luc, the objective no doubt to catch his reaction. "Right before you came and got me. If it wasn't you, you missed them by minutes, if that."

I turned my best accusatory look on Luc, but this was good—it was just as we planned. The more doubt cast on Luc, the more compelling I would be as the voice of reason when he made his suggestion.

On cue, he said, "I think you need to let everyone know there's a dangerous curse missing."

"*No.*" The alarm in my voice made three sets of eyes turn to me. Lightheaded with the risk I was taking, I moved to stand closer to Fran and Mario—a united front against Luc. "I can take it from here," I told him with a gesture towards the door. "We appreciate you letting us know."

Luc hesitated like he feared we weren't taking his warnings seriously, then gave a curt nod. "Alright. Good night, Valentina."

Then he was gone, and I was carrying this on my own. I chewed my lip like I was deep in thought and bought myself a moment to think of all the ways this could go wrong. What if I successfully put the plan in action and someone found out? What if whoever had done this wasn't fooled and destroyed the antidote without warning? But there was nothing for it; the only other option was being made someone's tool, and it was no option at all.

"No one can know," I said decisively. "It would be too disruptive for the soft launch." I didn't say that, if it *was* Luc, disruption seemed to be what he wanted, but I let the suggestion hang in the air. "But he's right about the missing curse being dangerous. Deadly, in fact. We need to find it."

"*Radar* shows no intruders and no staff in here at eleven thirty-nine," said Mario, a finger to his earpiece as someone in the security office fed him the details. "So this was one of your guests."

Radar was a security spell that identified and tracked people within a certain radius using a scale model. With a finger prick of consent, you became represented with a pin, gliding in real time around the model, your name hovering above you. It was mostly used in office buildings and on construction sites. At Fable, we used it to keep track of the many housekeepers, security guards, and event staff. If anyone was somewhere they weren't allowed to be, or an intruder appeared in the model, they would flash red.

Brilliant, except it wasn't tracking any of the guests. It would hardly be in the spirit of good hospitality to ask them to extend their finger and forfeit their privacy for the weekend.

"We need to add everyone else to *Radar*," I said. It was too late to find out which guest was in the office at 11:39, but surely we could catch the extorter at whatever they did next.

But Mario shook his head. "I've been asking to be able to add people for years," he said. "It's only set up for rotating staff. Your dad didn't like the idea of people seeing his or his guests' every movement. Now it's too late—he commissioned the spell, so he's the only one with access to change it." He nodded towards the hallway. "What we do know is no staff were on the top floor to see anyone enter or exit the office around that time, so that's a dead end."

"What if they came and went via the loggia?" I said, gesturing to the two long walls of arched glass doors. "Could the security cameras on the grounds have caught them?"

"There's some good coverage of this corner of the house. No footage of anyone out there in the minutes before the cabinet was opened."

"And after?" I pressed, sensing from his tone that there was more.

"Still nothing. But the footage is completely whited out for about six minutes during the fireworks. It's enough time to get to just about any room on this floor, so they could have exited that way."

No camera coverage if they reached my room via the loggia, and no witnesses if they went through the halls. I'd feared as much, but I didn't need to fake my aggrieved sigh as I turned to Mario and laid out my and Luc's plan.

"Your people will need to look for the missing items without alerting any of the guests that there's been a theft. It could cause a panic. If you search their rooms tomorrow during the hunt, when we're all in the forest, no one will need to find out."

Of course Fran was the one to try to ruin everything. She opened by making the smallest sound at the back of her throat. "You want security to go through your guests' belongings in secret? It's a terrible violation."

I rounded on her, instinctively mining for incriminating shades of feeling I couldn't reach without *Empathy*. Already tucked away in my room were the notes I'd started making at Daddy's desk. I'd added our observations from the ballroom while I was waiting for Luc to summon Mario, but they still began with a very short list of people with obvious motives. I hadn't forgotten who was on it. If we searched the guest rooms tomorrow and nothing turned up, that was information too, because by process of elimination, it was probably Fran.

In fact—

"*Radar* made a mistake," I said to Mario. "Fran was upstairs at eleven thirty. My friend Charlotte saw her."

"Actually," Mario said, "since she lives here full-time, she has resident status. *Radar* doesn't recognise her as staff." A shrug was his only apology as she cut an affronted look his way. "I'm just being thorough. You're not off the suspect list."

I turned back to Fran. "What were you doing?"

"The same thing I do every night your room here is occupied," said Fran, who could rarely be moved to any kind of urgency, at least by me. "I tidy after you before you go up to bed."

I had a sudden flash of discarding the packaging when I'd opened a fresh box of *Empathy* cartridges after dinner. When I returned to my room at midnight, it was gone—and so was the nearly full box of spells. Whoever planted the curse had cleaned me out so that I was forced to use the spiked cartridge, and I hadn't noticed. The price of my idiocy made the room tilt sideways.

So Fran had been in my room, minutes before the curse was planted, and admitted to it. It was an odd thing to do if she knew I would be looking for someone who'd been in my room around that time. Or was it? Had Fran done everything she normally would then gone back to plant the curse because the best story was the most obvious one?

"What did you do after that?" I asked.

Her expression didn't change, but her sudden stillness telegraphed her ire. She didn't answer; she always had an irritatingly firm sense of where her responsibilities ended. Instead, she said, "I think a quiet search will have to be tolerated. But my people have unpacked for our guests, and they'll clean their rooms all weekend. It would be more discreet, and less invasive, for *them* to conduct the search. Let's not invite security to traipse through their sanctuaries."

"Fine by me," said Mario, the way he said everything: on an exhale, as if it was his last, as if having to deal with this conversation was literally draining his life force. "As long as they do a thorough job, especially in Lucas Sayle's room. And Dr. Cabot will need to know."

"I'll tell her," I said quickly. "But not tonight—she doesn't need the distraction. I'll find the right moment."

I knew it was a lie. I'd known the instant the worst had happened that my mother wasn't going to hold my hand through this. Even as Fran and Mario retreated to organise a search they didn't know was only for the antidote—relief coursing through me to have pulled it off—a miserable fear was sinking in: that if I told my mother any part of this, she would still be thinking of the product launch.

There was something incongruous about those words: *sinking in*. They sounded gentle. But reality sinks in like a knife slipping under the skin. One moment you're whole; the next you're irreversibly marked, so fast the image of your dead former self, your unscarred skin, is still imprinted on your retinas.

I had died this death already. My therapist told me Mum had processed the sepsis that had almost taken my life the best way she knew how: by distracting herself with adjacent problems. The schoolwork I was missing, the real work she was neglecting while she was expected to be by my sickbed. In my gut, I had always suspected otherwise, but it wasn't until I started using *Empathy* that I saw the truth for myself: she recoiled from my need like it repulsed her. I was a distraction from her work she had hoped never to have. If I made a problem of my cursed blood—or even of the missing bottles, the fiction I had spun for Mario and Fran—this weekend of all weekends, she would likely never forgive me. And if I turned to her for the most comfort I had ever needed and she rolled her eyes, I would never forgive her either.

No, I was to be alone in this, I decided as I walked the dark corridors back to my room. Alone, but for the vampire.

7

I ran a bath, then sat on the rim of the tub with a candle in my palm until it was cold.

The veins of gold were a faint shimmer, only visible when angled just so in the light of the flame. They radiated from the pinprick where the needle had pierced me like cracks in ice, spreading under pressure. In the long hours that I watched, the gold webbing grew from a tiny circle to a pattern that covered the pad of my index finger. I wondered darkly if this wasn't what I'd always wanted: my blood turned to something strong and heavy, something that couldn't be taken from me with a tooth or blade or needle.

I hadn't thought I'd sleep this weekend with vampires under my roof, but I must have fallen into a stupor. I woke on the couch with the loggia doors open, the chill still clinging to my skin and to my heart. In snatches, I had dreamed of lying in a shallow grave. The scent of frost and the iron tang of earth filled my nose. Cold, crumbling soil barely covered my bloodless limbs. Crows landed, silent on their feet as they came to pick at my eyes but deafening with their tuneless shrieking as they caught the scent of the curse and fled in fear. All the while, the vampire crouched over my grave, preternaturally still and patient as he kept his vigil. When the paralysis of death lifted, I twitched my fingers towards him in a plea, and when his two hands wrapped around mine protectively, they were warm. When the shock of it wrenched me back to consciousness, it felt like a betrayal.

Crisp, clear light, an artist's light, filed the edges of morning into needles, hewed reality from denial. Breakfast would be underway, but the thought of eating made me heave, and besides, there was only one place I wanted to be.

The upper floor was quiet as I walked one wide stone hallway then turned into another, avenues carved through a mountain, all grey stone in gold light. Immaculate as it was unforgiving. Cutting through the very heart of the house, I passed a series of ephemeral canvases by an artist whose name I couldn't remember. Each twice as tall as me and rendered in textured oil paint, they were so many shades of white clawed through with erratic shots of pinkish red, like viscera. Like someone had taken nails to the walls, had torn themselves to shreds against these great swaths of seamless, enchanted marble, trying to get out. A chill shook me—I had never seen these paintings that way before.

The machines keeping Daddy alive spilled their noises into the hallway, warning me in advance of their disturbing presence. Jude was not as gracious. I found him asleep in a chair pulled up to my father's bed, still in his dishevelled tux, one elbow on the arm and his temple resting on his fist. A scowl marred his brow, and he wasn't completely at rest; his posture was stiff, too upright.

Sure enough, he came awake at the flutter of light behind his eyelids as I stepped up to the bedside. The morning surprised him; his eyes went to my father's face—golden, almost healthy in the sun—to the windows, to his watch. When at last they came back to me, he blinked several times. The absence of *Empathy* felt like having cotton wool plugging one of my senses, and my fingers itched to remove it.

"You were here," he croaked.

"What?"

He shook his head and sunk low in his chair, retreating. "Nothing. I was dreaming."

I'd hoped he'd leave and relinquish our father to me, but he leant back in his chair and recommitted to his vigil. There was nothing I could do—I couldn't have him see me leave again, like I thought it was enough to lay eyes on Daddy then go about my day—so I stood there, gripping my father's hand and watching him in silence.

"Who's his next of kin?" Jude said without preamble. Numbed by the question, I didn't answer. Jude closed his eyes ever so slowly, like he was falling back to sleep, and swallowed. "Claudia was handling it when neither of us were here, but it's clearly not her. Who . . . who are they going to ask when they want to turn him off?"

I curled my grief-weakened fingers around my father's and squeezed, ever full of hope that he would squeeze back, and ever undone to realise again that he wouldn't. Jude opened his eyes to a blank stretch of wall and stared, unseeing. There had been a time, years ago, when an adolescent Jude had woken every night screaming, sometimes more than once. But one day he simply decided to stop, and I doubted anyone had seen him cry since. Nor was he crying now, but I could see the question hanging from him, crushing his shoulders and rounding his spine, the hours and days he'd been wearing it. The issue was nothing urgent, and yet it was. He was asking to ask, because he couldn't not anymore.

Maybe a minute passed before he sighed and said: "I don't want it to be me."

"Well, I don't want it to be me," I snapped.

"Then what?" Jude shot back, his voice rising. "I'm not letting *her* do it."

I threw my hands up. "Then I guess he's not getting turned off."

Jude shook his head. He sprung from the chair like he meant to storm away, but instead he only went to the wall and slumped against it. "He wouldn't want this."

"I *know*."

"Please."

I flinched. I always felt as if I responded to Jude out of instinct. It wasn't my father's assets or the distribution of shares that told me he was the single biggest threat to my survival, but something evolutionary. But another instinct, foreign and unpleasant, hooked its claws into me now as he begged. I think it was the only time I'd ever heard that word from him, *please*, and it hurt, in my stomach and my throat.

"You can handle that type of thing, seeing as you're such an atrocious bitch." He rested his head against the wall, eyes on the ceiling. "I can't."

I didn't believe he meant it as a compliment, but any comparison in which he was weaker still felt like one.

"Fuck." I collapsed into the chair Jude had vacated, and the tears I couldn't summon for myself earlier finally fell freely. "Fine."

He didn't thank me—not that I wanted him to—but he didn't leave either. As I smothered my tears with the sheets of Daddy's hospital bed, I heard him sink down onto the floor. We stayed that way through breakfast, each in our own private grief.

As I was getting ready for the hunt, a housekeeper appeared at my bedroom door with a new, sealed box of *Empathy* I'd asked someone to fetch directly from the store. Only as I closed the door on her did I spot the black card under a corner of a console—as though it had skidded there when someone shoved it under the door.

I picked it up and flipped it right side up.

UNDER NO CIRCUMSTANCES LEAVE THE PARTY.

Redundant, but okay. Aside from the words, it was identical to the first: black card, gold embossed print. My murderer wanted to make sure the exits were sealed. No bright idea to slip the net and find help elsewhere would fly—if I'd even had such a plan. I was trapped in this house, forbidden from telling anyone, waiting for the axe to fall.

The card could tell me nothing else; I'd been in my room an hour or more as every suspect moved freely about the house. It would be the easiest thing to stroll down an empty corridor and slip it under my door without anyone knowing a thing. I read the message a dozen times, my frustration a physical pain in my chest, and then tucked the card into my jacket.

I'd asked the staff to bring me new *Empathy* cartridges in a Mythos bag with a receipt. The time of purchase was legitimate; the bag was new and uncreased. Still, I diligently checked the integrity of the plastic wrap on the box, then the edges of every individual spell for tampering.

Even then, plunging the needle of the *Empathy* cartridge into my finger had never been harder, but I needed every advantage I could muster to find who'd done this to me. I tried to suppress the memory of my blood dripping onto the marble. Because there was a fate worse than blood awaiting me in less than three days' time if I couldn't discover who had cursed me and taken the antidote. So I dosed myself with *Calm,* let out a slow breath, and pressed my finger to the dent like I had a thousand times before.

Sunshine burnished Fable's gardens as I stepped outside, cypress and wisteria spicing the air. Abutting one aspect of the house was the lawn, tennis courts, and the pool, which threw flecks of rippling light that decorated the shrubbery and startled butterflies from their rest. Adjacent were the border hedges and lavender of the English garden, where Daddy and I had sipped Earl Grey tea in the summers, drowning in the sweet perfume of roses. To the east was the Grecian garden—with rows of cypress trees, a pavilion, a reflecting pool the dark green of ivy—and beyond this, parkland—in the mornings brilliant with dew—sloped gently down until the estate was consumed by the forest. Centuries ago, someone had seen fit to hem the woods behind a low stone wall, which rippled as it followed the undulating contours of the earth like a sea serpent cutting through unknown depths. Before the stones were ever brought here and stacked, there were the trees. Spruce and hemlock. Alder, cedar, maple. They stretched their knotted, lichen-encrusted limbs over the wall towards the hunting party gathered below them, branches reaching as if they could point out the murderer in their midst.

Base camp for the afternoon was a scattering of Persian rugs, scarlet and gold and emerald green, their silk edges damp from lapping up dew. A mismatched array of armchairs and low tables was scattered across them, and from a refreshment tent spilled the scents of coffee and butter. The guests sipped from steaming china teacups, nibbled petit fours, and inhaled *Revitalise* as the gamekeeper dispensed rifles and team-colour armbands. A little ways off, a Mythos Blue sheet concealed what at first glance might have been a domed pavilion like the one in Fable's Grecian garden, except that a tinny scuffling was coming from inside. The scuffling rose to a squawk, and then a *giggle*, prompting anticipatory glee from the guests and a cry of "There it was again! You heard it this time?" from Nicola Burton-Shaw.

I picked out Hunter. He was at the gamekeeper's Land Rover, handling every rifle arrayed on the truck bed before he chose one, unhurried by the queue of guests still waiting to claim their guns. When at last he turned—a rifle like all the others slung under one arm—his attention passed over me like a rain cloud, at once hostile and indifferent. Then he crossed to join his team without a second glance.

Hunter—to keep his job. Those were the words I'd etched in harsh, trembling letters at the top of my notes. He was staring down the barrel of forced retirement. He was about to be unseated from an empire he had helped forge, usurped by me. Aside from Jude himself, who at Fable had more to gain from threatening my life?

If Hunter was the person hoping his trap had been sprung, he was playing it very cool. Even in the glancing moment we had been making direct eye contact, not a hint of anxiety or anticipation had brushed the feelers of the *Empathy* spell. But wouldn't that be easy enough to do with a little focus, maybe a Xanax? Whoever had done this knew that I regularly used *Empathy*, and Hunter had known me since I was born. As far as Daddy was concerned, he was family, since he had no family of his own; just a bevy of ex-wives who, by some stroke of awful luck, happened to be the four most vile and bitter women on the planet, if you were asking Hunter. (I only remembered the last. She volunteered at a nursing home and took me to get my first manicure.) As such, he occupied the role of an uncle with whom you shared awkward silences whenever you both looked up and realised everyone else had left the room. He and Jude enjoyed a friendly relationship, but it had never once occurred to Hunter to ask *me* how I was getting on in school, or if I was seeing anyone, or what I did for fun.

But that didn't mean he couldn't have noticed how I stood square on when I was talking to someone, the way one did to get the best result out of *Empathy*, a spell *he* helped launch. Or the way my eyes unfocused when I was concentrating on a person's emotions.

People were dividing into colour-coded teams. Hunter joined a group sporting red armbands and sipping coffee. Jude was among them. Charlotte was too, dressed in jeans and an oversized hunting jacket that belonged to my father and must have been leant to her by Jude. As she stepped away from the others to go claim a rifle, I thought of the clandestine search beginning back up at the house and an idea came to me.

I couldn't flaunt the rule on the card and confront him directly, and I didn't know what Hunter was capable of. But perhaps there was a way I could get him—or even Jude, if he was in on Hunter's plan—to show their hand.

I came up beside Charlotte as she was stepping away from the Land Rover, gingerly clutching a rifle. She tipped her chin at the giant bird cage. From this angle, the sun pierced the sheet and barely sketched the chimera of limbs and other unidentifiable parts swarming inside.

"Just when I was starting to wonder why I had to sign an NDA to be here," she said with feigned brightness. As she narrowed her eyes at me, her feelings swirled with concern. "Everything alright? Any *really bad* hickeys this morning?"

In my haste to fight back, I'd forgotten I would be walking into an interrogation.

"Sorry about last night," I said. When an explanation failed to trip off my tongue of its own accord, I added weakly, "I'm fine."

"Okay? Because at seven, you were about to combust with terror over the thought of vampires in your house—"

"That's a mean exaggeration." No, it wasn't.

"—and by midnight you were . . . what? Trying to drown out your grief with one? Did you sleep with him?"

"No," I said too quickly, and so it sounded like *but I tried to* and *you're wrong but you're not wrong*, and a little like *not yet*. Time to change the subject. "What did you find out about Jude?"

Charlotte managed not to glance his way as she steered us around the refreshment tent and out of Jude's line of sight.

"He *does* have a plan to win CEO," she said when she stopped. "But I couldn't get him to be specific about it. I think he only said anything at all because he drank so much."

My heart rate kicked up. A plan—one orchestrated by Hunter? Charlotte's emotions were coloured with the same cocked-ear anxiety I was feeling. Jude was up to something, but whether or not it involved cursing me, we didn't have the information to know.

"What else did he say?"

"He—"

But she cut off as Eric emerged from the breakfast tent, full of bubbly "hellos" and "good mornings" and "how did you sleeps" (the sweetheart). But he was a sweetheart who may have cursed my heart to turn to gold, and I wasn't about to pass up the opportunity to pry a little for a motive.

"Eric and Nicola are newlyweds," I told Charlotte before turning to Eric. "You must be so thrilled to get to spend eternity together."

There was a bittersweet edge to Eric's emotional reaction, but it didn't show in his smile. "Yes! What a privilege." He hesitated a moment. "I'll always wish Amelia could have had the same opportunity. Shame about the timing."

What a diplomatic way of confessing he'd rather step into eternity with a different wife. Charlotte and I made mournful, noncommittal noises.

"What with the tonic, Nic and I are talking about having children," he added. "I thought I was done with all that. I have my boys, my grandchildren. But with immortal life, what's stopping us now?"

Oh god, were we doing that? Having another cycle of kids every few decades? I'd always thought of having children as a necessary sacrifice for the preservation of the dynasty, probably because Mum had described her own decision to have me in those exact terms more than once. But what if Daddy wasn't dying and had felt otherwise? I cringed at the thought of dozens more Maddocks to compete with, then felt a guilty stab of relief at having escaped a thing I hadn't known to fear.

"Will you retire?" asked Charlotte.

Something crossed Eric's face, but since it was in response to Charlotte and not me, *Empathy* couldn't tell me what it was. Intrigued, I shifted so he and I were face on. If I wanted him to react to me like that, I needed to push him.

"More time to spend with your new family?" I said.

This time, Eric's expression was nothing but genial, but he felt a stab of something like an insult, and a clawing possessiveness, as if I'd tried to snatch something from him.

Power can do funny things to the nicest people.

He only laughed. "We'll see. I've been saying I'll retire for twenty years, but it's hard to build something up for decades and then walk away."

A doorway: an opportunity to bring the subject around to succession—and maybe Eric's stake in mine. "I bet your sons are clamouring for the chance to take over."

I was struck with his knowing assessment, like he could tell at once the comment was really about me. On its heels were shades of aversion and disappointment. As he replied, his tone took on a greater depth of sweetness—to mask the feelings, perhaps? "I've always encouraged them to be their own men. To make their own successes. That's what it is to love as a parent—you embrace your children for who they are, not how much of yourself is in them." His feelings turned wincing, as if he feared he'd said too much. "Excuse me."

As Eric went to claim a rifle, Charlotte turned to me with a raised brow. It was the confirmation that she'd heard what I had—a slight against Oscar Maddock at his own party. But what did Eric Burton-Shaw know? He had probably seen how my father played favourites and drawn his own conclusions.

But was it suspicious? Did Eric disapprove of me inheriting my father's empire enough to try to stop me? He was old and bereaved and facing death—maybe he'd developed some kooky philosophies that could drive a man to such a thing. It might not even be incongruous with his nature as a stone-cold softie—if he truly believed what he'd said about his sons, could he see extorting me out of my inheritance as a kindness?

It was a gossamer-thin motive. I would have to keep digging.

"Lovely guy, but the vibe I'm getting from that Nicola girl is she expected to be a widow within a decade," said Charlotte, sotto voce. To drive home her point, she rubbed her fingers and thumb together like she was massaging cash.

"Back to Jude?" I pressed.

"Right. When he mentioned his plan, he used the word *disruptive*," she said. "And *scorched earth*."

There wasn't a lot of unscorched earth left between Jude and I, if any, but cursing me to die would certainly put a torch to anything left standing.

"Did he say anything about Hunter?" I said.

"Only that Hunter was backing him. He said Hunter's never been a big fan of Claudia, even before she became interim CEO."

The last part wasn't news. The only major disagreement Daddy and Hunter ever had was when my father made the unilateral decision to accept my stem cells in exchange for Mum claiming the Head Magician job. I remembered it vividly, because it was also how I learned Hunter Corcoran was not *my* ally either.

It had been my first weekend with Daddy after getting out of the hospital. Still weak, Jude and I were both supposed to be napping, but I'd become a junkie for the amount of attention I'd been getting at Fable for saving his life. That evening I'd go back to Mum's, where the nanny wasn't supposed to spoil me; it only made me needier, said Mum, who'd obviously been correct (if not in the right).

I was coming down the stairs of the west quad. Daddy and Hunter were in the big living room; I could tell from the shape of the echoes as they talked, firing off remarks I didn't understand at the time, aged seven. Things about the board, and oversight, and how was Daddy planning on keeping Mum on a leash now that she was newly in charge of Mythos's entire lab?

"You should've taken my advice and fired her when you divorced," said Hunter, supremely pissed off. "Then we wouldn't be here."

"And I wouldn't have had any leverage."

"*Suing her* was your leverage, Oz."

"So I could force my own daughter to get a ten-inch needle punched into her bone?" hissed Daddy, now just as angry.

"Mark my words: with that woman, it would have been a much lower price than you've paid."

I only understood three things at the time: that Hunter wanted Mum fired years ago, that he thought Daddy should have sued her, and that hurting *me* was acceptable collateral.

If he really had threatened my life to lift the company from under Mum and me, it was nothing we hadn't seen before.

"Is Hunter involved in Jude's 'scorched earth' plan?" I asked Charlotte, matching my volume to hers so we wouldn't be overheard. "Was it his idea?"

She shook her head. "He didn't say anything like that, but maybe. Want me to poke around with Corcoran?"

"Actually," I said, stepping closer, "I had another idea."

With light brushstrokes, I painted a picture of what I needed her to do on the hunt.

"Sounds easy enough," said Charlotte with a shrug. I sensed her curiosity tugging at her to ask questions, but she shoved it aside. "I'll let you know how it goes. And look," she added, turning bashful. "Me and Jude—"

"It's not serious," I said. I'd only meant to finish her sentence, but it came out with the ring of a command. Charlotte bristled. I tried again. "I mean, it's not, is it?"

Charlotte flashed a smile as she rearranged her feelings into the kind of acquiescence that would get her what she wanted from all this. "Right."

"Right." I returned the smile. "Then I don't need to know anything about it."

This seemed to be all she needed to hear. She relaxed, visibly and emotionally, and we parted so she could rejoin her team.

It was then that a lull struck the party as Roman joined us. He came stumbling into the camp with his tuxedo jacket slung over one shoulder, a half-drunk bottle of champagne in his other hand. Several guests tried to greet him or fold him into their conversations, but he waved them off.

"Jude. Where's Jude?" he called over the talk and the tinny rustling from the cage.

Jude—who was arranging his red-team armband so as to look as roguish as possible—looked up wincingly. Roman threw his arms in the air as he spotted him, champagne leaping from the neck of the bottle to spatter Nicola Burton-Shaw's boots. "The *elusive* Jude Maddock," Roman slurred.

Jude came to meet him and attempted to rein Roman in with a lowered tone. "Couldn't you have changed at least?" he said as he tried to drag his friend out of the middle of the party. There followed a murmured exchange, and everyone else went back to their conversations. Jude seemed to be explaining to Roman that there was no space left on his team. He indicated the other guests in red armbands, Hunter Corcoran and Charlotte among them, the latter of which was a lengthy point of contention; Roman's gestures in her direction managed to convey both scorn and incredulity at once.

Jude's patience thinned as Roman ranted and swayed. I knew several people who'd attended Yale in the short-lived age of Jude and Roman, and their assessments of Roman were all the same: that he was incredible fun until the moment he wasn't. It seemed even his closest friend thought so.

"I'm not in the mood, Astor," said Jude eventually. He turned and walked away.

"Fine!" bellowed Roman after him. "You are a misery to be around lately, anyway. Good luck to her." Conversations stalled as he threw back a swallow of champagne and sprayed it viciously in Jude's wake.

Somebody must have sensed that the mood was about to turn and scrambled, because seconds later there was activity around the cage and Roman's antics were forgotten. The gamekeeper and three assistants had taken up a series of ropes, and the sheet gave a rustle as it started to unfurl. The crowd gathered, necks craned. Those nearest the widening vantage point released a collective gasp that rippled through the party. With one final flourish, the sheet was pulled away, and before us two dozen men and women crammed inside the cage struck melodramatic poses; feats of contortion and balance, blown kisses and obscene gestures, eyes a little wild, smiles too intense. A little freakish, a little alluring, just like the spells worn by each of them.

Masquerade was a commercial product used mainly in the entertainment industries; a cousin of *Polish*, but temporary, circumventing the need to hand out coveted Moths as if they were candy. Custom looks ranged in price from a couple of hundred if you wanted to sprout cat ears and whiskers for four to six hours on Halloween, to upwards of a million if you were shooting a superhero movie.

For that afternoon's entertainment, Mythos had spared no expense.

Some of the performers in the cage had wings: sheer and iridescent, or leathered like a bat's, ragged at the edges or coming to lethal, boned points. Others had horns, ridged and towering, goat's legs with cloven hooves. One appeared as if she were formed of leaves, the shells of her ears and webs of her fingers veined and translucent in the sun. Another had purple and silver scales arrayed across his shoulders and down his naked abdomen; they caught the light like shards of a mirror. All wore very little, save the spells and their impish demeanours.

As I was already sorely aware, it was nearly impossible to come by a real faerie anymore. They had retreated so far from humanity that they were no longer seen. So we had hired professional dancers and made them look like faeries.

And now we were going to shoot them with paintball guns.

I did not care one bit for shooting. Daddy had taken me on trophy-hunting trips for years as a child. He liked big game: moose, rhinos, lions. It was macabre. All those poor animals, their lives forfeit to somebody's idea of a good time. If Jude hadn't wailed like a baby at the sight of his first bleeding animal carcass and refused to hunt ever again, I wouldn't have kept saying yes to the trips for as long as I did. But like I've said, everywhere Jude might fail, there I was swooping in like a hawk.

It was a compulsion. It didn't matter if I hated the frightened screams of a shot zebra, the smell when a bear released its bowels. I liked the praise and the attention. I liked the rare opportunity to have my father to myself.

The faeries were released into the woods to a round of applause. While they got their head start—dancing and cartwheeling away as the trees swallowed them—the last of the party organised themselves into half a dozen teams. As bodies shifted, I caught sight of a mysterious figure languishing against the wall in the forest's shade; a sickly stranger, withering inside a waxed jacket too large for him, his eyes hidden behind pitch-black glasses, smoking a cigarette.

It was Luc. Thinner, paler, with exhaustion writ across the curves of his shoulders, the weight of his limbs. An umbrella rested against the wall beside him. He raised one hand in a lethargic greeting, and I went over to him.

"I had the impression vampires didn't come out in daylight."

"You don't have a good grasp of witch magic, as we learned last night," he said, "and it seems you don't have a good grasp of vampires either. It's almost like your family hasn't been in the business of magic for a century." When I ignored the dig, he smiled and relented. "We don't. Not if it can be helped."

He turned his head, and I followed his gaze along the wall to the deepest patch of shade, a hollow behind the refreshment tent. It seemed being stuck at this party continued to be a burden of terrible weight to the Gothenburgs. They were sprawled dramatically like a pair of high schoolers acting out the closing scene of *Romeo and Juliet*. Mariah—who was wearing the largest sun hat I had ever seen—clutched Randolph's drooping head to her chest as she waved a fan with the other. They, too, were both smoking cigarettes; perhaps it soothed the wasting effects of the daylight.

Or perhaps it just couldn't kill them.

Luc turned his attention back to me.

"Wouldn't you rather be"—I paused, suddenly afraid I was about to reveal another ignorance—"*sleeping?*"

"I love sleeping," Luc confirmed. "I wanted to see how you were."

"That's gallant of you, but I would hate it if you dropped dead on my account."

"But I'm already dead." He grinned, but it was more of a rictus of pain. The hollows of his cheeks were severely more pronounced than they'd been the night before. "It's just that under the sun, I lose most of the magic that makes it otherwise. I can't feed in daylight hours—I lose all my strength." The grin became sharper and more agonising still. "I can't be anything but what I really am. A corpse."

That must be how I got the idea vampires didn't come out in daylight. They didn't, not really. If I met Luc in a sun-drenched lane, or on the stoop of a shuttered bar, I could knock him over with a breath.

It was a delightful revelation, that my weekend-long sentence of sharing my home with vampires would be cut in half.

"But you're not going to—" I gestured at the sun.

"Mummify? Burst into flames?" He tilted his head as he considered the possibility. "The way I'm currently feeling, I live in hope. But I made it across the grass, so I fear I'm in it for the long haul."

I might have pitied him, but it was hard to feel anything other than relief when my fears had been reduced to literal husks of themselves. "You look how I imagine raisins feel."

His brows appeared above his glasses. "Well."

"It's like turning on the light and discovering that what you thought was a monster at the end of the bed was a raisin the whole time."

Despite his patent discomfort, Luc chuckled warmly.

"I doubt you could hurt me if you tried right now," I continued. "Besides, there are more serious threats to my longevity."

All amusement dropped from his face. "No sign of the antidote yet?"

I shook my head. "They'll start going through the rooms as soon as everyone's down here."

"And you're sure you don't want to let your mother know?"

The thought was vaguely nauseating. I smiled tightly. "As soon as I want reminding that I'm being dramatic for the attention, I'll bring her in on it."

I had the sense I was being scrutinised behind those glasses. "Too much to hope she'd shut the party down?"

I laughed. The alternative was showing Luc the grown woman who still needed her mother, who just wouldn't learn. "I'm not the favourite child—*Immortality* is. She's psychologically incapable of helping me right now. I could slit my wrists in the entrance hall and her heart wouldn't break until Monday."

"So, also supremely unlikely that *she's* thrown a wrench in the weekend by cursing you."

"Exactly. Oh, and there's this."

I produced the second note—UNDER NO CIRCUMSTANCES LEAVE THE PARTY—and handed it to Luc. His brow creased as he scanned both sides of the card for any other message.

"I thought that was the whole idea," he said. "I heard everyone signed something to say they understood they couldn't access *Immortality* for a few years if they left before Monday."

"Including me, but what if I might not make it past Monday anyway?" I said as I took the card back. "Would that agreement still stop you leaving if you were facing imminent demise?"

He grinned. "Depends on my mood."

"Or maybe, somebody thought the agreement didn't apply to me because I'm family, and wanted to make sure I stayed where they could keep controlling me." I bit out the last three words through clenched teeth.

"I don't get it. They want *something*—or they want to make you think they do—but they won't come out and say it. You don't have *any* idea who that could be?"

"I know who it *wasn't*," I said, "given the window of opportunity is between eleven thirty-nine and midnight last night, the entirety of which I spent with you."

It was a bad idea to mention last night. In the daylight, the memory of my *Empathy*-spiked mania, my blood on his lips, my mouth on his, all looked especially unhinged.

Like a gentleman, Luc breezed past it.

"Well, that puts you and me in a very unique position." He dropped his cigarette and crushed it under his toe. "I'm the only person here who you know for certain couldn't have planted the curse, and you're the only person here whose blood I can't consume. That fae magic in your veins is poison. I doubt it would end me, but it would make me very sick, possibly permanently."

"And would the same be true of . . ." I nodded towards the Gothenburgs, who were trying to climb a stile like a pair of drunken mountain goats, all their moonlit grace and ferocity vanquished by the sun.

"Any of us, yes," said Luc.

It was one small weight off my mind not to have to worry about vampires while I was worrying about fae curses.

"I suggest we team up," he went on. "If no one's calling in the cavalry to find whoever cursed you, perhaps I could be of assistance."

I studied him, but there was little to see behind his dark glasses, and despite my habitual prodding for emotion, *Empathy* stubbornly returned nothing. But I hadn't forgotten Luc's secrets. He still hadn't shared how he had come by an invitation to Fable, or why he'd accepted it. He denied knowing Mariah and Randolph, who'd clearly recognised him. Whatever had spurred him to attempt a friendship with Jude had passed; at least, it was no longer Jude he was trying to impress.

"Why would you help me?"

He shrugged. "I think you and I could both help the other get what they want out of this weekend."

"What an eloquent way of saying nothing at all. How, exactly, would I hold up my end of the bargain?" I pressed.

"It's not a quid pro quo, only an offer of friendship."

Was my friendship the thing Luc wanted out of this weekend? I was forbidden from telling anyone about the curse, but this vampire already knew; that made him the only ally I was likely to get. And if he wanted to stay close to me, perhaps the best thing I could do was let him and see where it led.

He eased off the wall with a movement that looked painful; the pull of his jacket across his shoulders gave away just how much his flesh had withered. I reached out as if to help him, but he waved me away. "It's alright. I'll get some strength back the deeper we get into the forest."

"Valentina!" came a cry. I turned to see Athena bouncing on the balls of her feet and waving an armband in the air; black, to match the one on her arm. "Valentina! Join our team!"

Next to her, in his own black armband, Graham stood crestfallen. I watched the will to live drain from his face and wondered if I looked as horrified. What game was Athena playing that she wanted *me*—the woman her fiancée had tried to leave her for—on their team?

"These two are on the suspect list, right?" said Luc, coming to stand by my shoulder.

"They both probably knew about my father's crude magic collection. Athena's known me since school and Graham almost definitely uses *Empathy* at least some of the time, so they could both have noticed that I do."

"And he's in love with you?"

I glanced at Luc sidelong. "Graham's only in love with himself. When it comes to women, his dream model has a surplus of wealth and a dearth of self-esteem. If he was less ambitious he'd realise Athena suits him just fine." Athena was still on tiptoes, waving in invitation, Graham slowly withering at her side. "I just can't work out what either of them would get out of cursing me. Or why Athena's being so nice."

Luc shrugged. "Whoever did this hasn't actually made any real demands. Maybe something else is going on. Can't hurt to feel them out."

He was right. I'd laid a snare for Hunter; I may as well poke at some other leads while I waited to see if he'd get trapped in it.

"Fine," I said, starting towards them. "But you're coming with me. I need a buffer."

By the time we reached them, Graham had recruited his own buffer in the form of Roman. With his champagne tucked precariously in the crook of one arm, Roman inhaled a cartridge of *Revitalise*, then knocked back an espresso in one.

"Black team!" he hollered. "Let's do this."

Luc winced at the volume but fell in behind Roman and Athena as they made for the wall. I started to follow, but a minute pressure on my coat sleeve made me glance around. Graham was hanging back; his eyes pleaded with me to do the same. Whatever he wanted was breathtakingly urgent; his fingers barely touched my coat sleeve, but his emotions were raking at me furiously, like the claws of a struggling cat. Maybe this was about the curse. Maybe he wanted to warn me about something Athena had done. Intrigued, I waited with him until the others were over the stile.

Without taking his eyes off Athena's back, Graham murmured: "About . . . what I said."

My hope extinguished, replaced with revulsion. There was nothing I wanted less than to give him another opportunity to embarrass himself like he had last year, especially whilst his fiancée held a paintball gun and I was wearing custom Chanel.

"If you can't summarise your point in ten words or less, I'm walking away," I snapped. "And it better not contain anything resembling the words *I love you.*"

His resentment thrashed as if he were trying to wound me with it. To prove I was serious, I turned my back on him, but I hadn't taken three steps before he blurted, "Don't mention what happened in front of Athena."

I swung around. "Of course I'm not going to mention it! Do you think I'm an idiot?"

"No—but I—"

"Graham!" called his betrothed from the shadow of the woods. Our team had all turned to find us lagging. "Let's go!"

I gave Graham the filthiest look I had in my arsenal—which, given my new, harsher face, was filthy indeed—and went after them. I had just landed on the other side of the stile and started picking my way over protruding roots when I heard the soft pop of air as a paintball left a rifle. Pain split my spine. A string of curses fell from my tongue as I twisted to try to see the damage. I'd been hit in the centre of my back, but a spatter of red had crept onto my arm.

"Finger slipped on the trigger, did it, Corcoran?" I heard Luc say, accompanied by a snicker of laughter that was distinctly Jude's.

I turned, only to be assaulted by Jude's malignant glee and Hunter's barely stirred humour; it was a wonder what he even got out of being so awful.

"Oops," said Hunter, holding his hands up. "Thought you were a faerie."

"The fucking audacity," I muttered as I stalked into the forest, Luc hauling himself after me.

For a dozen paces, light filtered through the canopy and the grass slowly receded underfoot. The earth softened, layers of castoff cushioning our steps. Then the earth sloped down and the trees stretched up, and we were plunged into the viridescent gloom of deep forest. The air, scented with sap and loam, took on a chill. The crack and cry of shifting bark, of talking giants, was a litany chanted all around us. Moss reigned; it furred the tree trunks like a mantle. It crept over fallen branches and into hollow logs. Ferns, some growing as high as my chest, crowded between the trunks, dew pearling on their fronds.

These weren't the woods where my great-uncle went missing. But they were just as old, the in-between spaces just as watchful, and people still thought of Fergus when they climbed over the wall. They wondered how many of the trees had once been children, how many skulls had turned to stones, grown over with lichen, crushed underfoot. Any magic that had once been was now surely gone, and nothing remained to tempt a wanderer off the trails until they were lost. But every knot in a tree was a thumbprint, every scuff in the earth the impression of long, clawed toes. The memory of magic lingered.

The other teams were fanning out across the forest, and it wasn't long before the first shots pierced the hush, cries of victory and pain ricocheting from trunk to trunk and reaching us from all angles. We picked an unclaimed path—southeast, where the estate stretched on for a dozen miles—and set out in search of faeries.

The dancers had made the most of their head start. Half a dozen times, we seized with readiness at the snap of a twig, only for a bird or squirrel—or once, a young buck—to burst from their hiding place and disappear into the gloomy green. All that vigilance, and when—after fifteen minutes of walking—we at last met a faerie, the first we knew of it was when she stepped right into our path, her hands raised.

"I'm already caught, please don't shoot me again," she said in a single sob as we levelled our rifles at her. Sure enough, several pellets of green paint had burst on her skin in spectacular fashion. In defence of the girl being perhaps the first to fall, she'd been made up to look like a living bonfire. Red bled into orange and then yellow down her naked limbs. Her fire-toned hair was radiating from her skull like a sunburst. She'd be lucky to make it back to base camp without anyone else taking a shot at her.

"We're behind," said Graham as she scurried off. "Let's speed up."

Another five minutes passed, Graham the vanguard of our single-file line. The trail here was overgrown—it could have been a decade since anyone trod this particular ground—but Graham cut a path like the prow of a ship, and the rest of us let him. His reward was the first kill.

"Faerie," he barked, and we all followed the line of his rifle with our own; except Athena, who'd been rubbing the corner of one eye absently and fumbled hers while spinning wildly.

She was already too late, whereas I spotted the mark just in time to see Graham's paintball burst on the chest of an Adonis-looking dancer with enormous lacy wings. The air left his lungs with a grunt, and he fell backwards.

Graham squinted through the trees. "Did I get him?"

The faerie gave another groan. His wings emerged from the ferns as he climbed onto all fours. "Please don't shoot," he wheezed, followed by a cough.

"What did he say?" said Roman.

"Not to shoot him," said Graham, as if someone had told him he couldn't order steak in a grill restaurant.

The faerie made another protest, less coherent than the first. He seemed to be crawling through the ferns. I was fairly sure they'd been given instructions to frolic only.

"You already got him," I said. "That's one for us. Let's keep going."

"Stellar job, darling!" Athena skipped to the front of the group, to the position Graham had occupied. "Perhaps for your next project you ought to try trophy hunting. People make careers of that, I suppose?"

"Next project, Crain?" called Roman from the back.

"Yes, Graham's not had a lot of luck with his last few entrepreneurial ventures, have you, darling?"

I think I heard Graham pull in air through his teeth before he replied, the words so softened with wear that they came out in a perfect monotone. "People who understand the field know it's always a roll of the dice," he said. "You win some, you lose some."

"More like you lose some, then you lose some more." Athena chuckled, delighted with her own wit. Glances danced between Luc, Roman, and I, but she remained unaware.

"Sounds like a drag, Crain," offered Roman. "I'd give it up the second I got the ring, if it were me."

I didn't need *Empathy* to sense Graham's mood darkening. Even Athena, bubbly to a fault, tripped over the joke. She shot Roman an exasperated look that through some alchemy turned good-natured in a blink. "Roman! You're terrible!"

Terrible, perhaps. But if there was one thing Roman Astor knew, it wasn't entrepreneurship—it was identifying your meal ticket. And his might be about to lose the chance to control the biggest pot on planet Earth.

As soon as the path widened, I came up beside him. "Trouble in paradise?"

Roman's caramel gaze was both stupid with drink and sharp with *Revitalise,* giving him the look of a springer spaniel, unburdened by thought and lusting for chaos—which was probably what they'd written on his paperwork when they kicked him out of Yale.

"Pardon?" he said, tendrils of need already snaking out to wrap around my attention and pull me in. There was nothing there akin to the vigilance of pretending you weren't extorting someone, but then again, there wasn't much vigilance in Roman, full stop. He'd probably share nuclear codes with terrorists if it made him feel interesting for a moment or two. If he knew anything, this should be easy.

"You and Jude," I said. "Everyone heard what you said to him."

I expected scorn or gloom; even when it's not directed at you, you can still catch the shrapnel by raising the topic. But Roman's feelings leant in as if they were gathering to gossip, the top note that same hunger I'd felt the day before.

"It doesn't really matter," he said in a dismissive tone that belied the yearning. "You know you can say whatever shit you like to Jude and he'll be apologising to *you* the second he's lonely again."

I did not know this. "Jude's only ever apologised to me under duress. And not since we were ten." Eager to crack Roman open while I had him, I steered us in a straight line towards the point. "What does he mean by 'scorched earth'?"

Roman made a face, bemused and probably blaming the alcohol and anything else in his system. "What?"

"Jude's plan to inherit." I dropped the lure and braced to see if he bit into it. "Or doesn't he trust you enough to share it with you?"

Most of what he felt as his face twisted into a frown wasn't about me, but I caught shades of possessiveness, feral and desperate, like the very thought of me knowing Jude better undid him. I wasn't surprised when he took it as a challenge.

"He read your diary, you know," he said. "When you were, like, thirteen?"

I hadn't known, but neither was I surprised. (Adolescent nemesis and all-round thorn in young Valentina's side read her diary? Fork found in kitchen!) But I pretended hurt and betrayal anyway and let Roman lap it up. Just a little treat for spilling a secret to me.

"Degenerate, right?" he said with a rush of affinity for me; we were *bonding*.

I narrowed in. "I bet he doesn't appreciate everything *you've* done for him either."

Roman snorted. "Oh, man. Try being friends with someone who's never heard the word *no* in his life. I've been available for him every minute of every day for five years, not that he's noticed *once*."

A faint trickle of vulnerability—he'd told me something true and painful.

"I bet you'd do a lot to help him succeed," I said. *Like take me out of the running for CEO.*

But Roman just glanced at me sidelong—vaguely bored—before turning to watch the forest. "Thing is, he's always going to be lonely. You have to actually decide to *care about someone* if you want their presence to mean anything." He was swallowing down every morsel of my attention—juicy, nourishing, prepared just for him—and none of it was touching the sides. "Someone ought to tell him that you have to, you know, give something back? Instead of being just a bottomless pit of need."

You can talk. Even as he kept his eyes out for faeries, he kept looking over at me, checking I was with him, was listening. The grasping feeling only seemed to grow in intensity, as if he feared I would drift away the second he loosened his grip. And yet even with *Empathy*, I couldn't coax him into having a conversation on my terms. I wasn't a person with whom to engage; I was a sounding board with interesting prompts for complaining about Jude.

We passed through a thin shaft of light that had broken through the canopy; a pinprick of sun that flitted across Roman's collarbone and caught something there. I'd noticed the jewellery and assumed it was a chain, but it wasn't—it was a diamond tennis necklace. On Roman, who had no family money—none he had access to, at least—and had never had a job in his life.

"What if you bribe someone for their company?" I asked him, eyes on the string of diamonds around his throat. "Is that giving something back?"

The rifle dropped from his shoulder. *Now* I felt his scorn. He wagged a finger around as if he was scolding me, his feelings a punch of indignant disbelief, probably that I was not, in fact, on his side. "Don't twist this around. Trust me, I'm the one doing Jude a favour."

"And when my lawyers subpoena you in our inheritance suit, I suppose you'll swear you've never seen him snort ketamine off a Calvin Klein model's abs and that he'd make a perfect CEO?" I pulled him to a stop, irritated now that none of my expert manipulation was yielding real information. "How much loyalty does my family's money get him?"

Roman's hurt stabbed him so briefly that I knew he was practised in shoving it down. He hooked his rifle over one arm and stepped closer to me.

"You and him are the same, you know that? Just because someone expects the *trillionaire* at the table to pick up the check, you think you're buying people. Forget that I'm the only person who knows how to get him out of bed in the morning." Even now, he was enjoying this; the audience, the connection. I could feel his hunger to hold on to me even as the conversation soured. "Jude would be a fucking disaster of a CEO, and you can quote me to your board. He'll forgive me when he wakes up and realises he'd hate it."

So there went Roman's motive. I rolled my eyes, and as I separated from him, I was rewarded with a stab of dejection.

"Faerie!" squeaked Athena up ahead, and we swung our rifles towards the ridge to our left.

But it wasn't a faerie who appeared through the ferns; it was the sickly spectres of the sun-afflicted Gothenburg duo.

"Oh, hello there," called Mariah. Like Luc, both she and Randolph had gained some body mass this much farther from direct sunlight, and they were no longer curling in on themselves like dying leaves, but they still looked like the liveliest corpses in a mortuary. Mariah had fashioned into a lapel pin a yellow armband that could never have fit on her wasted arm. Randolph's head listed to the side as if he was one nod from falling asleep.

"Have you shot anything?" Athena asked brightly once they had picked their way down the ridge.

"Oh, no, dear. I'm not so talented with a weapon," Mariah said with a razor-blade smile that left little doubt what she meant.

"Get separated, did you?" said Graham.

"We separated ourselves. We were looking for you, actually." This last was directed to Luc. "We thought us three ought to stick together. Don't you think?"

We all glanced from Mariah to Luc and back again as he toyed with his rifle, boredom leaching from every line of his body. "No."

Mariah's smile stiffened as she waited in vain for Luc to continue. "No?"

"No, I'm in no hurry to mend fences with a house that's proven such a lack of fidelity as House Gothenburg. The road to earning back the trust you've broken is a long one. Don't you think?"

He echoed Mariah's aristocratic tone as he threw the words back at her. Yet again, I was scrabbling to make sense of what was passing between them. Mariah and Randolph were noble vampires—among humans, that would mean they had status that Luc, as a common vampire, didn't. Yet my murky instinct was that Luc wasn't pushing boundaries, but that he held the power here. They'd come looking for him, after all.

"Well. Consider us chastened, Mr. Sayle." It was hard to read her expression beneath her sunglasses and the capacious brim of her hat, but the unwavering stare in Luc's direction spoke for itself. After an endless moment, she sighed and turned to her companion. "Randy, darling, I feel like the bubonic plague herself. Let's stop this nonsense and lie down in a darkened room until sunset."

She mustered an impressive pace to stalk away from us, Randolph sluggish at her heel.

"If I didn't know any better," I said to Luc as we set off again, "I'd say you hurt her feelings."

"I think Mariah's too old to bother with anything as human as hurt feelings," he said.

"What did you mean about House Gothenburg? What trust have they broken?"

"Oh, no, don't," begged Athena. "After her ghastly stories last night about *culling*, I don't think I could bear to hear any more vampire business."

An opportunity to change the subject. To, for example, whether she or Graham had cursed anyone lately.

"How's wedding planning?" I dropped in as an opener. I locked eyes with Graham, who paled. "You both must be so excited."

"It's a drag," announced Athena on a sigh. "I want to have the wedding in Scotland in winter, because I have taste, and Graham wants to be married in the Bahamas, because he doesn't."

She winked at him. Graham laughed like he was choking on something and said to the group, "We're working on a compromise."

Other people's love lives—okay, relationships in general—baffled me. Why were people so keen to tie themselves up in a commitment where constantly having to *compromise* was not only the best you could hope for but the gold standard? The truth was, I eventually wanted a Graham type of my own, only . . . feebler. Someone to supply sperm once or twice, go on long golfing vacations without me, and eventually take the inevitable divorce payout with only a little negotiation, for his pride. Someone I didn't have to compromise for, but who inspired me to be mostly kind to him anyway.

Before *Immortality*, I'd had my B-class Graham pencilled in at the tail-end of my ten-year plan; now he was probably a few childfree decades away. But good lord, IVF and a donor would do if the alternative was the toxic mess Athena and Graham had found themselves in. Her abuse must have been the price Graham was paying for his indiscretion; in which case, this had worked out fine for Athena. She'd have no need to avenge herself on me. She had locked down the man she wanted—if only because his preferred option had passed on the opportunity—and if he wanted to keep her (and her money), he'd beg for scraps like a good boy. She criticised and berated him with every breath, while he held his tongue and bunched his shoulders in a way that suggested he was striving not to aim his paintball rifle between her eyes and fire.

Or was it *my* presence that had him so tense?

I slowed until Luc caught up with me. "Can you jab at Graham a little?" I said into his ear. "Let him wonder if I told you about him. I need to see how he reacts."

Luc dipped a nod and called out to Graham at the front of the group. I fell back as he said, "Any cold feet, Crain?"

Athena whipped round with twice the speed of her fiancé, her expression caught between a pout and a scowl as she looked at Luc, then me, then narrowed in on Graham. Distrust and betrayal stirred in her feelings as they passed over me, and I winced.

Graham, on the other hand, was six-foot-six of roiling panic. He smiled around gritted teeth and said, "Not even a chill."

Athena mellowed. But Luc wasn't done.

"I never did the marriage thing," he said as we walked on. I manoeuvred myself alongside Graham and watched him. "The whole idea of it freaked me out. What if you take the leap and then the moment there's a ring on your finger, something better comes along?"

Graham's gaze found mine only for a heartbeat, but I drew deep on his emotions and committed everything I found there to memory. He was taut as a drumskin, thrumming from the touch of every word. And there was a kind of clutching, a balancing, like he was barely holding on to something precious, something that threatened to spill.

Something like a secret.

"Do vampires get married?" said Roman, who appeared too buzzed to catch the undertones of the conversation, or the look I shot him for interrupting.

"Never," said Luc. "We understand taking what we want, living how we choose."

Athena, currently at the front of the party, decided she needed two eyes and all her attention on the conversation and hit the brakes, causing Roman to nearly step on her. Luc didn't look her way, or Roman's. He addressed every word straight at a stone-faced Graham.

"The immortal don't compromise," he went on, lingering on Graham's own word, my own train of thought. "When we want something, that's all there is to it. And as soon as it's not serving us anymore, we move on. Hard to do in a marriage." He grinned. "But it sounds like you're ready to settle down, aren't you?"

Luc lingered again, this time on *settle*, pulling tight on the beautiful knot of contradictions he'd tied Graham up in. How was he to project the masculine ideal—powerful, impressive, *un*compromising—and simultaneously avoid pissing off Athena, who wanted him on a golden leash? His attention landed on me in brief flutters, like an anxious fly. The usual resentment and tension were there. And that secret—it was like he could barely hold it in, but every time he focused on me, a sense of collusion wrapped around me, as if I were welcome to it if only I would reach out and pluck it from his fingers. I imagined the emotion to be the shape of an antidote bottle hidden in his weekend bag, a demand on a rectangle of black card. Maybe the thing he seemed desperate to share was what he wanted in exchange for my life.

Yes. It fit.

Athena was watching her fiancé, poised like a mountain lion waiting for a toddler to step off the trail. One eye squinted, like cartoon shorthand for someone about to snap.

"Well, Graham?" she said, massaging the offending eye. *"Are you?"*

"Over there!" cried Roman, and swung his rifle to the left.

I spun. It was the leafy woman, camouflaged like a giant stick insect; if she hadn't taken her chances and tried to run, we might never have seen her. Roman's first shot hissed past my ear. Graham had adopted a sniper's stance but wasn't having any luck. Athena, on the other hand, fired an endless stream of paintballs after the faerie as she cut away from us. One found her square in the spine, and she went down screeching.

"I got her!" Athena's victorious fists shot into the air.

"I'm pretty sure that was me, sweetest," said Graham, the pet name undercut by the petulant tone of a man about to get less than full credit for a mediocre contribution.

Athena made a disgusted sound at the back of her throat. "Fine, we'll ask her."

We waded over to the faerie, who was crouched on the forest floor. Dirt and leaves—new additions to her costume—littered her hair. Sucking in air through her teeth, she twisted to try to see the paint splatter on her back.

"Which of us got you?" Graham asked.

"In the back?" said the faerie sarcastically.

Graham sniffed. "It won't have been Athena," he said. "This just isn't the type of thing she's good at."

"Oh, fuck off, Graham," snapped his fiancée, before turning on her heel and stalking back through the ferns.

Roman stood over the paint-splattered woman and looked her up and down. "How much are they paying you for this?"

She shot him a cold look. "Twelve hundred for the day."

"Seriously?"

"I don't think that's very much," I told him.

"Do you get paid extra for every time you're shot?" As he said it, he let off another two rounds at close range. One hit the woman's clavicle, the other her stomach. She yelped at the first, but the second forced the air from her. She took several gulping breaths before she replied.

"No."

"Oh," said Roman, who deflated with remorse for all of three seconds before breaking out in peals of breathless laughter.

I shoved him in the arm.

"Well, look on the bright side," Graham told the faerie, who had rolled onto her side and gone still, having seemingly decided her best chance was to play dead. "At least now it's obvious you're our kill. That first paintball looked like it could have been mud."

The faerie nodded, which satisfied everyone that this acquaintanceship had run its course. As we caught up with Athena, Roman turned to Luc.

"Our friend here hasn't fired off a single shot."

"Shame, Sayle," said Graham. "Not much of a gunman?"

Luc let the question linger until it was almost uncomfortable. "I'm struggling to get past the faerie costumes, that's all."

"What do you mean?"

"I think it's in poor taste."

Athena gasped. "What! Oh, I think it's *so* fun!"

"I think I know what you're about," Roman said. "The vampire would rather we were shooting human beings, so he can get the rush of real hunting. Am I right?"

"You *are* shooting human beings," Luc pointed out.

"Oh, but it's *so* much more fun when they're in their little costumes!" chimed Athena. "Better if it were *real* faeries, but of course even the Maddocks can't get those these days." She stopped and spun to face me suddenly, causing Graham to have to swerve into the ferns. "Did you try to get real ones?"

Obviously no. "I don't know, but I think that might have been too much of an ask."

She wrinkled her nose. "Perhaps a little too unsettling for some of the guests too. I don't frighten very easily, but I hear real faeries are ghastly things."

"Full of disease too," added Graham.

"I'm sure that doesn't scare you, Crain," said Luc, coming to a halt. "So how about it?"

The others stopped, one by one, and turned to look at him.

"How about what?" said Graham, the first to notice the challenge in Luc's tone and helpless to do anything but meet it.

The vampire had taken out his cigarettes and was leisurely tapping one out of the packet. He spoke slowly, part taunt and part condescension. "Do you want to shoot a real faerie?"

It was hard to gauge what he was doing, his eyes hidden as they were behind his sunglasses. Athena, Roman, and I were silent, content to let Graham navigate this. He made a noncommittal noise that might have been a laugh, but only if Luc was joking. When that elicited no reaction, he said neutrally: "I don't see any."

Luc lit his cigarette and let the smoke rise from between his lips before answering. "That's because your generation will never have learned where to look." I felt his eyes find mine from behind his glasses, and shuddered. "Follow me."

He turned and, without looking back, strode off the way we'd come. For a moment the four of us exchanged wary glances.

"There aren't any faeries in these woods," I said, more to reassure myself than the others. There couldn't be, because I had slept thousands of nights a stone's throw from this forest, and if there'd been faeries here the whole time, I would have to raze it to the ground. I would scream.

Somewhere above, a bird cooed with the rhythm of a ticking clock. Then Roman wove a path between us and broke into the ungainly backwards gallop of someone for whom trips to the emergency room were stories to tell.

"Fuck it," he said, and followed after Luc.

I went next—a stubborn urge to prove to myself that Luc was full of it tugging me onwards—Athena on my heels and Graham bringing up the rear. Somewhere to our right, the staff at Fable were sweeping through their belongings for something they probably hadn't been invited to understand. Had the antidote to the curse been found yet? Did Graham have it? The temptation to offer an excuse and make a beeline back to the house gnawed at me. But reckless curiosity—and the persistent truth that the answers might be within this group—kept me two paces behind Roman.

Only a minute along the path, we came to a basin where the ferns thinned out and sprays of ivy and wild garlic erupted from the earth. A grandfather of a tree had been torn from its berth and lay parallel to the trail, its roots bursting from one end like the tentacles of some colossal sea beast. The trail swerved to avoid it, but now Luc led us around its twisting roots to the other side.

"Do you see that?"

We gathered in the lee of the trunk and looked at what was hidden from the trail. It didn't appear like much at first: a corridor, where the trees were otherwise dense. It might have been an intersecting path once, but now—secret as nature had made it—the forest had reclaimed it, wrapping its coat over once-trodden ground.

"What is it?" said Athena.

Luc pointed through the gap in the trees. "See the flowers?"

A scant few specks of white were visible before the corridor turned and disappeared from view.

"Snowdrops?"

"It's late for snowdrops," I said.

"Late. Early. I don't think they mind." He beckoned for us to follow him, and we started between the trees.

"What is this, Sayle?" said Graham, who was probably as impatient at not shooting anything as he was at being yanked around. "You don't really know what you're doing, do you?"

Luc looked over his shoulder as we reached the turn in the corridor. "You tell me."

Athena gave a high-pitched little gasp. The snowdrops were just the beginning of a thread-fine trail of flowers, white as a scar. Not a single flower had grown elsewhere, and though the thread unravelled in a drunken way, it was nonetheless with a purposeful determination. It tottered around the next turn, following the winding gap.

"That's . . . strange," said Roman questioningly.

Strange enough to be magic? Part of me didn't want to find out. Fable was at our backs now and calling me. Somewhere in the house was the thing I needed to undo the *last* bit of crude magic I'd had the misfortune of coming across. But another part needed to know. I felt a pang of loss for my father, for all the times I'd run to him with a problem I needed him to solve. Maybe if I found a faerie, he would recall those times and spring from his hospital bed and hold me to him, promise me these woods would be empty of crude magic before the sun went down. When Luc raised his brows in challenge and grinned, and Roman, then Athena, then Graham took up the dare, I followed.

No one spoke, but the not-speaking grew louder every time we reached a turn and the peculiar thread of snowdrops continued. Disbelief turned into uncertainty, which turned again to disbelief, because that was better than dread. For a long time, we wound deeper into the forest, meandering until I no longer knew the way to the nearest trail—or to Fable.

I didn't notice the forest change; it must have arranged itself behind our backs as we took one turn after another. When we rounded a final tree, we were somewhere else. The silence was like sleep; it came on so gently, there was no beginning. Gone too was the violent wrestling of root and fern and fungus. We were in a grove of lichened spruce, uniform as gravestones. The light here was blue-grey and diffuse, as if dawn had only just arrived, and through it, the farthest trees were a watercolour smear.

"Am I still drunk," said Roman, who had pitched his voice to nearly a whisper, "or is the vibe here kind of strange?"

"Both, Roman," said Athena, with none of her usual pep. "It's both."

Luc raised a hand to hush us, face turned to the trees. "Relax your eyes," he said quietly. "You won't spot them if you're looking."

Even the sounds of breathing had vanished now. Beside me, Roman's fingers flexed on his rifle. I tried to swallow but my mouth was as dry as chalk.

A laconic creak, like the twist of old wood, or the turn of an ancient head. Luc swung his rifle towards the sound; with a clatter of weapons, we fumbled to do the same—as if they weren't, in fact, loaded with paintballs. I could practically smell our fear, sour and incendiary. Seconds crept by. Nothing moved.

"You know," said Athena, "I rather think we better head back."

Graham, who hadn't once let the barrel of his rifle drop since we'd stepped into the grove, seconded this. "Agreed. You could really get lost out here."

Even Roman, who had set multiple buildings on fire, was drawing the line. He didn't confess to defeat, only turned and led the way back, Graham and Athena scrambling after him. Luc didn't follow, and I remained glued to the spot, alone again with the vampire. As the others' flight through the forest vanished from my ears, Luc turned to me.

"Well, *I'm* certainly not shooting one."

"No one is," he said. "There aren't really any faeries here."

I looked again at the peculiar light, the haze of unreality that hung between the trunks. An unnatural gloom seemed to gather between certain trees, as if to disguise something lurking there, watching. Now that Luc had planted the idea, it was hard to uproot.

"What about the snowdrops?"

He shrugged. "They most likely led to a faerie mound once. Now I think they're probably the only residual magic left in these woods."

"You were winding us up?" I said, half hope, half scepticism.

"Couldn't help myself. It was Athena and her hypocrisy."

Something inside me unwound a little. "Then let's go back. If the search doesn't turn up the antidote, then I have to either work out who took it another way or dance on the end of someone's murderous strings, and I'm not in the mood for the latter."

Luc shifted his weight to one leg. "Has it occurred to you that there might be another option?"

"What other option?"

"There are no faeries here, but I might know how to find one. They might know how to create an antidote for the Gilded Grip."

The adrenaline from the first potential faerie interaction had barely abated. Now Luc set my heart pounding again.

"Are you suggesting that I bargain with a faerie?"

"If it saves your life, why not?"

"Because you're talking about *faeries*." I sounded breathless and panicky. "They're dangerous."

"They can be, but have you ever met a faerie?"

"*No*. No, thank you."

"But—"

"Crude magic is nothing like Mythos magic. It's unstable, unpredictable, *unsanitary*. You never know what you're going to get."

A crease appeared above Luc's sunglasses. "Is that from the Mythos marketing handbook?"

I scowled back at him. "It's effective marketing because it's true."

He sighed. "Crude magic is your only way out of this, whether you find the antidote that belongs to your father or not."

But it was different, somehow. The missing antidote had sat in a human drawer for decades; had been identified and authenticated and labelled, by humans. Almost as important, it belonged to my father, the way Mythos belonged to him. What I couldn't explain to Luc—because

I couldn't yet explain it to myself—was that the antidote was enough steps removed from its origins as faerie magic that I could pretend.

But going to a faerie. Wasn't this how the tales started? A desperate girl begs the aid of magic and pays a price she couldn't imagine? What if I lived, but under a different curse? The permanent plaything of some cruel fae king. Mum's life for mine. Spines down my arms and ivy for hair, like some half-human creature.

"It's unnecessary," I said firmly. "The antidote is somewhere at Fable, and if we have to turn the whole house over, we'll find it. Whoever did this knew I'd start looking for a cure elsewhere and warned me not to. I can't leave the party."

"And if whoever stole it never planned on giving it back?" Luc said softly. "It could already be destroyed."

"No." *No* to all of it: the antidote being gone, a faerie bargain being the solution. "Come on, let's go back."

We traced the path of the snowdrops in silence and joined the trail back towards Fable, Luc always several paces behind me. I had vague plans of intercepting another hunting team and plying them with questions—say the right thing to the right person and something was sure to slip out, wasn't it? The flicker of an expression, a hesitation, perhaps something they weren't supposed to know.

But I didn't need to intercept anyone.

"Valentina."

I turned to Luc, and he tipped his chin at something through the trees to our right. Someone had left the trails and was crashing through the ferns, parallel to us but moving as fast as his septuagenarian body would carry him.

Hunter Corcoran.

He hadn't seen us. By unspoken agreement we froze in place as he pulled ahead. Eventually he would meet the trail we were on, but for now he was making his way as the crow flies, underbrush be damned.

"He's not heading for the base camp," Luc said. "He's going directly to the house."

Hunter's red armband flashed through sun and shade as he ran, but his team was nowhere to be seen. I thought back to the grove and the possibility of faeries. The possibility that Luc could be wrong, that something in these woods had reared up in fury at our presence, setting an old man running for his life and leaving Jude and Charlotte as nothing but mangled limbs.

But no. Hunter's focus was ahead of him, the only thing that could be spurring him on a seed I had planted to see if he would break cover.

And he had.

"This fucking guy," I muttered before turning to Luc. "He has the antidote."

Luc frowned. "How can you be sure?"

"Because back at base camp, I told Charlotte to drop into conversation that she'd heard security talking about searching guests' rooms for something stolen from my dad's office last night. I wanted to know how Jude and Hunter would react." I was already moving in pursuit, Luc trying to keep pace. A sound of violent disdain escaped me. "He's so obvious that I'm *bored*."

Hunter throwing a tantrum because a *little girl* was taking his job should have been my immediate second guess. He was probably still in cahoots with Jude, this entire half-baked plot the same familiar threat: that Jude would take everything, with Hunter riding his coattails to reap the benefits. I was comforted by the thought. And as dull as the whole plot was, a spark of hope had flared for the recovery of the antidote. This had been extortion all along, my death had never truly been in the cards, and he could be talked around to not spending the rest of his days in prison. This was Hunter, for heaven's sake. He was no formidable evil genius. He was a mediocre man who had spent his life doing the bare minimum. He'd probably be relieved not to have to murder me.

Luc—who, with his sunlight malady, was little better than a seventy-something-year-old—fell behind as we followed Hunter to the wall. He crossed a stile into the orchard beyond the Grecian garden, never casting his gaze back. From behind a tree, I caught a flash of his strained features as he threw one leg over the wall, and then he was off again.

In the interval, Luc caught up. His pallor had shifted from white to grey, and a mist of sweat coated his skin. We were at the very edge of the forest, where the canopy grew sparse. Unobstructed sunlight at its afternoon peak burnished the earth just metres away, its light reflecting off grass and reaching us among the trees. Before my eyes, Luc was decaying. His cheeks sunk in beneath his sunglasses until his face was fleshless and gaunt. The tendons in his neck rose until they appeared grafted to the surface of him—a corpse rerisen, a dead thing without the sense to be in the earth. He gave a groan of pain as he fell against the tree.

"Where's your umbrella?"

He tipped his chin in the direction of the base camp, a couple of minutes' walk along the forest's edge. "I have to go back for it," he said, defeated. "Hurry, or you'll lose him."

By the time I crossed the stile, Hunter had disappeared into the house. I searched my memory for which room we'd put him in and found, stomach sinking, that I didn't know. I burst into Fable at a sprint, its shaded cool swallowing me like a pebble down a well; the clatter of my footsteps, so muted on the soft earth, amplified to a violent cacophony.

Equidistant between two sets of stairs, I chose one at random and emerged on the deserted upper floor—breath burning in my lungs—and listened. The soundproofing of Fable's doors was absolute, but should he open one—should he try to slip back out with the stolen antidote—he would give himself away. After only a moment, I heard the click of a latch. But it wasn't Hunter; two housekeepers emerged from a bedroom at the end of the hall. They startled but relaxed when they saw it was me. One made a mark on a piece of paper as they filtered through the next doorway and shut it gently behind them.

The search was still underway, Fran's army of invisible underlings combing the house as swiftly and inconspicuously as possible. In a nearby hallway, another door opened and closed. A moment later, a second. They moved like the ghosts they were trained to be, never causing a stir beyond the soft but echoing fastening and unfastening of a latch.

But someone, somewhere, was running.

It came to me like a rhythmic scuffing, distant and disembodied, the afterimage of a thing just happened in the remote reaches of the house. I took off after the echo, but I had only gone as far as the first turn when suddenly it was everywhere. Before I could pick a direction, the glow of a distant Moth caught my eye.

Hunter was directly across the courtyard, a toy-sized man through two panes of glass—with an arm braced across his ribs and something tucked into his jacket. I'd been right, but I had chosen the wrong staircase, and now he was about to reach another junction and vanish again. With all the strength left in my legs, I hurtled down one hallway, then the next. Sounds were beginning to rise from the ground floor—the guests returning from base camp. Their voices ricocheted throughout Fable like hail striking tin, too loud and sharp as they sliced through the susurration of my breath, the whisper of doors opening and closing.

By the time I reached the corridor above the entrance hall—Hunter already vanished around the next bend—they had risen to a din. Shouting punctuated the hum of voices ahead and below. *Something's wrong,* I thought in a corner of my mind. But I still believed it was a problem for after I caught my would-be killer. I believed it right up until I careened to a halt on the landing and looked down on pandemonium.

8

The guests had returned from the hunt. It must have been all of them, plus the event staff and Fable security, all fighting to be heard in the ever-rising push and pull of voices. The thickest part of the crowd had gathered around Mum. Another group ringed Mario. Both were gesturing with open-palmed contrition, their manners an intended balm for the atmosphere of febrile distress.

As I placed a first wary foot on the stairs, Mum looked up. Our eyes met, and I was nearly bowled over by the force of her fury. She was weak with it, screaming a plea for me to *just not*. My legs went soft, and I gripped the marble banister as I continued my descent. As afraid as I was to know, I still couldn't help catching snippets of conversation, like droplets of sea spray breaking free of an angry wave.

"What kind of security concerns?"

"I'm so confused. Was something *stolen* or was something *planted*?"

"Were *all* our things searched?"

My stomach lurched. The world tilted sideways. Now *all* the guests knew about the room search—but how?

As I reached the bottom of the stairs, Mariah slipped from between two bodies, looking a little less sun-sick now she was indoors. The dark circles around her eyes had receded to a smudge, but she still looked painfully wasted. At her side, Randolph seemed like he was clinging to consciousness; his eyelids fluttered as if he might drop where he stood. Mariah leaned close, and I tensed as all the exposed skin on my body burned cold.

"I simply adore a mob," she said, eyes sparkling with barely contained glee. I looked over her shoulder at the gathered guests. Some clusters were eyeing me with feelings ranging from indignation to a baffled sort of pity, and for the first time in my life I imagined exsanguination might be a mercy. Mariah leant closer and murmured as if sharing a secret with a friend: "People are so *vulnerable* when they collectively decide to lose their heads."

I will say this of being in a state of heightened stress: it's easier to push past the unsettling admissions of a bloodthirsty vampire. "What exactly are they saying?" I asked.

"Well, the dominant rumour isn't my favourite, but it's that some anti-capitalist protestor got onto the grounds and you and your security people feared they'd planted something—a bomb, if we were really lucky, something far less entertaining if we weren't. Your biggest fans think it was perfectly reasonable that you didn't have time to gain everybody's consent before you rooted through their undergarments." Her face turned grave. "Though most still have questions."

"And—there's another rumour?" I said, my heart in my stomach.

Mariah's eyes flashed, mouth curling into a hyena's smile. "That you've gone positively cuckoo as a result of your father's failing health. Paranoia up to your eyeballs. I heard someone say you think one of us is trying to kill you." She shrugged. "I don't think it's either. I wonder if you just wanted to violate us all. If it makes you feel powerful. I, for one, would understand. Or is it simply a fetish?" Her gaze turned liquid and knowing. "If you wanted a bit of my lingerie that badly, all you had to do was ask."

I let a breath out through parted lips and forced appropriate words out after them. Mariah was here representing a board seat, after all. I might need House Gothenburg's endorsement to win CEO. "No one was supposed to be inconvenienced and everyone's belongings were treated with the utmost care," I said mechanically. "I don't understand what happened. How did this get out?"

Mariah tilted her chin towards the main staircase behind me. I turned. There on the middle step, gazing down on the entrance hall with all the vengeance and triumph of the righteous watching the sinful bound in chains, stood Jude.

Fury propelled me at him like an arrow. Cries of my own name chased me up the stairs, summons and questions and censure, but the impulse to answer them—to unravel each guest by the loose threads of their feelings until I found where to suture the wounds Jude had torn—was quashed by something louder.

I didn't stop where Jude stood but snatched him by the arm and kept moving. He didn't fight me off; he had his own brood of petty, smug little feelings he no doubt wished to unleash on me. He let me drag him by the arm along the corridor and out of sight of the entrance hall like it was his idea.

Once hidden, I rounded on him. But words momentarily failed me as I looked at his stupid, pleased face and sensed his stupid, vicious feelings and accepted that really, this was my fault, because despite all the evidence, I had treated him like he had a single brain cell to fire up and put to work.

"What," I said through clenched teeth, "are you doing?"

Jude leant over me like a dog about to latch onto my throat, lips drawn back in a snarl. "Out of curiosity, how was I *supposed* to react to Charlotte's gambit?" I was wading in a miasma of his self-satisfaction so thick I wanted to vomit. The arrogant smile that split across his face almost sealed the deal, but I didn't dare reply; I had already fallen for Jude pretending knowledge once this weekend and I refused to give anything else away. "Did you seriously believe you could pull off a play without me noticing? I knew about your little sweep this morning—I was just waiting to see where you were taking it. But after you had Charlotte bring it up to see how I'd react, I decided enough was enough."

"A *play*?" A laugh escaped me as I realised: he thought the room search was somehow a manoeuvre to inherit. Hunter must not have involved him in the plan to curse me at all. I poured condescension into my voice as I said, "You really have no idea, do you?"

But Jude couldn't be riled. His emotions continued to sneer at me from on high. "Your mistake, petal, is believing I need to." He swept an arm in the direction of the entrance hall and the roiling protest of voices still rising from below. "I don't. I can fuck your future up just fine without waiting for your expositional villain speech."

I was so full of poison for him I could taste it on my tongue. I drew breath to explain, in small words, how he hadn't fucked me, he'd fucked everything; how the board would never make him CEO if he destroyed the *Immortality* launch; how the entire future of the product was riding on the uptake of those people down there. But Jude's gaze shifted to the side and refocused, and I followed it over my shoulder to the person who had appeared silently at the mouth of the adjoining corridor. Fran—my unlikely ally in agreeing to organize the room search—glided to the railing and looked down on the chaos with detached calm. When she turned to us, I felt the flickering of her satisfaction, kin to Jude's.

Of course Jude knew about the search right away. Of course everyone did—why else had Fran been so amenable to helping me on my terms? If Jude hadn't given the game away, she would have, because she'd seen that the most effective way to fuck with me was to go ahead with my plan and let the fallout blow me to pieces. I should have been more suspicious, only I'd thought the danger of her lay elsewhere, in a cartridge of golden magic and the threat of some unignorable demand. It still might, but it was no good focusing all of one's attention on the claws when the tail is snaking around to strike.

"You seem unwilling to learn," Jude said in my ear as Fran floated on, vanishing into the next wing without a word or gesture, "so let me spell it out: this isn't your house. Whatever you're up to, feel welcome to give it your all." He stepped around me, so that we were closer—almost ear to ear—as he delivered his last words before walking away. "Because you can't blink inside these walls without me finding out about it."

If I caught Hunter with the antidote in one hand and his next demand in the other; if I saw him thrown in a jail cell and left to die there while the rest of us lived forever and ever; if I removed this curse and restored my blood to an unmagical red; and in the meantime Jude destroyed everything I was working towards, what was any of it for?

Jude hadn't succeeded in ending my bid to inherit—yet. I didn't know where the blessed "security breach" rumour had started, but Mum was running with it. Her schedule of meetings was reorganised to squeeze our most distressed guests in that afternoon. I knew what that meant: concessions. Possibly discounted doses of *Immortality* as recompense. If there was any justice, the blowback for the damage would land on Jude, a boy so unfit to take up his father's mantle he had almost destroyed the whole legacy just to score a point against me.

And yet I was the one doing damage control. I wasn't exactly apologising for the room sweep. That would be weakness, a concession to another's power. *You understand,* Daddy always said instead. *You know how it is.* He told people how they felt, explained—with his undoubting smile and his firm handshake and his valuable time that for the moment was theirs—that he couldn't owe them an apology because he couldn't transgress. That the world rearranged itself around his bad decisions until they were good ones, right and wise, if not always kind.

As guests disappeared one by one into Daddy's office with Mum and Hunter (fucking Hunter), and I waited with growing nausea to be summoned, I cobbled together lie after lie to justify the gross invasion of everyone's privacy. Yes, there was absolutely an anti-capitalist protestor on the grounds. He claimed to have planted a weapon. I definitely feared for everyone's safety. I would have informed them as soon as they got back from the hunt. They were welcome, by the way, for my quick thinking.

"But Jude told me you were losing your mind," said Zazie from a sun lounger by the pool. Jet-black sunglasses made it harder to read her emotions—direct eye contact was best—but I still caught the thirst for drama. Her smile was always knowing and a little superior—a veritable smirk—but right then it had reached maximum velocity and grown unstable, trembling at the edges.

My possible mental breakdown wasn't the only thing massaging her mood. As we'd made small talk, Zazie had all but confirmed Luc's suggestion that she'd paired up with somebody the night before. When I'd asked how she was enjoying herself, she'd grown looser, sinking in her lounger as if the memory of her good time were a heat lamp, she a melting ice cube.

"I thought you might have gone to bed early," I'd said, probing because I could feel she wanted me to.

"You could say that," she'd replied with a grin and a swell of self-satisfaction that she had a secret.

Now she was casting a lure for *my* gossip, for a glimpse inside the fraught, high-stakes world of the Maddocks.

"Jude has . . . ulterior motives," I said now.

"Oh, I've guessed. And I'm completely invested." She lowered her sunglasses just long enough to wink at me. "My grandfather retired after a stroke too."

That wasn't as bad as the truth of our situation—that Daddy would never wake up. I imagined the news spreading among the guests that Oscar Maddock would not reclaim the title of CEO and felt a flutter of panic. That kind of instability was always bad for a company.

"My father's healthy," I said pointlessly. "I mean, he's recovering—"

"Well, don't *panic* about it. By the time you give us our phones back and news spreads, you're going to have sold billions' worth of *Immortality*. Mythos stock isn't even going to notice the changing of the guard." She sighed. "God, I wish I had a sibling. Inheriting would feel so much sweeter if I had to duke it out with someone beforehand. How good it must feel to *earn* it. Nobody earns anything anymore."

I nodded vaguely and tried not to wrinkle my nose. I did not want to earn my inheritance—I wanted the world to recognise that I was the one entitled to it. Perhaps the grass looked greener from where Zazie was standing only because she couldn't relate, but I had a feeling someone with her naturally competitive leanings could make sport out of my situation, and win.

"I suppose not everyone gets to declare war like you two, though," she went on. "The Maddock situation is a special kind of fucked up."

Was that a dig about Daddy cheating with his wife's sister? Or was she talking about my entire ancestral line, dating back to the missing child who'd been kin to us both? But Zazie seemed in too good spirits to be stirring the pot. *Empathy* wasn't giving me any clues as to why—it wasn't about me. She was sprawled with an arm over her head and one foot tapping playfully, as though the room search hadn't phased her. I also had the feeling she was already drunk.

"Since you're so invested in the Maddock situation," I chanced with a grin, "have you picked a side?"

"Oh, *yours,*" Zazie said instantly. "I'm a sucker for an underdog."

"An underdog," I repeated, wondering if a blade between the ribs would have hurt less. "Excuse me."

I'd thought near debasing myself with explanations and excuses was working. And for the most part, it was; as I roamed the corridors of Fable, the dominant feeling was more akin to gratitude than derision. My quick thinking and leadership had protected the guests from a threat. But there were other feelings too. Here and there, I was buffeted by sidelong glances and asphyxiated conversations. *Stress,* was the whisper that carried on draughts and echoed from the lofty corners of rooms. I was a girl destabilised by her beloved father's health scare, driven to paranoia and erratic fancies by the strain of it all.

Unsuitable to step into Oscar Maddock's shoes.

I couldn't bear it. As the westering sun gifted the trees long shadows and shot fingers of gold through the loggia and into the caverns of Fable, I escaped to my room. Charlotte found me there, pacing so furiously I could have worn a groove in the marble.

"I think I might be fucked," I said around my bitten fingernails. Every time I tore a shred free, *Spotless* buffed the rest of the nail down to an even smoothness, so that I was gnawing into the quick in no time. I still had to recover the antidote from Hunter and square this episode with the curse away, and now I had to do it without causing even a soupçon of chaos for Jude to weaponise against me, all because I couldn't count on him to think it through.

"Can I say something?" said Charlotte from where she reclined on my bed, fingers running unconsciously over the white mulberry silk sheets.

I stopped my pacing. My arms fell to my sides, and I swear I heard my nailbeds sigh in relief. "Something I'll hate, I assume."

Slowly, like she was delivering a bomb into my hands, she said, "Is there the remotest possibility that you and Jude could work together?"

I was stunned into frozen silence. Jude and I—working *together*? Had she even met us?

Charlotte rolled her eyes. "In Valentina-speak: maybe you could negotiate an agreement that gets you both what you want."

I shook my head. "But what he wants is—"

"To *take what's yours*—I get it. You're mortal enemies, pistols at dawn, et cetera." She slumped down farther into the pillows as if I had exhausted her. "And *your* problem with him is he stole your dad."

Other people didn't tend to allude to my Jude Problem in such confronting terms, let alone with Charlotte's tone of irony, and I flinched. "What's that supposed to mean?"

"Look," Charlotte said to the ceiling, before seeming to decide I deserved eye contact while receiving her wisdom and pushing herself up onto her hands. "I may have a weakness for terrible men but I'm not oblivious. Jude has some of the most glaring character flaws I've ever seen in a person. When I mentioned that we didn't own a car when I was a kid, he asked how else my family got to Europe."

If there was a subject at which I thrived, it was Jude's character flaws, but I didn't quite understand Charlotte's point. "But?"

Charlotte chewed her lip. "Shit. But nothing, I guess. It's not appropriate for me to say."

It was then that one of Fran's underlings knocked on the door and summoned me to face my mother. Charlotte shimmied her way across the expanse of my bed and stood. "I just think you're blaming him for a lot of damage he didn't cause," she said by way of a goodbye.

Listen. I was aware of how Daddy ended up with two bitterly ensnared families. I knew Jude hadn't *asked* to be born or to get leukaemia.

But that Charlotte thought this was about any of that just proved she didn't understand. People make mistakes, but Jude wanted to ruin my life *on purpose* and apparently always had. There would be no bargaining with him—I refused—so I would have to find a way to win this regardless of Jude outing himself as too stupid to play by the rules.

Once I explained this mess to my mother, Hunter would be dealt with, and then I could focus on making sure Jude didn't get another clear shot at me for the rest of the weekend. Better yet, I could plan a little sabotage of my own. After all, only one of us liked class A's and criminal property damage; if this was a game of character assassination, Jude was signing checks he couldn't cash.

It wasn't as if I *decided* to reach into the drawer beside my bed before I went to my mother. My conscious mind hadn't even recognised the last *Empathy* cartridge had worn off until I was opening it. Like reaching for a cigarette; like biting your nails.

I hesitated, one hand still on the open drawer, and tested the idea of not loading another. Was I confident I could still read a person by tone and expression alone? Was *Empathy* only helping me hew away at a collection of little suspicions—that I was meek, I was prey, I would never be deserving of my father's power—that might have been little more than paranoia when I started?

It didn't matter; if there was a time to cut back, this weekend wasn't it. And if the idea of facing this without *Empathy* made my heart flutter with panic, that didn't mean there was a problem.

If I'd known someone had been in my room again, I would have been more wary of the spells. As it was, I only spotted the rectangle of black card as I was heading out. It rested against a vase on the console by the door, the gold lettering winking at me as it caught the evening sun.

THIS IS YOUR ONLY WARNING.

"Fucking Hunter," I spat as I snatched it up. My hands shook as I shredded the note, though whether out of anger or disquiet, I didn't know.

I should have expected some kind of threat. I had skirted the very edges of Hunter's edict to tell no one so that I could make the search happen. Perhaps I was lucky to have been given this much grace, when for all he knew I had spilled the secret that I was cursed along with the theft of the bottles.

But what did it matter now? I was about to have him marched straight from Fable to a jail cell. An hour from now—less, even—I would be holding the antidote, and this hideous chapter would be over. This disquiet, this phantom breath on the back of my neck—Death chuckling in anticipation—would leave me alone.

Mum was shut in the office with a guest when I arrived, so I lingered in the hall below the original framed concept sketches of the Mythos laboratory. Commissioned and built during Grandpa's time, the lab existed within a sealed mountain at a location unknown. The coordinates were recorded somewhere, in thirds or quarters scattered among safes or hard drives; I didn't know the details. The only way in was a *Swift*-enabled vehicle, which would land within a secure hangar inside the mountain. Should the specific spell's unique signature not pass the sensors, the lab went into lockdown. Should someone whom the facial recognition system did not identify as staff, clients, or approved visitors try to enter the lobby, lockdown. Cameras sought out and identified faces in every corridor, office, and laboratory floor of the building, and in forty years, no one had once come close to breaching it.

A pair of soft-slippered feet approached, whispering secrets to the stone. Fran. In her belted linen smock and trousers, she looked every inch like she was about to drop into a karate stance and roundhouse kick me in the chest. Her disdain said she'd like to.

Unfortunately for Fran, at that moment the office door opened, and Eric Burton-Shaw was nearly surprised out of his skin to find us waiting there. Something thorny ballooned in his feelings like a deadly airbag. Two spots of colour appeared on his cheeks.

I hadn't seen Eric yet since the revelation of the room search. If he'd been using *Empathy*, he'd have felt me shrink back in anticipation of explaining myself for the thirtieth time. Without it, all he'd see was a girl with her shoulders pulled back and an unflinching gaze.

I smiled my father's killer smile and said, "Eric, you understand—"

"The damned echoing in this place," he said at the same time, laughing bodily in defiance of his unease.

"Sorry?"

Hunter appeared by his side in the doorway and clapped Eric on the shoulder. "Perfectly soundproof," he said as he passed into the hallway.

I wondered if they'd been talking about his diagnosis. I wondered—my eyes sliding to Fran—if he feared his medical information leaking to the press and destabilising his pharmaceutical company.

"Of course," said Eric, his discomfort fading, my gross violation of his privacy apparently long forgotten. "She's all yours!"

I stepped aside for Eric, and Fran took the opportunity to precede me into the office, which wasn't against the rules of her position but still felt disrespectful. I followed and was about to close the door behind us when I realised there were two other men yet to leave. Dr. Chandler and Dr. Yang, the newly Mothed team who had worked with Mum on *Immortality,* both nodded in thanks as I accidentally held the door for them to leave.

"I didn't realise they were still here," I said, tipping my chin towards the door when Mum looked up quizzically.

"Just a little help explaining the science," she said as she slipped what appeared to be Eric's paperwork for his *Immortality* order into a file. She took it to the cupboard that housed Daddy's safe.

"Such a charming man," she said with uncharacteristic lightness as she punched in the code and deposited the file.

"What did he say?" I asked. *About having his personal property dishonoured* was implied, or so I thought.

She tossed a hand in dismissal. "Oh, you know how he is—I think if he didn't offer a compliment every three minutes he'd stop breathing." She was smiling to herself as she kicked off her loafers and curled onto one of the couches. Fran watched as if Mum was a jam-glazed toddler about to press every inch of herself against the spotless white fabric. "Eric started trying to make peace with his own mortality, but he said he was relieved beyond belief that I'd succeeded. He said—and I know it's just flattery, but it made me think about it in a whole new way—he said even God couldn't stop death, yet I had." She made a show of rolling her eyes, but barely. "I suppose you can't get old without growing philosophical about it all. You must remember Grandma Hazel in the last years."

I plonked down onto the opposite couch, some of the tension of being here leaching from my muscles. The second Grandma Hazel was brought up in the conversation, it was curtains. Even Fran drifted closer to the loggia, like she wanted to be ready to throw herself off it.

"After Georgia, she was obsessed with dying. She went on and on about regrets—mine, mainly. The ones she imagined me having in my old age if I kept working as hard as I did. It didn't matter to her that I loved my work, that I was doing something important. It seemed sometimes that it didn't matter to anybody but me."

She glanced my way then, and though her thoughts were so far away that *Empathy* couldn't reach her, I knew she was thinking about motherhood. About the ways it had inhibited her, boxed her in. Grandma Hazel had dedicated her own best years to science and regretted it. She always wanted Mum to be more like Georgia, who worked only until she was married. Which was odd, since that side of the family generally agreed that Mum and Aunt Georgia should have been *less* alike, at least where their taste in men was concerned.

Here's how I felt about her reluctant motherhood at this point in my life, after years of therapy: Rejected? Yes, obviously. I had spent the last eighteen hours quietly playing detective instead of asking her to go nuclear on the problem—police, interrogations, pulling the plug on the party—because I couldn't trust her to prioritise me. But guilty? If she had suffered in our relationship, she had paid it back in kind. It wasn't my fault I existed; it wasn't my fault I'd been cursed. And being seven and frightened in the hospital hadn't been on me either.

And yet still, I had come to her braced with my whole body to cause her inconvenience first and concern second. I knew it was coming, and I would take it like a serrated knife wrenched through my belly. It would kill me.

I focused on my purpose, on the golden poison creeping its way closer to my heart.

"I realised something when Eric was talking about it," Mum went on. "I've never believed I would die. Never. It just didn't seem like something that belonged in my future. It was fine for Gigi, and it was fine for my parents when their time came." I spared a glance for Fran, whose tranquil aesthetic was in serious jeopardy as Mum described Aunt Georgia's death as *fine*. A muscle in her jaw twitched and her arms pressed tighter to her sides. "Isn't that odd? Even before I conceived of trying to end mortality myself, it's like I knew." Her tone turned dreamy, her gaze faraway. "I always knew I would get here."

She didn't mention Jude, who'd done years of dying before the stem cell transplant. And she didn't mention me, who'd descended to the brink at a much more eager pace with sepsis. But we never spoke of it, so I didn't tell her that yes, it was odd; that I could not think of a moment in my own life when I'd been in denial about my mortality. That it was less like it followed me and more like she herself had shackled it to my ankles when I was seven. I tried to imagine a girl who believed she wouldn't die; who had never stepped foot in a hospital or watched newsreel footage of police tape around a beach, a driverless speedboat towed out of the water, her aunt in a misshapen body bag. Who lived without the pendulum of some celestial clock shaking the earth with each swing. Death had been there, just visible on the horizon, right up until the moment it arrived at my shoulder with a needle and a drop of blood.

Luc had said last night that some people feel truly alive only when they confront death. It was only now, as I compared myself to my mother, that I was forced to consider the possibility I was among them, simply because I knew no other way to survive.

"But, gosh, listen to me." Mum laughed at herself, always so bashful to be talking about her accomplishments yet managing it anyway, regularly and at length, the trouper. She uncurled from the couch, and the mood in the office sharpened. When I caught the attention of her emotions now, the anger that had seized her in the entrance hall simmered among them.

"So." She leant on the edge of the desk, Daddy's face on the cover of *TIME* looming behind her. He might have been her pet behemoth, the power she would wield to see her ambitions realised, just waiting for the command to strike. But instead, he looked like he was pursuing her; teeth bloodied, grinning from the thrill of the hunt, she centred before his mouth like his next morsel, ready to be devoured.

I dragged my attention to Mum, and Daddy blurred into the background as her emotions overwhelmed me.

"Mario's told me most of it," she said, her gentle tone belying her frustration. But it was frustration edged with vindication, almost satisfaction—like this was nothing but what she expected of me. Was this always how she felt inside when she sighed and rolled her eyes at my rebellions? A scarred-in wariness flared up within me, cutting through my conviction. My right eye started twitching again. "I understand the missing bottles haven't turned up."

"No," said Fran. "We paid special care in the rooms of the guests Valentina most suspected of having committed theft while enjoying your hospitality, but—"

"She"—I cut in, jabbing a finger at Fran—"told Jude that the search was happening and he told everyone just to fuck with my reputation."

Fran stared straight ahead, the stoic enemy soldier holding firm under interrogation. "This is his childhood home. He has every right to know what occurs under its roof."

"Oh, stop fucking lying!" She flinched like I'd cracked a whip by her ear. "You helped him almost destroy the whole weekend, on purpose. That's the only reason you searched the rooms—"

"You know Oscar wouldn't tolerate me being spoken to like this, young lady." That *young lady* was concentrated poison. She'd been *young lady*–ing me since I was born, but this was its debut in my adulthood. It slipped off her tongue like it had never left.

"Valentina," Mum said with coaxing softness, and I shrivelled inside. In defiance of everything she was feeling, she'd adopted the air of someone trying to soothe a feral animal. I was being handled, like a hissing cat that didn't know what was good for it. Like I was crazy. "I think that's all, Fran. Sorry to have kept you."

"In that case, I'll check on Oscar." She turned to leave, but her attention lagged. It caught on the couch, the desk, the floor, and then trailed her out of the room.

It wasn't until she was gone that I saw what Fran was seeing: Mum had continued to scuff up Daddy's pristine office. More stacks of paperwork had bloomed like mould. Several water rings branded the coffee table. The burnished copper of Daddy's desk, usually gleaming, looked like she had touched every square inch of it, or perhaps hired a sticky toddler to do it. Underfoot was a vast woven rug, the colour and texture of a freshly groomed bichon frise. Beneath one edge of the desk, it was clogged with a yellow-brown stain.

"What happened there?" I nodded to the stain, trying to sound conversational instead of offended to my core.

Mum had drawn breath to say something, and it took her a long moment to recalibrate, blinking at me and then the stain and back again.

"For god's sake, *I* don't know," she said, as if she wasn't certainly the one who had caused it. "Coffee, I assume. Teeny—"

"It was Hunter, by the way," I cut in before she could make me feel like any more of a nuisance; before I lost my nerve. "This wasn't for nothing. I made sure he found out about the search, and he reacted like a man who desperately needed to move some stolen shit, so I followed him. I saw him move it somewhere, but I don't know where. But it was Hunter," I said again, in case the bottom line wasn't getting past her fury. "I solved it. It's done."

As I talked, her feelings swirled with new shades of ire, these ones mutilations of discomfort, confusion, and concern—the latter of which might sound like what I wanted, but Mum experienced concern like a cat being made to swallow a pill. She was looking at me as if I'd sprouted a second head.

"Teeny," she said slowly, "what motive could Hunter possibly have for stealing from Oz?"

THIS IS YOUR ONLY WARNING.

I had come here with hope in my heart and my purpose fixed firmly in my mind: tell her Hunter was extorting me with the stolen Gilded Grip and that he needed to be arrested—but quickly and delicately, before he had a chance to destroy the antidote. I was meant to walk out of this office having solved the problem, so I could turn my attention back to Jude and our inheritance game.

But once I broke Hunter's little command and told her, there would be only one response that didn't risk the antidote: swift and forceful. Hunter in handcuffs, the promise of twenty-five to life if he didn't hand it over here and now so that I could reverse the curse.

And it was a response that threatened to destroy the party she had barely salvaged from my antics once today already. Now that I was before her, *Empathy* telegraphing every irritation, every facet of her impatience and indignation; now that she'd waxed lyrical about how enamoured she was with her own achievement, I could see my mistake. In my desperation to be rid of the curse, I'd forgotten I would never be more important than her success. What had I thought she would do? March the police in here to take Hunter away? They would want witness statements from everybody. Fable would become a crime scene. And my mother would see it all as another blow, delivered because I couldn't let her have a single weekend—this one glorious moment of triumph—in which I didn't need her attention.

The more likely scenario crept into my mind, like a spider through the crack in a window frame: she would point out we had until midnight on Monday night to recover the antidote. She would tell me to wait until the party was over and the guests went home—until she'd sold *Immortality* to every last person here and the future of her crowning achievement couldn't be stolen from under her by the obligations of motherhood—before she dealt with this secondary problem.

And that meant two more days in this limbo. Two more days for Hunter to figure out he'd been caught, that I had disobeyed, and to crush the antidote bottle under his heel.

I let her feelings buffet me like North Sea waves in winter. A feeling in my chest, like a phantom of what my beating heart would become at midnight on Monday, held my tongue. I couldn't tell her I was cursed. She might get me killed, but my heart would suffer either way.

"He has the Gilded Grip and the antidote," I said instead, the words tasteless in my mouth. "That's a recipe for extortion. He could plant the curse—in my drink or something and—"

"In *your* drink? If he's really done this, why wouldn't *I* be the one he curses? Presuming this *extortion* you fear is about his job?"

Her tone had an edge of mockery, and I snapped in reply: "Because he wants me to give up my succession claim and hand the company to Jude."

"So you actually saw him with the missing bottles?" When I didn't respond, a self-satisfied knowingness swept through her emotions. *Of course* I was exaggerating. When was I ever not being dramatic? "Because to point out the obvious, Jude is the person most likely to have to crime his way to getting the company off you."

"Jude's not smart enough for this. It's *Hunter*," I pressed. "The curse—it's a gambit to keep his job, I know it is. We need to confront him and—"

"Good god, Valentina! Absolutely not." She gestured like I was insane, and panic razored through her. "If Hunter got it into his head to bring some kind of employment case against us, he could walk away with half the company. He helped build it, after all. No, we need to keep him completely sweet until the door closes behind him."

"But—"

"If this is some sort of move on his part—and I'm sorry, but I can't say I believe your little theory in the slightest—then sooner or later he's going to have to show his hand. But until you have proof, do not even think about making waves." She rounded the desk and started sifting through the papers strewn there. "Better yet, let it go. I can see this is causing you anxiety, but it's simply not a priority. We'll have the event staff keep an eye on the food, the drinks, and the spells, and that's the best we can do. Just, for the love of god, don't do anything else outrageous in front of the board. If Jude told everyone just to smear you, he'll do it again. Don't give him anything else to work with." Her feelings turned smug. "Good thing I anticipated a little chaos from you, given everything with Oz and the week you must be having. But we'll call it enough, shall we?"

That explained the vindication limning her anger. Of course she had known I was a liability. Of course she had planned to have to *deal with me*. Gut-wrenching disappointment tore through me, but only briefly; hot on its heels was a protective numbness. This was nothing I hadn't already learned to hear. If anything, it was confirmation that I was right to withhold the full truth from her.

"As for our mysterious guest," said Mum. "Did you find out anything while you were . . . giving him a tour?"

I had wondered when we'd get to the subject of me and a vampire in a corner of the ballroom, close enough to share breath; disappearing from the party one after the other. Mum had nothing to say about it; just like the day I'd come home with a tattoo of a tiger over the scar on my hip, her ability not to react to my worst impulses was impressive.

"Nothing yet," I told her. "But he's interested in me. I can keep him close."

Her flicker of distaste thrilled me. It was her only emotion I wanted to remember from this conversation. The rest were a list of reasons I couldn't depend on her. I was too needy; she was too ambitious to care. So unless I had proof that Hunter had the antidote, I was alone in this.

If that was the way it had to be, then fine. If Mum needed proof, then I simply had to make some.

9

Night swept over Fable like a passing breeze; gently, silently, as the party pressed on. Clouds blotted out the stars, and when the forest was no more than a brushstroke of water on a black canvas, someone knocked at my bedroom door.

There was no reply when I called for them to enter, so I opened it. At my feet was a black box with a white ribbon, and my pulse kicked up. The antidote, I thought at first; Hunter had lost his nerve, perhaps found out the net was closing in. But then a door down the hall opened; a moment later, another. The guests emerged, answering their own disembodied summons, collecting identical packages from in front of their own doors with a chorus of murmured curiosity and laughter.

The door directly to my left didn't open; Jude wasn't in his room. Maybe he was with Daddy again, or somewhere conspiring to make more of a mess of the weekend.

In my room, I opened the box. It contained a simple black domino mask, its surface matte but emitting a faint blue aura when I held it at an angle. I put my dress on and donned the mask, then went to the mirror.

That night, I wore vintage Dior: a silver gown with scalloped folds cascading down the skirt like the petals of a flower, each limned with sapphire-blue sequins. The bodice cinched in my waist, and the straps revealed the sharp-boned lines of my human shoulders and human clavicle, so that the grotesquely oversized head of a rabbit seemed to balance precariously on a too-small frame. The fur was a sandy grey, the shining eyes a rim of brown around blown-out pupils. One ear was standing at attention, the other wilted. It was deeply disturbing, too realistic and yet almost exactly wrong, like a puppet or taxidermy. When I touched it, it was solid, real, but just under the socket of the rabbit's eye was an invisible crease I could hook a finger under to lift the mask away. The moment I removed it, as light as anything, it was an ordinary black mask again.

I needed one last thing; then I was ready to find Hunter, to find the antidote. I crossed to the bedside drawer—

Where a second, nearly full box of *Empathy* had vanished from my bedside table.

I stared—paralysed, unsettled—into the open drawer, where a dwindling box of *Calm* and some *Revitalise* remained untouched. Then around the room. Nothing had been amiss when Hunter's most recent note was planted, but now? That lamp usually faced the other way. The tray of perfumes on the vanity had been rearranged, as if someone who didn't know their order had toppled them and tried to set them right. The ring handle on a chest of drawers was askew—I would never have left it like that.

Decisively, I shut the drawer. I knew exactly who to ask this time. Fran would be making her presence known to the event staff, probably by berating them for their treatment of the kitchen, so I would head there.

When I left my room, a slow, dreamy beat was being pumped through the house. As it grew, so did the scent of loam and mushrooms, until I turned into a corridor not of marble but of moss. I stepped over the roots of a tree growing in a doorway and into the depths of an enchanted forest. A canopy of thick, twisting branches snaked across the ceiling. Vines hung from them, and ethereal blue lights, like will-o'-the-wisps, hovered under them. What had been a couch was a tiny hillock blanketed in crocuses and toadstools; another had transformed into a log. In the shadowy corner, a badger in Tom Ford and a white-spotted fawn in green chiffon had found a mossy patch of earth on which to sit and whisper to each other.

I passed through the room and into the next, searching. Enough of the house had been enchanted into a forest to throw the party guests far and wide, to hide them from one another amongst the ferns and creeping branches. In one room, the green of the forest was outdone by the blush pink of millions of roses as they crawled over everything and dripped from the ceiling. In another, the toadstools towered like trees. Faeries—the same ones we had shot that morning, cleaned up but bearing bruises like purple and black sunbursts all over exposed skin—wove through the party with trays of violet cocktails, canapés, and vials and cartridges of magic.

I passed bison, cats, squirrels, wolves, and a single being with a human face and inhuman heart. Luc's mask dangled from his fingers. When I revealed myself, he caught my eye over the heads of a ram and an ermine who had trapped him in conversation, and held the mask up to his face. Nothing happened; the enchantment didn't recognise him.

We stared at each other. In the dark, the vivid grey of his eyes was drowned in shadow. The boyishness of his features was sharpened to a sombre intensity that lifted the hairs on my arms and the back of my neck. Did the lights among the trees fall on him just so, or did the vividness of him live somewhere in my ancestry, an evolutionary recognition that the thing that mattered most was the vampire who was watching me? If so, on the outer edge of fear was a trembling, fevered thrill not unlike desire. The threat of a bloody death was a constant knot in my abdomen, one not loosened by the fact that my veins carried poison. But I didn't want to loosen it; I wanted to tighten it until it snapped.

Still, I tore myself away and continued on through the party, my enchanted mask dangling from my fingers.

Fran was right where I expected her: pointing out specks of grime on a marble countertop to a stupefied young caterer in rumpled kitchen whites.

"Did you go through my things again?" I said as I came up behind her.

Fran turned as if she had been expecting me. She folded the cloth she was holding and handed it over to the caterer. "And don't neglect the edges," she said in dismissal. "Valentina. Did you need something?"

"I need to know if you've been in my room again, moving things. *Taking* things?"

"No, I haven't." I tensed as my mind starting racing through the possibilities, all worse than Fran interfering. Had Hunter planted another curse? One I might brush against? Breathe in? One to dispose of me before I could incriminate him? "But I asked one of the girls to retrieve the *Empathy* fetched for you this afternoon."

"Excuse me?" I spoke it like an accusation.

She tutted. "It seems no one thought to tell you. Given that curse that's strangely gone missing from your father's office, the spells in your bedroom have been discarded. For safety reasons, we won't be restocking some of the more inessential items again until the guests leave." The movement of her eyes as they travelled up and down me was masterfully subtle. "Including *Empathy*."

Outrage trembled through my limbs. Not this. Not now.

"On whose orders?"

"Your mother's, of course."

No, this wasn't her. I knew in my bones what was happening, because Jude had already promised me it would. "And on whose suggestion?"

Fran smiled. "He worries about you. He and I discussed it, and I took the idea to Dr. Cabot, who thought both removing the spells and . . . cutting you off were reasonable courses of action."

I slammed my hand down on the countertop. I wanted her to fear me—*needed* her to—but my voice trembled with desperation. "And how did he *know*, Fran? Isn't it part of your job to have some fucking discretion? What happened to maintaining boundaries with your employers?"

She bristled; at any other moment, I might have been fascinated that *this* was how I'd finally gotten a reaction out of her, but I was somewhere too far above apoplectic to care. "I don't work for you. I work for your father, who is still alive. I don't need to explain myself to you—"

"Yes, you fucking do."

"—but that's never been mine and Jude's relationship, as you well know. I am not an *employee* to him."

In the aftermath, I can see how foolish it sounds. How unlikely it had always been that Fran would do as house staff did and keep my habits to herself. And yet that's what I'd expected, despite everything, because that's what money had bought us: the privilege of cutting through the world without resistance, unmolested by time, distance, entropy, the wills of others, and, in the case of house staff, by the knowledge that we, like any other animal, had base needs and made waste. They were the unseen hands that allowed us to be something purer than they were, and they left no trace; no fingerprints, no consequences. That was *the deal*.

I tried to imagine what Daddy would have done, but this would never have happened to him, because Fran loved him. He had treated her like family.

"Who else knows?" I said. "Hunter?"

She breathed a laugh. "Oh, I'm sure anyone can tell. All this talk of discretion. Perhaps look to yourself as the first culprit."

"He is trying to fuck with me," I said through gritted teeth. "Believe me, you are making a ruinous mistake by getting involved. When I inherit Fable, I will fire you faster than you can say *mummy issues*."

"I do wish I could help you." The feigned obsequiousness was pouring off her like woodsmoke now, impossible not to breathe in. She took half a step closer. "It's not my place, but . . . this is a good thing, Valentina."

"You're right," I said tightly. "It's not your place."

I could feel an anxiety attack coming on, and the pressure of tears building behind my eyes. No *Empathy*. The twitching of my eyelid was like the frenzy of a trapped butterfly. My eye watered; my vision burred. I turned to stalk away, the panic of helplessness building like steam—but I couldn't. I stood paralysed, staring into a bowl of chocolate ganache on the counter. I had to find some equilibrium at once, to banish my real, fragile self before she and I made eye contact and I did something truly unhinged, on a stage in front of the board, under a spotlight lit by Jude. And even that was weakness—that I had to hold myself upright and poised in this cage I'd let him fashion for me. It was all a prison.

And so I did something vile.

A caterer was reaching for the ganache, piping bag in hand. But I was quicker. He watched, stunned, as I plunged my whole hand into the bowl and scooped up a fistful. Fran sucked in a breath between her teeth, which delighted me. I faced her, watched her try to keep her expression in check as I slapped the chocolate against the newly pristine counter edge and spread it along the side.

"Okay," the caterer said with a sigh as I took the ganache to the underside of the counter. I shoved my fingers right into the notch I found there between the marble and the unit underneath and dragged them along. When I was done, I shook my hand, which was the signal to *Spotless* to let every trace of the mess slough from my skin. I was perfect again before the flecks of confectionary hit the floor, and the counter, and the sunrise-pink linen of Fran's tunic.

"Don't neglect the edges," I told her impassive face, and I left the kitchen, temporarily soothed.

But still without *Empathy*. Somewhere near the ballroom, I collapsed back against a tree trunk, disappeared again behind my rabbit mask, and breathed through the mounting panic. The vibrating of my eyelid mocked me, jabbing a finger at my delusion. Because what had *Empathy* done for me so far? Driven me into the arms of a vampire just so I could feel powerful. Reminded me what a nuisance my needs were to my mother. Entertained Roman Astor for ten minutes. Probably atrophied my ability to read people by their faces alone.

Yet not using it would be like not having enough air. I pictured facing the onslaught of Jude's promised character assassination without knowing how it was received by the guests and fought back the urge to heave. If *Empathy* was a crutch, I couldn't walk without it.

There had to be a cartridge of the stuff *somewhere* in the house. The bathroom nearest the entrance hall: there was a cabinet which held essentials—*Revitalise, Calm*—for right when you were heading out the door. Daddy might have kept some *Empathy* stashed there too, for business appointments.

I practically ran there—hopping streams as they trickled down corridors, cutting an arm through curtains of weeping willow in my path—locked the door, and got on my knees in vintage Dior to ransack the cabinet. Boxes of vapours and powders and tonics toppled as I swept an arm through them, searching. Most were half empty; all were unsealed. *For safety reasons,* Fran had said. Well, Fran could choke, because the only spells she'd discarded had been stolen from my bedside drawer.

There at the back—a box the right shape. Reaching, I closed my fingers around the pack of needle cartridges and dragged them to the front, weak with relief. I pressed the release and the lid opened—a dozen spells, but grouped in pairs. This wasn't what a box of *Empathy* looked like. Already wilting, I took out one of the cartridges and read the product name on the side.

Incognito, it read. And below it: *Moth off.*

I sat back on my heels, the petals of my gown pooling around me in a sorry heap, one oversized ear still visible in the mirror above the counter. *Incognito* was for hiding your Moth: the first cartridge in each pair made it vanish; the second made it visible again. I bet these were Jude's, forgotten since he'd moved into his own place: a private island in Polynesia. Daddy revelled in every second of his power; he'd never want to be mistaken for someone of less importance. But Jude liked to slip his bodyguard and his Moth and find some anonymity in a dive bar or strip club or hookah lounge. I'd been catching him at it since we were sixteen—not that I'd ever told. I'd learned by then that Jude was allowed to do whatever Jude wanted.

Besides, back before I was imaginative enough to place my bleeding finger on a vampire's tongue, dive bars and vanished Moths had been a go-to quick fix for sixteen-year-old Valentina when she went felon. So I wasn't going to be a hypocrite about it.

I stroked the dent in the rim of the cartridge where the needle would emerge and felt an unsettling sort of hunger. I couldn't have *Empathy,* my safety blanket of thorns, my ugly little violation in a needle . . . but the rush? The sharp reminder that the memories might haunt me but that they were mine to summon, biddable as a child? It was madness, the needle a fresh trauma every time—and yet hadn't I been rushing to greet it with growing frequency? Hadn't I always chased the feelings that threatened to undo me, be it beneath a tattoo gun or the mouth of a vampire, or in a dive bar without a bodyguard, *Shield* turned off so a stranger could touch me?

As always, to think on it too long was dangerous. And I didn't. Without choosing to, I had already snapped a stick of *Calm*—I hadn't lost my mind *entirely*—and positioned the *Incognito* cartridge with trembling fingers. One deep breath and I pushed down.

A sharp rush of pain. The images raced before my eyes as I wrapped my hands around the insides of my elbows. My nausea was rising, but with it a sense of relief, of control.

I wobbled to my feet and straightened my gown. Beside the rabbit head, my Moth had vanished, there but hidden. It unsettled me. This was the valueless prize my self-harm had bought me, and still I would have to forge on without *Empathy*. I considered reinstating my Moth—a second moment of blood-soaked memories. But in the aftermath of the choice, as always, I felt small and ridiculous. Embarrassed, alarmed with myself, I left the second *Incognito* cartridge in the box and went to join the party.

I was wending a path through an overgrown garden—flower-choked bushes climbing one another like roughhousing children—eyes open for Hunter, when a string of venom-tinged words—most definitely Athena van Thiel's—came to me from beyond a magenta thicket of bougainvillea. I peered through the blooms; a mouse in a feathery yellow jumpsuit was arguing with a tuxedoed rooster. Whoever had thought to transform Graham Crain into a literal cock deserved some sort of award. Genital-adjacent folds of flesh wobbled under his chin as Athena hissed at him and he shot back indecipherable accusations of his own.

I was skirting the bush in search of a better aural vantage when the towering visage of a moose, antlers spread like the jaws of a Venus fly trap, appeared in my path. My heart tried to leap from my chest; I stepped backwards into the bush, making it tremble. On the other side, Athena and Graham fell abruptly quiet. I was caught.

"Is that Valentina?" said the moose. The mask was lifted away, revealing Eric Burton-Shaw. Out of politeness, I removed mine too. His eyes flickered to the empty space above my shoulder, but whatever it stirred in him that I had vanished my Moth, it wasn't mine to know. "Apologies! I wasn't trying to startle you, but—" He rummaged in the inside pocket of his tuxedo jacket. "I hope I don't offend you, but earlier, I happened to notice your . . ."

He found what he was looking for—a blister packet of two pills—and pointed to his right eye. My hand went reflexively to mine, still throbbing as my body begged for *Empathy*.

"Is it that noticeable?" I said. And then: "It's tiredness, that's all."

"Oh, I know, I know! Rest assured, I'm more observant than most. But if it's irritating you, these work like a charm. They're a variety of muscle relaxant we launched last year. I take them as I have a tendency to frown, right here." He rubbed the vertical lines between his brows. "Causes me headaches sometimes. But they'll be good for your thing too. These are spares, if you wanted to give them a go." He placed the blister pack in my palm.

"That's very kind of you, Eric. Thank you." I put the pills in the pocket of my dress. "Have you seen Hunter?"

"I haven't a clue!" Eric laughed. "What kind of animal is he?"

I forced a smile. "Right. Never mind."

He replaced the moose mask and disappeared into the trees. Before I could escape, the cock had stepped into his place. "Those things can give you a stroke, you know," he said, whipping off his mask and nodding to the blister packet in my hand. "He tried to give some to Athena too, but I flushed them." He drew breath to continue, but before he could say another word, I put my palm square in front of his face.

"I do not care about the state of your relationship," I said firmly. "There are no circumstances in which you could persuade me to care. So unless whatever you're hiding is about something else entirely, I don't want to hear it."

Would you believe, the man ignored me.

"There's something I need to tell you about Athena." The words rolled into one another, like if he said them fast enough, maybe I wouldn't have time to notice that he was pissing me off. "After what happened between us, she commissioned a *Recall*."

My palm dropped. "*Recall*," I said, stunned.

Memory alteration. The client told Mythos's technicians what they wanted gone and, if necessary, what they wanted to remember instead. A few sensory details for the brain to latch onto, and the mind did the rest. The spell was loaded into an applicator and brushed onto the temples; in a heartbeat, their lived reality had altered.

"She struggled, afterwards," Graham hastened on. "We were back together right away, but she was making it difficult. I did everything right—including couples' counselling, for Christ's sake—anything she said she needed, but nothing was good enough for her. So eventually she did the sensible thing. It was minor."

It was the most controversial and highly regulated spell to come out of the company to date. So regulated we weren't allowed to list it among our products and services on the website or advertise it in any way. You just had to hear about it; which was difficult, since anyone who'd gotten *Recall* inevitably knew less about it than you did. The main avenue for the uninitiated was through therapists. That was strictly how the spell was used, after all: for therapeutic purposes. Every professional body under the sun had vehemently denounced it, but the wealthier you were, the easier it was to find healthcare professionals who would take your money to tell you what you wanted to hear or treat you with whatever controversial miracle cure you wished to be prescribed. All Athena would have needed to place an order was a psychiatrist to confirm she was of sound mind and acting of her own free will.

And I would shoot myself in the eye if she'd been honest about the latter.

"What a marvellous idea," I said. "Come up with that one by herself, did she?"

All expression leached from Graham's eyes. I tried to imagine what he was feeling on the inside and pictured a beast fanning its spines. Yes, I was missing *Empathy* like a limb, but it didn't make the Graham

Crains of the world any less predictable. The only thing he was capable of feeling towards me was anger.

"You don't know her as I do. She needs to be given permission before she'll really consider a course of action. I only suggested it as an option. She took *herself* to the lab. She didn't even ask me to go with her."

That last part had probably been Graham's idea too. Because what could be worse, while trying to convince people you were forgetting a boyfriend's indiscretion of your own free will, than all six-foot-six of said boyfriend standing over you as you did?

But for all knowing this made me want to shudder, one mystery had been solved: I had sensed conspiracy in Graham's feelings in the woods that morning because, against my will, he and I were in one. And Athena had no animosity towards me because she had no idea Graham had wanted to leave her for me.

"Listen," he said tightly. "I'm only telling you so you know there's no reason to say anything to her, alright?"

Was that an implied threat in his voice?

"Graham, dear, I don't know how I can be any more clear," I said as I replaced the rabbit head mask and stepped around him. "I don't think about you enough to want to ruin your life."

He made the dismayed sound of someone scrabbling for a comeback and had to settle for: "Fine by me."

His misused fiancée had cut a path through knee-high tufts of blue-green grass and perched herself on an oversized toadstool to sulk. Her giant mouse head hung down, its enchantment flickering as she bothered the corner of one eye.

I imagined wiping the worst things that had been done to me from my memory, the way Athena had erased Graham's abandonment. Once, not long after I'd come home with a tattoo over my hip and angry questions tripping off my tongue, Mum had selectively overcome her aversion to excessive magical modifications and agreed I could forget the whole stem cell transplant. She'd taken me for the prerequisite psychological evaluation, where I had wilted against the couch whilst a psychiatrist gently explained that magic could not untangle what I'd believed was a straightforward complaint. Childhood memories, especially those that bred the kind of neuroses I was carrying into young adulthood, were not only dangerous to tamper with, but nearly impossible to remove *well*. The psychologist had asked two or three perfunctory questions about what I remembered of my role in Jude's recovery, and I answered honestly that it was startlingly little. I didn't know why, when I dreamed of the hospital, the dream so often featured the back of my father's head. I couldn't account for why a certain hand action Mum sometimes used made me cold with dread. The memories were, by this time, beside the point. To remove what they'd left, if such a thing were possible, would be to remove me. And if this wasn't the me I would've chosen, she was still the only one I had.

I'd regretted the whole thing immediately. It had closed a door that had always been there; one through which I could step and be reborn. I could almost sense her, that other Valentina, unchipped, unmarked, as hard and flawless as a diamond.

But looking at Athena, I was both sadder and oddly comforted about the loss. She had returned to her state of unbroken perfection, and here she still was in a loveless relationship, as miserable as ever. *Recall* had fixed nothing. Perhaps neither of us had been a cracked vase to begin with—what if we were clay instead, destined to warp with every thumbprint? I imagined for a moment that the stem cell donation had never mattered, that I hadn't been robbed of my imperviousness by a break; I simply didn't have it to begin with.

It was not as dismal a thought as it sounded. Clay could be fired. I could yet be made into something perfect.

I was starting to get restless with my search for Hunter when the scent of sweetness and salt, sticky and savoury, overpowered the loaminess of the enchanted forest. The fingers of a weeping willow—swaying uncannily like reeds underwater—blocked the dining room door, but as I grew closer, they parted with a soft rustle and I gingerly slipped through. Inside, lights like fireflies—bobbing, buoyed by every eddy of the air, winking in and out of existence—lit a feast fit for a faerie court. A rustic wooden table appeared to have grown out of the moss-robed ground, its legs entwined trunks that separated into nests of roots beneath, and its top laden from corner to corner with glistening maroon and burgundy fruits: plums, pomegranates, blood oranges, wine-soaked pears. Nestled in the fruits was an embarrassment of meat, dark-glazed suckling pigs interspersed with giant roast birds I was fairly certain were swans. Not a popular slaughter, or so I would have thought; half of the beasts had already been rendered bone by intrepid guests. I was curious myself; the meat looked dark and succulent, a richer bird than I had ever tasted.

But a man with the head of a badger was picking at the leg meat of the nearest; aloft in his other hand, a Manhattan.

It was his cocktail of choice.

For the plan to work, I had to get Hunter to follow me. I'd prepared a lie about needing to talk to him, about using the search as an opportunity to have my mother's laptop scoured and what had been found, how it might hurt the company. It was a gossamer-thin plan—I had not instigated a one-on-one conversation with him in my twenty-three years—but then another idea presented itself. Because I was standing there, and Hunter had looked over, and he didn't know it was me at all. His giant badger head had dipped as his eyes fell from my rabbit mask and landed, presumably, on the naked skin above the neckline of my dress.

I tried my hardest not to dry heave as I crossed to the glass doors leading to the gardens and shot a coquettish look over my shoulder—which is difficult to do when your face is hidden behind a rabbit's, so in case the message wasn't clear, I curled a finger in invitation. Like a dog called to heel, Hunter set down his drink, wiped the grease from his fingers with a blood-red napkin, and followed me away from the safety of Fable. And if the turn this had taken made me deeply uncomfortable, it helped to think about the thread count of prison linen; of the decades of discomfort Hunter was in for as soon as I'd caught him red-handed with the antidote.

Outside, cool, fresh air rinsed away the fecund tang of deepest, darkest woods. I cut around to the path that led to the gamekeeper's hut, to the same trail I had chased Hunter along that afternoon. I passed through the Grecian gardens, along a gravelled trail between neat rows of lavender and cypress trees, to a stone fountain of a woman pouring water from a jug.

Beyond this was a grove of fruit trees. As I waited for Hunter to catch up, I stepped behind a plum tree and delicately toed the grass and clods of earth off the thing I had buried there earlier. My heartbeat was slow and steady as I held my clean and perfect purpose like a static charge. Birds rustled the branches; glass clinked in the caterers' setup around the other side of the house, by the kitchen. Beneath it all, the bass-heavy music pumping through the house was a bell jar keeping the guests from the goings-on outside.

The crunch of gravel told me Hunter had reached the fountain. It almost disappointed me, how easy it was to lure him out here, this mediocre man who thought he could steal away all that was mine, who thought he deserved it more.

I waited to be sure we hadn't been followed, but this was a masquerade and I'd been careful not to show Fran my disguise; if her army of spies were looking for me, they were doing so blind. I stepped into the path, and Hunter crunched to a dead halt, instinct propelling him to throw up his hands.

Probably because I was pointing a rifle at his chest. Yes, I was doing another ambush.

He dropped them instantly as he saw the rifle was one of the paintball guns we had used that morning in the forest. Hunter threw off the mask. "What the fuck?"

Grinning, I took off mine. Hunter didn't recoil as I'd hoped—I suppose he thought nothing of visually groping a girl he'd known since infancy. He only let his shoulders fall and released that humourless grunt that passed for a laugh. "Revenge, is it? You got me." He slapped his right arm and turned his shoulder to face me. "But I sleep on my left, so try and get me somewhere on this side."

"In that case, I better do a practise shot first." I nodded at the fountain behind him.

Hunter scoffed. "All those hunting trips with Oz couldn't make a shooter out of you, then?"

"Do you think I can hit her in the face?" I said, pretending the girlishness he imagined of me.

I got a little closer to the fountain and took my time lining up the shot. I was ready for the kickback, and when I pulled the trigger, the bullet hit the statue square in the face. Stone exploded.

I told you I didn't care for shooting. I never said I wasn't good at it.

Hunter leapt, which was gratifying enough, even before he lost his balance and went sprawling on the gravel. I lowered the rifle as fragments of rock toppled down the decapitated body of the water carrier and plunked into the fountain. By the time Hunter had risen to his feet—laboriously, like the decrepit old man he was—I was aiming the rifle at him again. Behind the stone walls of Fable, the music pounded on.

"What the fuck?" Hunter said again, brushing gravel dust from his tuxedo. His instant and audible fear was a temporary balm for my lack of *Empathy*.

I'd chosen the rifle from the gamekeeper's hut a couple of hours before. The moment my eyes landed on it, I'd known it was the one. It was almost identical to the paintball guns.

Not that it had to be. I'd just wanted Hunter to look right past the threat of me one last time.

"Where did you hide it?" I said levelly.

"I don't know what—"

"I *watched you*, you tiny, miserable man. I followed you out of the forest when you learned about the search and I watched you move it. *Where is it?*"

He was looking at the rifle, not me, maybe in fear, but it still felt like a dismissal, which he confirmed when he drawled, "You're not going to shoot me."

Maybe I was a little out of practise, because the second warning shot—aimed past his shoulder—skimmed his sleeve. The bullet struck a pear tree behind him, sending shards of bark flying and Hunter covering his head.

"Jesus. Alright." He patted at his arm, seeking a wound. I must have been a hair's breadth from tearing through him. "It's in my car, alright?"

Success. I let my father's grin break free. But I didn't just need a confession; I needed the antidote. I jabbed the rifle in the direction of the garage. "Lead the way."

We left the Grecian garden beneath a long, arched trellis wrapped thickly in vines like the resigned prey of a colossal snake. It creaked beneath the weight of its burden as we passed through a darkness fragrant with the musk of wisteria and barely touched by the soft illumination of Hunter's Moth. I kept the rifle lifted, the barrel pointed at Hunter's back. There was nothing I trusted myself to say; without *Empathy*, I couldn't guess how the wrong word might inspire him to stop cooperating, even to destroy the antidote once and for all.

The path veered past the tennis courts, nestled in bursts of white hydrangeas, ghostly in the blue night. They crowded the gravel trail and brushed my skirts like the hands of admirers, soft as breath. The hum of the party was a distant thing now, its music little more than a vibration, like the midsummer work of bees amongst the blossoms.

Eventually, we came to the squat warehouse of the garage. Security had been instructed to guard the garage at all times and summon the persuasion party—Mum—immediately if anyone looked like they might leave. Like cats called to their dinner, two guards materialised as we stepped into the forecourt. Glances bounced from the rifle to me to Hunter without reaction.

"Miss Maddock?" said one.

"You're really going to let her point that thing at me?" said Hunter, his volume rising. The more agitated he grew about the rifle, the more I was enjoying holding it.

"Mr. Corcoran has what we've been looking for in his car," I told security. "Lead the way, Hunter."

His glance travelled over each of us. With a sigh, he led us into the garage, where dozens of nearly identical black SUVs—bulletproofed and glistening—waited for their owners. A young attendant in a grey polo rose hesitantly from the desk in one corner when Hunter pointed to him.

"Open my car."

As we waited, Hunter stared at me inscrutably. I glared back, steadfast and angry. My arms trembled from holding the rifle.

The SUV unlocked with a happy bleep. Hunter opened one of the rear doors and lifted his briefcase out of the footwell to place it on the seat, then stepped back and gestured in invitation. Still, I didn't lower the gun, even as the attention of the security guards burned holes in my back.

"Unlock it."

Hunter tipped his head at the security guards. "Tell them to back off."

"So you can destroy it before they can stop you?"

The gun pointed at his chest had not compelled him to focus on me like he did then. For the first time in twenty-three years, I'd become interesting to him; I just didn't know how. His expression was too many things, his feelings a mystery without blessed *Empathy*.

"Because the contents of that briefcase are confidential," he said at last, in the same tone one would say *because the sky is blue*.

I found the face of the attendant hovering behind a guard. "Take the car key," I told him, a corner of my mind gnawing on a fretful feeling. "All of you, give us some space."

Reluctantly, they moved away. Hunter entered the combination on the case and opened the lid. Lowering the gun—but clutching it close—I pawed through its contents, my desperate heart in my throat.

A laptop. Some outgoing mail. A fat document wallet the glossy white of Mythos papers, marked CONFIDENTIAL. And an unmarked manila envelope that looked promising but turned out nothing but a flash drive when I upended it with trembling hands.

I tossed each item onto the back seat as I dug—the mail sliding across the leather like a fanned pack of cards—but there was little to excavate before I ran out of corners. I pawed at the velvet interior for a catch, a hollow, a secret compartment. The gnawing feeling intensified. It was trying to draw my attention to the superstitious focus with which

I was pressing my will against the moment. It pointed out—in a voice too fearful for me to heed—that there was no magic to be drawn from the force of belief alone.

When I turned, I knew I was failing to keep the panic off my face. Hunter watched me with that unreadable interest, but a crease had appeared between his brows. I realised later it was from effort. He was trying—and failing—not to glance at the flash drive I had tossed aside.

"What is it?" I said, nodding at the drive.

A muscle jumped in his jaw, but he didn't reply. It wasn't the antidote—that wasn't here, because Hunter didn't have it, a reality to which I was growing blessedly numb—but he had brought me here when I demanded what he'd taken.

He'd thought I was talking about this flash drive.

I knocked his briefcase into the footwell and pulled the laptop towards me. I couldn't fire up the drive while holding the rifle, so I put it across the seat where Hunter couldn't snatch at it. When I booted up the laptop and connected the drive, a folder of half a dozen files appeared on-screen, each titled with a sequential code I recognised. These were product development documents, records of design sessions in a Mythos lab. I clicked on the first one.

The first words that jumped out at me were *full-body paralysis*. I was already opening the second. *Docility. Suggestibility.* Then the third: *neurotoxin*. All had the name of the magician, alongside the date and lab number, printed in the top right corner.

Claudia Cabot.

The abandoned seven-year-old I had once been reared her head, ears pricking.

"What are these?" I said, as if I didn't already know.

Hunter appeared torn. After drawing breath to speak several times, he at last said, "Just a sample of the things your mother gets up to behind the closed doors of her lab." He cleared his throat. "I downloaded them from her hard drive last night during dinner. I had the drive in my room until this afternoon."

When he'd found out about the search. I clicked through the files again, but I couldn't bring myself to look too closely at the contents; the voice in my head—the one that belonged to the future CEO of Mythos, still stubbornly alive, oblivious so far to the fact that the antidote was god knew where with god knew whom, for *who even fucking knows* what reason—whispered two words.

Plausible deniability.

"Mythos doesn't make weapons," I said, like tying a pretty scarf over my eyes.

You know already there were industries Mythos hadn't yet revolutionised: telecommunications, for example. Logging, textiles, information. Things we had set our sights on but not yet developed the spells to conquer. But then there were the arenas in which we'd cut deals. That is, the perpetual money trees of our biggest investors. The Eric Burton-Shaws of the world, who had seen Mythos tech disrupt industries and topple giants in energy and shipping and construction, and who had funded our labs, defended our patents, and backed us against regulators and state interference.

In exchange, Mythos didn't tread on its friends, the holy trinity: agriculture, pharmaceuticals, and defence.

We had not revolutionised food. We had not revolutionised medicine. In case you thought warcraft was a moral boundary.

"Well, with the company under your bitch mother, maybe we do," said Hunter. He made a series of scornful throat sounds, like misogyny morse code. "Set aside the conflicts of interest for a moment—the public sentiment around just the possibility of Mythos entering the defence space? They'd bring back the guillotine. I'm not talking boycotts; I'm talking about handing politicians their entire campaign platform. I'm talking court challenges, renewed anti-trust reviews, the whole circus. All with the defence industry leaving Mythos in the mud and us deserving it." He thrust an arm at the screen. "I mean, look how fucking insidious all this shit is. She's a psychopath."

He was gathering steam as he went on, talking with twice the energy I had ever seen him commit to anything. And I let him do it, as if I needed convincing, because I'd be damned if I'd admit Hunter Corcoran was right about something.

He was *too right*, though. The idea of Mythos's clandestine step into defence was too egregiously dumb, the framing of all this too convincing. Of course my mother, the woman more committed to her craft and driven by ambition than anyone in history, was crossing lines in pursuit of her glory. With this curated little collection of documents, wasn't it all so obvious?

Mythos's magicians engaged in basic research all the time. They strung together different combinations of code, new ideas, and recorded the output from the AI in development documents like these. There were archives' worth of discarded spells; things that weren't practical, or marketable, or *safe*. If we were lucky, some of it found a new use or was cannibalised down the road.

No, there might have been slivers of the truth in what he was telling me, but there was no honesty.

"I get it. I see the play." I snapped the laptop shut and pulled out the flash drive. "You leak one or two of these documents to the press, the board fires Mum for the sake of damage control, and then—*oh, look!* You're interim CEO, you set Jude up in your old job, and he guarantees your future when he takes over."

Sneering, Hunter came closer, until I could smell the whiskey and meat on his breath. "I helped build this company. I won't watch it fall into the hands of a woman so that she can drive it into the ground." His eyes flickered down to my cleavage again, in case it was unclear that he was talking about me as well as my mother. His voice grew deeper as he went on. "Do yourself a favour: take your chunk of Oz's shares at the astronomical price they'll be worth when we launch this product wide and be satisfied. Better than being CEO of a company your mother will have spent a year destroying every way she can manage."

"I've got a better idea," I said. I took the rifle off the seat and handed it to him. "Stick this up your ass. I'm taking the flash drive. And this."

I grabbed the glossy white document wallet, which I had to assume also contained some manipulation that could get Mum fired over nothing.

Hunter had other ideas.

"Not that!"

He lunged to snatch it from me. I leaned away until I was wedged in the hinge of the car door, the file held above my head. For one transcendently real moment, the rifle was pointed casually at my jaw. The next, it went off with a bang that shook the world like a cup of dice.

Darkness. An ache in my shoulder.

I threw my hands over my ears, too late; my eardrums shrieked their horror.

And then it passed.

"You *stupid*—"

Hunter bent to scoop up the file, a brick of bound pages two fingers thick. It had hit my shoulder as I dropped it. Behind him, a security guard was looking up at the ceiling, where one of the hanging strip lights swayed from a support, dark now. Pebbles of glass littered Hunter's car and the concrete.

"What the actual fuck?" I shrieked at Hunter. "You almost killed me! Over—"

I gestured to the file he was clutching to his chest. The card wallet had torn, revealing the blue-covered heft of a lab report. It was a document detailing the programming and specifications of a new spell. Such reports were part of the mise-en-scène of my childhood; they had lingered on footstools, been stacked haphazardly on shelves, rested on the breakfast bar with the covers folded back on themselves in Mum's kitchen. This despite the reports being proprietary information, hence the bold, black letters stamped across the wallet and both sides of the cover.

Immortality, read the print beneath the stamp on this one.

"*You*"—he jabbed a finger at me—"are not authorised to have this."

I stepped towards him. Hunter stepped back, angling his body protectively around the file as if it were a chicken bone, he a starving dog.

I recalled what was so groundbreaking about *Immortality*: it was the first Mythos product based on a magic that wasn't Martin Maddock's. Contained within that document—alongside the pages and pages of code that made it compatible with Mythos's manufacturing process—was the method for distilling eternal life from vampire venom.

The document contained something replicable.

"You're going to sell the method," I said, shock blunting my tone.

For a beat, Hunter was frozen. Then a mocking sneer of a grin painted his face. "You know what?" Casually, he extended the lab report to me. "You want it so badly? Enjoy."

I didn't reach for it. My fist around the flash drive clenched rhythmically as I turned the offer over in my head, but I couldn't see his angle. I could barely think at all as another question pounded its fists against the moment, drowning everything out: Where was the antidote? Who had done this? How would I find it before the Gilded Grip alchemised my heart?

Before I could decide what to do, Hunter's expression flickered rapidly through several emotions I still couldn't read, and he withdrew the report. Turning on his heel, he stalked to the attendant's desk.

"Give me a lighter," he barked at the attendant, who patted his empty pockets and turned wide, beseeching eyes on the guards. One of them stepped forward, fishing a lighter from his inside jacket pocket, and handed it over.

Hunter held the report aloft above a trash can and set the flame to one corner. Fire licked gleefully up the edge, curling and blackening the cover and then the pages beneath, one by one, gaining strength with every bite. With a glare in my direction, flat and full of casual loathing, he let the report drop into the can with a heavy *thunk*.

He hadn't been planning to sell it. He just didn't want *me* to have it.

Hunter tossed the lighter at the guard, straightened his tuxedo jacket, and stalked past me on his way out of the garage.

"Now fuck off."

10

My wretched, dying body carried me back to the house. I barely felt it.

It was supposed to be Hunter. He had motive; he'd been hiding something. Even with the truth, fumbled into my hands at the end of a gun, I couldn't accept it. Reality butted against the diamond conviction that this was supposed to be simple because I wanted it to be. I was a Maddock; I was my father's daughter. Problems bowed their heads and shrank into the corners at the sound of my approach.

I stumbled, catching myself gracelessly on a stone bench.

It was supposed to be Hunter.

A scream built in my throat. I gave in and let it tear free, curling my fingers around the stone as if to crumble it to rubble.

When I had burned every ounce of my breath and my throat was raw, someone swam into focus in the corner of my vision. It was a kid on the catering staff, maybe sixteen or seventeen, carrying a trash bag. He saw me and tensed like he had stumbled upon a bear. I stared him down. I was so far beyond explaining or excusing myself; let him tell someone who would tell Fran who would tell Jude. If I was going to be dead in two days, what did it matter?

Wherever he was supposed to take the bag—a dumpster, presumably—the boy lowered it to the ground where he stood and backed away, only turning his back on me as he reached the corner.

I went to the bag. Hunter's flash drive was still in my white-knuckled fist. I let it fall to the floor, and I drove the whole weight of my body into it with my heel, again and again, until it was in half a dozen pieces. I didn't know what a tech person could do with the scraps of a storage device, so I threw half of them into the bushes and only half into the bag of trash, which I kicked, because *fuck Hunter,* that time waster. An entire day was gone, and I had no suspect, no motive, and no evidence of where the antidote might be.

And the curse.

Around a bend in the rows of cypress, the approach to the house had been lined with torches. I tottered for the nearest—my heels on gravel joining the race to murder me—where I thrust my arm close to the flame. At first it was like looking into a crucible. Blinding gold light reflected off my gilded veins. I pulled back, and the pattern revealed itself. They were as delicate as a lace glove, burnishing my skin as high as my upper arm, creeping ever closer to my heart.

Like a burning fuse.

I had no time to waste on this pity. The culprit still hadn't revealed what they truly wanted, but capitulating to them when they did would be the end for me. I could never call myself my father's heir after baring such an unforgiveable weakness. It was off the table. I may as well have died.

There were other potential suspects, other motives. Hunter was a dead end. Graham might still have wanted to ensnare me somehow—for revenge, for money—but the *Recall* suggested he was committing to Athena. And now she didn't remember I'd ever been a threat to her impending nuptials, so there went her motive too. Eric had noticed I was antsy and offered me pills—could it have been a test of some kind? A threat? I didn't have the first clue what he might want from cursing me, but I couldn't rule him out yet. Roman didn't seem to think Jude should be CEO—but maybe that was because he saw a future in which Jude became too busy, maybe even too fulfilled, to need Roman anymore. He knew his meal ticket depended on Jude's attention, on his need. I could not conceive of Mum dragging this out, or doing it this weekend, or in fact going to such lengths to manipulate me when she already held my future in her hands. And if this was House Gothenburg,

I didn't know their motive either, nor had they the means—they hadn't met me before yesterday to clock my *Empathy* habit, and they likely didn't know about the crude magic collection.

Fran and Zazie still had motive. Fran needed Jude to inherit Fable if she was going to keep working here, and Zazie might be looking to right the hundred-year-old wrong of her bitter family's invention—maybe owning Mythos's future CEO was a path to restitution. Or maybe—and my heart leapt to my throat at the thought—this was straight-up revenge, a life for a life, and I was never going to see the antidote again. The first note—TELL NO ONE—might have been designed to stop me from going to the police, but it didn't explain the second one telling me not to leave Fable.

It was somewhere to start. I headed back to the house, but once I was enveloped again in the green and resinous scent of forest, the somnambulant beat of the music—Fable had been changed.

I'd entered the way I'd left: through the dining room, I was certain of it. Yes, there was the banquet table, still laden with food and fragrant with the salt of roasted meat and the syrup of ripe fruit, red-black in the dim of the midnight forest—but now it was half sunken into the rolling earth, as if a thousand years had passed. One of the legs had swelled into a mature and bulbous oak tree, its presence so quickened, so vital, I thought I could hear it whispering under the music. Its leaves appeared to twist and turn with aching slowness. They obscured the ceiling—that is, if the ceiling was still there. The very structure of the house had shifted under the enchantment, and where the door to the hallway had once been there now was a cliff face of tumbled stone dressed in ivy. But the opposite wall had partially crumbled, creating a treacherous opening to the next room.

"Motherfucker." I bent in a graceless crouch to crawl through the space the fallen stones had made, balancing on my hands and the toes of my shoes. This was not easy to do in a ball gown; at one point I almost landed on my face when I stood on the hem. I should have emerged near the entrance hall, the main stairs right ahead of me. Instead, I was in the grand ruin of a pillared hall. Some thick and fragrant vine—bitter with

a tang of poison—was making slow work of the ceiling and supports. Some columns still held; others were diminishing like candles. They stretched on and on—dozens, perhaps hundreds of them—all throttled by the creeper, which was the green of deep and stagnant water. Loose stones wobbled underfoot—and that was enough; I took my heels off and tossed them. The stairs still had to be this way, so I started through the hall.

But the spell in this part of the house was profoundly uninterested in the concrete reality of Fable's floorplan. A quality of the shadows, or the spacing of the pillars, or perhaps a sixth sense within me told me I was moving down the hall and not across it, but this waxed and waned every time I turned my head and lost my bearings. Twice, I came to a place identical to where I'd started, and once to a wide stream. I turned back to the pillars, but by the time I'd gone ten paces and decided to brave the water—at least it wasn't *this*; I'd sooner have been wet than stuck here any longer—the stream had vanished and the hall stretched on.

There were others in there with me; I saw them in flashes between the columns, their animal heads chiaroscuro monsters in the light of their Moths. For a while, a guest in a tuxedo and a fox head appeared between every column as I walked, as if they were stalking me.

When I at last recognized the string of diamonds at the fox's throat and called out "Roman," one of my best suspects had already vanished. Or perhaps it hadn't been him. Perhaps no one had ever been there at all. Perhaps the others in here were part of the enchantment too. By that point my frustration had me by the throat and was applying a little more pressure with every breath.

I might have given up on my senses, or else relied too heavily on the glow of a Moth to tell me when someone was coming, because Mariah was upon me before I saw her. Nightfall had restored her to a picture of full health. Her skin was bright, if ghostly pale against the silver beading of her dress. She was holding—my insides squirmed in alarm to see it—a *living bird*, its wings pinned to its sides, its heart beating so hard I could see it pulsing in its breast.

She dropped her hand to her side like it contained nothing more than her car keys and tutted.

"I saw someone without a Moth and thought you were that youth with the darling Midwest accent." Her gaze explored the length of me and came back to mine with a new shine. "Though you are quite darling and fresh yourself, aren't you?"

A chill raced across my skin, suddenly too exposed. "Do you know which way it is to the stairs?"

"Yes." She grinned, the teeth behind her red lips pearly and ordinary. I looked around, and all my strength melted away when I found no one nearby. I stepped back and bumped into a column, and Mariah rolled her eyes. "Oh, please, with the shrinking-damsel thing. How medieval!" The bird made an attempt at freedom, thrashing against the cage of Mariah's fingers, and she cooed at it and stroked its head until it stilled. "When I took the gift, my maker promised me it was a new age. She said that when everyone caught on that it was magic and not the devil, you little dears would be *begging* us to feed on you. It was the nineteenth century! Freedom was on the rise!" She held the little bird before her face and looked hard into the black marbles of its eyes. It was still now, its energy spent. "Two centuries later and you're still so desperately in need of correction."

Slowly, she gentled her hold on the bird, until it lay in the palm of her open hand, its head turning this way and that as it seemed to weigh its chances. Then it sprang to its feet and—stayed there, balanced on Mariah's open hand, where it remained even as she brought the creature to her face and kissed it. She smiled, satisfied, and came towards me, hips swaying out of time to the beat of the music, the bird nuzzling her cheek.

"You're supposed to be *eager*," she said with a sigh. "I know I was, in my day. I was an acolyte to the gift." There was something vulnerable in her face now, a hesitation as her heavy-lidded gaze flickered to my neck. "I know how it feels. I can describe it to you first, if you want."

I tried to shake my head; nothing happened. I screamed such a feral scream that my lungs caught fire, yet no sound escaped me. *I'm poison,*

I warned, but no attempt at moving my mouth made the words real. Some magic had fixed me where I stood, robbed me of speech, except this wasn't the predatory trick of a vampire. It was the magic of fear, whetted until it gleamed, handled compulsively until to hold it was the only thing that soothed. I pictured Mariah the acolyte, twenty years old at most and still brave enough to name the void within her and let another's bloodlust fill it. Then I pictured myself, locked beneath her bite, her teeth two cold needles in my vein. I couldn't. I would die.

But I was dying anyway. The curse in my veins would ruin Mariah, but the curse in hers might save me. My eyes fluttered closed. My breath came in shallow gasps.

She was upon me now, so close I could feel her cool breath kiss my cheek, could smell the honey and amber musk of her.

"Ah, but you don't need me to. I can smell it on you, you good girl." She bent her head towards me, and I was going to break. I was going to dissolve into tears and begging. "I can smell your surrender."

A cold hand closed around my arm. Mariah gave a theatrical sigh of irritation. When I opened my eyes, Luc was there, and the other vampire was strolling away, one index finger petting the breast of her little bird like she'd never had an interest in me in the first place.

I leant into the pillar, drawing deep breaths until I was no longer aware of the blood pumping beneath my skin. Luc's fingers still held my arm. Another vampire, but at least this one knew I couldn't be bitten. The curse had granted me that much.

"I thought it was over." My life. My ceaseless circling of an end I felt I'd written for myself by wearing a groove in my thoughts of it. Inexplicably, tears sprung to my eyes. I blinked them away.

"She knew not to take it further than you'd allow," Luc said as he released me. I couldn't tell if he'd understood exactly what I'd meant, but he gave me a scrutinising look, as if he was trying to. With the setting of the sun, he too had been restored to an imitation of life. The shadows beneath his eyes were gone, as were the hollows under his clothes. He seemed to consider his words carefully before saying, "Sometimes fear is . . . complicated. You can't stop it eating away at you, but you can step into its mouth and let it consume you whole. That's the only power you have."

The memory of the needle on a cartridge spell I didn't need. The way I'd hungered for the rush of fear.

"Is that power?" *I can smell it on you.* "Sounds like surrender."

"Maybe." He flashed a regretful smile, gone as fast as it appeared. "But maybe it's also the only way to live. Let's dance."

"I— What?"

He nodded to where the light changed, an ethereal purple glow permeating the myrtle shadows of the ruins. A white mist spilled through the rows of pillars. Why the enchantment was showing me the way out now, I didn't know, but I didn't want to be stuck here when Mariah came back, so as Luc set off, I fell in step behind him.

Somewhere in the fog, new shapes began to take form. We were in a forest of silver birches. Beyond the hall of pillars, the shape of Fable had been restored, and the walls—though shrouded in flora in most places—were where they should be. The light was the colour of sunset, and the milky mist rolled across the floor, eddying as animals cavorted through the trees. A peacock swayed drunkenly, light blazing in the mirrored sequins of her dress. A lynx was wrapped around an owl, their bodies flush as they moved, hands wandering where they pleased. Damp, cool air caressed my skin. I breathed it in like it was medicine, felt it cleanse me from the inside out. I was grounded again—focused—so when Luc extended a hand in invitation, I shook my head.

"I don't have time to dance. My lead was a dead end. It wasn't Hunter."

That focused him too. I relayed everything that had happened since the afternoon: Hunter disappearing with his hidden contraband, Jude's interference, the real, less interesting betrayal our CFO had been working on (though the last I sketched with corporate delicacy). Luc wanted every detail and asked questions with the efficiency of a surgeon: Had there been more instructions? No, oddly, not yet. Had Jude given any indication he knew more than he was letting on about the missing antidote? Not in the slightest; he was as oblivious as they come. Could this be about the *Immortality* tonic somehow?

"In what way?"

He gave me a look I couldn't parse. "The cost."

"You think someone wants to get their hands on *Immortality* by threatening me instead of simply buying it?" My mind leapt to Charlotte, but no—she had been with Jude when the curse was stolen. Besides, she hadn't even known it existed until the party.

Luc smiled, but a hardness stayed in his eyes. "No, maybe not."

He didn't need to ask if Fran's spies were watching me that very moment.

"The girl at the edge of those trees has been collecting up glasses and putting them down again the whole time we've been talking," he said with the barest nod in her direction. "I noticed her following you through those ruins."

Her uniform was the precise shade of Fable's walls and floors and ceilings, all the better to shift through the rooms like air. In this enchanted grove—the atmosphere glittering, blush light through vapour—she was a smudge of dullness. I wondered if she'd watched me cower from Mariah, if she'd feed word of my weakness back to Jude.

I should have put the rabbit head back on. Now it was too late.

"You need to breathe," said Luc.

"Is that a vampire joke?" I said to deflect from the fact he'd noticed I was wound tight as a fist. I forced my shoulders to relax, forced Daddy's grin onto my face.

"Do you want to be led around on the string of whoever did this?"

The grin shattered, my mind short-circuiting as a trap of my own neurotic invention appeared before me. *Led around on a string.* The very idea was a punch to the gut, just as Luc knew it would be—his expression of satisfaction told me so. He had identified my worst nightmare, had found my buttons and decided to press them all. He may as well have been using *Empathy*.

"Or do you want to let them come to you?" he went on. "When you find out what they want, you'll be on the path to who they are."

I was reminded of Jude, of the casual accusation that I was nothing but my mother's tool, lobbed like a grenade to destabilise me. It didn't matter that Luc thought he was helping. He had still trapped me in a catch-22: be transparently manipulated by his perfect read of me, or do the first thing, be led around on a string. Neither of which left me holding the power.

Looking back, the biggest surprise of that weekend might be that I didn't twist myself to death.

But there were other wants pressing on me at the moment. Luc extended a hand again, and I trembled at the thought of being held by him.

Step into its mouth. Let it consume you whole.

Could he sense her too—the part of me who wanted this feeling, who only became herself at the tip of a needle, terrorised but alive? Before I knew it I was placing my hand in his—cold—and letting him lead me through the trees. Mist danced around our feet like a murmuration of birds, swelling and flinching. We reached a space among the silver birches where other couples swayed. He threaded an arm around my waist and pulled me in, its weight pressing coolness into my spine. My heart pounded at his nearness. My blood was on fire. A few inches closer, a dip of his head, and his teeth could be in my neck. It was a fantasy—or a nightmare—nothing more than a product of this thing that was both fear and fascination, but no less vivid for the promise that it couldn't be true. I could still sip on it. I could taste him as he was forbidden from tasting me.

"So, Mythos's miracle product." I snapped out of the creeping fantasy when Luc spoke. "It really can't be ready before the curse reaches your heart?"

I shook my head. "The kicker is, it *is* ready, technically. The spell is just code, then the code gets imbued into a substance like a tonic or vapour with our hardware, and boom, magic. My mother and her team finalised the working spell a couple of months ago."

Luc tilted his head. "So the problem is the doses haven't been manufactured? How long does that take?"

"A matter of minutes—once the code is uploaded. The upload's meant to begin on Monday, but the longer and more complex the spell, the longer the upload takes." I shifted my gaze to look over his shoulder. "*Immortality* will take five days. Even if I'd run to the lab myself and hit *upload* the second I knew what was in my veins—"

"It would never be ready in time," finished Luc.

I fixed a false smile in place. "And before you say it, the irony of facing death at a party to celebrate *Immortality* is not lost on me."

"The irony of being a vampire at a party to celebrate *Immortality* isn't lost on *me* either."

I pulled back to look into his face. "Irony? Vampire venom helped make the tonic. It makes perfect sense that you're here."

A long moment went by, the music filling the quiet between us with a dreamlike unreality. Luc led me in slow circles around the floor, but our dance had grown detached, mechanical.

"When I was about your age," he said at last, "me and five other men—well, boys, some of them—attacked what we thought was the hideout of a rival gang. But you can't kill vampires with lead bullets, and lead was all we had."

Cold shuddered across my skin as if Luc had unlaced our hands and run his fingers up my arm, across my clavicle, lingering at my throat. I could almost—but not quite—admit that I leaned into the feeling. "They were a gang of vampires?"

Luc laboured over his reply, like the choice of words was crucial. "They were a family of sorts. Nobodies, an offshoot of strays from an old line of House Thebes trying to make something of themselves. They kept us there I don't know how long. It could have been a couple of days, it could have been a week. Either way, it wasn't long enough that I ever stopped believing I would live, even as the others started dying. I'd gotten through prison, hadn't I? I'd gotten through all the shit with my dad, because I'd refused to stop fighting." The flutter of a muscle in his jaw belied his casual tone. "So I fought. Turned out, that was what my maker liked about me. I reminded him of his kid brother, Etienne. He'd died at the Somme."

"Then he should have let you go," I said, as if I could change a story decades—perhaps more than a century—old by speaking a plain truth.

Luc gave a laugh—easy and warm—and I was reminded of the impression I was doing of my father, of the smile that wasn't really mine. His fingers pressed harder into my spine—I don't think he knew he was doing it. "Vampires aren't so good at thinking in such sane moral terms. We're famously existential, prone to longing. Most of us were given the curse at moments of extreme anguish in our makers' lives, because they followed an impulse that convinced them that was the cure for what they were feeling—that they could feed their pain to another and it would be an act of love." The easy smile curdled into something equal parts anger and loss. "Yves was nothing if not anguished." He seemed to shake off the memory. "The point is, I was never allowed the choice. In fact, I focused so hard on staying alive, on not dying like I'd watched the rest of them do, I didn't even see it coming. I passed out like I'd been passing out for days, except the next time I woke up I was dead.

"The more time that passes," he went on, composed now, "the harder it is to know what that young man would have wanted if he'd known what was coming, and yet I find myself thinking about it more and more. If you manage to reverse the curse, you'll get the choice that was stolen from me: to live forever, or to die."

"That's an easy choice to make," I said. "Who wants to die?"

"Oh, I know plenty who would. It's an easy choice to make at the time. I get it. But take it from one who knows: when you gain eternity, you give something up too."

"Change," I said instantly.

Luc's eyebrows rose in surprise. "Yes. That doesn't intimidate you?"

"*Change* is another word for damage."

"Maybe," he said carefully. "But did you ever think it's damage worth taking? Right now, you're chasing the idea that maybe everything could be perfect. Living people—you strive, because you want your life to be good while it lasts. Every chance is moving past you. And as futile as it is, chasing that image of perfection, it pushes you forward. There's an intensity to it. It presses on you, forces you into new shapes. But all of that's gone when you stop moving through time. Allowing yourself to be changed by anything feels . . . *trivial,* because everything you experience is just so fleeting, and the after stretches on and on." He smiled as he took in my expression. "What's so funny?"

"You're describing everything I want," I said. "I'm twenty-three, and being changed by what happens to me already exhausts me. I want to be stone, Luc. I want to be diamond."

"You want to not care."

"I want to not *bruise.*"

He looked at me strangely. "It's more complicated than that. When you're not malleable anymore, eventually the only shape you're capable of being is a more distilled version of whatever you were already."

"And what were you?"

His eyes unfocused as he slipped into thought. When he returned to the moment, it was with a belying smile on his boyish face. "Angry."

Without meaning to, I put some distance between our bodies. To stop striving was the whole point of *Immortality.* It was completion. Contentment. *Certainty.* But what if the distilled version of myself was someone ravaged by fear? What if I would always feel weak, for eternity?

"Yves and those vampires," I said, the question forming even though I thought I knew the answer. "Where are they now?"

Our dance had slowed, like Luc's smile. I couldn't tell if he was pleased I'd asked or was about to deflect until he said, with just a flicker of pain, "They're dead." His gaze kept catching on something over my shoulder. "I don't think you'll like this, but . . ."

"What is it?" I asked.

"The man over there with the iridescent scales."

I looked over my shoulder. A wiry faerie was lurking in a darkened archway holding a tray of *Good Time.* His eyes were black in the low purple light, and they were fixed on Luc.

"What about him?"

"He's been there for some time." Luc drew breath to speak but hesitated, his eyes on mine. "He wants me to feed on him."

My heart gave a jolt. An incoherent noise escaped me as I dropped Luc's hand and slid out of his grasp. "How do you know?"

"I just do. Call it experience. There are always curious people. Not enough of them, but a few."

I was an acolyte to the gift.

I looked at the man again. Now that Luc had told me, it was impossible to ignore. He was watching him with the intensity of lust, coloured with something different. His throat bobbed as he swallowed.

"He doesn't . . . he doesn't want you to kill him, surely?"

"They rarely want that. Not at first, anyway. But sometimes giving less than everything isn't enough for them." After a beat, he added, "I won't go that far, of course. Not in your home."

"I don't understand it," I said on a breath.

I hadn't taken my eyes off the man. Luc was closer than I thought, his chuckle almost against my ear. "I still don't believe you. I think you do." Closer still, his body a solid presence pressing close to my side. His thumb found the pale inside of my forearm and caressed it. "That close to the edge of death, living is euphoria."

Luc's touch travelled higher—too close to the crease of my elbow—and I flinched away, willing down the rising images.

"I'm sorry, but I'm not in a position to reject him. After being out in the daylight this afternoon, I—"

"Just go."

If the words came out curt, there was nothing I could do about it. Luc crossed the room, weaving around the trees. As he whispered in the man's ear, the faerie's eyes fluttered closed, the bliss of anticipation already descending. They looked like lovers, not predator and prey, but perhaps the difference was not as marked as I wished. I rubbed my thumb over the healed fingertip I had sacrificed to *Incognito,* to an impulse I was too ashamed to name.

There was release in letting your demons consume you.

There'd been respite in dancing with them too. Luc's hands on me, his mouth inches from my delicate skin had been like a drug, or a cobra, rinsing my mind clean and arresting my full attention. But as soon as he was out of sight—the promise and threat of him leaving my body—reality descended. I couldn't do as Luc said; I couldn't wait for the curser to reveal themselves. It wasn't Hunter, so I needed to look at the next most likely person on my list.

To decide that, I needed the notes I had tucked away in my room.

Another incident like the labyrinthine hall of pillars and I would lose my mind along with my bearings, so it was for the best that a staircase made itself known in the hall just beyond the grove. I would go straight to my room, retrieve the list, then hunt down the next best suspect if I had to rip the animal mask off every guest in the building.

At least, that was the plan. I was two corridors from my room when I came across the first faerie and careened to a dead halt.

The spell on her appearance had at last sloughed off, but I identified her as a faerie by the blue and purple circles dotting her naked back. She might have been the leafy creature we had shot that morning. She was moving in an odd shuffle away from me, her arms spread and waving as if she was trying to get someone's attention in slow motion.

"What are you doing?" I said.

She spun in surprise and said something I couldn't hear through the sudden pounding in my ears. Dripping blood spelled out a word from her shoulder to the opposite hip, across the bruised and blue-veined skin of her breasts and stomach.

JUDE.

"What are you doing?" The shouted words scraped against my suddenly dry throat. She tottered towards me, a zombie clamouring to feed. A piece of white table linen was knotted at the back of her head—a blindfold. I stormed towards her. She shrieked as I tore the thing away.

"No! I can't cheat! I can't cheat!" Eyes wide, she scrabbled to snatch the blindfold back. Her fingernails clawed at me, and I tried to speak, but I was absurdly afraid that if I opened my mouth, she would put something in it and infect me with whatever had driven her insane. I relinquished the blindfold, which she hastily replaced despite her shaking fingers.

"They can't think I cheated," she gasped out. As I backed away, I found smears of red on my arms and dress. It wasn't blood. It was paint.

"There's no one here," I said loudly and slowly. The naked woman was on drugs, surely. She already wasn't listening; she'd turned away from me and continued shuffling around the corner, the name branded on her now smeared.

I followed her. The pace was interminable, but I was afraid to approach her again and get an eye clawed out or an ear bitten off. When we turned into the next corridor, a second girl, also blindfolded, with bruises on her legs and someone's dress shirt covering her to the knees, was disappearing around the next corner, in the direction of a moaning, mumbling scream. It was so distant it seemed to come from everywhere, from the walls themselves. Compelled onwards by a sense of wrongness and a sick, buzzing feeling beneath my ribs, I overtook the first girl, then the second, whose shirt was also defiled. *ATHENA* was printed in rough, dripping letters from corner to corner. There was also a doodle of a love heart.

I came to the balcony above the ballroom, which dripped flowering vines. Birds and squirrels crowded the railings, their chatter replacing the music, which had been turned down here. The screaming was coming from the bend of the nearest staircase, where another dancer—painted with the name *ROMAN*—was sprawled, his mouth mutilated by pain and the rest of his face shrouded in the linen blindfold. Yet another blind dancer with an astonishingly black, football-size bruise over one shoulder was attempting to descend around the first's prone body, and the creeping vines, and the spilled paint decorating the step.

Except it wasn't red paint this time. I gripped the railing as I looked down at a shock of jagged white protruding from his ankle.

"Oh god, it's broken," he was gasping. "Oh god. Oh god."

The man trying to get past him was also chanting. "I'm sorry. I'm sorry, Isaiah. I'm sorry."

More zombies had reached the opposite balcony. With sick fascination, I watched them risk the fate of Isaiah, not one removing their blindfold to see or to help him. Most were almost naked, though some had found a T-shirt or a tuxedo jacket. *ZAZIE,* said the paint across the front of one. *NICOLA,* said another.

A bleating laugh sounded from somewhere below before smothering itself. I navigated around the zombies as I took the stairs, muttering an apology to Isaiah as the skirt of my dress touched his fracture and he bawled. Under the spell of the party, the floor of the ballroom had transformed into rustic slabs like the stones of a medieval castle. Moss grew between them; some were overrun with ivy. The infinity pools had turned into wells or fountains, the only blessing in this death trap being that they would be harder for the blindfolded dancers to fall into as they tottered towards a long table in the centre of the room, laden with—

Trifle, a layered creation of berry red and pale creams in a raised glass bowl. A nightmare cake, iced in mint green with delicate violet piping, swirls of buttercream, and glacé cherries, their stalks rising from the top like the prongs of a crown. A pyramid of choux buns encased in spun sugar and dripping with caramel. A baked Alaska.

The parade of desserts went on and on. And beyond them, languishing across chairs and loveseats pillaged from elsewhere, Jude and a dozen guests had done away with their masks and watched on in unblinking fascination. They didn't appear to see me, their eyes fixed instead on the *ATHENA* dancer, who was clawing her way down the final step and jerkily rounding the banister. Behind her, Isaiah, still whimpering, had hauled himself onto one foot.

I stalked past the table of desserts and made for Jude, who lounged in a chair like it was a throne. Roman was draped over the arm, one hand lazily caressing the skin beneath the unbuttoned collar of Jude's shirt. I could see the edges of the tattoo that started at Jude's shoulder; just the knuckles of a skeleton's hand, a couple of sprigs of the wildflower bouquet clutched in its bones. It covered the site of the venous access port that had delivered chemo drugs and later my stem cells, and the scar it left behind.

Neither Jude nor Roman took their eyes off *ATHENA* as I approached, but the former held up a hand, halting me. I ignored it.

"What on earth is this?" I said.

Someone shushed me. Someone else smothered another manic giggle. Athena herself leaned forward in her seat, mouth hinged open. I half expected to see drool at the corners.

"They have to be the first to eat a whole dessert," Roman said under his breath.

"And then what?"

"They get a prize. But they can't take their blindfolds off or they're disqualified."

"And the prize is?"

Roman looked at Jude.

"Fifty mil," Jude said tonelessly.

It was probably life-changing money for a dancer who'd accept twelve hundred to get battered with paintballs. I had never really been a fan of game shows, but with all the added blood and zeros, I suddenly understood why people *were*. The world wasn't ending, the timer on the bomb wasn't running down, but for the contestants, the stakes were just as real. How much desperation would they show? How funny or mortifying or obscene were they willing for their debasement to be? Isaiah had reached the entrance hall, but now he faced crossing the floor to the dessert table—if he could find it—without anything to hold on to. He clung to the end of the marble banister, smearing blood on it, and drew ragged breaths; in preparation to hop, I guessed.

I knew, in whatever part of myself I kept my common decency, that I was supposed to avert my gaze—to leave Isaiah and the others to their painful humiliation and pretend ignorance—but that was exactly why I couldn't. It was like a domestic argument in public, someone too drunk at a party, a wardrobe malfunction, but many times worse. Not to mention what a headache this could turn into. Could someone bleed out from a compound fracture? I looked at the floor, at the evidence of Isaiah as he approached. It seemed like a lot of blood, but it wasn't as if I could stop him. The man might be about to win fifty million, if anybody actually gave it to him when this was over. (And they'd have to give him something. This was how people got sued.)

Graham, who lounged on a couch, one ankle crossed over the other and his hands balancing a scotch and a cigar, made a sound of competitive male glee as *GRAHAM* appeared at the turn of the opposite staircase. He was scrabbling down the stairs like his life depended on it. Despite the blood already spattering the ballroom, now that I understood the game, it was a wonder they weren't all moving that fast. But then *GRAHAM*'s feet slipped and his head hit the bottom step with an echoing crack. The spectators let out a collective gasp, I with them.

"For fuck sake, man," Graham groaned. Roman snorted. *GRAHAM* rolled onto his back and stopped moving.

"Pull up a chair, petal."

I recoiled. "I'm not part of this."

But I also didn't leave. *ATHENA* had reached the table, letting out a shriek of relief; she groped until she found the nearest dessert, the ugly green cake, and tore into it with her fingers. Isaiah had adopted a crouch partway across the floor. He was sweating and trembling, and appeared to be muttering a pep talk, or a prayer. I wanted to tell him to give it up. There was already some hush money coming his way.

I had a memory all of a sudden of a thing my father used to say: "One zero is nothing. Enough zeros is *nothing happened*." He'd said it when he was fined for the elephants at his birthday party; when a former assistant sued him for wrongful dismissal; when a paparazzo said something about Aunt Georgia and Jude had broken four of his teeth. I'd always assumed it was a joke, that he was trying to make light of a situation that might seem grave. But there are jokes, and then there are true things people say to be funny.

I didn't need to stop this; Daddy certainly wouldn't. Besides, I wasn't about to be the monster who stood between one of these people and fifty million. I couldn't march over there and tell Isaiah he could have maybe a hundredth of that because I was worried he was staining the marble. If the worst happened, perhaps someone would have the sense to keep the rest of them blindfolded and save us all the nuisance.

As I was about to flee the scene, I realised: I didn't need my list—most of my best suspects were right here, ignoring me. I took the opportunity to study each in turn, seeking unnatural posture, an aborted sidelong glance.

With Charlotte elsewhere, Roman was making the most of having Jude to himself. The way he was touching him—fingers seeking skin, his whole body folded possessively around Jude's—was far beyond friendly. As if he wanted to remind him that the Charlotte situation was a fling, a weekend thing.

I'm the only person who knows how to get him out of bed in the morning.

Roman's affection might have been bought, but he wanted to own Jude too. But for love, or the love of money? It couldn't be the first alone—it would be too much of a coincidence if the person whom disinherited Roman Astor happened to want was a Maddock. Then again, I knew firsthand how helplessly he was drawn in by indifference, and for all that Roman was hanging off him, Jude barely seemed to know he was there. He claimed to believe Jude would be a terrible CEO—said I could quote him on it to the board—so that wasn't what he wanted. What if cursing me was meant to be the stunt that finally earned him the love he'd been denied everywhere else? He was certainly capable of such reckless damage if it got him noticed.

Zazie was stirring a martini so dirty it was practically a pizza, one concertinaed anchovy slicking grease through the liquor as she swirled the cocktail stick. She was a Crowther on her mother's side. They were the Montagues to our Capulets, our generational enemies—or so they'd cast themselves. From our side, they were a mild irritation that popped up on talk shows or in documentaries every few years but had stopped causing real waves long before I was born. And Zazie might have been part of the clan, but barely. Because she was a Reynolds too, the heir to a *Fuel* dynasty worth tens of billions, all built on a foundation of Maddock magic. It didn't take a math genius to work out how much more that was worth to her than a stale grudge.

And like all of us, Zazie liked her money. She was into racehorses. She owned a share of a Formula 1 team. Surely wealth had been more formative for her than a family conspiracy about a third cousin gone missing. Or did her competitive leanings make the idea of squaring an old rivalry too compelling to resist?

Then there was Athena, who'd given up her memories for the sake of her relationship. It wasn't out of character for her. She'd sported Jessica Rabbit curves for a year for a college boyfriend. She'd funded a D-list actor's gambling addiction for five months. I wanted to shake her by the shoulders and jab a pointing stick at Graham's (admittedly all internal) flaws. Was anything different this time? And if she truly had no idea what he'd done to betray her, could it have anything to do with the gold in my veins?

One of the gathered guests *was* shooting nervous glances my way, but it was probably because I was so focused on his fiancée, whose loyalty to him I held in my hands. Graham had volunteered this vulnerability to me—had probably known he'd have to come clean about Athena's use of *Recall* when they accepted the invitation—so it no longer made sense that he'd planted the curse for a related reason.

But that didn't mean he didn't have one. I had seen the truth of Graham in the way he'd tried to rise even higher than the van Thiel billions. Nothing would ever be enough for him if someone else had more, and who had more than the Maddocks? We were a symbol of success the world over, but to the likes of Graham Crain, we were icons of his own failure. Perhaps my extortion wasn't about what I could be made to do but simply about making me do it. About seeing me dance.

So how would he react if I publicly refused?

How might any of them react?

The party wrapped up after breakfast on Monday morning, and yes, it stood to reason that some time before then, whoever had cursed me would name their price for the antidote, just as Luc said. I could wait; I could make them come to me.

Or, I could lure them out.

UNDER NO CIRCUMSTANCES LEAVE THE PARTY.

They had made a point of confining me here when the rules of the weekend had already done so—why? Where would I go, when the antidote was right here at Fable and the instructions for getting it back would be too? Why write the second note at all—or the first, for that matter—if there wasn't some delicate balancing act at play, something they couldn't get from me without first manoeuvring the pieces into place?

And what if I shook the board?

Without giving myself time to reconsider, I announced as if to no one, "I'm going home."

Half the onlookers cut blank looks my way, while the other half remained fixated on the action behind me, where another blindfolded player had just slipped in blood and let out a string of stuttering curses.

"You mean bed," said Jude absently as Roman continued to trace spirals across his clavicle.

"No, I mean home," I said, and this time I crossed in front of them so they would all have to watch me heading for the door. "I've had enough of this party."

"But you can't leave," said Athena. I turned to study her and found half a dozen or more inebriated faces staring back at me. I at last held more of their interest than the game behind me—though Zazie was still making wincing faces as she kept half an eye on *NICOLA*, who had reached the table and was cracking the caramel shells of choux buns in his teeth one after the other, yellow custard bursting like the jelly of an eyeball from each one.

But without *Empathy*, I couldn't read any of them. I needed my poisoner to give something away.

"Why can't I leave?" I challenged Athena.

Her eyes widened urgently. "Because we don't get the tonic if we leave before breakfast on Monday." She tilted her head to one side. "But maybe you didn't have to agree to that?"

I almost asked if that was her only objection, but then my threat to leave would look too much like a transparent attempt to draw someone out.

"You're right, I didn't," I lied instead, at the same time Jude interjected, "She did."

There was a note of petulant command in the words. He fixed me with a look that said: *What are you doing?* But it was happening now: I was threatening the structure of the party and thus the structure of my future—potentially—as well. But a curse that would turn my heart to gold in less than two days threatened it too. Nothing to be done about the slip-sliding lurch in my stomach but grip the wheel and pray.

Swallowing my dread, I turned on my heel and announced over my shoulder, "Then feel free to try and stop me."

I resisted the urge to look back as I swept from the ballroom. Keeping the wall to my left, I headed east, seeking the front door. We were deep into the night now. Platters of glasses and vials of *Good Time*, half of them empty, lay waiting for a cleanup operation I knew would occur, as if by magic, in the pre-dawn hours. Those guests who preferred their energy organic would have taken themselves to bed already; everyone else was on their second or third dose of *Revitalise*. I hoped whoever had cursed me was among the latter, busy as they were conniving. I hoped, in truth, that they'd seen me stalk from the ballroom.

The forest enchantment diminished the nearer I got to the entrance hall, until the walls were bare of moss and ivy, and underfoot no roots or hollows lurked to snare a heedless toe. Only a cherry tree—anchored at the top of the main staircase and weeping silently, its blossoms fragile as flesh—spoke to the enchantment over the masquerade. The petals whispered against my skin as I crossed to the front door and pulled it open on silent hinges.

In the bright light of the porch lantern—worshipped by busy insects—the forest inside became a dream I'd woken from all at once. Sweet night air brushed its taste from my mouth, its cobwebs from my skin. A security guard, black-clad and armed, stepped into view like the answer to a question I hadn't asked yet.

"Fetch my car," I said as if it wasn't a question at all. "I'm leaving."

To my surprise, he moved away to murmur into his headset without a word of protest. I stepped off the porch. Gravel daggered my bare feet but I moved out into the drive until I could stand before the house and see the whole, hulking façade; until I knew I would see my curser coming.

It was reckless; a half thought-out gambit at best. But someone needed me here, and I was about to take off and leave all their careful planning in the dirt.

Let's see if they tried to stop me.

Minutes passed, the thrum of the music lower now, turned down as if to not scare away the dawn. Somewhere on the upper floor, an open door spilled chatter onto the loggia and over the rail like mist. I braced for the sound of my name or approaching footsteps to cut through the voices and chill me.

Instead came the crush of wheels on gravel (my SUV was *Swift*-enabled, of course, but unless they were drivers, most staff had never worked *Swift* in their life). My stomach tightened. *React*, I willed, *before it's too late*. But it wasn't my car pulling into the drive. A golf cart carried another security guard, who pulled up alongside me and climbed out.

"Everything okay here?" said Mario, bored out of his mind.

In many ways, Mario was the antithesis of Fran. Both had firm boundaries about what their job entailed, but while Fran's encompassed a courteous manner and only minimal cooperation, Mario went above and beyond but would kill us all and then himself before pretending he didn't hate it.

"I asked for my car," I told him.

"I know."

"Well, where is it?"

He folded his arms across his barrel chest and sighed. "What's going on, Valentina?"

There could be no *wink-wink, just play along* with Mario. He'd probably have my car here twice as fast just to be free of my shenanigans.

"What's going on," I said, "is that I've been standing out here for three minutes now and I still don't have my keys in my hand."

"You were asked to stay until Monday, just like the guests."

He watched me blankly, like it almost didn't matter what I said next; he would read from the script, then get back to more important things.

"I don't care," I persisted. "I'm leaving."

The corners of his mouth turned down in displeasure. For a beat I thought I was wrong—he would unwittingly buy me time as he attempted to manage me. Then he dipped his head to the mic on his collar.

"Bring Valentina's car around," he said. "She's leaving."

As Mario moved away—still radioing instructions to his team—I squared myself to the building and waited. A minute passed, then another, my heart beating an anxious rhythm to keep time. Onlookers appeared—in a ground-floor window of the east wing; framed by an arch on the floor above; at the outermost corner of the upper loggia. They were solitary, anonymous figures, backlit by the lights of the house and stood as far from the railing or as close to the window's edge as the angle would allow, like they didn't wish to be seen. I squinted at them, at first unsure why they were so cloaked in shadows.

But of course, they had no Moths.

The house staff. Jude's army of spies. Were there others I couldn't see? Shadow-cloaked eyes lurking deep within the recesses of the arches? The sharp edges of Fable's roof were framed by nothing but sky, making it into a mountain, a cliff face, and all at once the place looked ominous.

This time, when the churning of gravel announced an approaching vehicle, the gambit was up. My car was brought to a stop beside the golf cart where Mario sat waiting, and another guard emerged from the driver's side. He left the engine running and held the door. I took a single step towards the car and stopped, looked back at the house, then out at the gardens, like someone might dive out of a bush the moment I got behind the wheel. I couldn't actually *leave*, not without the antidote, not while its return was being held over my neck like an axe. At the realisation that someone had called my bluff, my defiance dropped away like a pebble in deep water, out of reach before I knew it had slipped from my fingers.

Movement on the upper loggia snagged my attention. One of the Mothless watchers had been joined by another, and when she stepped up to the balustrade, the lights of the drive just kissed her face and her short crop of white-blonde hair.

Fran bent her head to listen to her underling's report, but her eyes were on me; I could *feel* it. Had they fetched her to bear witness to the happenings in the drive?

Had Fran asked to know if I tried to leave?

She had been upstairs right before the curse and the antidote were taken from the cabinet—Charlotte had seen her. She lived at the house, in rooms on the ground floor of the west quad that *weren't searched* that afternoon. She had everything to lose if I inherited Fable (and didn't she know it—I'd promised to fire her myself). And she was watching my every move.

I took a step towards the car, too fixated on Fran to notice the stones serrating my bare feet. Would she call out if I tried to get behind the wheel? Or would she cut her losses, let me go, and quietly dispose of the antidote somewhere it couldn't be traced back to her?

I never found out. Before I could take another step, the front door opened then swung shut, its heavy echo skittering away through Fable like so many mice when you turn on the light. Jude stood on the porch, Daddy's nurse cringing behind him. He looked like he'd run here, the terrible weight of the news he was carrying to me held behind his eyes.

I knew before he sunk to his knees, before the nurse crossed the drive and whispered in my ear what she had told him first.

Somebody had unplugged Daddy's life support.

He was dead.

11

A zen fountain stood in one corner of Daddy's room, trickling merrily. It must have been there the day before, and the day before that, but now that the beeping and the hiss of oxygen had fallen silent, I was hearing it for the first time. But a waterfall couldn't have filled the quiet.

The tubes were gone. The Moth that had kept its stubborn vigil since the stroke had vanished. All that was left was Daddy—aged and diminished without *Polish*—and the three of us. His nurse, pallid with stress, stood at the foot of the bed. Jude was opposite me, though pressed against the far window like an opposing magnet. He looked horribly sober.

I stood over my father's bed, too close to pretend the body in front of me was only sleeping. You don't notice how a living person is never still until you're keeping company with a dead one. Looking at my father, I couldn't restore him to his big, bright life however hard I tried. I could think only of my grandparents in open caskets, of the pieces of Aunt Georgia in her closed one. Of big game, magnificent beasts made trophies in a single, needless moment of violence.

This had been a needless violence as well, to murder a man on his deathbed. And yet it had served someone; it meant something. And unless there were two would-be killers at Fable that weekend, it should have meant something to me. I placed my hand in Daddy's. I stroked his arm like I was committing him to memory.

But I was searching.

"Your mother said she would come," said the nurse as I stroked my father's hair, and I tried to make it look natural when I slid my hand beneath his pillow before pulling away. "I think . . . I think she needed a moment. She was sleeping."

"Someone—" Jude's voice grated in his throat, and he coughed. "Someone did this to him. Why were they able to just *unplug* him? Isn't there an alarm? A backstop?"

As I kneaded the blanket around my father's supine form, I heard the nurse drawing short, ragged breaths, as if she was fighting back tears. "Perhaps we should wait."

"That woman's not even his family," snapped Jude. "*She's* his next of kin."

I froze, aware I was suddenly the focus of their attention, and tried to keep my hand on Daddy's sternum perfectly still as I looked over at them. It was difficult, because beneath my palm, I had just discovered what I was looking for: a rigid rectangle of card between the blanket and Daddy's chest. My mouth had gone dry. My heart was thrashing against my ribs. Jude stared me down, but I couldn't recall the thread of the conversation until he prompted, "We want to know what happened, don't we?"

I fought back an acid laugh. I didn't want to know what was happening here—I *needed* to, and I was fairly certain I had five fingers on the answer. But *we*? When did he and I become *we*? Was it the morning before when he'd said *please*? He was dishevelled, unrested, the tattoo on his chest still partly visible under the open collar of his shirt. He'd gotten it for Aunt Georgia—something trite about flowers that bloomed in May, when she'd had her accident—and I wondered if he'd get a matching bouquet for our father. I did not wonder if he'd get one for me, should I fail to do whatever this card asked of me.

I needed to get at it, which meant I needed to be rid of both of them or risk flaunting the rule on the *first* card, to tell no one. But maybe the details would yield a clue. I turned to the nurse.

"Tell us everything."

I hadn't noticed Jude circling closer, or the nurse moving away. But now he and I stood on the same side of the bed. Together.

"It happened"—she checked her watch—"seventy-five minutes ago now, at most. I check on him every hour." Each syllable shook. She was crying heavily, tears trembling on her lips and gouging streaks through her makeup. No *Spotless* to keep her together. "But your housekeeper—she showed me a room I could rest in during night shifts. She said there was no need to be with him every moment. He was stable. There had been no changes! Nobody ever mentioned a security concern. I would never have—"

She cut off with a sob. I wanted to hit her—not for abandoning Daddy, who should have been perfectly safe in his own home, but for crying in fear for her job, fear of a lawsuit, when my father was dead. But I forced down the urge and feigned civility as I said, "The housekeeper. You mean Fran."

She nodded a confirmation, but though it was the answer I expected, the pieces refused to fit together. Had Fran really lured this woman away from Daddy's room to create an opportunity to unplug him? I could believe she had cursed me, but murdering Daddy? Even if she hadn't doted on him, what could she have to gain?

The card beneath the blanket was a white-hot flame in my awareness.

"You can go," I told the nurse, who turned and fled almost as quickly as the dismissal could leave my lips.

"I'm getting the police," said Jude, making to follow her.

The laugh I couldn't bite back this time surprised us both and brought him to a stop.

"To tell them what?" I sounded like silverware rattling in a drawer, metallic and discordant. "That your *as good as dead* dad is now all the way dead? Think, petal: Oscar Maddock can't die at the launch of *Immortality*."

His eyes flashed, and I felt my mistake in my body, like the sensation of falling. While I raged against pain with rebellion, Jude sunk things. Boats, usually, but what if a company would do? If he'd already risked the weekend for the chance to embarrass me yesterday, then now—over Daddy's deathbed—inviting the police to interrogate the guests and throw everything into chaos would be the silver lining to his loss, Mythos be damned.

But as he started again towards the door, a better—and worse—tactic struck me.

"There'll be an inquest," I blurted.

Jude caught himself against the doorframe, pressing his weight into the stone like a man bleeding out and determined to die on his feet.

I pressed my advantage. "They probably won't let us bury him until they've done a full investigation." And how long would that take? Everything the speedboat propellor had left him of his mother had lain on a slab in a refrigerator for weeks before they could put her to rest. Georgia didn't exit the news cycle the entire time. Police fought their way through the media staking out the driveway every few days with more questions. They took her journals, read her every secret. I softened my voice, a thing I had never done with him. "Daddy wasn't waking up. Maybe . . . we decide that someone meant this as a kindness? Aren't you ready for this to be over?"

I braced for his worst. But when he turned, he wore that unguarded look, like he'd forgotten he hated me. The hollows of his cheeks were the same ones grief and puberty had scooped out in the years following Georgia's death. Now that entire boy had returned—vulnerable, lost, too dazed by his agony to question my motives.

"Don't let them do that," he begged. "An inquest, don't let them—"

"I won't," I said, pushing aside my growing discomfort.

I would. As soon as I had the antidote back, the full force of the law was coming down on whoever had done this. If it broke Jude's mind and spirit once and for all, well, then, I'd be killing two birds with one stone. A wreck of a man couldn't run a company.

Worse had been done to me for his sake. I just wish he wasn't looking at me like that; like all I'd ever had to do was be kind—even for my own reasons, even for a moment—and he would forget that we were nemeses.

Jude rubbed both hands over his face and came back into the room. The spell was already wearing off, his vulnerability slipping back under his shell of apathy.

"Fine," he said tonelessly, and turned to brood by the window.

I took my chance. At once desperate and terrified, I squeezed Daddy's cooling fingers in apology and reached under the covers for the note resting at the centre of his chest, this violation that had made a message of his death. The starched under-sheet crackled, loud enough to my ears to make Jude turn. Wincing, I whipped the note from its hiding place and put my back to him to examine it.

Black card, just like the others. When I turned it over—my breath captive in my lungs—the embossed gold lettering caught the light.

REMEMBER OSCAR MADDOCK HAS NO HEIR.

Fingers shaking, I flipped the card over. But that was it. No demands. No instructions. I took in the scene again, expecting whatever I'd missed to obediently catch my eye. But it was just my father's corpse, serene now that the machines weren't mechanically filling his lungs and pumping his blood. No more cards and no more clues.

Biting the inside of my cheek to stop from sobbing, I let my legs give up and sank to the floor. Was this all just a game? What was I supposed to understand from a reminder on a corpse of something I already knew? Assaulted by grief, I wanted to give up, concede defeat. And yet I couldn't even do that, not until I knew at whose feet I needed to fall. And they were giving nothing away.

I was crying now, fat, silent tears. I begged those instead, tried to persuade them to please not humiliate me in front of Jude. But they wouldn't listen. Instead, I kept my head turned away and down, and when my eyes landed on the smear of gold against the silver of my hem, it appeared as a thousand diffuse gems of light through water.

I blinked hard and let *Spotless* collect the tears from my lashes. One of the sequined petals at the front of my skirt was dusted with a brilliant gold glitter. The floor where it had dragged was dusted with it too. *Some detritus of the forest enchantment,* supplied a corner of my mind, even as a larger part stilled in recognition. I brushed my fingers over the hem and brought the stuff closer to my face.

It wasn't glitter. It looked like the finest sand, glowing with its own uncanny luminescence. I rubbed it between my fingers and sucked in a breath as it stung my skin.

Glass.

Swivelling in a crouch—my gown dusting more of it over the floor—I found the faint trail of powdered glass I had walked into Daddy's bedroom. It winked against the matte grey of the marble floor, brighter than it had a right to be, because it was making its own light.

Heart in my throat, I rose to follow it.

"Petal?" Jude huffed when I ignored him, and around clenched teeth said, "Where are you going?"

The trail was easier to spot in the hallway, the gold a beacon in the dim. I traced it as far as the ballroom, where it vanished among the crumbling, moss-edged flagstones, a tapestry of light and shadows. The bloody chase had mercifully ended. The table of desserts—half clawed apart—remained, but any trace of blood had been cleaned away along with the injured. Had they let paramedics in, or had they delivered Isaiah and *GRAHAM* to an ambulance at the gates, hauled clear of the party by a housekeeper holding a limb each?

Nicola Burton-Shaw alone tended to the leftovers. She sat on a tree stump, one arm steadying the trifle in her lap as she took shaking, morose mouthfuls. I stretched out my gold-dusted hand, the question forming on my lips.

"I can't do it." She hiccupped. "I have to tell Eric I can't do it."

"Can't do what?" I said warily.

"Be immortal." She dropped her spoon into the slop and slapped her hand to her mouth. "I didn't say that. Pretend I didn't say it. Please."

My first thought was automatic: that begging was an invitation to leave an impression of power. If I could work out who Nicola was—what impressed her, scared her, awed her—then she was mine. But something clenched behind my ribs as I remembered: I was without *Empathy*, and that was how I was doomed to remain.

"Do you know what this is?" I said, indicating the glass dust on my fingers. "Where it came from?"

She gave me an inscrutable look and shook her head. Frustrated, I swept on towards the stairs, retracing my earlier path. In the entrance hall—back beyond the reaches of the forest enchantment—I found the trail of glass again, scuffs of it everywhere my hem had brushed the floor, improbably fine, redolently gold. The veins of my right arm hummed with recognition. The path snaked out of the front door, then back in again—I hadn't picked it up in the drive. I crossed the entrance hall and kept going.

Through the lavender-lit birch grove. Back into the hall of pillars, shrunken and diaphanous at the edges as the power of the enchantment started to wane, my former path marked by incoherent curlicues of gold dust. At the crumbling wall of the dining room, I recovered my shoes. Just as I'd suspected, on the sole of the right was a compacted coating of powdered glass. I had ground some of it into my hem when I stood on my dress climbing over the wall. Heels in one hand, I clambered over the fallen stones again and on the other side found a conspicuous trail of shoe prints that led me out into the garden.

I knew where the crumbs were leading me, though I'd forgotten the abandoned trash bag until the moment it came into view. I had started turning the latest note over in my mind. REMEMBER OSCAR MADDOCK HAS NO HEIR. Not a demand, but a foretelling. A declaration that this was never what I'd believed.

The bag had a tear in it, one I hadn't noticed in my moment of anguish. Something glowing with the burnished gold of my veins had ripped the plastic and tumbled out onto the path, where I had crushed it unwittingly beneath my shoe.

I knew, even as my body dragged me closer as if I were a thing made of lead. I knew before the bag fell open with one weak tug and there they were, like fireflies, or fairy lights; like somebody had decorated balled-up tissue, floss, a condom wrapper with the shattered pieces of the bottle that had once contained my fragile life.

I knew. Because if the great Oscar Maddock could die at the press of a switch, nothing in this world would save me.

12

I would die.

I don't remember leaving the garden, only that I took a piece of the antidote bottle with me, trapped gently against my palm as if it were a butterfly. A cotton-wool feeling started in my ears and spread to fill my throat and lungs. It bound my limbs, covered my eyes.

It didn't matter; I was not in my body. No conscious desire bade me seek her out, but something evolutionary instead; an instinct I had long known was faulty.

When Mum wasn't in her room, I knew at once where I would find her. Daddy's nurse had left. Jude was gone too, no doubt to white out his grief with drink and god knew what else. She was a tiny thing, curled on a loveseat with her knees pulled to her chest, staring across the marble at my father's body. Only when she wiped clumsily at her nose with the back of her hand did I realise she was crying. I had lifted my closed fist to show her the piece of glass inside, but I stilled.

"Mum?"

She reached for me, like she could bridge the gap, then settled for patting the space beside her. "Come here," she whispered.

I went. As I reached the loveseat, I could see the loss in her eyes. I couldn't recall if this was expected: Mum undone by the death of the man who had wronged her in the most essential way.

"I'm fine," she said, a hopeless lie to answer a question I hadn't collected myself enough to ask. "It's shock, I think, but I'm fine. It's just . . . they're both gone now. Somehow, I imagined it would all be made right in the end, but it won't. And with the . . . the party, and the product, I suppose I've been too busy to process all this. Now it's hitting me and . . . I don't understand how he could die when he and I—"

She hadn't stopped crying, but here she was interrupted by a heaving breath that shocked her into silence. She shook her head.

"I'm so sorry, Teeny. I'm being selfish. I lost your father decades ago, and you only lost him tonight." She wanted my hands, but one of mine still cupped the shard of golden glass. I let go of it—let it fall between the cushions of the loveseat—and put my hands in hers. "It's my fault. This is all my fault."

"No, Mum—"

"I keep thinking, if only we had run the upload a little sooner. Who knows if they'd ever have been able to heal his brain, but maybe we could have kept him with us, just in case. It wasn't much of a hope—I just thought there'd be time to decide. If *Immortality* had only been ready. Don't you see, Teeny? It's *my fault.*"

She descended into sobs as she forged through her speech, but she never let herself lower her head or look away. It was disturbing. Each stumbling, mewing sob rent holes in my numbness. She would lose me too, long before these convulsions of sorrow had abated—and I couldn't bring myself to tell her. I couldn't cause her any more suffering. She'd been gentled by needing me, by her own vulnerability, but she was hardened by mine. So I would take these wet, tragic bits of love and make do.

"This isn't your fault. But, Mum," I said, squeezing her hands tightly—even if I couldn't break her heart, I needed her to hear me, to understand that something awful was happening. "This is important. The same person who did this to Daddy took the curse from the collection." Four notes, all of it a game; they had never intended to return the antidote, and now Daddy was dead—who was next? "We don't know what else they might do."

"Yes, yes, you're right," she said, collecting herself. Her breath still trembled, but she pressed her fingers to her lower eyelids to collect the last of her tears and straightened. "We'll call the police. Just—not yet." She gave a choking laugh. "I mean, for god's sake, what a time for a Maddock to die."

It was too soon for me to laugh at the irony. Everything in me seemed to fold in half at the thought of her learning, less than two days from now, that I was gone too.

"Almost everyone has bought *Immortality*, but this would be a stain on the product forever," she went on, brow furrowed as she thought through the ramifications aloud. Her tone grew more concerned, her gaze distant as she said, "*Immortality* would be a punch line. We could fall short of our projections and then . . . No. Oz wouldn't want that." She met my eyes. Hers were full of hesitation. "We'll find a way through," she said. "But on Monday, after the guests leave."

I'd braced myself for what I'd known she would say, but I still felt it pierce me. Despite her grief, my father's death still mattered less to her than this weekend, and I couldn't change her mind without confessing that I would be right behind him.

But there was something else I needed to tell her. Without mentioning the rifle or the confrontation, I explained that I'd caught Hunter with design documents he was going to use to get her fired. I told her about the flash drive, the incriminating spin he tried to put on the contents, how Jude had promised him he could keep his job.

As Mum listened, a crease deepened between her brows. She was shaking her head absently, as if she couldn't believe how close she and I had come to ruin.

"Those design sessions," she said when I finished. "If they're the ones I think they are, he's misrepresenting them."

"I know," I said in a rush, though the child she'd scarred had thought otherwise at first. "I know what basic research can look like. It didn't mean you were going to use those spells. Mythos doesn't make weapons."

"No, we don't," she agreed, taking my hand again. "Still, it's a good thing you stopped him. I'll talk to legal, but it sounds like grounds to remove him sooner. Well done, Teeny. And listen." She flicked the last of her tears away. "I'm going to insist to the board that we expedite the CEO issue. I'm going to ask them to decide tomorrow."

It was excruciating: the clenching panic—had I made my case? Was the timing right?—followed by the thudding realisation that it no longer mattered. Less than forty-eight hours from now, I'd be dead. The empty words on the final card—REMEMBER OSCAR MADDOCK HAS NO HEIR—turned in my mind. A threat? A warning? Had someone planned for Mum to react just like this to Daddy's death—and what then?

"In fact, Hunter's antics are perfect fodder," Mum went on, gaze soft and distant like it was when she was thinking out loud. "He has to go immediately—well, Monday, I suppose, but I'll let the board know right away—and then things will be far too unstable not to name a successor quickly." Remembering I was there, she shifted to face me. "I know your chances are . . . tenuous right now, but I'm making some changes to the program tomorrow that will remove Jude as a contender. I'm going to prove once and for all that he's unstable and unfit. The best time for the board to make a decision will be immediately after, with everything fresh in their minds. Just trust me. Perhaps there's a silver lining to the timing of your father's death, after all."

I couldn't imagine what she meant, but I tried to think of something happy—fireworks, a tropical sea, Daddy riding an elephant—to infuse my forced smile. Tears welled, and when Mum's face creased with rare pity, I let myself believe that was all *Empathy* would show me. She reached for me and stroked a thumb down my wet cheek.

"I think I'll get some sleep," I said.

"That's a great idea. Good night, sweetheart."

It started the moment I left the room. I had been precariously balanced somewhere above myself, and now I toppled into the reality of my death. I trembled violently, the vibrations filling both my psyche and body like a swarm of bees.

I couldn't die. I refused. The feeling started to smoulder—the one that ended with a tiger inked on my skin, or a vampire on my lips. The one I called "going felon." A reckless idea was reached one step at a time, and with the antidote gone, the precipice appeared right at my feet. A solution, one I could never have dreamed of an hour before but that now seemed obvious.

I went directly to the kitchen, where just two red-faced and harried chefs armed with Mythos tools were catering for the entire party. Our assembly line tools could replicate a simple motion once shown. With a little supervision they could flip steaks to a timer, stir sauces, caramelise crème brûlées. They were expensive, but Mythos had undercut the cost of hiring actual people when we invented them, so every good caterer used them.

It was around four in the morning, and they had already started on breakfast. They looked up from their mini quiches and muffin batter and must have read on my face that I wouldn't ask for their help or appreciate their interference—I could see what I needed the moment I stepped foot in the kitchen.

They were lined up on a long, magnetic block above one steel counter. I could count the times in my life I'd chopped food on the number of fingers I was about to have, but I knew which blade would suit my purpose. I think it was a cleaver: a thick square of steel on a hefty grip, weighty and correct when I pulled it from the wall.

"Does this cut bone?" I asked. The blade of the cleaver threw back an opaque, jagged version of my face. Somebody stopped whisking, but nobody answered. *"Anyone?"*

"Uh, it can," said the chef to my left, followed by some other things I didn't bother to hear. Waiting was the enemy. Thinking would be the end.

It was too far to my room; too long to hold my sanity at bay. But I needed privacy—the hidden hollow of a tree, a paddock of tall ferns—somewhere I wouldn't be apprehended. I found myself in a corridor curtained on one side by silky, aquatic vines—the green of new grass—studded with magical flames that flickered like the petals of golden flowers. The vines were disturbed in places where people had found the doors behind them; a purple glow emanating here, the trickling of water coming from there. I moved along the corridor, seeking, until a section of the wall swelled to life. Grey butterflies, maybe a thousand of them, took flight as I disturbed their hidden spot. I covered my head as the swarm passed on hushed, papery wings. The vines shuddered back into place in their wake, but not before I saw it: a flat outcrop of rock—perhaps a console by day—at the mouth of a cave.

I pushed through the vines, my gilded veins winking where the blooms of fire struck them. They were as soft as organza but hid me entirely when they fell back into place. Yes, it would happen here, now, before the curse reached my shoulder. I slammed my golden hand down on the rock, adjusted my grip on the cleaver, and angled myself to bring it down on my upper arm.

This is the secret truth about recklessness: once the notion takes hold, there's no peeling away its claws. To reach a precipice one stupid decision at a time is not, in fact, to make a choice at all. You are propelled there by the thing that is chasing you, a version of yourself you cannot bear to look at. A once-perfect thing disfigured by her memories, her gloss smudged by little touches of harm. Haunted, angry, helpless.

Dying.

My body went cold and still. I could think of exactly one thing worse than fixing this here myself, and that was dying. It wasn't a choice at all, and there was something calming about that. Dreadful, but calming nonetheless.

But the blood.

When I thought of breaking myself open and releasing the curse from inside me, an instinct honed with experience screamed at me that it was wrong. That it was mine and *I needed* it; it belonged in my veins and nowhere else. Fable was spinning as my body, desperate to live, took matters into its own hands. The hand with the cleaver raised it high. Bile pooled at the back of my mouth. I heard a broken, guttural cry, like the wail of an ensnared animal. It shocked me, to hear that sound come from my own throat, and my fingers fumbled their grip, just slightly.

A cool hand wrapped around them.

"It won't work," Luc said close to my ear.

He was behind me, close enough that his shirt scraped the beading of my dress with a sound like butterflies' wings. His other hand was on my waist. He held me with a pressure that said there would be a struggle if I tried to keep to my plan.

"The curse is already in your blood." He brought the knife down gently, and I let him, relinquishing it to the stone when he tentatively released my fingers. "Cutting off the gilding won't stop it."

Luc turned me and placed his hands on my shoulders. I focused on the pressure of his fingers on my skin, cool but reassuring. This was real; it wasn't magic. He let his hands slide down my arms—also not an illusion—and I felt the touch in every pore of my body, the sensation like ripples from a stone. The desire for a different kind of cure for my weakness seeped into my body, the habit rising up to wrap me in its arms, comforting and familiar. It was a bad idea—and wasn't that the point?—yet it felt increasingly like the only possible path, so inevitable I'd been creeping towards it since before we met, a single question driving me onwards one reckless decision at a time:

How much fear could my body bear before it killed me—or turned into something else?

I could already feel it transmuting at the edges, cold to warm. The tension that so often stilled me with dread now begged me to move, so long as it was closer to him.

Let it consume you whole.

Surrender, Mariah had called it.

Need, I called it.

My hand pressed against Luc's abdomen as I stepped into him.

He stepped back, his fist closing around the wrist of my audacious hand. We hung there, suspended, waiting for the wind to change. His eyes on mine were probing. I was the one to break the standoff. Using his grip around my wrist, I pulled myself into him, my other hand finding his body again. I let my fingers trail up his chest until they reached his open shirt collar, his throat, his jaw, his lips. He didn't move, except for the rise and fall of his chest, quickening the longer I touched him. I leant closer, marvelling at the barely perceptible flow of air between his parted lips, the cool breath that brushed against my skin. I cared little for the question of whether his life relied on it, and more for the building volume, the little catches, the rush of confidence that he would come apart as thoroughly as me if I continued.

I closed my eyes; this was easier when I couldn't see him. Fear still gripped me—making everything taut and oversensitive—but prying open its ribs was a theory, one pieced together from moments of breathlessness and stabs of cruel fantasy; teeth in my skin, helplessness pinning me beneath a hungry mouth, the images played over and over like a compulsion, the sensations induced by needle when there was no other way. Arranged just so, it didn't look like fear at all.

I gripped his face between my fingers and brought my lips to his, my mind filling with the cool, mineral taste of him. His lips parted for me; his hands found my hair. Luc made a sound of surrender as his tongue dipped between my teeth and found mine, and heat rushed to my core.

The kiss grew urgent, and so did my need, until the moves of our dance took on a familiar, crystalline simplicity; drenched in madness or passion, the cure was the same. I broke away and led Luc into the cave. The lilac glow I had seen came from formations of crystals that grew in clumps on the moss-lined walls. I pulled Luc against me again, pushed the hours before further away. His hands moved over my arms, my waist, then found the wall behind me and hemmed me in.

As I grappled with my dress, his mouth found my neck. I gasped as his lips brushed against my pulse. I was not even sane enough to be surprised by the plea that escaped my mouth. Luc did as asked and grazed his teeth against my throat; then, encouraged by the helpless sound I made, drew the skin into his mouth and bit down. He didn't break the skin. A mark maybe, bloodless, soothed with his tongue before he did it again. It had been what I wanted, and now it wasn't enough. An ache was building, and it would break with blood or ecstasy.

And my blood was poisoned wine.

The bodice of my dress wouldn't budge, so I unhooked the straps from my arms and freed myself. Luc's fingers found the edge and tore it down—I heard the terminal rip of fabric—and then his mouth was on me again. I sucked in a breath and clawed at my skirt as he trailed kisses down my abdomen as far as he could reach.

He steered us to a flat outcropping of moss-covered stone—a table, probably, in another life. As I perched on the edge, my hand met something—a glass—and sent it to the floor. It shattered against the stone, shocking Luc upright. I took his shoulders, tried to bring him back, but he didn't move. Some doubt had found its way between our bodies and ensnared him. I bit my tongue, teeth holding sharply to a plea.

"This doesn't matter," I blurted, desperate. Not to the secrets he was keeping. Not to the things he usually did in these darkest hours. I imagined his hands clinging to a dying woman the way they clung to me, but as long as I could keep feeling this, I didn't care. Stop, and one way or another, death would sweep in. Luc's hand traced the invisible gilded veins around my wrist, along my forearm. When he reached the awful, vulnerable dip behind my elbow, I flinched. His thumb paused above white flesh, then skirted to the outside of my arm, coaxing the hairs there to stand on end.

"This doesn't matter." His voice was hesitant, questioning, but his hands were already moving again, tackling the layers of my skirt and finding skin beneath. I grabbed the back of his neck and pulled his mouth to mine, entangling us frantically, hungrily, before he pulled away and sunk to his knees.

I shuddered at the touch of cold against searing heat. I grasped for thoughts of escape, but also of surrender, so that in the end I thought of nothing at all—knew nothing but the feel of his mouth and the sweet, aching tension building beneath it.

Still not enough.

I brought him to his feet. He kissed my mouth again, pressing himself against me until I could feel his readiness between my thighs. We scrabbled greedily to unbuckle belts and shift fabric. There was danger in the in-between moments, in losing the mindlessness of anticipation. I raced through them like crossing the corridor when the bathroom light went out.

When he sunk into me, I let myself fall back. Luc braced his hands against the stone, and I dug my fingers into his forearms, wrapped my legs around his waist, and lifted my hips to control the rhythm. *In the lilac gloom, he could be anyone,* I told myself as I rocked closer to release, but it wasn't true. I had not wanted *someone*. I had wanted darkness, a danger more tempting than the golden one I faced in the light.

I had sought teeth.

Everything I had wanted the first night—envy, power, to be dangerous—was a distant memory. All except the tug of some insanity I had denied at the time. *Some people only feel truly alive when they confront death,* and in the arms of the vampire, poison running through my veins, I was clinging to life with bleeding fingers. When release came, it was with startling vivacity, a white thunder cracking my mind in two, no thought of how I would piece it back together.

I had been right; fear was not so different from lust. Neither behaved as if the sun would rise.

13

Moss fell in chunks from the walls, turning to mist as it hit the floor. We had stumbled to what was slowly turning back into a couch, where we sat for an hour or more, watching the cave crumble bit by bit, the stone giving way to towering bookshelves, a row of arched glass doors. A log propped on its end became a ladder for the upper shelves.

We were in one of the libraries, and the endless night was over. Long fingers of dawn pierced the windows, melting magic where they struck. Peace had finally fallen with the last dregs of twilight, the music replaced by birdsong. The guests would be showering, dosing up with *Revitalise*, or maybe getting a couple of hours sleep just to fill the lull before breakfast. Fran's staff would be restoring Fable to its former flawlessness, as if none of the indiscretions of the last few hours had happened.

Luc pulled himself heavily off the couch to straighten his clothing, as if his body was as pleasantly spent as mine. And maybe it was, but with the sunrise, he had also weakened. He looked strung-out, like a man who'd had no appetite for anything as healthy as food for months.

"Do you remember what I said?" His glance cut towards me but didn't meet my eye. "About there being another way?"

In monotone murmurs, I'd confessed to him that the antidote was gone, smashed, probably disposed of as soon as it had been stolen. No one was ever going to save me.

"What other way?" As I said it, our conversation in the forest the previous morning struck me like a mallet. "You mean . . . a faerie."

"It's not a guarantee. They might not be able to help you. But if they could, it would be worth it, wouldn't it?"

His suggestion hadn't crossed my mind once. It had been perverse, unthinkable. Crude magic was a beggar's refuge. It was loaded dice. Even with a cleaver raised above my arm, no survival instinct had sprung into action and pulled forth the possibility Luc had floated just hours before, so dismissive had I been of the idea.

But the antidote was gone. So far, my only plan for survival had been to force whoever had done this to me to reveal themselves and get it back. Now the extortion was a ruse and Daddy was dead. The untouchable Oscar Maddock had been made helpless, and then he'd been killed. If such a thing could happen to him, I couldn't pretend at control anymore, couldn't brute force my way to having the upper hand. I was losing, and I would die if I kept pretending at a power that hadn't even saved the man I'd borrowed it from.

My memory conjured Isaiah, broken and blind, hauling himself towards a future he'd bartered for with his blood; the grossly compelling depths of his need, his determination. I was him now. Nothing was beneath me. As much as I shuddered to think it, that included crude magic.

My hope was ugly, laden with dread, beset by problems—how would we escape Fable without anyone knowing? What would be the price?—but there was hope. When it crested the mountain that was my looming death, I could have wept.

"Yes," I said, shuffling upright on the couch, my heart pounding. "Yes, it would."

Luc nodded, but for a long moment said and did nothing. He was gazing across the floor, deep in thought, yet I had the unshakable sense that *I* was the thing being evaluated, that he might decide any minute not to help me. Was it what we just did? Had he found himself in deeper than he'd planned when he said he'd help me live? I held my breath, at a loss.

At last, he stood up. "Alright then."

Luc scooped up his suit jacket from the floor, but as I climbed off the couch his eyes alighted on the rip down one side of my bodice.

Spotless could repel a stain or smooth a wrinkle—it couldn't do anything about this. I tried to arrange the fabric into something decent, but it was unsalvageable.

"Here."

He passed me his jacket—a bare-minimum courtesy, but also fatally close to a tenderness that would ruin this entirely. I recalled his teeth against my neck and a thrill ran through me as I accepted the garment and slipped my arms into its sleeves.

"So where are we going?" I said.

"The thing is . . ." Luc ran his fingers through his dishevelled hair in a nervous gesture. "I don't know where to go if you need a faerie, not off the top of my head. I only know that I have people who can find out."

"Ah." I sighed, and added the problem to the list, right above all the others. "You need your phone back."

"You're sure that's where they're keeping everyone's devices?"

"Sure enough," said Luc. "I saw them take my phone up there when I handed it over."

I had changed into a sweatshirt and jeans (I wanted to be ready for our breakout at a moment's notice) and met Luc in the entrance hall as he'd asked. The awkward aftermath of my decisions lingered like a third member of our huddle. I couldn't look too closely at what I'd done, who I'd been as I'd begged to feel his teeth against my flesh, but my body felt different. I still wore my awareness of him like a second skin, but now it held a spectrum of tones, darkness and light, terror and ecstasy. As we stood in a corner of the entrance hall—our whispered conspiring multiplied to a frenetic hush, like so many dried leaves stirred by the wind—my urge to keep a distance between us warred with the desire to feel it all again.

"And you can get in there?" I asked, glancing towards the CCTV monitor room on the landing above the entrance hall. "What if they lock it?"

"Let me worry about that. Just get rid of the guard." His gaze cut to mine, and I nodded. "What are you going to say to them?"

"I have a task in mind," I told him, heading for the stairs. "I'm trying to kill two birds with one stone."

Finding the remnants of the antidote bottle—seeing my salvation as the con it had always been—had consumed me. I had wanted to think of nothing, *be* nothing but sensation and feeling. But then Luc had introduced new hope, and the sun had risen on a fresh clue; and though it couldn't cure the curse gilding my veins, it might still lead me to the person who'd put it there and then killed my father.

REMEMBER OSCAR MADDOCK HAS NO HEIR.

Was it nothing but a taunt, an outstretched arm inviting me to look upon the chaos they'd wrought? I'd imagined myself the target because the curse would harm me and therefore benefit Jude. But I had to assume killing Daddy served some purpose too, and how it helped Jude secure the company wasn't nearly as clear. If anything, it would soon prove better for *me*, given it had inspired my mother to take Jude out of the running once and for all. Maybe the other shoe was about to drop, a final turn I couldn't see yet that would pull the rug—and the empire—out from under me. But another fear was forming: What if it wasn't me they wanted to destroy?

What if it was Mythos?

What better way than to kill the man who was supposed to deliver *Immortality* and make a mockery of the product on which all our hopes for the future had been pinned? What if Daddy and I were just dominoes in an attack that would turn everything Martin Maddock had built to rubble?

I refused to let that happen. The very thought was so disturbing that (and I would perjure myself on pain of death before I said it out loud) I would rather see Jude claim everything than watch it be destroyed. I wished I'd never met that realisation—it was a betrayal of myself—but it was one thing to see what you wanted handed to your worst enemy, and another entirely to have it expunged from the earth, removed like a limb or a lung or a memory. I needed the Maddock empire to exist, because I needed that complete and unadulterated power I had chased all my life to be real. Daddy had died with a sigh instead of a hurricane, but his mortality had been his only weakness. If I reversed the curse and lived to take the tonic, the same weakness in me would be healed. I could still keep my grasp on who I was, who I wanted to be, so long as his legacy was alive.

First, I needed that bag of garbage—and the boy who had abandoned it—to lead me to my father's killer.

When I knocked on the monitor room door, Mario himself answered. A glance over his shoulder told me he was the only person in there, which was good; at least I had to distract only one guard.

"I need to find one of the event staff who was working last night," I said without preamble. Mario did *not* care for preamble, or niceties of any kind. I once asked him what was in his smoothie and he handed it to me and walked away. "You've got a list of them, right? You know where everyone is?"

"What's the name," he asked, except he didn't trouble himself with an upward inflection, lest he sound too curious.

"I don't know, but he was blond, I think." That got me nothing but a hard stare. "And young. Sixteenish?"

"Tell you what," said Mario. "If he's here, he'll be helping with breakfast. It's in courtyard one."

He started to retreat into the monitor room, but I put a hand on the door to keep it open.

"Where are you going? You have to come with me."

"Why?"

"Muscle." I flashed a grin. "I think he knows something about the theft, but we might have to lean on him." Mario was unconvinced—he gave a long, long blink, and I wondered if he was doing one of the meditative exercises from the book Daddy had gotten him three Christmases ago, as a joke. "Mario, there was dangerous shit in those stolen bottles. This is a security issue. It's quite literally your job. Let's go."

I turned and started towards the stairs. With a sigh like the foghorn of a cargo ship and a word into his mic, Mario followed. I peeked over my shoulder to see the camera room door swing shut behind him. He hadn't locked it. I panicked at the idea that the devices were in a safe inside and Luc would have no way to get to them. No, I told myself, willing truth into it. Mario was just sick to the back teeth with this party and having an off day.

Breakfast was an extravagant buffet in the shaded, palm-treed first courtyard. Forty hours into the party, the most popular station at breakfast was the fresh juice bar, where staff blended greens and coconut water with powdered cures: charcoal, açai, algae, rare mushrooms. One of the attendants' sole job was shucking kilos and kilos of ginger. The aroma spiced the entire courtyard as Mario and I stood in the loggia, scanning for the catering assistant. I tried not to notice Hunter, who was at a table directly across from me and was chewing an espresso—the bovine masticating felt personal, like he'd noticed I hated it—as he stared me down. I knew he hadn't told anyone about the interlude with the rifle, because that was the lesser crime of last night, and the longer my threatening him stayed between the two of us, the longer he held something over me too. One day, the perfect time to make me look crazy would be upon us. I had a feeling it was probably about six months from now when he'd be booted from Mythos's offices.

Eric and Nicola Burton-Shaw were also enjoying breakfast. The former looked fresh and rested, hair damp from the pool and an egg-white omelet disappearing before him. His pretty wife was faring poorly. Two bruise-coloured streaks cupped her eyes, and she had the sickly pallor of someone neck-deep in a hangover. Eric was stroking her arm reassuringly, his head bent close as he murmured a stream of words to which Nicola smiled weakly and nodded her agreement. Slowly, reluctantly, it seemed she was coming round to immortal life.

"Keep an eye out for the boy," I told Mario, who had no time to mention that he didn't know who we were looking for before I was wending my way between the tables, one fist in the pocket of my sweater. Inside was as much of the golden glass dust as I'd been able to scrape off my shoe. I scooped out a pinch and, as I stopped at the table Graham and Athena were sharing with Zazie, sprinkled it onto the tiles.

"Oh, Valentina!" said Athena as Zazie attacked the buffet. She put a hand on her fiancé's arm. "Graham and I have our appointment to place our orders this afternoon. I can hardly breathe."

Gone was the melancholy after their fight last night, but Athena had never been one to dwell, especially when she was determined to have fun. I'd seen her recover from insults and heartaches and disappointments as if she'd flicked a switch and restored herself to factory settings, which in Athena's case was a brand of giddy and unserious most people could achieve only with hard drugs.

And yet—here *I* was, hosting a party and pretending it hadn't been the worst week of my life. Maybe Athena wasn't this way because nothing touched her—after all, she'd subjected herself to memory alteration when she couldn't let Graham's betrayal go. Maybe, instead, seeming frivolous was what served her.

"Congratulations," I said. "How did you enjoy the party last night?"

"Oh, it was spectacular," she replied with wide-eyed enthusiasm. "Jude throws the *best* parties."

It was hard to control my tone when I replied, "I don't think Jude had anything to do with planning this one."

Athena flapped her hands. "Oh, no, of course not, I just mean it's always a good time when he's there." She tilted her head to one side. "Will your dad retire?"

The change of subject jarred and wounded me. What I would give to be living in Athena's world, where my father was still alive—or was it an act? Was Athena changing the subject because she was scatterbrained, or because appearing scatterbrained and none the wiser was a good way to pry for information? "Sorry?"

"Before he was ill, Jude was talking about hosting a whole year of parties. One a week," she said. "A whole weekend and a different country every time, starting and ending on his island in Polynesia."

"What does that have to do with my father?" I asked.

"Just that if he taps Jude to replace him, then the year of parties is probably off." Her lips formed an exaggerated pout. "One of you has to take over Mythos if he steps down, don't you? Isn't it . . . magically binding or something?"

She blinked up at me, all innocence, and my hunger for *Empathy* was a physical ache. If Athena was the one trying to bump off Maddocks, and it *was* with the goal of decimating Mythos, then the details of the blood rule were key information. I had to make her give something away, so I said, "Yes. Magically, it has to be me or Jude."

Graham scoffed. "It doesn't," he said, cutting into a turkey sausage—one of *six* on his plate, as if maintaining his ginormous and completely illusory figure required a lot of protein.

"Excuse me?"

"If Mythos could do that spell, you'd be selling it." He waved a fork at the assembled guests. "You think most of these people wouldn't pay an arm and a leg to ensure their shareholders couldn't take their parents' and grandparents' companies off them? They're going to be immortal. The thing to do would be keep pumping out kids, installing them to control your holdings, and have a tighter rein on greater wealth than you could have hoped for otherwise. Isn't that the whole point of this? Growth?" He shrugged. "It's what I'd do."

I didn't bother correcting him—Mythos hadn't manufactured the blood rule spell for itself; it just . . . *existed* as part of Martin Maddock's deal. Instead, I watched Athena take this in as she sipped her green tea, but whether her tight expression meant *I am not having two dozen of your worker babies* or *That's a kink in my dastardly plan* was hard to say.

At last, Zazie was on her way back. She had a plate piled high with bacon and eggs, and the air of a cat in a sunbeam, a self-satisfied little smile playing on her lips, her hips swaying as she navigated the tables.

I waited until she was close (might as well catch as many suspects as possible) then looked down and said, "It looks like one of you is trailing something."

Three faces followed my pointed finger to the tiles and the scatter of gold I had dropped there to catch someone's reaction. I watched

Graham first, partly because I liked him most as a cold-blooded killer and partly because he immediately stood and started checking his shoes and trousers with some concern. Zazie frowned down at the glass like she couldn't make sense of what she was seeing.

"Is it glitter?" said Athena. "I'm somehow covered in glitter after last night. It's like I rubbed myself all over one of those faeries." She snorted a laugh. "I hope it was that skinny guy with the really green eyes."

Graham stopped patting himself down and made an affronted face. "*Why?*" The least faithful men were always the jealous ones.

I touched Athena's shoulder to wrest her attention back to the ground. "Was it glitter like this?"

"Maybe? I think it was more orange than gold. Why is it glowing?"

It was then that Zazie swooned. Her breakfast plate smashed on the tiles, shattering the quiet refrains of the courtyard. Graham's and Athena's heads whipped towards her, away from me and the glass dust. Zazie crumpled sideways, falling into a board member at the next table, who helped her into a chair. At once, the number of servers in the courtyard doubled as they swarmed to sweep Zazie's breakfast out from underfoot, and the event planner appeared to ply her with juice and try to persuade her that she needed medical attention.

"I'm just on my period," Zazie announced loudly and imperiously when she'd had enough of the fuss. "I'm *fine*."

The fussers dispersed, taking the porcelain shards and scattered egg with them. I couldn't fault their thoroughness—every speck of the glass dust left on the floor was gone now too, my gambit thwarted.

I would have to hope the boy with the garbage had some answers. But would I even know the one I'd seen if he was here? It had been dark and I'd been busy screaming. As I returned to Mario, he checked his watch. I didn't know what excuse I'd come up with next if he tried to return to the monitor room too soon. I shifted my weight from foot to foot and resisted the urge to chew my nail.

Charlotte stepped into the courtyard and, spotting me, followed the loggia until she was at my side.

"Where's Jude?"

"Good morning to you too."

"Sorry. Do you know where he is?" She tossed her hair around in the way I'd seen her do before an exam, or in the final, pre-dawn hours before a deadline.

I angled away from Mario and murmured, "I thought that was your job." I was still scanning for the boy, not to mention a signal from Luc, and probably sounded too curt.

Charlotte frowned, her eyes roaming my face as if she was chasing what was wrong. But when she spoke, it was to ask something else entirely. "Is everything okay with him? I saw him in a corridor a little while ago and he completely blanked me."

She was sleepless in the same way all the guests were, but while everyone else was decidedly unwound, Charlotte had an air of toil. There was tension around her eyes. I might have warned her about Jude—that he bored easily and cared for no one—but I'd thought Charlotte was smart enough to determine that on her own.

"Nothing's ever okay with Jude. He's a bottomless pit of need," I said, repeating Roman's words from the previous morning. "He's a miserable brat. I've told you."

Colourfully disparaging Jude usually brought a little jolt of catharsis, but this time it unsettled my stomach. Jude had been orphaned in the night, but I wasn't telling Charlotte that.

"Shit," said Charlotte. She gazed penetratingly into the middle distance like she was doing calculus.

I felt a pang of guilt for deputising her in my Jude Problem. "Are you having fun?" I asked. "I know you've been busy lately, but you can relax a little. It's only a few days."

Charlotte's concentration broke, and her eyes snapped to mine. "Then back to the grind, right?" She smiled at my querying look. "I called my parents during the week and told them you were training for a C-suite position at Mythos straight after graduation. Do you know what they said? That that would be me one day. Like, what is that even supposed to mean? That I would get plucked up by the CEO of a mega-corporation who happens to be my mother and handed all this power and money because I asked for it?"

A scoffing laugh escaped my lips before I could stop it. "It's my family company. It's my legacy."

"They really believe in all of it," she went on. "I did too. And then yesterday, I was telling Jude how smart you are—defending you to him. I told him you were top of every class, aced every assignment. Turns out there are just spells for that."

Focus was permanent magic. Parents tended to make the investment when their children reached school age. It offered a twenty to thirty percent boost in concentration and memory. It was also helpful in the workplace and in developing skills in general.

Mum didn't know I had it. She's been raised by old guard intellectuals, the kind who believed that when a thing that was difficult got easier, something sacred and conveniently indefinable was lost. Daddy had had to sneak it onto my Moth when I was ten.

"You knew about that," I told Charlotte. "It's common knowledge."

Her eyebrows jumped up her face. "Is it? Then how come it never came up once in all the months I've been telling you *I can't believe your stamina* and *Wow, you have, like, a photographic memory?* Jude says all the schools know about them—that it's allowed."

"Right. So what exactly is your problem?"

A brilliant, sharp-toothed smile spread over Charlotte's face. "There's no problem. Would you believe it, I'm still going to be fine all on my own."

She made to pass me, and I grabbed her wrist. Charlotte's head snapped round, eyes wide at the audacity.

"You're still spying on Jude, right?" I said, panicked. "Because he has the whole staff—"

Her laugh cut me off. She yanked her arm free of my grasp. "Hey, fuck you."

She stalked away. I stood there, retorts tangling in my head. I would have chased after her—however unbecoming that would be of a

Maddock—if I hadn't known with humiliating certainty that I would only make it worse. I couldn't tell a *fuck you, I'm in a bad mood* from a *fuck you, we're over.* I couldn't claw back the upper hand without knowing everything she felt, and even then, the controls for Charlotte were in a foreign language.

If we were over, she'd made it sound like my fault, but I knew it wasn't. It was Jude's. Whether because he was onto the fact I'd sicced her on him or just to spite me, he'd found the weakness in our friendship and snapped it over his knee. He'd turned her, like an enemy spy snuck into my garrison, and it had been easy because Charlotte saw nothing in me that she couldn't get from him instead.

I rubbed my sternum as if I could ease the ache beneath. But there wasn't time for me to dwell on the hurt, because at last a server I recognised had stepped into the courtyard, a silver platter of croissants held aloft on one hand.

"You!"

He spun. I took in his sandy-blond hair and acne-scarred face and was reasonably sure this was the kid I'd seen last night. I crossed to intercept him near the continental station.

"I need to ask you about that rubbish bag you ditched outside."

His Adam's apple leapt as he swallowed. "Oh, hey, I'm really sorry—"

"Where did it come from?"

"S-sorry?"

"The rubbish bag. Where did the trash come from?"

He shook his head slowly and repositioned his platter. "Uh—I have no idea."

Just as I felt my lack of patience about to boil over, Luc appeared in the shadow of the arches across the courtyard. He gave a minute nod before retreating into the house, away from the daylight, and a breath of relief escaped me. We were one step closer to a chance to save my life.

I patted Mario on the arm. "I can take it from here."

"If you say so," he said, already walking away.

I rounded on the boy. "Alright," I said, and let out a slow breath. "Where did you pick up the bag? Someone's room?"

Eyes wide, he shook his head. "No, no way. I didn't go upstairs, I swear. We're not allowed."

I raised both palms placatingly, even as I was deep-breathing through my frustration. "Where did you get it, then?"

"It was left outside the kitchen." He pointed vaguely that way, the platter tilting dangerously in his other hand. "I was passing through for my break and that lady told me to grab it."

My heart pattered. "What lady? With the headset?"

"No, she's not event staff, she's one of yours. Not like that's stopped her breathing down all our necks. I don't know her name. Like, bleach blonde? Dresses kind of like a monk?"

"Oh, for fuck's sake."

"I can't fathom why you would need to know that."

"You don't have to *fathom*, Fran, you can just tell me. Where did the bag come from?"

I had tracked her to the far-flung reaches of Fable where the corridors were narrower and the staircases, rather than standing proudly like sacred cairns, were slotted into corners. Here she had a small suite of rooms that were all hers. I'd never been inside; whenever I knocked—four, maybe five times, as I'd been instructed when Daddy wasn't home and Jude started screaming in his sleep—Fran had thrown the door wide, then narrowed it to the width of her face when she saw it was me. So I knew what it looked like: a cocoon of rugs and wall hangings. Dark wood warmed the grey stone, and globs of candlewax bled onto ceramic dishes. A strong odour of sandalwood leaked into the hallway.

Her moss-green linen ensemble was rumpled from whatever pile of blankets she had crawled from to answer the door. Discovering Fran had cursed me and destroyed the antidote would be the most unsurprising revelation in the world, but I was yet to convince myself she could have hurt Daddy, and her anguish wasn't helping. Her face was horribly splotched and puffy from crying. Yet, on seeing me, she managed such a feat of mind over matter that I had no choice but to be impressed. She pulled herself tall, fixed that look of imperious serenity in place, and faced me down without a hiccup or sniffle.

And now she was back at what she did best: barely answering my simple and direct questions.

"Danica was taking it out when the fire alarm went off," she explained. "The alarm was in her corridor, so I told her to leave the bag and run straight back there to check. Then the boy passed through, so I told him to take it."

"The fire alarm didn't go off," I said. "I would have heard it."

"Of course," said Fran in a tone of revelation. "You've never lived here, so you wouldn't know. The alarm doesn't sound throughout the house right away, only in the service areas."

She was enjoying herself now, crying jag long forgotten. Or perhaps there was just always space in her heart for a dig at me.

"Fine," I said through gritted teeth. "But where did the bag *come from?*"

"If Danica had it," she said with condescending slowness, "then it was rubbish emptied from the bins on Danica's corridor."

Mine and Fran's final goodbye could not come soon enough. "Gosh, thanks. *Which guest rooms?*"

With the smile of the persecuted but brave, Fran shut the door in my face. She was back a long moment later with a printed list of guests and assigned housekeepers. Danica was responsible for a stretch of the house in which six guests were staying, in five rooms.

Athena and Graham, Roman Astor, Charlotte, and a room each for the Gothenburg vampires.

My heart leapt. This was my suspect list, at long last whittled down to only a handful of names. That is, if Fran was telling me the whole story.

"Where were you at eleven thirty-nine on Friday night?"

She smiled. "I'm glad you asked," she said, before handing me a printed image in black and white—Fran on the gravel path outside the kitchen door, two caterers with her, their kitchen whites unbuttoned at the collar, cigarettes in hand. She was gesturing in the direction of the catering tent set up just out of view. I couldn't see the details of her expression, but I got the gist: these caterers were getting a dressing down for smoking along the same path the food took to the kitchen.

"Look at the time," she said.

But I'd already seen it—and felt an oily flutter of frustration at another dead end. The image was a still of the CCTV footage, and in the top right corner were the words KITCHEN WEST along with a date and time. Exactly 11:39 on Friday night.

"I obtained this from security as soon as I learned about the theft. I've been expecting you and your accusations from the second you showed me that cabinet."

"How do I know you didn't doctor this?" I said without much conviction.

"The recorded footage is all saved for two weeks." She folded her hands in front of her with an air of smugness. *And that was that.* "Check it yourself."

"I will," I lied, thrusting the photo back at her.

"One more thing."

She put a third paper object into my hand: an unmarked, unsealed envelope. Impatiently, I ripped the single sheet out and scanned the short typed letter.

"This is your resignation."

"Never say that I haven't known you these long years, Valentina. I know what happens now, and I don't want to stand helpless and watch my fate decided while you drag Jude through court to snatch his childhood home from him. I want to hold space to be there for *him* through all of this. Perhaps you'll succeed and perhaps you won't, but I won't wait around to be fired by you, should you get your way. So I'm leaving."

I had daydreamed of this moment my entire conscious life, so I could hardly believe the emotion that rushed up to greet the news. Fran was one of the few people left in that house whose feelings I always knew, even when her face was as placid as the eye of a storm. The only thing I wished to elicit from her was hate, and she never let me down.

Being within these walls when Fran wished me elsewhere and could do nothing about it was the surest power I had ever had over anybody, and I was losing it. Fran was leaving, and I was not jumping for joy. I didn't feel free.

I was devastated.

"You'll go and work for Jude, I suppose," I said dully. "In Polynesia."

She was silent a long while. Something not at all in keeping with her usual façade seeped into her features. "My work visa is unlikely to allow it."

"Well, that's nonsense." It was not kindness, but merely a sense of responsibility—a concession to my own power, if you will—that made me say, "I'll make some calls."

Fran didn't quite do a double take, but her expression slackened for all of a millisecond. It was unsettling to see her so caught off guard. "I— Thank you."

I nodded, gestured with the list of housekeeper assignments by way of excuse, and strode away.

"Valentina." When I turned, Fran had placed a reverent hand against the stone and was gazing at it, watery-eyed. "Hire someone who'll love this place as we do."

I didn't know who *we* was—the family, which she'd decided herself a part of, or just she and I?—but I couldn't wait around to find out what I would do. I was worried—but no, it was absurd, impossible—that I was about to tell her to stay.

14

Luc had his phone, but he was still waiting to hear from someone who could tell him where to find a faerie that would bargain with me.

"But they're on it," he told me, shut in my bedroom behind a soundproof door. "We just have to sit tight."

I nodded, like the idea of "sitting tight" didn't make me feel so restless it caused me physical pain. We were plodding our way towards noon—thirty-six hours until my heart turned to gold—and my pacing traced the same circle I had worn yesterday. "Who is *they*?"

"Friends."

Luc, by comparison, leant against a chest of drawers with that unsettling calm. The further the thrill of him touching me receded into the past, the more my anxiety over the curse ratcheted up, the more unstable the girl I'd been last night looked to me—and yet the faster she was circling back. I'd led him into that cave the night before with the object of getting him out of my system. Looking at him now—a touch fragile, no less steeped in death—I realised I'd done nothing of the sort. I'd proved to myself that there was pleasure in fear; that I needn't run from the tremor down my spine when I imagined his teeth in my flesh. But there was more to this—and it was embarrassing in its mundanity: I was imperilled, needy, and therefore clinging to the most eager body. I was in pieces, and Luc had offered up his hands to hold me together. If I was fifteen, I would have believed myself in love. But I wasn't, and I could see it for what it was: a sparkling forgery, a quick-burning match that would turn to ash just as fast.

For all my knowing, I was no less in its thrall.

I wanted to press my lips to the place on his neck where he had bruised mine. I wanted his arms to encircle me and bear my weight like they would his victims'. He was watching me like he wanted to.

And yet, when I looked at him just so, I thought I saw the monstrousness beneath the mask.

"Were your friends also invited this weekend?" I said.

He smiled wearily. "I told you, I don't know who any of the other invitations went to."

"But you could guess." I stopped pacing and faced him. "Couldn't you?"

As he watched me watch him, his expression morphed into a challenge. Here he was going out of his way to help me, as he had time and time again, and I could still barely pretend to trust him.

"You know I didn't do this," he said. Not a question, but a reminder loaded with several others, unspoken: that he didn't have to do *this* either, that he hadn't had to steal back his phone or chase Hunter through the woods or scoop me straight out of Mariah's waiting jaws.

But the loudest: that I didn't have a choice. I could trust him to lead me to a faerie, or I could die. It was true Luc wasn't the killer I was tracking—he was, in fact, the only person in the house I could vouch for myself. But what of his other secrets? I wanted to press harder for the answers. Had this conversation happened last night, I might have, too convinced I could fake my way to being my father to acknowledge the danger. But now my father was a corpse, the fearlessness, the shine, the *magic* of him stripped away until all that remained was pallid skin wrapped around lifeless organs. It's what would become of me too if Luc couldn't find me a faerie, and though allowing him that power over me was agony—a pressure that threatened to crack my ribs and rip the air from my lungs—I would bear it if it meant I got to live. I would hold my tongue until I no longer needed him.

"I know" was all I said, and turned away.

I had paced another two circles—my mind turning over Fran's list and how I'd eliminate any of the guests on it—before Luc spoke again. "What were you doing when I was getting my phone?"

"Tracing the antidote bottle," I said. "I've managed to narrow down the suspects."

I explained how I'd found where the rubbish bag came from and the six people it implicated: Charlotte, Roman, Athena, Graham, Mariah, and Randolph.

"Charlotte was with Jude and didn't even know the curse collection existed," I told him. "And I don't have solid motives for the others, but it has to be one of them." Luc gave me a look I couldn't parse. "What?"

"You're dead set on not involving the police until tomorrow? After the party?"

"Since I'm now hoping to *live*," I said, my emphasis underscoring how much I was relying on him, "I can't let this launch fall apart. So yes, no police."

Luc shrugged. "Then you can't do anything about the curser until then anyway. And you don't need to find them to get the antidote anymore. Why keep hunting them when Jude's trying to make you look paranoid and unhinged? Why not wait it out?"

The truth was a weight on my lungs. I drew a heavy breath. "They killed my father," I said with my back to Luc. "They unplugged his life support. The chances of him ever waking were slim after the stroke—perhaps they were nil by last night. But somebody wanted him dead so desperately, they couldn't wait. They even left . . ."

Thinking on it conjured the hopelessness of the night before, so instead I took the note from where I'd stashed it under my mattress and thrust it at Luc.

"'Remember Oscar Maddock has no heir,'" he read, frowning. A long moment passed in silence while he turned the card over and back again. "What do you think this means?"

"That this was never about extorting me," I said. "This is about something bigger. It's about my family."

My father was gone, and soon I might be too. A possessive kind of fury gripped me at the thought that, if I couldn't find who was killing us, they might keep tearing through the Maddocks until there was nothing left.

Luc's eyes lit up with revelation. "You think Jude might be next," he said.

I hadn't put it like that in my head, afraid the words would unmoor me. And they did; my psyche struck the idea that I was in a position to save Jude's life again like an exposed nerve meeting steel, heedless to all the ways this was different, cognizant only of the ways it wasn't.

And Jude could *not* get himself killed, not after all the trouble his life had cost me.

This was a lot to explain to Luc, and all of it vaguely embarrassing. I opened my mouth to speak long before the only words I had emerged. "It's not like I want him dead."

Luc accepted this with a nod, as if it could be that simple. "Then you should warn him."

Jude wasn't in his room, which I braved despite the risk of finding Charlotte there, or a whole tangle of bodies, or someone snorting cocaine off him. The late risers were still at breakfast in courtyard one; others were swimming, their aqueous noises drifting in from the pool. I checked neither. I knew where he would be.

I hadn't been prepared for the trolley, the body bag, the undertakers dressed up as catering staff. As I watched, bracing myself against the doorway, they threw table linen over the bag containing my father's body and turned him into a macabre buffet, something we might uncover later at lunch.

Jude sat on the far side of the room with his head in his hands, but he looked up as they wheeled the trolley past me, and our eyes met; his a fanciful blue, mine an equally false violet, both dull grey in another life.

"Fran knows," I said by way of greeting, "that Daddy's gone. I assume you told her, but you need to make sure she keeps it quiet."

He didn't hear me. His bleak eyes had already tracked past my shoulder to the empty hospital bed where Daddy had lain for five days. A sudden tightness pushed its way up my throat. It looked like he'd gotten up to use the bathroom, the blankets peeled to one side, the pillow dented.

Jude spoke, but I didn't catch a word of it; he had put his face back in his hands.

"What?"

The silence stretched as he scraped his hair away from his face, gripped the nape of his neck like he was shoring it up, and finally let himself fall back into the chair. "I said, we should do the funeral in Iceland. On that beach he always said was his favourite, with the black sand."

"His favourite beach wasn't in *Iceland*," I said. I had no idea where his favourite beach was, and for that reason alone, I hated the idea. Even worse, I hated that Jude didn't bother to argue with me, like he knew he had nothing to prove. He had known our father better and I was just another relation with an opinion no one asked for.

"And the undertaker said dear Aunt Claudia wants to arrange a viewing at the funeral home," he said instead, styling out his trembling voice with a supercilious sneer. "Tell her she can't."

"Why not?"

"Because I don't want people ogling him on the suggestion of the PR department. Besides, it's not up to her. It's up to us."

There it was again: us. We were tangled in ways I could never undo, but we'd slipped the most inescapable knot: Daddy was dead. He'd always hoped a fix existed for his fractured family life, as swift and governable as every other problem that touched him. By his decree, Jude and I had exchanged Christmas gifts—a scarf or bracelet for me, some artsy ceramic trinket for him—joined him for dinners and "lockdown vacations," during which our drivers were given the week off and instructed not to *Swift* us out of there even if we begged them. All in the belief that with proximity, our differences would prove themselves surface level and they would heal.

But what had festered between Jude and I was not just paper—birth and stock certificates, lists of assets. It was blood and bone. We were not squabbling children—we were haunted, our phantoms a pair of seven-year-olds who had almost died together.

Now that our father was gone, we should happily never see each other in the same room again.

And yet Jude was edging closer.

Please.

He'd made me next of kin, even though it would hurt his case for CEO with the board. I had never been able to read Jude, even with *Empathy*—it was all just hate. But that was enough to remind me not to fall for any of it.

"Look," I said. "I know we would both rather the other could trade places with Daddy, but since that's not possible, I may as well tell you that you need to be careful. Somebody in this house has an agenda and there's a good chance you're in the way of it."

Jude's face closed. His eyes narrowed. "What agenda?"

"I don't know."

Very slowly, he said, "Then why do you think you know that?"

I scoped around for something honest I could say but found nothing. There was a reason I hadn't warned Jude before now, and it wasn't spite. It was that he'd used everything I'd done and said this weekend against me. I couldn't trust him to take this seriously or not to tell Roman, who still remained on my narrowing list of suspects.

"Tell me, when you were watching your demented blindfold race, was everyone there the whole time?"

I saw his eyes flicker towards the hospital bed, saw the cogs in his wine-soaked brain thunk into place. The look that crossed his face was the one he made when he wanted to say something cutting and aggressive. Instead, he said only, "Yes. We were all in the ballroom the entire time."

"You're sure?"

"I don't know. Maybe I'll think on it harder if you tell me what's going on."

"What's Roman up to?" I blurted, wondering if my brashness might spark an honest reaction.

Unfazed, Jude slipped something from his pocket. "You mean, apart from"—it was a sheet of paper, which he unfolded one way, then another—"trying to marry me?"

My suspect list. I remembered the quiet disarray of the room the night before. The housekeeper who took my second box of *Empathy* spells on Jude's orders must have swiped it while they were rifling through my things. I thought of what was on it—Graham's betrayal of Athena, for one; vague accusations about half a dozen other guests—and grew dizzy thinking of the damage Jude could do to me if he circulated it.

Jude saw me panic, and a cheerless smile crossed his features.

"Tell you what," he said. "You can have the company. Not the house, that's mine, but I'll let you take the company. I'll stop trying to fuck everything up for you. And I won't circulate this." He held up the note between two fingers, then folded it back into his pocket. "All you have to do," he said, his expression darkening like a thundercloud, but his voice small as a boy's, "is say it was worth it. Say you're glad you saved my life."

I recoiled like he'd hit me.

"Is that a joke?" I whispered. "It was the worst thing that ever happened to me."

Because it wasn't even *about* Jude, and he needed to understand that. He could claim leukaemia, but I wouldn't let him diminish my sepsis, my fear, my emotional abandonment, just because they got in the way of me being *grateful* to have saved his life. He got to *live*—he did not get me being happy to have suffered for him.

Obviously, I hear now how it sounds.

At the time, I only heard a cheap trick, and not even a very imaginative one. Jude would not give up on his quest to ruin my life just because I gritted my teeth and said I was glad for what was done to me. He had already dropped it, his red-rimmed eyes sliding off me like I was furniture. I'd warned him as best as I could manage; I was done.

I turned to leave, but that forsaken hospital bed snagged my attention again. "He hated hospitals," I said, mainly to myself.

"You're projecting."

"I'm not. I remember." I paused, surprised by myself. Because now I was doing it too, probing the wound we had left to fester and blacken. Silence fell, as if even the zen fountain was stunned into listening. "He could barely stand to step foot inside."

"What are you talking about?"

His tone of true surprise compelled me to turn. I watched him move through confusion to a realisation that made him flush—one he reached long, long moments before I did.

He had more information, of course. I'd had only the *absence* of my father, a seven-year-old's vulnerable mind, and a lie planted in his place for me to take hold of: that Daddy hated hospitals. Everyone had said so. The nurses, the paediatricians, both sets of grandparents; even Mum had done what self-sacrificing ex-wives always have and saved my opinion of him. He bore the burden of visiting as often as he could, but it was never enough for me. The shape of those days and weeks in my hospital bed was drawn by my mother—her distance and impatience, her endless suffering of me—but they were shaded by his absence, by my infant longing for him.

He had been with Jude. This new truth was so very obvious that it didn't even hurt. What was there to realise? That I wasn't the favourite child? That he had never even tried to pretend? It wasn't even very scandalous. Mum had custody and full control of my medical decisions. The only place Daddy had had any power—the only place he could be himself—was by his son's bedside, with his second wife.

It didn't hurt. What hurt was that Jude understood it all in one glance, that he knew now that Daddy hadn't been there for me the way he had for him.

That his face now coloured with shame—that was a feeling I couldn't name.

"He loved me more," he blurted.

Some part of my mind broke off, like it knew what I would do—what I would say—and didn't want to. I swept towards the door. "Fuck you."

"No, *wait*." He rushed on before I was clear of the room. "You never understood. You only saw that he loved me more and never saw that he overcompensated in your favour, but *I* did. He had fifty-six *years* to write a will, and he couldn't put in writing that Fable should go to me. He wanted you to feel like this was your home so badly he forgot that it was *mine*. That *he* should have been mine because he was all I had."

I shook my head. "I only came to tell you to be careful—"

"Do you think there's a difference between love and envy?"

I turned over every word of the question, expecting to find the thread of the conversation stuck to the underbelly of each one.

"I mean all-consuming . . . *soul-crushing* envy," he went on. His voice was pained and full of meaning I flailed to grasp on to. "Because I'm not sure I do. Think about it. Being consumed by how different you want things to be. Sifting through everything they do or say, just for crumbs, no matter what it does to you. When you miss someone who's standing right in front of you, is it because they mean fucking everything to you, or because you want to turn to gas and seep through their pores? You want to live in their body—"

"Disgusting."

"—in the existence they take for granted. And what if that feeling is the biggest part of who you are? If you were only alive because of someone"—he leant so far out of his chair that he may as well have fallen to his knees on the floor—"and you knew for the rest of your life that you could never make that equal, no matter how far you would go for the same power over them, because that's how badly you need them to feel what you feel—is that love? Gratitude? Is it supposed to hurt?"

"You're still drunk."

"It sounds like envy, right?" He rose, passing me on his way to the door as if he had casually run out of depraved things to say. "It is seriously, deeply improbable that it's love, but what's the difference? It's my entire fucking personality. Either way, you're the most important thing in the world to me."

The reply sprang to mind: *I didn't save your life on purpose*. But it was too cruel, and it didn't need to be said.

He already knew.

"And you wish I was dead instead of him," he said, reaching for the door handle. "Makes two of us."

"Wait."

I didn't expect him to *actually* wait. But as he turned to face me, open expectation lighting his features, that unguarded absence of a loathing he claimed was love, I realised—he thought I was going to correct him.

Swallowing heavily, I said instead, "You can't circulate those notes. Every bit of chaos you cause hurts both of us. Hurts *everything*." As his disdain rose again to the surface, I continued. Mum had promised the board would name me CEO today, but Jude didn't need to know that. "They're not going to make you CEO if you destroy the *Immortality* launch. Not with the entire future of the product riding on the uptake of those people out there." I stabbed an arm in the direction of the door. "Trillions of dollars are on the line at this party. Our stock value is going to depend on—"

I broke off as his ugly laughter struck me like an open palm across the cheek.

"What don't you understand?" He enunciated each syllable with a tender delicacy. "*I don't care*. I don't care about Mythos and I don't care about being CEO."

Whatever he saw in my reaction—bewilderment, panic, instability, as if I had looked down and found what I'd taken for solid ground was a groaning rope bridge, buffeted by the wind—brought a grim smile to his face.

"Yes, you do" was all I could think to say.

Jude shook his head slowly. "*You* care. *You* want CEO. All I wanted was to stop you getting what you want. And I don't need to sit behind a desk and sign shit for eternity to do it. I can cost you everything that matters to you just by destroying it."

The trickle of the zen fountain became the roar of blood in my ears. Jude didn't want CEO. He didn't want any of it. I could feel my mouth moving like a guppy's but I couldn't control it. I imagined what *Empathy* would show me—Jude full to bursting with satisfaction—but I couldn't pull myself together enough to hide what this revelation had done to me.

I *lived* to claim back what Jude's existence had stolen from me: my father. His legacy. I'd always known Jude's motives were weaker than mine. He wasn't hungry, didn't live on scraps of Daddy's time, the morsels of love that were left over. He'd never been called Jude Cabot by unknowing teachers, didn't experience being told he looked like his mother with a sting of exclusion. While I had been born into an already fractured family, Jude had never known anything but belonging uncomplicatedly to our father. He had nothing to prove, had never been denied. But I'd believed he was defending something, even if the only way he could conceive of its value was by believing it was his by right.

But if he'd never wanted it . . . was this just about claiming back some power he believed I'd taken when I saved his life? Did he need what I coveted because my own twisted envy nourished him? And was this pain I caused him really all that kept him in this locked-horns, bone-breaking embrace of ours?

I didn't get the chance to ask any of it. Before I could pull myself from a state of shock, the door snapped shut, the echo like a gavel coming down.

I stood in the empty room, the air so death-choked it clogged my throat, holding in the urge to rush after Jude and beg at his feet for understanding. When the handle turned, I knew I wouldn't be able to stop myself.

But it wasn't Jude in the doorway. It was Luc.

"It's time to go," he said.

15

Fran drove a *Swift*-enabled Mercedes that Daddy had gifted her. She liked to park in a secluded spot to the south of the house with the keys in the sun visor.

"No one's going to notice it's gone?" said Luc, nodding towards the car. We were lurking in the loggia, him leaning heavily against an arch as the sun tried to reduce him to a walking corpse, me looking every which way for house-staff espionage. I'd stopped feeling their eyes on me this morning, as if Jude's will to thwart me had died with Daddy.

"Forgiveness, not permission, et cetera," I said as I crossed to the car and slid in behind the wheel. Luc got into the passenger side and sighed with relief as he closed the door on the sun. "I don't get *Immortality* if anyone finds out I left the party early, but I can't take it if I don't live into next week anyway. One problem at a time." The display in the centre console glowed blue as the options appeared, and I selected the navigator. "Where to?"

Luc input an address, and a map onscreen confirmed the location.

"I brought a bracelet my father gave me," I said around a sudden lump in my throat as the flare of the spell engulfed us. "Out of the stuff I have with me, it has the most sentimental value. They like that, don't they? Taking something that means a lot to you?"

Luc grinned. "Did you bring cash?"

"Uh—no."

"Then change of plan. Take us to an ATM first."

We materialised in an empty downtown *Swift* lane in a metropolis

I didn't recognise, under a steel-grey sky. In the driving lanes, a thick flow of cars were moving at a steady pace, most with a Mythos Blue glow emanating from the strips along the chassis, but none *Swift*-enabled. The pulsing strip of a *Fuel*-powered tramline ran halfway up the street and made a turn. At the distant top of the gentle slope, speeding cars flashed beneath a colossal Mythos billboard. It was old; that generation of *Calm* hit stores eight months ago.

Swift lanes were usually in the parts of town where *Swift* users wanted to be, and if this was the city's best offering, it was no wonder I'd never been here before. The pervasive colour was an almost identical grey to Fable, except in concrete instead of marble, the edges weathered with neglect. To our right, a dozen people waiting at a tram stop had whipped out their phones as we appeared, like they expected us to high-tail it straight out of there again and wanted to catch the spell in action. I took my sunglasses off my head and hid behind them as I pulled out of the lane and drove a couple of blocks to an ATM.

"This is better, actually," said Luc as I pulled wad after wad of notes out of the machine. He pointed down a perpendicular street, to a tower block such a feeble grey that it looked insubstantial in the hazy shadow of the skyscrapers above it. Only the violent colours of the graffiti rooted it in place. "We can walk from here."

I swallowed down a sick feeling of dread and reminded myself why I was here. "Then let's go."

The lobby of the building smelled like smoke and urine, and the elevator made a worrying, constant hum as we climbed to the ninth floor. There was graffiti here too, and the grease-soaked packaging of someone's fast food in one corner. Even the light was ugly, in a way that was both too yellow and uncannily dull.

"Cash?" I asked as I stood with elbows tucked in, careful not to touch the walls.

Luc was watching the floor numbers rise. He appeared completely relaxed in our current environs, but my question curled his lip into an unfriendly smile. "You devalued their only currency. They don't have a choice but to use yours."

The elevator opened on the most claustrophobic corridor I had ever been in. There were no windows, and the low ceiling was studded with fluorescent strip lights that all flickered, or were dark, or were in pulverised pieces on the floor. I had only seen corridors like these in literal horror movies. Outside one door, a man lounged on a folding chair with the distinct air of a bouncer. Behind him, the door was ajar, and a jam of bodies formed as a man stumbled out towards the elevator, carrying with him the chemical stink of burning rubber. Luc stretched an arm behind him and pressed me back against the stained wall as he passed. I remember because I have not felt clean since.

"Oh god. If I'm in a crack den, I'm going to cry."

"You're not in a crack den," said Luc. He glanced through the open door as we skirted the man on the folding chair and continued. "You're *outside* a crack den."

The apartment we wanted was, to my horror, right next door. Luc ushered me to one side as he knocked. "Let me speak to her first."

I'd thought I was already hating this, but in the interval before the door opened, writhing dread came alive inside me. A faerie—had I completely lost my mind? This could only end badly.

A chain scraped, and the door cracked open. Luc—seeming to understand how small and fragile our window of opportunity was—applied some pressure to keep it there. "Can we bargain?" he said softly through the gap.

Then he'd stepped inside, and the door all but closed behind him. Only his knuckles holding onto the frame stopped it from slamming in my face, leaving me with a crack person in a folding chair. A crack person with a gun tucked into his waistband, I now realised.

"Luc." I tried to push the door open, but he held it firm. Either a negotiation or a mortal betrayal was taking place in murmurs on the other side, and the crack person had risen curiously from his chair. Suddenly the vampire-infested faerie lair looked like the nicer of two deaths.

Just before fear became screaming, I was pulled into the apartment. Humidity and the loamy scent of vegetation engulfed me. We were in a short, dark corridor, and whatever was here with us had already retreated to the room at the end; I could see its warped reflection in the glass of a display cabinet. Despite the close heat, my every hair stood on end.

"Be respectful," Luc said, his voice low. "She knows who you are."

We passed a tiny bathroom with pink fixtures, neat but for a broken window, deadly nightshade spilling inside and over the tiles, and a bathmat that appeared to be growing algae. A second door was pulled closed. At the end of the corridor was the main room, a combined kitchen and living space with one occupant.

A woman was seated at a little round table and was smoking a long pipe. She was alarmingly gaunt, with the leathery, wrinkled skin of someone who had had too much sun in her life but the complexion of a person who had had none, ever. Yet underneath her skin texture, it was hard to pinpoint her age. Her eyes were clear and dark, and followed me with the quality of a wary child's as I came into the room. Her lank hair was golden blonde—or looked like it would be, rinsed of the heavy grease that pasted it to her skull; a skull too large for her frame, but only just. A human woman, by appearances, wearing a lilac dressing gown and smoking something rancid.

Luc introduced me. "This is Valentina."

"A pleasure to meet you," I said weakly, eyes roving about the tiny apartment. There was a humming here too—but louder and emanating from several corners of the room—and the same sickly yellow tinge. The windows above the kitchen counters looked out on a narrow, north-facing light well—darkness, in other words, made darker still by the plants crowded on two rows of shelves between us and the glass. It wasn't working out for them; most were browning along the edges of their leaves or shrivelling altogether. Dozens of other plants on shelves, surfaces, and the floor were faring about the same. A long terrarium stood against one wall; I didn't want to know what was in it, but I saw them anyway from the corner of my eye: monstrous snails, as big as my palm. I vowed that if I left here without seeing one ground up and thrown in a cauldron, I would call it a win.

"You have a curse on you," the woman said, her voice as high-pitched as a child's and filled with omen. I looked at my gilded hand, normal beneath the overhead light, and shuddered.

"How did you know?"

She took a languid pull from her pipe—it was ivory, or perhaps *femur*—while dissecting me with an unblinking stare. Then she tipped her chin towards Luc, sour smoke pouring from her lips. "The vampire told me, idiot."

There was a *snap* from somewhere behind me. My heart, skin, and brain all leapt in an offbeat canon, jangling me like marbles in a jar. I jumped a second time when our hostess brushed past. She took a plate from a shelf and a plastic tub of butter from the fridge.

The *snap* had been a toaster. As our hostess hooked a piece of charred toast out of the relic of an appliance, my eyes snagged on the socket. It looked broken to my eyes; so did the socket beneath, where a blender was plugged in. Neither was ringed by the glow of power.

I finally made sense of the odd dullness, the humming. This building used real electricity. There was, in fact, no tinge to the lighting, just the absence of one. So much of the world as I knew it had the faint glow of magic that without it, everything held a gloom.

I knew that not everywhere in the world used *Fuel* yet. I'd just thought that meant . . . I don't know, Yemen or something.

"There's one way I'll even look into helping you, and that's if it pays my rent for a whole goddamn year." She pointed a butter knife at Luc. "You're a piece of work, bringing her here."

"Will this be enough?"

I held out the folded wad of cash, and her fingers—her nail beds were blue, like a dead woman's—brushed mine as she took it tentatively. I'd withdrawn the maximum two dozen times but hadn't counted how much was there; a few thousand, maybe. She looked from me to the money and back again, her face carefully neutral, then tucked it into her dressing gown and went back to buttering her toast.

At least I'd assumed it was butter. Whatever she had filled the old container with had the consistency of apple sauce but was a pale, fungal grey. Once she was done, she tossed the knife into the sink and picked a fragment of shell out of her breakfast. I tried to swap glances with Luc, but he watched her return to the table with impassive calm. His diet was worse, I suppose.

The faerie took a bite of her toast, then flapped for me to come closer. "Show me."

As I rolled up my sleeve, Luc produced his lighter. Our hostess bared her slime-coated teeth at it and shooed him away. "No flames. No fire."

"But it's Gilded Grip," I said. "The veins only show—"

I cut off as she snatched my hand and pulled it close. Instinct made me struggle, for all the good it did; her grip was a vise. I started to panic. She kneaded my fingers as if she was looking for something, which revealed itself to be a solid grip when she took my index finger into her mouth, positioned it under a canine, and bit down.

After that, I don't know. I fainted, obviously.

I came to in a limp heap on the couch, Luc kneeling in front of me. My arm was moving, but it was several moments before I realised *he* was moving it; another few more before I understood he was bandaging my forearm—close, too close, to the vulnerable crook of my elbow.

"*No,*" I tried to wail, but it came out an asyllabic moan. I didn't have the strength to pull away, nor could I armour the area with my left hand, which was stuck under me.

"It's done," Luc said. "It's over. I told her to take what she needed while you were still out. Here."

He picked up a glass from the side table, its contents a nebulous, anaemic red. Nausea flooded my mouth with saliva.

"It's grapefruit juice. It's all she had."

Shakily, I rolled to a sitting position. The bandage wasn't quite in the crease but below it on my forearm, which was the saving grace of my sanity. A second wrapped my finger, and stinging pain burned under both.

"That thing fucking bit me," I said, knowing the thing was somewhere behind me in the kitchen. I could hear her handling glass, the opening and closing of the fridge.

"What's getting bitten to the likes of you?" she said. "How did you think I would know what was in your blood?"

I lowered my voice to exclude her and leaned towards Luc. "She could have cursed me again. This is more or less how I contracted the first one."

Solemn, Luc looked at his watch. "It was always a risk, but if it's going to sprout, it'll be within the next few minutes. If you feel a pressure in your tailbone, let me know."

It took a long moment, then another—the inevitability of the situation I was in stealing my breath—for me to realise he was mocking me. Luc smiled a cruel smile, and my terror transformed into irritation.

"She took a vial to make an antidote to help you," added Luc. "So let it go."

He pushed the grapefruit juice at me again and I took it, but my hand shook too much and I placed it back on the table. I couldn't drink it anyway. Noxious panic was swimming through me so fast I was dizzy. The air tasted too thin. As Luc went back to the kitchen, I let my head fall between my legs. Years of therapy went out the window as I decided this was the time that would kill me.

"Bit dramatic for a vampire's pet," I heard the faerie say to Luc. After a pause, she added: "Or is the biting only hot when it's by something pretty in a human way?"

Luc's reply was too quiet to hear. It was several minutes before I was sure I wouldn't pass out again and could raise my head. Doing so immediately brought new horrors. On the wall straight ahead was a tall mirror—its carved frame spray-painted gold—and in it, behind me, was the faerie.

Reflected in the mirror, she was nothing like the creased and lank-haired human woman she appeared. Nor did she bear a resemblance to the *Masquerade*-clad dancers we had hunted through the forest. Antlers, blue-grey with lichen, scraped the ceiling. Her face was hidden entirely by a curtain of Spanish moss growing from her like hair. Skin the green of clay was sloughing off in papery husks, revealing a reptilian gleam to limbs like attenuated branches, impossibly narrow. I couldn't hear the words she murmured to the empty kitchen, but when she gestured, it was with fingers twice as long and twice as jointed as mine.

Luc's reflection wasn't in the mirror. He was there—I knew it deep down—but I still had to turn and see him for myself. Because in the mirror world, vampires didn't exist, and I was alone with this eldritch beast.

"She stirs," said the faerie in her human guise. What kind of evil magic could do that? Did Luc see the glamour when he looked at her? "It's going to take me some time to produce something that will reverse your curse." She produced the wad of cash from her dressing gown. "This is half. You bring the rest tomorrow at dawn."

I rose from the coach. Thank you, *Revitalise,* for the dregs of energy I could still muster.

"Tomorrow at dawn is too late," I said. "I'm dying."

"She thinks I can't count to three," she replied with a sardonic glare.

The fact my three days wouldn't run down until midnight tomorrow was beside the point. I stepped closer, willing her to understand. I was vaguely aware of Luc coming closer too. "I can't wait all day to find out if my heart's going to turn to gold tomorrow or if I get to live. You took my money, you give me something *now.*"

She grinned, revealing teeth that I knew to be sharper than they looked. "I already have your money, girlie. The time to negotiate has passed."

Panic, indignation, the unbearable pulsing of the wound in my finger; they all crystallised into rage as I threw myself at her. My fingertips brushed the lapel of her dressing gown before I was wrenched roughly away. I staggered, catching myself on the back of a chair. The faerie was backed up against the fridge, Luc protectively in front of her, his face a picture of animosity unprettied by magic.

My hand flew to my chest as if I were a scandalised biddy. The only person who had ever put their hands on me was Jude, and we'd been children. And I'd have understood—I did attack *her* after all—if Luc wasn't radiating outrage. If he hadn't shoved me harder than he needed to. I tried to take stock, but under the adrenaline I couldn't tell if I was injured.

It turned out later that I was fine.

"You're magic," I said to the faerie, breathless and beseeching. "You know things, I know you do. I bet you can tell me who did this to me."

She folded her arms tight across her chest, still pressed against the fridge as if *she* was afraid of *me*. But there was also a screwed-up mulishness to her expression. She did know something. Perhaps I could still learn who'd put me through this; could still claw back some control by looking them in the eye come Tuesday and showing them they'd failed.

"Give me *something*," I said, pointing to where the cash had disappeared into her dressing gown, "and I'll pay you double that tomorrow morning."

She hesitated, tapping her fingers against her sleeve. Then she sniffed derisively. "I know something." Her gaze tracked to the side, to Luc. "But it's *their* business."

I huffed a sigh. "Do you want my money or not?"

"You're hosting House Gothenburg, aren't you?" she went on. Luc tensed. "They're playing your co-conspirators in all this."

A prickle travelled up my neck. "What about it?"

"Buyer's remorse. Your compact has cost them the favour of the other noble houses. We have all heard how House Gothenburg would do just about anything to atone." She fixed me with a dead-eyed stare. "I'd say taking out a Maddock is probably a start."

Taking out two would probably be better. I'd discounted House Gothenburg as serious suspects because they had no way of knowing I used *Empathy* or about the crude magic collection—but what if they had? I'd been paying a housekeeper to spy at Fable. Who was to say House Gothenburg hadn't managed the same? Who was to say they hadn't been spying on *me*?

"We're done here," said Luc. "Thank you for all your help."

The faerie pointed a cadaverous finger at him. "You tell no one about this, vampire. Some would see me meet the same fate as House Gothenburg. Or Waerloga, even. I won't be a pariah."

"Trust me," said Luc, with a glance my way that excluded me, "the Maddock heir isn't telling anyone they sought help from a faerie."

He ushered me towards the door. The faerie followed, probably keen to lock us out as fast as possible.

"Waerloga?" I asked as Luc and I spilled into the hall. The man on the folding chair still waited, but he was a minor horror to me now, since he was eating a breakfast burrito and not growing moss from anywhere. "You're talking about the witch who sold my great-grandfather magic, aren't you? Her name's Waerloga?"

"Not a name," said the faerie from behind us. "Just what we call her." She looked me up and down, already closing the door. "It means traitor."

16

There'd been a change of plans for the afternoon.

The new plan announced itself with a pulse of Mythos Blue light that filled a sky turned grey, as if for one moment magic had come to cast the rays the sun would not. In its wake, waves rippled across the dark surface of the lake a quarter mile north of the house, and a colossus of shining white landed like an oversized swan.

"I heard it once belonged to Grace Kelly," Graham said as Luc and I slipped back in among the guests arrayed in a loggia, watching the swells of the lake settle.

I didn't think they had superyachts in Grace Kelly's time. The torpedo-shaped behemoth my father had christened the *Adieu* had been designed to spec some years earlier. It slept thirty and had a spa, a movie theatre, an art gallery, and a swimming pool, which existed—I assumed—for its ridiculousness. It looked as out of place on the lake, under an uninspiring sky, as a great white shark in a babbling forest brook.

As the guests piled into golf carts that would take them down to the shore, Luc turned to me.

"Where can we talk?" he said. He was staggering slightly, but as we stepped into the cool fortress of the house, he regained some solidity. He was taller; his shoulders filled out. I didn't know what happened now, but if I had to apologise to get him to keep helping me, I would have to swallow that. I had needed him to get me the antidote, and I needed him still if the only other vampires at this party were involved in poisoning me.

We found ourselves in the same library in which we'd greeted the dawn, with its marble shelves full of books nobody ever read; the long, low couches in coffee-toned velvet; the busts of great thinkers, bone white. Luc meandered through the space until he passed too close to a sunbeam and flinched.

"If I ever see the fucking sun again after this weekend, it'll be too soon," he said as I went along pulling the curtains to.

Once we were in relative shade, I leant against the back of a couch and faced him.

"What the faerie said about House Gothenburg," I said. "It finally makes sense why Ansgar isn't here, and why Mariah and Randolph don't want to be either. If partnering with Mythos, which is essentially partnering with the Maddocks, lost them the favour of the other houses, do you think killing us might have been the offered price for putting them back on an even keel?"

Luc stood with his arms folded, still except for the rhythmic tapping of his fingers on one bicep.

"I don't know," he said at last. "Nothing about it sounds like how the houses operate."

"What do you mean?"

"I mean vampires are the same as these people," he said, gesturing in the direction of the lake and the mega-yacht hosting a bevy of billionaires. "They care about the same things, they backstab in the same ways. It's all money and empire-making—I'm sure it's why House Gothenburg partnered with Mythos in the first place. *But,*" he said, running a hand through his hair, "when they want to do violence, there's a way that feels natural."

I nodded that I understood, because I couldn't bear to hear him say it, not with the memory so fresh: blood. Teeth.

"Of all the ways someone could have chosen to kill you, they picked the Gilded Grip," he went on. "That's got to be significant somehow."

"And what's the significance of my dad being unplugged while he lay in a coma?" I bit back.

"I don't know." He looked like he meant to say more but stopped himself. There was a flatness to his tone, a lingering anger. The subject was about to turn to me trying to attack the faerie, Luc attacking me; I could feel the sudden tension ratcheting up. At last, I decided to get ahead of it by being the one to go first.

"I was frightened."

"I was impatient. I'm sun-sick and I need to sleep." He gestured to my bandaged finger and arm, which I wished he wouldn't do; I was working very hard to ignore them. "Are you alright?"

"I'll be fine. There's some *Calm* around here somewhere." A silence. Nothing seemed solved, yet the quiet stretched on and neither of us offered a better apology. At last I chanced to say, "You'll still help me, then?"

"Of course I will." He smiled, if it could be called that. Under a benighted sky, I'm sure it would have been flawlessly convincing, but robbed of his magic, it was painfully strained. "How about this: you go down to the yacht and try to talk to the people on Fran's list. The Gothenburgs will be in the house somewhere, since no vampire on Earth is going out on the water."

He paused expectantly. I could see what he was doing, making me the naïve little rich girl to prove some obscure point. My lack of knowledge about vampires fascinated him, like he was a ten-year-old boy and I a tarantula behind glass. I could feel myself ceding even more power to him, bleeding myself dry, as I was forced to ask, "And why not?"

"It's almost as draining as sunlight, worse if it's flowing. So I'll stay here and find Mariah and Randolph."

"Oh, do tell! What mischief do you hope to catch us up to?"

Our eyes met, dismayed, as we turned. Mariah stood in the entrance, her hand resting high on the doorframe like she was posed for a glamour shot. Her maroon dress was a draping silk that fell just past her knees; too mature and elegant for her, but it wasn't her fault she looked like a teenager. She must have had it made to fit her slightly wasted daylight form. Randolph hovered behind her like a good dog, there by someone else's design but happy to be dragged along by the neck.

"Go on. Randolph and I love a juicy cat-and-mouse story. Don't we, Randy?" She didn't look at Randolph and he didn't reply.

My heart sank. If they were behind this, now they knew I was suspicious and would never let themselves be caught.

Luc let his hand brush my spine, the smallest touch of support.

Or maybe there was another way, a Hail Mary: talking this out like adults.

"We know why Ansgar didn't come," I said, forcing strength into my voice even as my body noticed how outnumbered I was by vampires. They couldn't hurt me, not during daylight hours. "We know House Gothenburg regrets its decision to partner with Mythos. I understand there have been—repercussions."

"Ansgar didn't come, dear, because Ansgar is dead." She tilted her head to one side and gestured vaguely at herself, Randolph, and Luc. "And not in the sexy way."

I went still, like a prey animal sensing danger. Ansgar was *dead?* "I'm—sorry for your loss."

"Darling, thank you." She sauntered to a couch, where she curled her legs beneath her and stretched an arm across the back. I could see the cascade of little efforts she made not to tremble or look sick. Randolph moved aimlessly in the direction of a bookshelf, where he picked up and inspected a miniature bust. "To tell the truth, it's been a perfectly awful time, what with having to clear out the other lines."

"Clear out . . . Sorry, what?"

Her eyes widened, and she leaned forward like someone about to dispense the hottest gossip you'd ever heard. "Oh, you don't know! Losing a Maker is *carnage*, darling, pure carnage. We don't call the head of the house *Maker* for nothing, after all. They're the one every other vampire in the house descends from—do you see the problem?"

"I—no, not quite."

Mariah sighed, displeased with me, so Luc cut in.

"Below the Maker are the Ancestors—those they sired themselves—and then there are other generations below them."

"Right, like any family," I said.

Mariah made a face. "Typically, we're all touching each other too much for that analogy to hold, but alright."

"As I understand it, a Maker has an heir among the Ancestors," Luc went on. "Not always the first sired, often just a favourite. Should the Maker die, the heir takes their place and . . ."

"And the rest have to go!" said Mariah, grinning in a way that looked painful on her daylight form. "It's positively exhausting. We've been decimated—worse! We're a quarter the size we once were. And Ansgar was only the first Maker to go. House Thebes are *still* coming for us."

"Thebes?" I said. The oldest and most reclusive noble house. "House Thebes are killing you?"

Mariah looked at her lap, where she was rearranging the fall of her skirt. "Not that it matters which of the houses it was. They have the full backing of all the others, and they've been making a jolly meal of it. Six months ago, I was a first descendant." With a flourish of the hand, she looked up and smiled, though a tension remained around her eyes. "A little jostling, a little regicide, and you're now looking at the Maker of House Gothenburg. May she reign longer than her predecessor."

I hoped she hadn't expected a little curtsy or something. I stood there open-mouthed and blinking. "All for working with Mythos? Why?"

Mariah dropped her chin so that she was looking up at me. "Oh, poppet, I shouldn't have to tell you that. Really."

I looked to Luc imploringly, but he gave a shrug and turned to the Gothenburgs.

"Where were you both between eleven and midnight on Friday?" he said.

She had a naked and unflinching stare, unselfconscious as a child's. It moved between Luc and me with unhurried interest.

"Well, let's see. I suppose I was in the ballroom." She tipped her head against the back of the couch, exposing her pale throat, to address Randolph behind her. "What about you, Randy? Where were you between eleven and midnight on Friday? Sherlock Holmes and Doctor Watson here would like to know."

Randolph put the bust back on the shelf and turned it just so. Then he came to stand beside Mariah, who slid a hand into his and stroked his knuckles with the other. When he met my eye, it was with a gaze more ordinary and mild than I imagined. He looked even sicker than he did in the dark, but some of his strangeness had fallen away, as if it had been an act. *Or is this the performance?* I thought with a shudder. In the end, I was more disturbed for how less disturbing he'd become.

Even his voice was that of *just some guy,* neither anachronistic nor rough from disuse as he said: "Feeding."

I tried to seem casual—not dizzy, not suddenly aware of every inch of my fragile skin—as I leant against the couch. "So, not in the house at all?" I said hopefully.

"No, I was in the house. In my room, with a guest."

I made a noncommittal noise, which was all I could manage while trying to steady myself. Distantly, a dreadful fact was settling in, more dreadful than the thought of vampires feeding under Fable's roof, just a few rooms away from me: that if the Gothenburgs were telling the truth, neither of them had planted the curse, and I still hadn't caught my murderer.

Luc, stood behind my shoulder, put a hand on my elbow and cut in. "What time did you go up?"

"It was just before the fireworks began, so . . . around eleven forty-five, I think."

"Did you see anyone else on the upper floor? Or anything strange?" pressed Luc.

The Gothenburgs were both still, their patient faces turned questioningly to Luc as if he'd malfunctioned. I glanced over my shoulder at him; the stare he had for Mariah was equally impassive. I considered repeating the question, but after a moment that lasted an age, Randolph looked down at Mariah, his entire demeanour an obvious bid for instruction. Mariah tapped her nails against her thigh, a tiny smile on her lips.

After lengthy consideration, she said: "Tell them, Randolph, dear. It's alright."

Randolph looked up at us. "I saw the intruder."

The question that almost tripped off my lips was, *What intruder?*

Then I remembered the rumour Mum had harnessed to quell the outrage over the room search: she had let everyone believe a protester had made it into the house and may have planted something dangerous.

But how had Randolph seen someone we made up?

"Saw them where?" I said neutrally.

"Out there." He tipped his head towards the wall of glass doors. "They were hurrying, and they knocked over a plant pot right outside the window. I heard it smash, and then they ran on."

I pushed off the couch, my earlier dizziness gone with a snap. "Which way were they going?"

He considered, then imprecisely gestured towards the third quad. "West."

My room was at the westernmost corner of the house. Randolph hadn't seen some trespasser—he'd seen the killer.

And failed to recognise them.

"What did they look like? Did you see their face?" I said. Urgency strung the words together so that they fell over one another. Randolph's brow creased in confusion at the questions. We were supposed to have caught the intruder—why would I need him to tell me what they looked like? "Please, it's important."

"Just their silhouette through the curtains," he said. "Nothing to identify them by. The fireworks had started by that time and the flashes distorted their outline."

"Who was with you? Could *they* have seen something?"

Randolph's mouth pressed into a hard line. "When a person offers to sustain me with their body, I consider it an act of selflessness. An honour. I won't betray them."

"What Randolph's saying is he's a terrible *prude*, darling." Mariah patted his hand before he snatched it away, his expression dark. "He could have a writhing young thing pinned beneath him, panting in his ear, and he still doesn't go in for the notion that he's getting them off. He doesn't even fuck them." She shot Randolph a goading smile he ignored, then turned her head to me. "But it was Zazie Reynolds."

"*Mariah*," Randolph pleaded.

"Oh, *what?* She's a miserable, clingy thing, anyway." She rearranged her skirt again and sniffed. To me, she added, "Some people lose all sense of decorum when they get a taste. They turn into raging addicts the first time they bleed for us. That's why I prefer to drain a person until their heart stops for good and remember them fondly. Otherwise you risk them knocking on your door at god knows what sunlit hour, isn't that right, Randy? You learned that lesson this morning, didn't you?"

"I wasn't sleeping," Randolph said weakly.

That explained Zazie almost fainting at breakfast, and alibied her for planting the curse. It also raised the question of who Mariah might have eaten this weekend, if she was of the *drain them* school of bloodsucking. I wondered whether I would have been informed if a member of the catering staff went unaccounted for and realised I probably wouldn't.

"Suffice it to say," Randolph said with painful tightness, "there was nothing for either of us to see. Like I said, the person was a distorted shadow through a curtain."

"And when you heard what they might have done, you still didn't tell anyone?" I said.

I was ignored. Or perhaps I had asked a question I didn't understand. It was suddenly like being a stranger among old friends, the rhythm and cadence of a secret language washing over me, the meaningless sound prickling my skin. I glanced over my shoulder at Luc but saw nothing in the look that passed from him to Randolph. Mariah had taken up her unblinking stare again, seemingly unintelligent but purposefully so, I thought. Some unspoken rule, some dynamic of culture and hierarchy governing how vampires interacted, was playing out before my eyes, and I may as well have had them closed.

"Tell the Maddocks, you mean?" Mariah had heard me speak, after all. "Because we did not wish to put another foot wrong. House Gothenburg is ready to discuss how it can make amends to the houses. Until that happy occasion, we will do exactly nothing."

But if they'd kept the incident to themselves to avoid helping us, why tell me now?

Before I could ask, Luc muttered in my ear, "Let's talk in the hall," and propelled me by the arm out of the library. Once we were out of the Gothenburgs' earshot, I turned to him.

"Randolph saw the killer."

"During the fireworks," said Luc. "They planted the curse while you were on your way to your room. You very nearly caught them at it."

"Fran came up here, then Jude and Charlotte, then Randolph and Zazie, then me," I said, trying to visualise the timeline. "And somewhere in the middle, the killer."

There was no way onto the upper floor from outside, but Fable had staircases in every wing. The corridors formed loops through each quad in which to double back or change direction. The walls passed echoes from place to place, alerting anyone engaged in subterfuge to the presence of witnesses. And should someone find themselves trapped and about to be discovered, all they had to do was duck through the nearest door—every single room led to the loggia. We'd given the killer a vast labyrinth in which to play, and they'd taken full advantage.

"I need to go down to the yacht and tell Mum everything that's going on in House Gothenburg." I shot a glance at the library. "What was all that about?"

Luc shook his head, deep in thought. "Let me talk to them again alone. If they're looking to cut ties with Mythos, maybe there's something they'll tell me that they don't want to say in front of you."

"Thank you." I made myself smile through the feeling in my gut. Maybe the offer was innocent and whatever House Gothenburg said would be relayed to me. But there was an implication in the things Luc didn't say, in the wordless shake of his head, and it was a lie. Luc wouldn't say outright that he hadn't understood more of what had happened in there than me, but it was what he wanted me to believe nonetheless. I might not have known that in moonlight; as it was, with sun and cloud battling overhead, it was a much-needed reminder of Luc's secrets.

But how many other times had he let me hear only the answer I wanted? Which truths concealed an underbelly of dishonesty?

A deep discomfort settled in my gut as I imagined a battle of wills with this vampire and all his quiet purpose, and I realised afresh something I had always known: Luc would decide to trust me and show his hand, or he would devour me. Something warned me this wasn't the moment to demand his secrets and hope for the former, but I sensed we were reaching the precipice. Maybe I needed to call time on his usefulness and get far enough away before it was too late.

Luc watched me leave, his face giving nothing away as I rounded the corner, headed for the *Adieu*.

With or without his help, I was a step closer to ending this.

17

I rushed like a draught through the halls of Fable, and Luc's secrets chased me.

Whatever had passed between him and House Gothenburg was a cold reminder that I still didn't understand why he was here. That first night, I'd clocked that the vampires knew each other, but not how. However House Gothenburg had alienated the other noble houses, their insult clearly resonated with common vampires like Luc too. *The road to earning back the trust you've broken is a long one.* Those were the words I and three others had heard him sneer at Mariah and Randolph yesterday morning in the forest. He'd dismissed the idea of even being around them, so they couldn't be allies.

Or had we seen only what they showed to us? It struck me then: how easily the incident could have been a performance. House Gothenburg had made their reluctance to be here obvious long before confessing that Ansgar and others had died; if they regretted helping Mythos produce *Immortality,* why show up at all unless they'd been given another reason? And had that reason presented itself in the form of Lucas Sayle?

However little I could trust him, one thing I still knew for sure was that he couldn't have planted the curse. I had to concede that Randolph had also effectively ruled himself out. The intruder on the loggia, his teeth in Zazie's flesh—too many places for his story to fall through if it was fiction, too incriminating if it was a version of the truth. I had no doubt questioning Zazie would confirm Randolph's alibi. She'd told me she was interested in him on Friday night, not long before he granted her that first taste of death.

I made for the drive, where the last golf cart waited. I powered up the cart—the glow of *Fuel* bursting from the underside—and floored it down the path to the lake, air whipping my hair.

Athena, Graham, Roman, Charlotte, and Mariah. One of them had destroyed the antidote and thrown the pieces in the trash.

Mariah claimed to have been in the ballroom. It could have been a lie, but after our conversation, I was confident Mariah believed killing us all could cause more problems for her and House Gothenburg than it would solve.

Charlotte had been with Jude; Fran had seen them entering his room a little before eleven thirty. Charlotte would have had to make an excuse and leave him there only a few minutes later to get across Fable and steal the bottles by 11:39. As soon as Fran blabbed to Jude about the theft, he would have put two and two together, and I couldn't fathom anything that would persuade him to stay quiet about her subterfuge after someone unplugged Daddy.

That left Athena, Graham, and Roman, all of whom Jude claimed to have had in his sights when our father was killed. A realisation landed: I was going to have to tell Jude I had been cursed. He was the only way to narrow it down. I had to let him in on how serious this had gotten and hope that he cared.

As the path sloped towards the shore, the last of the trees fell away and the *Adieu* came into view, roped to a long temporary pier. The yacht couldn't tour the lake or in fact move at all. The waters were only deep enough in the spot where she floated.

The whole thing was patently ridiculous, but it hardly mattered. The *Adieu* was attraction enough. She had featured in everything from tabloids to interior design publications, and the on-board art gallery was just as, if not more, famous. Daddy's decision to house Botticelli's *The Birth of Venus* on the yacht had famously spurred his insurance company to cancel their coverage of the painting, and no others had taken up the mantle. The fact that one of the most famous paintings in the world was uninsured was now one of the first things discussed whenever the topic came up; like the fact Van Gogh had died penniless or Caravaggio had killed a man. The controversy meant the Maddocks well and truly *owned* the painting, in deed and in the zeitgeist, and that only made the appeal of seeing it aboard the *Adieu* even greater.

I was handed a life jacket as I boarded, which I threw on top of a stack of others. Most of the guests were sipping cocktails on the sun-deck under the blanket of clouds, low and faintly grey. A seafood buffet had become the centrepiece of the afternoon; not because the guests were ravenous, but because it was being served on the naked bodies of a dozen immobile, expressionless people.

They were a new crop of living props; I imagined the faerie dancers had been dismissed with payoffs after the Chantilly cream and blood-bath in the night. These new masochists had been arranged in a heap of knotted human flesh, like a nest of baby rats, their limbs, stomachs, backs, even in some places their faces, arrayed with the bounty of the sea. One woman, folded over another in an admirable chakrasana, balanced a ring of oysters on her stomach; ice melted between them and dripped in tracks down her pinking, gooseflesh skin onto the body below. Another had caviar heaped on her breasts. Nigiri and sashimi and tempura prawns were spaced along lounging arms. A man curled on his side formed a living basket for half a dozen lobsters; their claws draped his limbs as if they were trying to climb their way free. As I watched, the Italian duke scooped some caviar onto a cracker, dropping a dollop on the woman's face. She continued to stare expressionlessly into the middle distance, no doubt at a thorough retrospective of her life choices.

Mum wasn't on the deck, so I looked for her in the gallery, a temperature-controlled room of gleaming teak and silk-panelled walls, where a dozen paintings hung behind glass, a Matisse and a Goya among them, not to mention the *Venus*. She was resplendent in the centre of the room, always larger than I imagined. I pictured her stepping from her seashell onto the shore of Greece, grounded and safe, and her face—once so mild and at rest—seemed to stare witheringly. She looked done with our shit. Seeing no sign of Mum, I slipped back out.

I was about to head belowdecks to the bedrooms and wine cellar when I spotted Roman. He was leaning one elbow sulkily on the gunwale, tearing shells off shrimp and flinging them overboard, his fingers shiny with butter. I thought of his claim in the woods yesterday that he didn't want Jude to inherit the company—then of Jude's claim that he didn't truly want that either, that burning the thing to the ground would do just as well if it put paid to my dreams.

Roman hardly reacted when I stopped in front of him. If his gaze passed over my arm as he peeled his next shrimp—wondering if he could see the evidence of his curse as it spread—I didn't catch it.

"I talked to Jude," I said, pouring as much omen into the words as I could.

Still nothing. Roman discarded a shell with a snap of the wrist. "Makes one of us." As I started to speak, he said, "What is she even doing here? She's *poor*."

"*You're* poor." That earned me a contemptuous look. "When you said Jude would make a terrible CEO, did you know he only wanted it to stop *me* getting it?"

Roman's face twisted, but I couldn't read it. I had always experienced him as the overwhelming sensation of his feelings, smothering and starved. Without access to them, he was a cold presence, a void.

Is that why I'd been cursed with an *Empathy* cartridge? Did someone whose every need was telegraphed with the *Empathy* spell think they could turn me off using it and avoid giving themselves away? Someone like Roman?

"Jude and I don't sit around swapping sob stories about how our families don't love us," he said sharply. "You're not the centre of his universe, you know? Just because you gave him something nobody else could and it saved his life."

Apparently, I was. Roman's obvious jealousy said he knew it too. His possessiveness might be his fatal flaw if even *I* was a threat to him. I decided to push him.

"Aren't I? Because he told me this morning I'm the most important thing in the world to him."

He narrowed his eyes. He didn't believe me, or didn't want to.

"I thought it was strange too, given how close you two are." I shrugged. "And now he's freezing you out for Charlotte."

"I know what she's doing," he spat. "And deep down, he does too. It's like a self-harm ritual. He gets drunk on a new flavour of attention, like he thinks this is the person who'll finally heal him; then he figures out he's being used and he's hurt all over again. It's like clockwork." He took another shrimp off his plate and shook the excess butter over the side of the yacht. "It's his mess to make, so I leave him to it, but it's hard to watch."

I snorted a laugh. "You don't actually care," I said. "You're just pissed he knows you're using him too."

Roman placed the shrimp back down. When he looked up at me, he was so profoundly bored I almost felt scolded.

"You know, my dad's first wife was my mother's college roommate." He curled his lip in disgust. "He's an asshole. He has five kids by three women and we all hate him. And I was an art history major."

"What does that have to do with—"

"Jude and I have things in common. We're the same." He shrugged. "Except Jude always had more time for his shitty father."

I almost hit him. My hand made a fist. I imagined the soft give of his stomach as it connected. In the back of my mind, I heard motive, but what I wanted most was to tell this unrepentant gossip that Daddy was dead and catch his reaction, and that would be a mistake. I needed to draw out something solid.

"Yesterday," I said through gritted teeth, "forty people heard you call Jude a misery to be around. The week his father had a stroke."

Roman reared back. "So *what*? People don't talk to each other like that unless they care. A lot." He looked me up and down and found something that brought a smirk to his face. "I mean, you should know. Nothing like a sibling if you want someone to take for granted. Someone you have a connection to no matter what."

"What? That's not—"

"I mean, Charlotte was your barnacle before she was his, wasn't she? Must be lonely being a Maddock." Roman leaned close, and that edge of jealousy returned to his voice as he said, "He told you that you were the most important person in his life, that he would change everything about himself and become a fucking desk jockey just to hurt your feelings, and you came running straight to me to brag about it? It gladdened your lonely little heart that someone cared that much."

The threads of my interrogation—Roman resented the type of man my father was, and he truly cared for Jude, or believed he did—dangled just out of reach, my mind spinning. Where did I even start? I didn't want to explain myself to this walking misdemeanour, and yet I felt the explanations welling up inside me like a dam about to burst.

"You don't—know anything about me," I said stutteringly.

Roman smiled like I was caught. He tipped his chin at something over my shoulder, and I turned to see my mother beckoning for my attention. When I turned back around, Roman was walking away, his half-eaten plate of shrimp abandoned.

Fine. It wasn't like he could get very far. I'd tell my mother everything I'd learned about House Gothenburg and come back to this with a clear head, prepared for his mind games.

Mum met me in the middle of the deck.

"Teeny. Where have you been?"

"Up at the house." I almost said more, before remembering she wouldn't thank me for harping on about the stolen curse and its antidote. "There's something you need to know."

I led her down a set of steps to the promenade deck. A second set of stairs led farther below to the bedrooms. I eschewed it and followed the promenade towards the stern until we found a quiet spot where the rhythmic, guttural slap of water against the hull overpowered the chatter from above. There, I told her what the metropolitan faerie had said, surreptitiously mixed in with House Gothenburg's own confession to obscure the source: that the noble house was looking for an out.

"Ansgar's dead?" she said quietly when I was done.

"Not just Ansgar. It sounded like House Thebes are decimating them. Mariah's their *Maker* now. There's no one more senior left."

"Well, that explains one thing: Oz's assistant confirmed that the extra invitations he sent on Monday all went out to vampires. Montreal, Avignon, Lahore, Cuzco, *Thebes*—they were all invited, and then I assume some select others."

"Daddy invited the noble houses? Why?"

"I can't even guess, but at least now we know why none of them showed up." She swore under her breath and stared out across the lake. "Ansgar always referred to working with us as a high-stakes investment. Laying a bet. But he never once suggested he was breaking rank. It doesn't make a lick of sense—House Gothenburg approached *us*." She gestured in disbelief. "And they simply confessed this all to you? You're *sure* they implied they're not our allies anymore?"

"That part was perfectly clear." I lowered my voice. "Randolph saw whoever stole the curse on Friday night. They decided not to tell anyone because they don't want to risk pissing House Thebes off any more by offering us further help."

"He saw them?" All my incredulity was mirrored in the crease of her brow as she waited for it to sink in: there had been a witness all this time. "So you know who it is?"

"No, he couldn't identify them. He just caught a glimpse of someone he thought was our fake intruder on the loggia, heading towards the third quad, sometime before midnight."

"Of course. The loggia," she said, nodding absently. "I assume you've checked the footage?"

"It was during the fireworks," I said. "They whited everything out. It might be they were using the fireworks intentionally for cover, or they might just have not known the exterior CCTV could catch them, given the angle of the roof."

"Then can I make a request?" I gestured in invitation. "Will you please let this lie until tomorrow? Despite everything with Oscar, the weekend is a resounding success so far. All of our guests have committed to doses of *Immortality* for their whole families. And . . ." She lowered her voice conspiratorially. "I'm possibly moments away from disqualifying Jude entirely as a future head of the company. We're so close to the end now, and I want it to go off without a hitch."

I looked out at the lake so that I didn't have to lie to her face. "Alright." But I could not stop; I couldn't let it lie. So long as the murderer was undiscovered, she was still in danger, and so was Jude. "But please remember to—"

"Be careful. I am, I promise." She patted me on the shoulder as she passed me on her way back to the main deck. "Be sure to be at the ball this evening. I have a final surprise for the guests and I need your help."

"What is it?"

She grinned wickedly as she started to leave. "If I told you, it wouldn't be a surprise." She turned away. "And, Teeny? Put on a life jacket."

She left at a purposeful clip. I wrapped my hands around the polished teak of the railing and checked my watch. Sixteen hours until I could return to the faerie and pay my way out of this. By then, with any luck, Jude would have helped me identify the killer, and the police could be summoned to arrest them quietly. Tomorrow at 9 a.m. I could call my lawyers and tell them Daddy was dead, and the fight to inherit Fable would begin in earnest.

"I can't believe you would ask me that."

"Shhh."

I backed away from the railing until I met the wall. The voices came from the stern of the boat, just around the corner. It must have been an accident of the breeze and the lapping of water against the hull that I hadn't heard them approach. I edged closer, thankful I'd not found a chance to turn my Moth back on and give myself away with its glow.

"Let's be honest for a second." It was Jude. "You can whisper about how I deserve so much more and how I've been so mistreated in between making me come, but you're in this for the money. Fine with me, that's what I need you for. But sorry for wondering if it crossed your mind how many extra zeros you could squeeze out of me once I inherited."

"By *killing your dad* while he lay in a coma?" hissed Charlotte. "You asshole."

"You had the perfect opportunity. I was covering for you myself during that contrived little game last night. I looked Valentina in the eye and said you were there in the ballroom the whole time."

"I can't take you seriously. A hundred million and you think I want *more*? Actually, forget that. You're right: I regret not saying a billion. You wouldn't have blinked, would you?" In the pause that followed, I almost ran; I thought I'd been caught. Then the slow tread of heeled feet was followed by lower voices, as if she'd moved closer. "I've done everything you asked of me. Why would I jeopardise that now? Think."

"Fine. I believe you. But we have to be careful. Valentina's worked some of it out, I'm certain." I pressed myself harder against the wall and strained to hear over the rushing in my ears. "Are you absolutely sure no one saw you go into my dad's office?"

"I'm not stupid. No one saw me."

My mind tumbled over the details faster than I could slot them into place. Charlotte had snuck into Daddy's office at Jude's behest. Charlotte, who was staying on the corridor where the antidote bottle was later shattered and thrown away; who was seen upstairs by Fran minutes before the bottles were stolen from the collection; who had hustled her way into this party in the hopes it would help her make her fortune.

Charlotte, who'd been invited by Jude—whose only alibi was *Jude*.

I had stopped breathing. I had stopped *listening*. I shoved my spiralling thoughts down and tried to focus on the conversation, but it was almost over.

"Eight o'clock," Jude was saying. "My room. Now get to shore."

"You're not really doing this, are you?" she asked. Jude said nothing. "This yacht costs . . . I don't even *know*."

"Boats sink all the time."

"I think you have a skewed impression of how often that happens when you're not around. You are playing right into her hands. This is a setup. Fall for it, and all of this will have been for nothing. You'll never be CEO."

"I don't *want* to be CEO."

"Then why—"

"I'm not giving you a head start. Do the sensible thing and let my guests know it's time to disembark."

"Jesus Christ, you're messed up. FYI, therapy would be cheaper," said Charlotte, closer now. She was heading this way. I had five seconds to dive into the nearest room—a linen cupboard—before she swept past, a shape in emerald green, abstract between the slats in the door. Jude never followed, even as I held my position, breathing from my diaphragm and trying not to keel over at the first surprise wave of a disembowelling grief.

But there wasn't time to recover from it. Less than two minutes had passed before the *Adieu* gave her first jolt of injured shock, and my mother's reason for changing the plan this afternoon came into focus. Bracing myself against the wall, nausea swelling in my salivary glands, I followed Charlotte back to the main deck.

She had already torn through; the yacht was emptying, guests snatching up life jackets and skittering for shore. Smoked salmon and tuna tartare and crab salad were sloughing onto the deck as the human platters became a naked maelstrom of panic. Roman remained at the railing, Zazie beside him, both holding martinis aloft and staring down over the side of the boat. Even as I crossed to join them, the floor took on a lean. The roaring sound I had thought was in my head was coming from the boat as water attacked it below. Something previously battened down had been opened, and however Jude had done it, the *Adieu* had obediently begun to drown.

"How do you even sink a yacht this size?" said Zazie conversationally.

"I wouldn't know, I'm not totally fucking unhinged," replied Roman.

Zazie made a tutting noise and patted his cheek. "Oh, sweetheart."

The *Adieu* gave another mortal tilt, and even Roman Astor was forced to admit it was time to join those scrambling to disembark.

I wondered if everyone else felt it: the sense of unreality as we fled the sinking yacht. I heard questions volleyed about the safety of the Botticelli; some whispered that they'd thought Jude's penchant for art would protect the *Adieu*. I might have been similarly stunned, if I hadn't seen Oscar Maddock's sickbed emptied that morning, his body quietly claimed by an undertaker while the rest of the house was at breakfast.

At last, an incredulous hysteria rippled through the onlookers like the lake water batting at our feet. Word was spreading that *The Birth of Venus* wasn't here among us; that she was returning to the water, as if she'd taken a single step out of her seashell, looked around, and thought: *hard pass*.

My mother had conjured this like a witch. Take the corpse of one parent, mix with an indelible grief for the other at precisely the moment her nephew cracked in two, and she had sunk a billion dollars and any future he may have had at Mythos. Our incredulity was the entire point, for what kind of madman would do such a thing, and how could he ever be trusted at the helm of the company? I wondered numbly if she'd killed my father for this, but found I was too wretched to care.

She was down at the shoreline, deep in conversation with half a dozen members of the board. As I watched, one broke free and joined a gaggle of others. Something was being passed around with the speed of consensus, frictionless as oil. The only dissenter was Hunter, and though he looked like he was putting up a fight, from his posture, it was half-hearted. The decision was already made. Mum found me in the crowd and gave a single nod.

It was mine. I was the next CEO of Mythos.

I waited for the dreadful grief to transmute; for victory to ball it up and toss it away with a *fuck you*. I had won. The company was mine. The house would follow. Tomorrow morning I'd be rid of this curse. Healed. *Complete*.

I waited as the bow of the *Adieu* sunk beneath the surface, leaving nothing but a churning foam as the guests dispersed towards the golf carts.

I waited, but the relief never came.

At last I was the only person on the shore. I watched Jude. He stood on the pier, a wrench dangling from his fingers, oblivious to us all and to the wind whipping at his clothes. How I hoped it hurt.

An accomplice. A match made in hell. I was sick to discover that in some damaged corner of my soul, whether out of kinship or the unspoken rules of our dance, I had trusted Jude. I had trusted him, and I had conceived of Charlotte as some pitiful bee, struggling to climb out of a glass, as yet unaware that her stinger had been spent and she was dying. I hadn't imagined that to combine all of his need with all of hers could kill me.

But I wasn't dying because Jude wanted the Maddock empire. My crime was being the most important thing in the world to him. I hadn't heard the declaration for what it was; hadn't understood how often he thought about the two of us, and Aunt Georgia, and the stem cell transplant, and wondered what it would take to stop feeling the way he did. Envying me, with an obsession that left no room for anything else—it was misery. I knew because I would be living it too if I felt for Jude what he did for me. I just hadn't known how far he would go to never have to think of me again.

But I did now. And just in time too.

18

Luc had gotten House Gothenburg alone, and then House Gothenburg had left. Without the threat of withholding a product they didn't need, nothing had been keeping them here. In the end, security had been too afraid of making enemies of vampires to stall them and alert my mother.

My anger was a balm. It gathered up all my hellish feelings of weakness—everything that had risen to the surface as the *Adieu* had gone down—and forged it into something distracting and useful: a blade I wanted to plunge into Lucas Sayle's neck for whatever had happened after I left the vampires alone.

It wasn't that Jude had tried to kill me—it was that I'd allowed it to happen. I had had a vulnerability for years and never even recognised it. Of course he would have noticed the *Empathy* cartridges. Of course he wanted me dead. I had been stupid and pathetic and naïve not to realise it. I had been a child crying for her mother, waiting for her father, refusing to discover that nobody would protect her. Never learning.

But I had learned now.

And while I was culling weaknesses, I would start with one that felt like less of a psychic wrecking ball: the vampire and his lies.

I swept into the vast formal sitting room. As the clouds thickened and the wind picked up, the fireplaces at either end had roared to life. Luc stood alone over the flames, an arm resting against the far mantel. I passed beneath the chandeliers—weeping glass structures, fungal and alien, their tendrils reaching for the people far below. I passed guests gathered on the clusters of couches, sipping coffee, whispering about Jude and the *Adieu,* conserving their energy for one final bacchanalia when the sun went down. They grew dim as I approached the roaring fire and Luc turned to face me.

"They're gone," I said.

Shadows played across one side of his face as the flames leapt and writhed. "Yes."

Why? I wanted to scream. *What did you say that I wasn't allowed to hear?* But I couldn't let myself. I could swallow my weakness when I believed he might be my ally, if it would help me live. But he wasn't on my side, I was certain of it now, and to betray the storm behind my ribs was one indignity more than I could bear. I folded my arms and held it in.

"Did they tell you anything?"

"I had to read between the lines, but I don't think Mariah has a handle on things as Maker. House Gothenburg are divided on how to proceed. There's a faction that think they should stay the course and keep working with Mythos. Then there's Mariah and her side, who are looking for an out. I think she was persuaded to come to the party. Maybe she thought it would pacify her detractors and avoid another round of slaughter." He looked into the fire. "She'll need a lot of luck, I think."

I let the silence linger—fractured at the edges by the rumble and snap of the fire and the conversations of the other guests, made formless as they echoed off the marble—but he said nothing more.

"And what would you do," I asked at last, "if you were them?"

The question surprised him; his gaze snapped my way like it hoped to snare something. "I don't know what you mean."

"Oh? You say you don't know what House Gothenburg will do. It looks to me like they've already decided. They left. Whatever you said to them made up their minds." Luc made no reply, but a tension crept into his features. "Explain something to me: What will be done to your reputation by *you* being here? My father sent invitations to a dozen vampires, it seems, but you're the only one who showed up. Are the houses going to come for you like they have for House Gothenburg?"

He shook his head slowly, as if I were a mountain lion that might pounce at any sudden movement. "The houses don't concern themselves with the activities of common vampires." He glanced at the room—no one was watching us—then came closer. "If you have something to say to me, then say it."

God, I wanted to. And why not, if he could already see under the edges of my control? How could I expect myself to keep playing a future CEO when all I wanted to do was howl?

"How did you know my father?" I pressed again.

"I didn't."

"Then how did he know you?"

"I don't think he did. I think when he sent out those invites, he was anticipating a problem and trying to solve it."

"What problem?" He waited, stone-faced, for me to understand him. "You. Vampires."

Was that really what had been playing on Daddy's mind in the hours before the stroke? That Mythos needed the support of the wider vampire community? Why? The tonic was nearly complete; the vampire venom donated by House Gothenburg had long ago played its part. If Gothenburg had disregarded some obscure practise or broken faith in doing so, what concern was it of ours? What problem, exactly, had he anticipated?

If Luc knew of one—if this was more than a theory about the workings of Oscar Maddock's mind—he clearly wasn't sharing. My frustration started to boil over.

"Say something," I snapped.

"What would you like me to say?"

"That you've been using me."

I had no proof. No motive. The accusation erupted from the black bile organ of all my worst fears and hung between us, sparkling in the firelight. As much as the words surprised me, I meant them. What if the end he had in mind by helping me benefitted him more? What if, in thinking I was the one keeping him close, I had left myself vulnerable to harm?

What if Jude and I had never been competitors and I was somehow still losing?

Luc came close enough that his breath tickled my cheek. "I've been using you," he said against my skin. Through the loose and drunken feeling, I grasped that he was mocking me. Slowly, he bent his head, and a shiver moved over my ear, then my jaw, to my neck. I swallowed, but it didn't shift the anchor in my sternum pulling me closer to him. His hands found my waist. Mere paces away, the other guests droned on, but I didn't care. "We've been using each other, haven't we, Valentina?" His lips brushed my throat. Barely there. Not enough. "Haven't you got what you wanted from me in the bargain?"

A taste of a new kind of fear. It hummed through me now and set me trembling. I was helpless to stop myself as I took his face in my hands and brought his lips close to mine.

But he pulled away. Into the space between us rushed my anger and despair. Luc gripped my shoulders—exposed by the straps of my day dress—and tilted my right side towards the fire. A metallic flicker gleamed in the corner of my eye; the same that had caused Luc to pull away from me.

"Look," he said, urging me to turn so that my cursed arm was closer to the fire.

Bit by bit, I tilted my body towards the light. We watched the flame strike gold, first on my fingers, then my wrist, then up the length of my forearm and past my elbow. The gilding shone under firelight like real metal inlaid in my skin as far as my shoulder and beyond.

The threads crept nearly the length my clavicle.

"It's too far," I said on a breath, afraid if I spoke too loud, I could disturb the veins of gold and make them bleed even farther. "It's too far."

Luc spread his palm wide and walked his fingers across my skin, measuring. When he lay his hand over my chest, his thumb above my heart, a tremor of something shuddered through me again.

"The Gilded Grip is supposed to take three days," he said, his voice low to match mine, "but it's moving much faster than that. If it keeps an even pace . . . I think it's going to reach your heart in exactly two."

The fire cast flecks of gold into his eyes, illuminating an understanding I knew he saw in mine.

"Tonight."

He nodded.

My insides tried to flip over in panic. I checked my watched; it was three in the afternoon. Nine hours until midnight. "How?"

Luc bit his lip as if he was remembering the taste of my blood. "The decay of the magic? I don't know. I'm not an expert in fae curses."

"Then I have to go back. Right now."

"I'm coming with you."

"You're not."

"Valentina, let me—"

"I don't need you," I bit out as I marched away. "Stay here and hide in the shadows."

19

"I said dawn."

And yet she'd unlatched the chain and let me in without a flicker of surprise. Now we sat across from each other at her kitchen table as the sour, rotting scent of her pipe seeped into my clothes. To my right, the prehistoric contents of the terrarium moved under the humming electric light.

"It's become a matter of greater urgency." I removed a brick of cash from my bag and placed it on the table. It was double the thickness of that morning's, as agreed, but she barely glanced at it before drawing deep from her pipe and turning away. The carved bone instrument trembled.

At the corner of my eye, one of the snails became unbalanced and toppled from a stick. The faerie made a sound of sympathy and rose. Clicking her tongue like she was luring in a cat, she reached her fingers into the terrarium and lifted the ugly beast out.

"Can you have it ready now?" I pressed.

She said nothing, only petted the snail, a litany of reassuring nonsense pouring from her in a whisper. It went on a long time—so long that I think I began to understand.

"Yes and no," she said at last. She put her lips right to the slick flesh that would be the snail's chin and kissed it. Both the snail and I recoiled.

"Meaning?"

She was silent still as she replaced the ill-fated thing in its habitat and drew the lid closed. I'd made a brief study of the room. The evidence of work having occurred and been completed was tidy but there: a pestle and mortar, something like a crucible upturned on the draining board. The place was cleaner than it had been that morning. The smell was the same: damp and vegetal under the reek of the pipe smoke.

My host went to the fridge—still she didn't look at me—and removed something palm-sized. It tinkled like glass.

"Your curse is not what I was led to expect."

"It's not Gilded Grip?"

She came to the table, but instead of taking her seat, she hovered by mine. I saw the anxiety on her face and pretended it wasn't there. "Yes and no," she said again. I fidgeted, restless. "I cannot tell a lie. You know that about my kind, don't you?"

I knew almost everything about magic. What the code it was written in looked like, where the cartridges and packaging were made. I knew how often Mythos serviced installations of *Fuel* and *Swift* and *Edifice* and all our other products embedded in infrastructure and industry. I knew we'd be the only provider of power and transport technology within ten years.

I didn't know a faerie couldn't lie. I hadn't known they lived in high-rises or that vampires hated water and wouldn't crumble to ash in the sun. I had a playground knowledge of crude magic: fairy stories and cautionary tales. The truths in them were accidents, and to believe them seemed naïve. Even then, a part of me believed—hoped—that I would look back on this one day and think I'd remembered it wrong; that magic had always come in lacquered white boxes and the world had burst into being in a blaze of trademarked Mythos Blue.

I nodded anyway.

"Good. Because I tried, do you hear? I wanted your money. I agreed to take it, didn't I?"

Was she asking me? Exploiting a loophole by phrasing it as a question? No, she was after a verbal waiver. Another bargain, that I wouldn't punish her.

"What are you saying?" I said, though I already knew.

She placed a bottle in front of me, smaller than a shot of liquor, its contents a diluted gold. It was in my hand a moment later, its weight and coolness the proof I needed that it was real.

"I'm saying if that doesn't work, don't come back. There's nothing else I can do."

I held the bottle tighter. "Why wouldn't it work?"

The faerie tapped the table with her false fingers, swallowed. "I told you: the magic in your veins is not what I thought. Make no mistake, it'll kill you. But it's foreign. Do you understand me?"

"No."

"You said matters have grown more urgent. How?"

"It's progressing too fast," I said. "I was told Gilded Grip gave the victim three days to live, but the gilding is nearly at my heart already."

She nodded as I said this but hesitated to reply. "That's because what's cursed you is different. *Damaged*. I did my best to match it with that"—she gestured to the bottle enclosed in my fist—"but if it doesn't work, it's because the magic can't be reversed. It's not my fault."

It had to work, so her warning registered as advice meant for someone else. Small print. I pushed the wad of cash towards her. The faerie stepped back.

"I don't want it."

I laughed, shaking my head. "But that was the bargain. It's what we agreed."

"Keep your money. Just scrub me from your memory." She leant over me and grabbed my arm roughly. "I won't go up against this power. I don't want its notice."

I was numb to her nails digging into my flesh. What ancient magic could scare even her? A god? A celestial being? Had Jude somehow bargained with powers the likes of which even Martin Maddock had never dealt with?

"You have to take my money," I begged. Or else the bargain wasn't struck. I didn't know how it worked, only that an antidote that would save me had to be worth the agreed-upon price, and this one wasn't.

It was worth nothing, I realised, as the faerie produced the cash I'd given her that morning and forced it into my hand.

"Tell no one we met. Tell no one I tried to help you." She pulled me to my feet and towards the door. "Please. Take your tonic and go. I don't have anything else for you."

"Where do I go if it doesn't work?" I said at the threshold. "You have to tell me who'll help me."

"No one," she said, already closing the door. "No one can help you. No one can fix this."

With a click, the door closed, the faerie's final truth ringing in my ears. The light in the hallway was different. The smell of forest floor had been replaced with the artificial aromas from the crack den next door. If not for the glass bottle sweating in my fist, I might have dreamed it. Under the fluorescent lights of the corridor, the liquid had an aquamarine iridescence. The bottle itself looked bought in bulk—probably online—and was made of clear, unornamented glass with a black metal screw top. Nothing like the gold, glowing glass of the shards Charlotte had discarded.

I unscrewed the bottle. The tonic smelled grassy and astringent. Everything I believed of crude magic reared its head, and for a brief flash I recognised myself to be insane. But I remembered I was dying anyway, pinched my nose, and poured the whole bottle into my mouth. I swallowed heavily and nearly choked. The inside of my mouth tasted of citrus rind and the mineral tang of seaweed. Nothing seemed to happen, but that had been true when I was cursed too. There was only one way to be sure.

The folding chair creaked. The crack person from that morning was still here and watched me apprehensively. He was thick-set, with a varsity jacket and sleepy, jaundiced eyes. My fear of him—and the gun in his waistband—had been so overwhelming that looking at him now was like remembering a childhood nightmare. Convenient, because he could, without a doubt, get me a lighter.

When I put this request to him, he stared at me as if I'd said I wanted to tour his crack den, please. I pulled the two stacks of cash out of my bag—was it twenty thousand? Fifty? I hadn't counted—and offered them to him. "This is everything I have." He tensed, his eyes on the money and then my bag. I put the money inside and offered him the whole thing—wallet, Montblanc pen, hand sanitiser. "Take it. Take everything, just get me a light."

Money is so often where the pity of strangers ends. They can smell what you're striving for, because they want it too: a life without pain or misfortune. Money and power enough to insulate them against everything from a paper cut to heartbreak. They delight in every indication that you don't have it yet, because they sense how much closer you are than them and it makes them sick with envy. Your suffering is mocked. Your exploitation—should they get the chance—is fair game.

So when the crack person took my bag from me, I started removing my earrings. My Moth was still on *Incognito,* but he might recognise that my baseball cap cost a few hundred—was that worth taking? Were my shoes?

"Lady, stop." He fished out the cash, which he tucked into his jacket. The bag he returned to me, shaking his head with something between disapproval and sympathy. Then he was gone. A moment later, he was handing me a cheap plastic lighter. He tipped his chin at the apartment next door. "If *she* can't help you, this sure as hell won't." Perhaps fearing I would come to my senses and demand my money back, he shut himself into the apartment and I was left alone.

So this was where misfortune trumped wealth: outside the home of a faerie, with an empty bottle of magic and a five-figure handbag I couldn't give away. A door, shut in my face by a drug dealer who'd identified—correctly, I feared—that I was the most wretched, hopeless soul in this building.

And that was before I flicked on the lighter, held it to my arm, and confirmed the antidote hadn't worked.

20

When the pulse of Mythos Blue faded from Fran's car, and that colossal monument to the life I might have had loomed before me, Mario was waiting.

He stood at the head of the carport looking unimpressed, thick arms folded across his chest, eyes boring through the windscreen and into mine. With a lazy flick of his hand, he gestured for me to get out, and like a zombie I obeyed.

"Come with me," he said with a sigh. There could be no more consequences for a dead girl walking, so when he turned and made for the house, I followed.

It was four o'clock in the afternoon, and I had eight hours left to live. The truth of this was so large that it was meaningless. That I would certainly die was no hairpin turn, but a final, gentle bend at the end of one. But my murder, and at Jude's hand? *That* had hardened and clarified until it was sharper and realer than anything I'd ever known. He had taken enough from me. He needed to pay.

Charlotte too. It had to have been Charlotte who planted the curse; her room was on the same corridor as Randolph's. What had convinced her to kill me in the course of an evening? How long did she think about it? A hundred million, she had said. Pocket money. Did they fuck before Jude propositioned her? Or was it after, to seal the deal? Had she betrayed the hustle, or did this count? I catalogued my questions in service of the confrontation that was coming, a developing plan for the paltry remains of my future: exacting vengeance.

I'd thought Mario was taking me to my mother, but when we climbed the main staircase, he ducked into the security office and held the door for me to follow. It was a dark, windowless room with a wall of CCTV monitors above a control panel. Quiet aspects of gardens, the perimeter wall, rows of ivied arches filled the screens. And on a table in the centre of the room, glowing faintly with Mythos magic, the two floors of Fable laid out in miniature, a three-dimensional blueprint populated by firefly-like pins that moved slowly about the table as *Radar* tracked them.

Mario moved around the *Radar* setup to the monitors and wordlessly indicated for me to look at one as he hit a button on the control panel. "Recognise this?"

I didn't. It was an anonymous corner of the garden, with a hedge running down one side of the screen and a small outbuilding in the corner.

"No."

"How about now?" he said as a pulse of blue light flared then faded, the source just out of shot. Suddenly the tiny corner of the garden *was* familiar—that was the outbuilding Fran parked behind. I checked the time stamp on the screen—it was from this morning. He'd caught me sneaking out of Fable *twice*.

"Why didn't you say anything?" I asked.

"Because you just lost your dad. Figured you needed a breather. God knows I do."

As he spoke, he clicked through to another angle—an image of me hotfooting it to Fran's car, alone. At least he hadn't caught me sneaking Luc off the premises with me. Right before I exited the frame, I looked over my shoulder as if to talk to someone, but it clearly wasn't enough for Mario to realise there was a vampire with me, invisible to the camera.

"Are you going to tell my mother?" I asked.

"I was thinking about it."

I imagined staring down her disappointment, her gutting lack of surprise, and found I had no space for any emotion but my anger at Jude. She could no longer wound me with her indifference or frustration, now that I'd taken a mortal injury that—to my infinite surprise—was so much worse. I knew Jude could ruin my life—I hadn't known he could hurt my feelings.

No, Mum couldn't touch me now, but she could still get in my way. She could fill my last hours with arguments and restrictions. She might even decide to eject me from the party once and for all. And I had business here at Fable. There was justice to claim.

"Don't tell her," I said, the words weak and small. I was at his mercy. "Please, Mario."

For just a beat, he softened, as if I'd caught him by surprise.

"Didn't know that word was in the Maddock vocabulary." He splayed his hands on the *Radar* setup and stared unreadably at the model. After an endless moment, he said, "If it happens again—"

"It won't," I cut in. "I swear. Thanks. And . . . sorry I never say please."

He gave a single nod, so terse I was afraid he was about to change his mind. I needed to get out of there before he did, but if there was a way to nail Jude and Charlotte for what they'd done to me, it was in that room, the security hub for all of Fable. They had to have slipped up *somehow*. I took in the *Radar* spell that refused to incriminate either of them, the wall of CCTV feeds that hadn't caught a thing.

"No footage from outside my father's room when he was killed?" I asked.

Mario shook his head. "Not a flicker of movement."

I'd thought as much. Despite what she'd claimed to Jude on the yacht, I was certain Charlotte had gone rogue and killed Daddy too. She knew not to approach from the loggia a second time—that getting in view of the cameras without the fireworks would get her spotted—and she knew to leave a note identical to the first three. Those two facts together—plus my certainty that Jude would never have killed Daddy—made her the only suspect.

But as evidence, it was worthless. I couldn't show the police the damning footage of her *not* getting caught on camera. The only physical evidence they would have were the notes and the solid-gold heart of a dead girl.

Unless Jude and Charlotte had needed to communicate by illicit means.

"Have you checked that you still have everyone's devices?" I asked. If someone had noticed Luc's missing, I could pretend I knew nothing about it.

"No need," said Mario. "They're under lock and key at the gatehouse. At least two of my people are always there, and no guests have been anywhere near it."

The last part was no surprise—the gatehouse was at the other end of a drive over a mile long. Since they'd all arrived by *Swift*, the guests wouldn't even have passed it.

But the rest of it? I glanced around the monitor room and all at once realised how bare it was. No cupboards, no shelves. Just the control panel along one wall with the monitors above and *Radar* running on the table in the centre.

"You're not keeping them in here," I said. Not a question but a realisation that came down on me with a thud.

"We don't keep valuables in the security office." I don't know what my face did to draw interest from Mario, of all people, but he added, "What?"

"Did Lucas Sayle hand in a phone?" I asked.

"Yeah. Why?"

That morning in the library replayed in my head—Luc's hesitancy, my sense that I was being assessed. Even after what had happened between us, he'd been unsure whether to trust me, and he'd decided against it. Everything that followed had been a performance, a lie designed only for me.

"It was a decoy," I said numbly. "Luc's had his phone the whole time."

He was sleeping when Mum, Hunter, Mario, and I arrived at his room. He made us wait outside while he put some clothes on.

"I don't know what this one's supposed to do against one of them," said Hunter, nodding first to Mario, then Luc's door. He was shifting his weight, straightening his shirt collar. Mario was still, but his eyes betrayed a faint anxiety as they failed to settle on anything.

"Nobody's doing anything," Mum said. She was more composed, but her words were clipped and firm the way they were when she was trying to force a truth. "He's a guest and we're his hosts. This'll be awkward but civil and that's all there is to it."

Except that wasn't all there was to it. We were confronting a vampire, one I'd convinced them had conned his way here. I'd known Luc wasn't to be trusted, but there'd been no one else, so I'd cast him as an ally—maybe even a friend. I'd been so desperate not to be alone, so weak for the promise of comfort that even a vampire would do.

This was how Jude must have done it, I realised; how he'd swathed his pain and heartache and obsession in crafted skins of rage. My anger at Luc was a skin too, a coat of paint over black mould, a safe thing to feel instead of hollowed out, just for now. Just until the terrible thing I'd almost decided to do solidified.

The door opened a second time, and Luc stepped back to let us in. He tried to catch my eye as I passed, but I didn't know what I'd do if I saw another lie in his, so I swept by like he was a doorman.

"Wait out here," Mum said to Mario.

Luc closed the door on him, and the sunlight from the hall was banished. Every floor-to-ceiling curtain along the loggia wall was carefully arranged to let in not even a sliver of sunlight. The only light was from two bedside lamps.

Aside from the bed—roughly made while we waited in the hall—the room didn't look or feel like it had been occupied for two days. None of Luc's belongings littered the surfaces and chairs. No scent of cologne or sleep or laundry hung in the air. It was like he made no impression on the world, as he made no impression on a mirror or a reel of film.

If Luc knew what was happening, he gave nothing away. He joined us in the centre of the room with his hands on his hips and waited. Mum held up the phone Mario had retrieved from the gatehouse, the one Luc had handed in on arrival.

"Does this even work?" she said.

Again, he tried to catch my eye, and this time I let him. I needed him to see that I knew, that I'd caught him. I hoped he saw an enemy in my face, one who'd go to her grave cursing him.

His smile was half grimace as he turned back to Mum. "I need to pack, don't I?"

"We have a few questions first," she said.

Luc went to the bed and perched on the edge, as calm as he'd been when he arrived on the threshold on Friday.

"I'm working on a theory," Mum said. "And I want you to tell me if I'm right."

He gestured for her to go ahead.

"All the invitations Oz sent out on Monday appear to have gone to vampires. I think Oz had perhaps grown attuned to a . . . dissatisfaction in your community. I think Mythos have unwittingly insulted not just the noble houses but vampires in general by accepting House Gothenburg's offer of partnership and taking them into the company. Am I close?"

"Yes," said Luc. The moment stretched on as we waited to learn how hard he would make this. After a long minute, he continued. "House Gothenburg are young. Ansgar founded his house not even four hundred years ago, but he's been unsatisfied with being a low-status house for half of that. He saw a chance to elevate himself"—here he pointed to us—"and he took it."

"How was helping Mythos supposed to elevate him?" said Hunter.

Luc shrugged. "The usual ways. Money. Power. You're the biggest company in the world and the only one dealing in magic, and now House Gothenburg are the only vampires with a seat on your board. The only thing is, most of us don't consider them entitled to unilaterally enter into that deal, so yeah, people were pissed off."

Mum frowned. She started to speak several times before settling on, "You're saying Mythos should have made an agreement with *all* the houses?"

Luc broke out that unfriendly grin, and I marvelled at how I had ever forgotten that Jude wasn't my only predator.

"We certainly wouldn't have gotten here if you had. But this isn't just about house politics." He gestured to himself. "We all have a stake in this. I've never met Oscar Maddock, that was the truth, but I came to represent many of us." He nodded at my mother. "I think you're right. I think Oscar somehow recognised the fracture he accidentally helped cause and invited us here to offer some concessions. I only kept a phone on me to keep contact with some other interested parties."

At the mention of concessions, Mum had drawn a breath, and in the quiet following Luc's speech, all eyes turned to her. Her face cycled through shades of confusion before settling on something like chagrin.

"There'll be no concessions," she said tightly. "Mythos won't deal with dishonest parties. There's no trust here."

"Understood." Luc rose, and I thought helplessly of some fanged beast unfurling itself. The sudden tension in Mum and Hunter told me I wasn't the only one. Luc's gaze settled for a long, unblinking moment on my mother, then Hunter, before he said, "Trust is . . . everything in matters this delicate. Isn't it?"

Something snapped in Hunter, and he stepped closer to Luc, his shoulders bunched in unspent aggression.

"Make no mistake," he said, falsely civil. "The full force of the most powerful entity on this planet will come down on top of you and your associates if you even try to move against us."

Luc laughed. "I don't doubt you mean it," he said, hands raised. "But I swear, it's never been my intention to damage your company."

Mum went to the door and brought in Mario. Just Mario, no miniature army of quaking security staff to frog-march Luc from the building. The air of doubt and absurdity was palpable, yet we all ignored it. Yes, Luc was a vampire, but more important, he was a guest, and so the normal rules of hospitality applied. He would surely understand he was no longer welcome—between equals, what bearing could the spell broken on the threshold possibly have on that?

Mum folded her hands together, then refolded them. "I'm sorry about this," she said, and I felt my face twist in displeasure. Daddy wouldn't have apologised; Luc didn't deserve it. Even as the words landed, she seemed to reconsider them; there was more bite in her voice as she said, "But Mario is going to see you off the premises."

Luc only gave a resigned nod. Mum was already making for the door, Hunter on her heels, as he turned to the closet and brought out his weekend bag. I lingered in the gloom until they were gone, then crossed the room to Luc.

"Why me?" I said, shaking with rage.

He glanced up from the dresser, where he was stuffing socks and a sweater—normal things—into his bag. "Sorry?"

"You targeted me. You came wanting Jude, but then you picked me instead." I swallowed down my dread and asked what I could hardly bear to know. "Is it because you thought I was the weaker mark?"

Luc smiled, this time with the edges filed away. "No, Valentina. It's because you're Oscar Maddock's heir, not him."

It would have warmed me to the core if it was true, but I couldn't think on the idea at all—I would combust. I only turned and fled, and Luc asked nothing about my second visit to the faerie or the progress of my murder. Whatever purpose I'd served for him, he'd been thwarted, and we were through. When I shut the door behind me, it closed like a book.

Mum squeezed my arm. "Well done, Teeny." She shot a triumphant look at Hunter, who threw back daggers. First the yacht; now I had neutralised a threat from the vampire community at the eleventh hour. If the CEO race hadn't been over before, it was now.

But I couldn't stop Jude taking it, not even by using my final hours to have him arrested for my murder. I pictured handcuffs, paparazzi, a televised trial. The media salivating over the end of the story of Jude and Valentina Maddock. And what a finale. Jude with a dozen star lawyers arrayed around him and no physical evidence. Charlotte, right there to take the fall, her money having never materialised to suggest a connection. Newsreels sharing photographs of a brave and smiling seven-year-old boy, hairless from the chemotherapy; the decade-old footage of a speedboat hauled from a lake, for colour. And pictures of my old face, before my last *Polish*, because I had been dead for months.

That wasn't justice. Real justice was nothing less than the same correction I had been demanding my whole life: Jude paying in full for what he'd taken. Fear and denial were the silt I rinsed away until, underneath, the shape of my want started to show itself, unthinkable and perfect: an annihilation, at once horror-drenched and soothing. Every reckless impulse that had ever gotten its claws in me, every self I had run from—they were meek, grey things, but this new and shining beast trembled at its own daring.

Or was there any daring in it at all? I had been saved from any reckoning by the curse in my veins. How poetic, that my death would provide the opportunity to restore balance, to make this fair.

A life for a life. It was mine to take back anyway.

21

Dinner was to be served at seven, followed by a candlelit ball until late.

The guests wiled away the gloomy late afternoon playing billiards and cards, or in the home spa we had crammed with massage therapists and facialists for the weekend. A croquet match was attempted on the blustery lawn but was abandoned amidst peals of Athena's shrieking laughter when no one could score against the wind.

I didn't try to enjoy anything. I didn't say any goodbyes. Both required a kind of peace with what was about to happen, and if there'd ever been a chance of that, then it would have had to start two days ago. If I tried to savour the scent of the lavender or the birds chirruping from the forest now, I may as well just start screaming until my lungs were raw, because that's where it would end. No, it was too late to make anything of these last hours but revenge. Whatever I couldn't exorcise with blood, I was taking to the grave.

With six hours left until midnight, nothing could hold my attention but the preparations, so I began. The kitchen was full of witnesses, chefs and serving staff I had been prepared to encounter. I strode in with my cupped hands held up before me like an offering. Warily, the half dozen staff downed tools and stared at me. Or rather, stared at my hands and the items spilling from them. A sapphire earring fell to the floor, landing with a glassy smack.

"You didn't see me," I said, dumping the jewels on a counter. "Got it?"

The catering staff exchanged looks. A big guy came closer, eyes on the bundle of diamonds and other precious stones. I'd cleaned out every jewel I had with me, including the bracelet from Daddy that I had almost bargained away to a faerie. I wouldn't need it anymore.

"That's it?" said the big guy. "You weren't here?"

"That's it," I confirmed.

They descended.

"No squabbling now," I said as I went to the strip of knives. I chose long thin ones, two of them. Behind me, one of the white-smocked staff said something about getting straight to a pawnshop.

"No." When I turned around, they were all looking my way. If any of them had a thought in their head about what I was up to, it was *look how much cash those knives have made me*, because none of them said anything. "You have to finish here. That's my other condition."

I couldn't have the catering staff dipping out and triggering a change of plans. They accepted this with little fuss. I wrapped the knives in a dish towel and returned to my room.

Dusk was falling fast. The clouds hastened the failing of the light, but the wind droned on, heaving them across the heavens. A scar of orange bleeding into pink was tearing open on the western horizon. A final sunset. That felt like a good omen, even if I couldn't bring myself to dwell on it or look too long. When I did, a feeling like I was barrelling too fast towards a drop-off overcame me. There were many things I couldn't think on for fear of that feeling. Jude—for better or worse, my brother—having murdered me was one of them. Me murdering him, another. I had to let this sense of fate, this righting I felt was an obligation as much as it was a choice, pull me onwards.

Shortly before seven, I changed into leggings and a T-shirt. There were two of them, and there was a chance they were both stronger than me. My advantages would be surprise and weapons, but the ability to move unencumbered by the gown I'd planned to wear that evening would also be a plus. It's not like I was heading down to dinner. My Moth was still hidden with *Incognito*, so I didn't have to worry about hiding its light.

By the time I stepped out onto the loggia, the clear sky had gone from a crease at the corner of the world to a widening swath of indigo stretching my way. It was still thirty minutes until eight—four and a half hours until the end—time enough for me to scope out a hiding spot and be ready when they arrived. I clutched the knives, still swaddled in the dish cloth, and edged along the wall to Jude's room. A couple of lamps shone inside, but it was empty. The door to his bathroom, hanging ajar, showed that was empty too. The first in the row of glass doors opened smoothly at the turn of a handle, and I stepped inside.

I rarely had occasion to go into Jude's room, and I'd forgotten how heinous his taste was. Before I could close the door, the breeze set a macramé hammock swinging and a chime tinkled in the corner. An honest-to-god *futon* lay under a canopy of some homespun, sand-coloured linen. There was nothing that resembled a chair, just the hammock and a plethora of Moroccan floor pillows.

Between a jade statue of the Buddha and a collection of rain sticks mounted on driftwood shelves—because apparently Jude had never met a culture he didn't want to appropriate—was a folding screen in painted silk. It was almost perfectly positioned; someone would have to venture right into the corner of the room to look behind it. I stood a good chance of cornering them if it came to that, so I turned the latch on every loggia door to narrow the avenues of escape and crouched behind the screen.

Never let it be said that Valentina Maddock couldn't stage an ambush.

Every minute might have been an hour for how they crawled by. I avoided all introspection by playing out different scenarios in my head: where they might stand, how I might get a few crucial feet closer before I was seen, whether to play it cool when I showed myself or lunge, knives out. If I acted innocent and kept my weapons hidden, I could incapacitate one of them—Jude first; we had the same fine-boned Cabot build, but he had the longer reach—with a knife to the gut before all hell broke loose. It would be better to be underestimated, but striding out, blades in hand, might make them panic and act stupid. The loggia doors would unlock with a turn of the latch, but if they were already in a frenzy, maybe that would be enough to convince their fear-addled minds they were trapped.

Whatever the scenario, I only saw myself winning. In hindsight, suffering anything from humiliation to grievous bodily harm was the more likely outcome, so I suppose it's a good thing it didn't play out like that.

Jude got to the room just before eight. I held my breath as he passed the folding screen, his languid stride visible through the cracks. He didn't pause or give any indication he knew I was there, but went straight to the bathroom, casting aside his shirt as he did. A moment later, he started running the shower.

The water shut off just as the first tendrils of steam began to escape through the half-open door. It must have been exactly eight when Charlotte let herself in. A mirror hung in my sight line on the opposite wall, and she stopped to look at herself. She had rotated back to the same red dress I'd seen her in on Friday night, but twisted her hair up for a different effect (like that would stop anyone noticing). Nothing in the eyes she made at the mirror as she curled a tendril of hair with her fingers said she cared. I searched for the change in her—for a murderer—but of course I saw none. If you're bloodthirsty every day of your life, you'll never give yourself away.

Jude emerged wearing a pair of loose trousers, his blond hair sodden and darkened to a muddy grey. In slivers through the gaps, I caught flashes of the tattoo on his chest—a skeleton's hand clutching a bouquet of spring flowers. At certain angles, when the light struck his skin just so, you could still see the raised flesh of a small scar where the venous access port had been removed. Everything in me squirmed; there they both were. Nothing left to wait for. But quick and mindless no longer felt like the way to go. My chosen moment had to feel right. And it would; I was dispensing justice. I was balancing the scales.

Charlotte saw no reward for her bedroom eyes or the way she let a hand linger at her cleavage as Jude went to her. He only held out a hand the way he did for wine lists. Deflated, Charlotte shoved a large, heavy envelope at his chest and walked away. I'd been too focused on her murdering traitor's face to notice it. It was manila and unmarked, and when Jude peered inside, I could see nothing of the contents.

"There was some other stuff too," said Charlotte as she examined every bottle on Jude's bar. "A ring binder and some files. But you didn't mention anything else so I left it all."

"Good. This is all I'll need." A muscle in his jaw pulsed. "Did you read it?"

"Like I even could. It's pages and pages of code."

"So you read it," said Jude, voice rising.

"Oh my god, relax." Charlotte sighed. "I flicked through a couple of pages. More fool me, right? Sounds like I should've taken pictures." The blood drained from Jude's face so fast I was certain he'd faint. "*Which I didn't.* No phones, remember?"

The door opened again, and Jude tossed the envelope into a drawer as someone else entered. Heart pounding, I shifted to get a look at them, but all I could make out was the light of a Moth. I caught snatches of a man as he crossed the room, his arm full of glasses.

But he wasn't alone; the glowing of a second Moth revealed itself as they separated. Four people now, and me crouched behind a room divider with nothing but a pair of kitchen knives. Were they all part of this conspiracy? The speed with which Jude had stashed the envelope suggested not.

"Are we set?" said Jude to the newcomers.

"We're set." It was Roman. A baggie of what looked like cocaine dropped onto the low table amongst the floor cushions before he shifted into view. He was half dressed for the evening, his tuxedo jacket slung over his arm and his bow-tie undone around his neck. He discarded both and placed his cufflinks and watch to one side. "If you were talking to me, I could have told you the bottom feeder you paid two million just to get his ankle fixed sold it to me. Dude's got a thriving side business. You were had."

Jude made a noncommittal noise and started loading a record onto his turntable. This was shaping up to be something other than the plotting I had anticipated. That didn't change the truth, I told the flutter of panic in my stomach. Jude and Charlotte had still conspired to kill me. I had heard as much. I just needed to ignore the cramping in my legs and be patient.

"Probably only works in catering to meet clients," said a woman. Zazie. I angled to peer through another gap in the screen and found her. She wore a black dress with crystal straps barely clinging to her shoulders. She was steadier on her feet than she'd been that morning at breakfast, but a slumbrous quality still weighted her limbs as she crossed the room.

"I wonder how much he's making," said Roman as he piled the glasses onto the table, along with a bottle of something from Jude's collection. "I thought we might make an anonymous tip-off to the police, teach the vulture a lesson."

Zazie gave a delighted giggle that petered off at an unimpressed glance from Charlotte.

"I couldn't care less, Roman," said Jude.

"Right." There was a pause, filled with a tapping and scraping as he cut the coke into lines and Jude's predictably pretentious avant funk. "It's not that I care because of the money. It's the principle of the thing."

"You do what you want."

"I'll leave it, then?" said Roman, somehow both sarcastic and bereft.

But Jude barely seemed to know he was there. He sunk onto a floor pillow, his eyes lightless and far away. I understood this side of him: not wanting to be alone but not comforted by company. Self-soothing with his worst impulses. Jude and Roman had a lot in common—ugly family lives, nihilism, a taste for destruction—but now I understood that none of it was what inspired Jude to keep him close. Roman could bring the party, but he would never ask anything insightful or notice that your pain was swallowing you whole.

Most of Jude's friends were like that, now that I thought about it.

As Charlotte went to her knees by the table and did a line, Zazie and Roman were engaged in a swaying, grinding dance, glasses of tequila in hand, eyes too bright. Jude sat on the floor, watching them without seeing, until Zazie danced across the room and planted her feet either side of his hips. She moved over him, arms swaying, hips twisting, until Jude reached up and slid his hand through the high slit of her dress, exposing her thigh. His attention was fixed on the inside flesh of her leg.

"Holy fuck?" said Charlotte, scrambling closer. "You let one of them bite you."

"Why did you think she fainted at breakfast?" said Roman before doing a line. He looked up at Zazie. "Was it hot?"

Zazie let her head fall back as if she was remembering it. "I can't even describe it. It felt like . . . mourning. Like life is beautiful, but it'll never be enough. Still does. If he hadn't left, I don't think I would have been able to stop." Her lips took on a pout as she came back down to earth. "He wouldn't fuck me, though."

"It's still bleeding," said Charlotte with a shudder.

Jude remained fixated on the puncture wound, a twisted expression on his face. Time stopped, a held breath in which they waited for him to move or say something. I couldn't understand it, his transparent disgust even as he bent his head to Zazie's thigh and touched his tongue to the bleeding bite mark. Zazie gasped but didn't pull away. Roman was transfixed, head tilting to one side, his face a kind of serious I couldn't read.

As Jude lapped at Zazie's blood, Charlotte stood and backed away until she was standing outside the scene, looking in. I suspect I'd looked that way during the hunt, staring into that haunted watercolour grove, waiting for some phantasmal danger to take a shape I knew to run from. It was the same alarm I'd seen strike her the first evening as the guests had effected a frenzied applause for their immortal lives. The recognition of a difference.

Yet I was on the outside too. Maybe it was the blood; the way the room tilted and my hands trembled without having to see the mark or Jude's mouth on it at all. But I sensed a fraternity binding the three of them the way an adolescent girl senses a joke at her expense. I recalled the faerie's fear of the power that would kill me, and suffered vertigo at the thought of what Jude might have done to wield it. What offering he might have made.

When Jude pulled back, his tongue running across his reddened teeth, Zazie sunk to her knees in his lap. With his eyes on hers but an expression that conveyed very little engagement in what he was doing, Jude swiftly divested her of her dress. Roman joined them. He knelt beside Jude and Zazie's tangled bodies, took Jude's jaw roughly between his fingers, and kissed his bloody mouth.

Despite having been poisoned with a curse that would kill me in a matter of hours, I can say with confidence that being stuck behind a room divider at my brother-cousin's carnivorous orgy was the worst thing that had ever happened to me. And not just because of the way Zazie's fingers danced along Jude's waistband, the quick descent towards things I needed never to see. My chance was gone, my vengeance a poorly conceived scheme lost under a tide of blood, cocaine, and god-awful music.

They'd lost Charlotte. Jude made eyes at her as Roman's mouth moved to his neck, but she regarded him bluntly, topped up her drink, and wandered over to his record collection.

I couldn't just plug my ears and seethe. I needed to get out of there and regroup; there was just enough time left to come up with another way to get them alone and cornered if I thought fast. Still in a crouch, I edged to the corner of the folding screen and gauged the distance to the door. They were all occupied, except for maybe Jude, who while busy with his hands and mouth did not appear mentally diverted. I could get to the door in relevant silence and simply hope no one looked up, then run for it if the latch made a noise.

I had taken half a step beyond the screen when Charlotte turned around. She didn't scream as our eyes locked; she didn't even jump. She just pinned me there, at her mercy, as Jude, Zazie, and Roman writhed on the floor between us like a nest of snakes. Full dark had descended beyond the windows, and the invisible gilding of my veins tugged on my awareness. But not Charlotte's; if it crossed her mind to wonder how long I had left, the direction of her gaze didn't betray her.

"What are you doing, Valentina?"

Jude tore himself free, followed by the others, as I emerged fully from behind the screen. The reactions ranged from startled yells—Roman—to open invitation—Zazie, who raised herself onto her knees and reached a hand towards me. Jude grabbed the proffered arm and shoved it down.

"What the fuck?" he said to me. Not as shocked as I'd hoped he'd be, but if Jude lived prepared for the fact I might leap out at him at any moment, that would do as well.

It was too late for mortification, so I gestured to Roman and Zazie, scrabbling to untangle and dress themselves, and told him: "Get rid of them." Jude made a face, his first instinct to fight me. I went on before he could. "I heard your entire conversation on the yacht this afternoon."

His petulance vanished, replaced with a shade of the bloodless anxiety he'd had over the envelope Charlotte had given him earlier. My glance at the drawer was involuntary, the response in Jude a convenient accident.

"Leave," he said, getting to his feet. Zazie was already wriggling back into her dress, but Roman fumed.

"What conversation on the yacht?" He was addressing Jude, but his eyes were on Charlotte. It would have been him, I realised, if she hadn't wheedled her way into Fable this weekend and made herself the less volatile choice. However little Roman knew about the situation, he knew this.

"Just get out." Jude didn't even look at him as he handed down the command. Roman got to his feet, his mouth red and swollen from kissing him, and shot a final, stony glance at Charlotte as he grabbed his things. As they watched him leave, I took the opportunity to duck gracelessly behind the divider and retrieve the knives. They shook as I emerged.

"What are you doing, petal?"

They had both taken a step back and closer together, and I wondered who was more likely to throw the other into my path for a chance to escape. Jude, I decided. Not that I believed it had crossed either of their minds yet; both looked more discomfited than afraid, but there was time to remedy that.

That time was now. I had lost the element of surprise, but I was still between them and the exit. But the wall of arched doors to the loggia stretched on and on; I wouldn't beat them to the farthest ones. Now that this was happening, I didn't think I could keep them from slipping past me either; the room was vaster than I'd let myself believe. The echo of my shallow breaths rushed from corner to distant corner and came back to me like the attention of some behemoth creature come to thwart me. Jude's home, not mine.

I could get one of them at most, and it had to be him. Jude watched me as if he'd known this end was coming before I did. Perhaps he had. Perhaps he'd always understood the only way I could win was by taking back the life he'd stolen. It was fair, it was right, and I would barely have to live with it. But first, I needed to understand.

I turned to Charlotte. "I truly hope I'm not the one to break this to you, but he's never paying you that money. You understand, don't you, that he can't have a hundred million land in your bank account and still keep his hands clean? That that's all you were good for?"

She tried to catch Jude's eye with a questioning glance, but his were on the knives.

"What happened to your startup?" I asked.

Charlotte's eyes widened. She threw her head back in laughter. "God, you'd still sell me that bullshit, wouldn't you? Even now."

There was a beat in which I imagined I was supposed to defend myself, but I didn't understand the charge. "Do go on."

"When I got to this party, I understood within half a day what you'd never had the decency to mention. These people." She gestured like Jude and I weren't the only ones here. "The ones with companies that their families founded and handed down to them. Not a single one of them gets to be immortal because they worked for it. There's not a self-made pinkie finger in this hideous fucking house, because guess what? You can't get this rich in a lifetime. You can't work your way to this life." She laughed meanly. "And you were just going to watch me try."

"You want to be like us badly enough that you'd kill for it? That's pathetic."

Jude tensed. He started to speak over Charlotte, who had reared back, brow furrowed.

"*Kill?* If you heard our whole conversation, you heard me say I didn't unplug your dad." She turned reluctant. "Condolences, by the way."

"Charlotte's not killed anyone," Jude said redundantly. A tendon in his neck pulsed as he looked between us.

"The money was to slip away from the party last night and get into your dad's safe." She smiled, eyes triumphant. "And he's already paid me."

But it had to have been Charlotte. She was the only one of them who would have passed Randolph's room to get to mine. Unless, perhaps, Jude himself took a circuitous route from somewhere other than here to confuse the trail, in case he was seen.

I was trying to force the pieces together when I caught the slide of Jude's eyes towards the drawer, towards the envelope.

"Wait—"

I levelled a knife at his sternum and kept him back as I went to the dresser. Charlotte was hissing about having had it with our unhinged family as I wrenched the drawer open—shaking the whole dresser and knocking a ceramic sculpture to the floor, where it smashed—lifted the heft of the envelope out, and emptied it.

The contents landed with a smack: a thick, bound document with a quintessential blue cover. This couldn't be what it appeared to be; not again. Even as I turned the lab report right side up and saw the product name printed in capitals on the front cover—déjà vu doubling my vision; past and present, reality and the impossible—I couldn't catch up. Without understanding how, the certainty that I had failed in a dire and irreparable way ensnared me.

"The other night when I found you and that vampire in your dad's office, I was swinging by to check how difficult it would be," said Charlotte, her voice watery and undefined under the rushing in my ears. "I thought the plan was to threaten to leak it to some wannabe Mythos competitor if your mother didn't name him CEO." She addressed Jude. "But apparently you don't even want to be CEO. Do I have that right? Not that it's anything to do with me anymore."

"You're right, it's not. And I said I was going to leak it, but I didn't mean to Mythos's aspiring imitators. You just assumed." Air rushed from the floor cushions as Jude collapsed back onto them. I dragged my eyes from the report. He had given up his anxiety now that he was caught, and in its place was a familiar look of derision. "Fran saw your mother punch in the safe number yesterday when the three of you were in Dad's office. So me stealing it is on your mother, when you think about it. She should have been more careful."

With every new detail, my mind spun, desperate to tie this back to my purpose here, to tell me I wasn't wrong. I played the conversation on the yacht back—so damning at the time, I had been certain—and saw only a mirage, melting as I tried to grasp the pieces. I'd told Jude that someone at Fable had an agenda, but I'd denied him all the details and so he thought I was onto . . . *this*. This nothing scheme. This fatal distraction.

I had enough presence of mind to place the knives on the dresser before my trembling hands gave them up to the floor. My panic was a living thing in my chest. Distantly, I realised that whoever was slaughtering the Maddocks was still undiscovered, that Mum and Jude—I had almost *killed Jude*—were still in danger. But a larger, brighter horror whited it out: I was never going to know who killed me; never going to take from them what they'd taken from me.

"This can't be happening," I murmured as Charlotte said something from across the room.

"What?" said Jude, bored.

"I *said*," Charlotte intoned, "who were you going to leak it to if not Mythos's competitors?"

"The press, of course."

"Why?"

"The deal was not to ask questions."

"Never mind, then. I just realised I don't care."

This damned report, the same one Hunter had almost shot me in the garage to keep out of my hands. It was haunting me.

"No, wait." My voice was weak, but it quieted the patter of their insipid bickering. "Why the press?"

"You're joking, aren't you?" Jude's expression slackened as it dawned on him that I wasn't. His voice lowered, grew tentative. "How do you not know? The party's almost over. Everyone's supposed to know by now."

Mum used to leave lab reports on the kitchen table, half read, the pages folded back on themselves. This one was lifted from a safe.

"Know what?" said Charlotte.

"Shut up." There was no heat in the command; he just needed to forget she was there. The crease across the bridge of his nose had appeared. When he turned to look at me, it was to broker an understanding. It was an invitation to conspiracy. Jude and I had never conspired, not over shattered heirlooms or missing cupcakes—we were informers, enemy spies—but he looked at me now like a brother looks to his sister to abet him. Like he was calling on a pact we'd never made.

Someone's killed me, I wanted to say. *I thought it was you.* But what did I want him to say to that?

I'll avenge you.

You're forgiven.

He pushed off the floor and came to me, and in my grief-addled state, I thought perhaps I'd said some of it aloud. Then he reached past me, slid the report off the dresser, and dropped it into my hands. "Take it." His gaze passed over the fragments of the ceramic sculpture I had sent to the floor as he turned away. "I'm over this shit."

How do you not know?

I slipped out without a backward glance. As if in a daze, I floated past Zazie and Roman, hovering in the hallway, and fumbled my way into my room. I'd left a single lamp on, back before the last day of my life had turned to night, and I staggered through the dark towards it. There, I flipped to the back of the *Immortality* report. Charlotte had called the document "pages and pages of code," but she had never seen one before. She didn't know that after a few hundred pages, the programming came to an end and the specifications were more intelligible. And there was something there, something Jude believed I should know.

It's easy to imagine now that I already understood what I would find: a connection, a thread that somehow bound my death to the thing that had brought us all here. That with my last hours of life, I was frantically skimming pages of a Mythos document because I was on the cusp of understanding all of it. I don't think I was. I think I was lucky, and stupid, and I think I have Jude to thank for the fact I found it.

Or blame. Depends how you look at it.

22

I burned the report once I'd read it; sheared the pages out a fistful at a time and made a bonfire in the bathtub. I'm not sure why—my mind after reading it was a helium balloon, tethered to me by the pinch of a finger and thumb around the ribbon—but I think its existence seemed dangerous. After all, I had read it and now I balanced its truths in one hand and my sanity in the other, and I was moving lightly, inhabiting the world with the barest touch so that I wouldn't disturb the balance and break both open on the floor, where they would run together.

I made my way down to the party undressed, without makeup, hair undone. Echoes coalesced into a melody as I followed them down hall after hall shot through with daggers of moonlight from the tall, arched windows; the clouds had lifted. As I came to the top of the main staircase above the sepulchral stillness of the entrance hall, the melody changed. A loping mid-tempo tune in a minor key started up. Fiddles, and maybe that was an accordion. It made me think of a jack-in-the-box, of a spring coiling tighter with every step—winding, winding, winding.

The cathedral of the ballroom was draped in dark red velvet. Columns of it hung from the balconies on both sides like curtains, ready to be drawn and encase us here. It covered the windows too, turning the cathedral into a cave, or a crypt. Candles in clusters of dozens burned with a lambent light; it caught on jewels at throats, on teeth behind smiles. As the band played from a stage at the far end of the room, the guests danced in pairs; they were an animal mass, a murmuration shifting on the same cues. They spun perilously around the unlit pools, whose depths were blacker than night but whose surfaces winked with candlelight.

I sunk into the shadowed recesses below the balcony as I made my way across the room, searching, my steps falling in time with the winding of the music. At the side of the stage, I finally found her. My mother turned to me like some signal had been given, and passed through the draping velvet into the shadowy corridor behind to meet me. Her eyes narrowed slightly as she took in the T-shirt and leggings, the lack of makeup, the still missing Moth, before meeting mine.

"You lied," I said. My right eye twitched as fluorescent hospital lights flared across my vision. The backlit silhouette of my mother, hovering above me, there and gone again. "You lied about everything."

For a time, only the loping music filled the air between us. Mum folded her arms and, on an outward breath, said, "I see."

The figure of Mario appeared at her side. "A delivery has arrived for you, Dr. Cabot."

"Take it to Oz's office," said Mum with a bite of irritation. "Wait for me there. Don't leave it unguarded." Mario was quick to vanish. Mum turned back to me. "How did I lie?"

If I was silent, could I make her say it? My calm was almost completely evaporated, my sanity with it, and in my mind I held a cleaver. My knuckles tensed painfully around the memory of the handle.

"Valentina, I don't have the time—"

"You said *Immortality* had none of the effects of vampirism. You told everyone that."

"Yes. For good reason." She did something strange: she lifted a hand and stroked my arm. Soothing. Coaxing. She was here. She was listening.

I flinched away.

"Blood."

She shifted slightly, and the candlelight struck one side of her face now. The softness of her voice, the gentle attempt to comfort me; I had expected a look that was weary, tender. Pitying, perhaps. But the curl of her mouth that could have been sympathy was a smile, half suppressed.

"You want people to drink human blood."

She shot a look at the dancing guests and pulled me farther into the shadows. "*Want?* Want doesn't factor into it. What I've achieved is a fucking miracle. Eternal life, Valentina. I think the cost is more than fair, don't you?"

My ears were ringing. *It's not your blood. Not your cost. Who's going to be paying it?* I didn't think I had to say it aloud—didn't realise I *had*—didn't know, until she rolled her eyes and sighed, weary at my fragility and my disapproval, that I'd feared exactly that response.

Yet somehow it was even worse. Somehow, she was laughing at me.

"Who will it come from?" Was I in the light? I needed her to see my face, because then maybe I could make her understand me finally. "What do you expect people to do? *Please.* Please just tell me you understand that you *can't.*"

She looked at me askance. "Is that all it would take not to have this argument again?"

"'*Is that all?*' Is some compassion *all?*" She made a noise and moved as if she would walk away from me. I grabbed her arm, fingers digging mercilessly into flesh, and she hissed in pain. "If it's such a small thing, then why can't you manage it? What's so broken about you?"

I expected her expression to shutter, her eyes to dull with hurt. But instead, they caught fire, turning gold in the light. Her sly smile hardened into a sneer. She took the vise of my hand in hers and twisted until I let go.

"I'm embarrassed for you, Valentina. You know how awful I can be, don't you? You know what it feels like. You're *triggered*, you poor thing. Well, you can climb off that high horse, because let me tell you something: you and I both know you'll take the tonic like the rest of us."

I felt myself shrinking. "Why are you speaking to me like this?" I said, the words catching horribly on the lump in my throat. I sounded wounded and pathetic. Young. Her complaints had rushed from her lips like a great pressure had finally broken the seal, and now she looked sated, relieved, and I was scrabbling before her to keep my grip.

"*Because,*" she said, in a tone that settled the matter. She straightened to her full height, as if she were feeding off me as I crumpled. "You're ungrateful. You're judgemental. You're selfish. Tell me what you would have done, if you were a mother. Allow a child to die? Valentina"—my name was a plea and a curse, raw and accusing in a way that made me want to look at the floor, mortified—"you treat me as if I knew you would develop an infection if I let them take bone marrow. Your whole life, you've treated me like I'm a monster."

Words wouldn't come; I could only shake my head. Because, unfathomably, she understood me acutely. We weren't talking about consuming the blood of others, not quite, but about the limits of her callousness. About a suspicion I had been told all my life was wrong and ungenerous, because sometimes people cope in strange ways.

"You really, truly think you can sell your abomination to people?" I said, trying for the scorn she always suspected I had. Trying ever harder to hurt her.

But nothing worked. I couldn't grasp the upper hand, couldn't find even footing for a single moment. I called her work of ten years an abomination, and a weight lifted off her. All frustration, all pent-up injustices and rehearsed speeches blew away on a spring breeze, and she smiled. She was beautiful, benevolent.

"Yes," she said. "I do."

She turned me bodily to face the swarming dancers and twinkling candles. Holding me at all times, her fingers firm but gentle against my shoulders, she moved to stand behind me. Her voice was close enough to be coming from inside my head. "I've been working my way through our guests all weekend. As of this evening, every client here knows exactly what they have to do if they want to live forever."

I felt a wave approaching, vast and strong enough to sweep me up like kelp.

"They all want *Immortality*, Teeny. Every single one of them."

The dancers spun, and Athena's face appeared among them. She danced with Graham, her faithless fiancé. So much she didn't know, but she knew about the blood, and she would still claim her eternal life. Zazie—belonging to a family who knew the lengths we would go to before I was ever born—would be part of this. Eric Burton-Shaw. He was the kindest, sweetest old man. Dying, and prepared to hand down the toll to another. He stood to one side of the dancers, a glass of red wine in hand and a full-throated laugh escaping him. *Nicola*. She'd been told what she'd have to do. I had watched her falling apart over it the night before; by breakfast, she was coming round.

And Jude. He had known, and rather than object, he had thought of leveraging this to avenge himself on Mum. The company would have been forced to disavow *Immortality*, Mum with it. They would have blamed the formula on her and sworn ignorance.

With the weight of a blow to the chest, I realised what we were doing here. The soft launch. The private meetings, the lockdown, the phones relinquished at the door. We were crafting a conspiracy, each client and member of the board sat down, one by one, and asked if they were in. And they were, every last one. Everyone who knew the truth was in this ballroom, Jude's smoking gun was ash in my bathtub, and no one was going to the press.

"I can't be here," I said, one hand clutching my throat. I think I'd raised it to muffle a scream. "I can't do this."

"Do what?" Her arm was a warm weight around my shoulders, but her voice held a note of lurid eagerness.

"I won't be a part of this."

"Of course you will, Valentina." Her fingers stroked my arm in that peculiar way. "You're dying."

The wave broke. The world took on new meaning. It was as if someone had dimmed the lights, and in the gloom they were rearranging the stage. The same scene, a new angle, and yet when the lights came back up, the only thing changed was me.

Mum's fingers laced with mine. The dancers tilted out of view as I was moved again.

"My darling. Come with me."

23

A lamp on Daddy's desk cast a circle of yellow light that melted onto the floor and encased Mario. It burnt brightly enough to reduce the dim glow of Fable's stone to abstract shadows, strange and looming.

"You can go," she said as she swept towards the cupboard that contained the safe. "Leave the case on the desk."

He did as he was told, casting glances towards the darkened corners, the open loggia door where a curtain swelled in the breeze. Too much air eddied through the office, setting fabrics and paper and hanging things to dancing. Too alive. Behind the desk, Daddy's face loomed in the dark, the blood in his teeth black and heavy. A weight settled on my heart.

"Here."

She was handing me something, palm-sized and glossy white. A needle spell.

"Another curse."

"Teeny," she admonished. *Don't be dramatic.* "It's your memories. You'll want to sit down."

"My—"

Dread numbed me. I couldn't have. After that one devastating consultation at aged fifteen, the thought of using *Recall* had never seriously crossed my mind since.

Or had it? As I sunk into a chair, my fingers drifted to my right eye. It had begun twitching furiously just as the cartridge containing my memories appeared. The same way Athena's seemed to bother her.

I had put it down to the *Empathy*. But something unspeakable had happened here. Something worse than my blood-soaked abandonment in a hospital room.

I turned the needle spell over in my hand and tasted acid at the back of my throat. "I can't—"

"It's alright." The gloss of the powder cartridge between her fingers caught the light. *Calm*. Because she'd known everything—about the *Empathy*, about where to plant a curse so I'd take it. She snapped the stick of *Calm* for me as if I was a child. When it chased away my horror, all I was left with was an undiluted sadness I couldn't describe and shudder to recall. Plunging the needle of the cartridge into my finger was no easier or harder than all the times before.

"Is that a yes?"

In broad strokes, I had laid out my plan: she would place me in Hunter's job, set me up as the natural successor for CEO. She would return to being only Head Magician and train me in magic so that we could run the company together, the way only magicians would. I would snatch the Maddock dynasty from under Jude's nose, and every way she had been wronged would at last be made right.

Mum smiled, but a tightness remained at the corners of her mouth. "It's a yes."

My breath rushed from me in a laugh. I squeezed her fingers, looked into her eyes so that she could see the gratitude in mine, this woman who held my future in her hands. Who didn't need to know I was a Maddock in my heart.

Not until the empire was mine.

"Great," I said, standing, restless. "This is great. Let's have another drink."

"You make them," she said staidly, her enthusiasm trailing behind mine. "I'll be right back."

As I placed a fresh round of old fashioneds on the coffee table, she appeared in the doorway, a lab report clutched to her chest. I sensed her hesitancy, strapped down by a defiance, a refusal to hear her own doubt. Without a word, she came around the couch and presented the document with both hands. The title stared up at me.

Immortality.

"I suppose I need to be familiar with this before the weekend? Gosh." All four hundred pages of text dropped heavily into my hands. "Please tell me most of this is just code."

My self-conscious laugh tore straight through the thin silence as it fell, spoiling the moment like vinegar in milk. Mum took up her cocktail as she sunk back into the couch, curled her long fingers around the glass, and didn't speak. I looked down at the report—this puzzle box I was being instructed to open on my own—and spotted the neon-yellow strip barely protruding from near the end.

"You've tabbed a page."

Anxiety throttled all her other emotions; one squeeze of a fist and then it released. This was what she meant to show me. Balancing the document in the crook of my elbow, I coaxed it to split at the right page. Under the section heading "Maintenance Requirements" was a brief, pragmatic paragraph: one brutal revelation and the instruction to consult Dr. Cabot with further questions.

I read it once, then again. Then a third time, slower, still certain that a change of meaning would unspool between the lines. When it didn't, I looked up at my mother. Because of course, the text said very clearly where to find the additional information. Only she could tell me what this meant.

Her emotions were in a holding pattern, their attention fixed on me like a bank teller on the barrel of a gun.

"I am satisfied," she said, "that every possible alternative has been explored."

I believed with my whole being that she was about to tell me which one had worked. And yet a sense of violation, old and scarred over, ached between the bones of my spine, the insides of my elbows. A buried truth.

"I think, by this point, I understand vampirism better than any who've studied it. In trying to distil immortality from the venom, I've divided the constituent parts quite well. The death of the host is caused by a particular component, the intolerances—sunlight, silver—by others. Their ability to be perceived by us as non-threatening when they are in fact our only natural predators is a magic similar to a faerie glamour.

"But their stasis. It's almost not a function of their curse at all, but a product of the way they're sustained. Vampirism adapts the body of the host to harness—well, the *life-force* of blood. The two can't be unbound. Life simply cannot be sustained beyond its natural limits without it." She was alight with discovery, and all her hesitancy had burned up in its heat. "The science is undeniable. This is the only option."

Options. Alternatives. They would do everything, but when it all failed, they would do this.

They would take blood.

"It won't be much. Depending on the client's weight, a cup or so will sustain the spell for a couple of days, or thereabouts. The more the client consumes, the longer the magic is sustained, but only up to a point. It will need to be taken about every ten days, at the least, or the spell will disintegrate." She looked into her drink. "But it will need to be . . . incredibly fresh. Consumed from the source."

"And human," I said, feeling the beginnings of a smile at the corners of my lips. Because this wasn't real. I would play along until she told me this wasn't real.

But she continued to explain. There had been talk of acquiring a voluntary supply—of enabling clients to buy it—but the complications were endless. For one thing, anyone who would sell it was likely to be riddled with drugs or disease. These things couldn't hurt an immortal, of course, but think of the optics. Mythos couldn't attach its name to the provision of something so tainted and ask its clients to consume it. It was better if clients chose their own supply and thus absorbed the responsibility.

This was not the main issue with the idea of donation, however.

"I don't need to tell you that discretion is paramount," Mum said. She had relaxed in the face of what she must have interpreted as sober attentiveness. I had stood rooted as I listened, the report still open in my unshaking hands. "The exact specifications of the spell have thus far remained between a select few people. There's no question of regulators putting an end to *Immortality*—and in doing so, an end to all who've taken it—if the maintenance requirement became public knowledge. Such things are best managed by as few people as possible, and any sort of voluntary supply would require collaborators."

The only way, she said—though not in as many words—would be murder. The victims would be strangers; ordinary, innocent people who couldn't be traced back to those who had drained them of their lives, who perhaps wouldn't even be missed. There were billions of them out there, all over a planet Grandpa had opened up to us with *Swift*. If we were careful, we need never leave a trail that could be followed.

She rolled her glass between her hands and stared into the dark liquid. "I know vampires sometimes nourish themselves without inducing a fatality. That option is simply not available to us. I'm already working on several new products that will make it incredibly easy for everyone. Clients will sign contracts forbidding them from involving the help and obliging them to alert us at the first sign of suspicion." She twisted one hand in the air—*and that's that*. "We don't anticipate any issues. It will be a completely closed circle."

Silence fell. The punch line never came. I stared right into the heart of her and found nothing I could cling to. No shame, or recognition; no confession at all. And what else did I expect? I was hardly learning for the first time that pity did not move her, not if it stood in the way of her own glory. I longed for witnesses—therapists and family, my dying father reanimated, anyone I could turn to and say, *Isn't this what I said? Isn't this who I told you she was? You said I had to heal, that forgiveness would be good for me. You said the lessons of that hospital room were an accident, her abandonment of me an ordinary human flaw. But she once traded the use of* my *body for her own ends; that another life could continue had been incidental then too.*

"This isn't about you, Valentina."

I thought she'd read my mind. But the silence was freshly fallen, and my throat was raw. Mucus and tears and spittle clung to my face. The *Immortality* report lay open and twisted on the coffee table. I'd been screaming at her. My last few words came back to me—that I should have told the world what Daddy had told me: she only saved his son on the condition he made her Head Magician.

And she was shocked, hurt, furious. She was all the things she wasn't when I said it a second time. My mother had sat there as I screamed at her, looking so small, so sorry, so *done*. Done with my blame and my ingratitude. And when I was finished, all that was left to think about was blood. I sprinted, bile rising, to the bathroom, and vomited until I was empty, cried until I was dry. I was on the floor, my face pressed to the cool porcelain of the toilet bowl, the hum of the fan the only thing I could focus on, when my ruinous vengeance came to me.

My phone was in my pocket. I dialled a school friend whose dad was a famed investigative journalist. She didn't answer, but I left a message instructing her to put me in touch with her father, I had a tip-off for him. It was about Mythos, I said, and the world needed to know.

When I unlocked the bathroom door, the key sticking slightly in the original Victorian lock, I was calmer. I had a plan: I was going to expose her, force Mythos to disown her work, and stop *Immortality* before it lionised her. What would happen after that, I didn't care to dwell on. It wasn't that this was the right thing to do—I don't remember that thought once crossing my mind. It was that, in my mind, Mum meeting a reckoning for this was the same as her meeting a reckoning for the stem cell donation. The crime was the same—not the blood, but the indifference. If I hadn't been on *Empathy* that evening, perhaps it all would have gone differently. As it was, I was living on a crystalline and refined anger, and I stayed in it, where it was safe, as I opened the door.

She was there. She didn't step back or disguise the fact she'd been listening. A flash of astonishment crossed her face as she pushed me, palms flat to my chest, her whole weight behind them to knock me off my feet. I heard my head smack into the tile more than I felt it. Tears sprung to my eyes. I watched her pick up my phone and remove the key from the door through a film of water, but I blinked before she disappeared, bringing my mother into focus. That same astonishment was frozen on her face, like she couldn't believe what she was doing. I wonder if she wore it as she locked the door, as she called her team at the lab, as she explained to them what had happened, what needed to happen now.

I had bruised my hands and scraped my throat raw by the time I heard them arrive. It took hours, days, an eternity for the three of them to get themselves together, and all the while I sat against the bathtub and refused to believe. She could not have locked me in there. She could not have pushed me. Mum would never.

But I had no idea.

They came through the door as one: Owen Chandler and Jonathan Yang, Mum's team for *Immortality*, moving in synchronised haste to pin me to the tile. She had a glass of whiskey in her hand, and she was talking to me soothingly as she knelt, her knees bracketing my legs, and forced my jaw open.

"You and I had a few drinks, Teeny. We talked about making Hunter retire, and you taking over. Nothing else. Then I went to do some work and you started thinking about Oscar. You called a friend to cry to. She was worried, but you've texted her now, see? You've told her you're drunk, to forget the conversation and that everything's fine. You're going to clean yourself up and go home."

Liquor on the floor, muttered curses from the men overpowering me. And a pitiful, animal keening in my ears. I didn't understand yet how she thought I would just forget this, couldn't avail myself of the idea that *Recall* was for consenting clients, that it wasn't used like this.

Hands clamped my head. She was far above me now, watching at a distance as someone brushed magic onto my temples and my vision blurred. Losing my memories felt like nothing.

There's a fog after, a few long minutes of recovery swallowed up by the spell as collateral damage. In mine, I lay on the cold tile as Owen and Jonathan fled, watching Mum watch me. I was wiped clean, a newborn looking up at the only thing in existence. Free from all the resentments and accumulated pain, all the failures—hers and mine—that had grown like wild things over freshly toiled earth, left unchecked until we were ensnared in the briar, thorns piercing our skin. It was gone; she was only my mother, and so I was helpless before the animal instinct that made me reach for her.

She knelt over me, her reddened eyes coming into focus. I wanted to tell her she didn't need to cry, that we were alright. She moved as if to touch my cheek or stroke my hair, and I was filled with a soft yearning. I felt for her body with weakened arms, tried to pull her closer.

She drew her hand back and slapped me.

When the fog lifted I was weeping for my dying father. I washed my face, wondered at the redness already fading from my cheek, and left without saying goodbye, passing the closed door of my mother's office as I went.

She sat opposite me, framed by the open door, the gauzy white curtains made phantoms by the breeze. Only a few seconds had passed, my missing hours unfurling all at once, one moment on top of the next. It felt like the *Recall* had never worked in the first place.

Except that her reactions tonight made sense. My fingers went to my cheek and tried to massage away the echoes of the sting left by her palm. When I'd confronted her in the ballroom, she hadn't found the bleeding scar at the heart of me because she understood me. She had known because I had cut it open myself, right at her feet, and let the poison flow free.

She leaned forward and placed something on the low table between us; something that must have given itself away between the cushions of the loveseat in Daddy's bedroom with its impossible gold light.

"Why didn't you tell me you found the bottle?"

The shard of glass winked at me. Had she already found it when we talked on the *Adieu*? For a moment, I couldn't fathom how she had disguised the knowledge so well. Then the depth of the deceit came upon me all over again.

She had always known. She had been the one to kill me.

"I didn't mean to smash it," she went on. "I would have poured it down the drain like any normal person, but you know me. In all the clutter, I knocked it over."

I followed her gesture towards the desk, where the stain she'd told me was coffee still marred the rug. Had Fran lied to me about the provenance of the bottle?

No, the mistake had been mine, the only lie my inability to see my mother as a suspect. I had only asked about relevant guest rooms. I believed I didn't know which corridor they were on.

But Charlotte had told me her bedroom was next door.

"The notes," I said flatly.

Mum rolled her eyes. "Yes, I'm sorry for that bit of theatre. It was asinine, wasn't it? But I assumed once you cursed yourself, you'd try and tell me about it, and then what would I have done? I'd have had to fake a panic just to look innocent."

She laughed at the horror of that idea: disrupting the weekend with a pantomime of concern for me.

"Was I ever—" I swallowed back bile. "Was I ever supposed to live?"

Mum's look was withering. "Teeny," she admonished. "Do you truly believe I wanted to *kill* you? What do you take me for?"

A murderer. But she had swept from the couch and rounded the desk to where Mario had left the briefcase, slim and black, with a biometric lock. She pressed her thumb to the pad, entered the combination on a second lock, opened the lid, and stepped back.

"Well?" she said, impatient. "Come and look."

Weightless in my horror, I floated over to her and looked down into the case.

Nestled in the bed of foam were rows and rows of vials the size of my smallest finger, each containing a translucent red liquid. She slipped a vial from the crate as if it was impossibly delicate; one nail hooked over the top to prize it out, and the other hand pinched it between two fingers.

"It's here, Teeny." She was gazing, entranced, into the vial. In the light of the desk lamp, the tonic shimmered, oily and pearlescent. It seemed to move within itself, microscopic currents tugging the liquid in eddying spirals. "It's really, truly here."

Immortality. Salvation. Everything I hadn't known to beg for, right in front of me.

And drenched in blood.

My voice came out like a sigh of surrender. "I don't understand."

The upload was scheduled for tomorrow, when the board would approve production. It would be another five days before the first doses could be produced. If *Immortality* could have saved me, I would have gone to the lab to start the upload myself—I would have found a way, whatever I had to do—but there hadn't been enough time.

Just before the first pieces of the puzzle could shift into place, Mum folded herself into Daddy's desk chair and laid them before me.

"After the disaster of our conversation on Tuesday, I had to decide what I would do next," she said, still gazing into the vial. "The obvious answer was to withhold the maintenance requirement from you until it was too late. Which, I admit, entertained me for a while." She smiled tightly. "It would have soothed my pride to see the look on your face, but then what? Another ruinously bad decision from you, no doubt, because it's what you do when you're worked up. I mean, you must have known on some level that whistleblowing on the tonic would mean the end of your life as you knew it. You family's legacy in shambles, me in jail, probably." She wore an expression of superior amusement. "They wouldn't let you keep the money, you know. They'd seize the family's assets, along with the company's. That's what exposure would mean for you, and in your tantrum you tried to pull the trigger anyway."

She was right. I *had* known what talking to a journalist would mean, but in my frenzy to claw back some power, it had felt like a problem for later. I couldn't have stopped myself even if it meant my life or the lives of everyone who had taken the tonic.

"And I couldn't keep the tonic from you either," said Mum. "That would have been too conspicuous. What reason could I give that made it good enough for everyone else but not my own daughter? No, you had to know about the maintenance requirement and choose to take the tonic regardless. You had to be made to come down off your high horse." Her words had turned sharp, her face stony. "And how could I do that? By bringing you face-to-face with your mortality."

The truths were coming at me like sharks in murky water, dangerous and not quite real. This was never about killing me, or extortion. It was a violation so much worse. It was an enfeebling.

Mum tipped her chin towards the cabinet holding Daddy's crude magic collection. "When I remembered the Gilded Grip, everything started falling into place. Your little *Empathy* habit is, I'm afraid, quite well known. Your father and I had certainly noticed, and I understood Hunter and Fran had too. So slipping you the curse was child's play." She placed her elbows on the armrests, all the while toying with the vial. "But I needed to be able to control the situation. I needed to keep you where both myself and the tonic could reach you—*cage you* where your own recklessness couldn't get you killed. It had to be this weekend." She laughed bitterly. "When I was already balancing everything I'd been working towards, I had to account for you too. But what else is new?"

This whole time, I'd been discounting her as a suspect because I knew she wouldn't play games with the launch. Nothing could make her sow chaos in her moment of triumph, I was certain.

Nothing but a threat to her glory, and that's exactly what I was. This had all been about *Immortality*.

"There was just enough time if I could arrange it all that evening."

"Five days," I heard myself say.

"Quite," she said, pleased that she hadn't raised a *complete* idiot. "I went straight to the lab, sent an email around letting everyone know production floor two would be out of action for maintenance that week and no one was to enter, and I started the upload. Then I spent the rest of that night whipping up an accelerant for the Gilded Grip. Because I didn't *have* three days, did I? I couldn't access your belongings to place the curse before we convened here on Friday, and I couldn't let you out of Fable on Monday with a heart about to turn to gold—god knew what you might do before I could track you down. I could control for when you took the curse well enough—I knew from the rate of your *Empathy* use I could count on you needing a dose every few hours—but I needed this over by the last night of the party. By tonight."

The faerie had known, I realised with a dull thud. *This* was the power she wouldn't interfere with: not old gods or celestial beings as ancient as the universe, but Mythos.

"I realised if I made it look like you might get the antidote back, I could probably curtail your worst behaviour. Keep you from telling people, running off, self-destruction, that sort of thing." Her laugh was almost indulgent. "I mean, you made a good go of ruining my party anyway, but I always expected *some* antics. I always knew that I only had to withhold *Immortality* from the guests if they left, and I could keep this on course, despite you. Of course you'd try to find who'd done it, try to save yourself. But—" She gestured: *Oh, come on, you get it.* "That was the whole point, do you see? You needed to make your usual fuss, get it out of your system, and come to the conclusion, on your own"—her eyes hardened to obsidian, every insult I'd hurled shining in their surface—"that you'd rather get over yourself than die."

That she would put it in such blunt, venomous terms shocked me, but only dimly. I was barely aware of my body, arms limp at my sides, mouth open like I would speak—but I couldn't find anything to say, anything to feel.

Mum frowned. "How did you find out about the maintenance requirement?"

I snapped my mouth shut as if Jude's name might escape, but this—all of it—was about her. My reaction went unnoticed.

"I suppose it doesn't matter," she went on. "This isn't so different from what was supposed to happen. I was going to bring you up here this evening, just like this. I was going to open the briefcase and tell you what I've quietly told every client here as I've been meeting with them." She held the vial up between a thumb and forefinger, eyes so awe-filled and twinkling they might have contained a galaxy. "That we claim our immortality tonight. Together."

The room tilted sideways. I grabbed for the edge of the desk to steady myself. All those times I'd thought myself weak or helpless, I'd been a fool. In this house, dragged by chains into the folds of this conspiracy, surrounded by people I had never truly known—this was helplessness. After news of the room search got out, I'd assumed discounts had smoothed the waves, but it had been this—meetings brought forward to lock them quickly into the conspiracy. The guests could fuss and leave, or they could accept our explanations, stay for the rest of the party, and live forever.

"But first," said Mum, producing a one-page contract from a drawer and placing it on the desk, "you'd have signed this, just like everybody else. It says you won't discuss what was said in this meeting with anyone, or your access to the tonic will be revoked. *And*, that if for any reason you decide not to commit to *Immortality*, you consent to have your memory of this meeting erased with *Recall*. A formality, really. Owen and Jonathan would have been here to help restrain you if you resisted." She grinned as I recalled their unexpected presence in Eric's meeting yesterday. "I have you to thank for that idea."

She leant back in Daddy's chair. "You're my last meeting, Teeny. The last person I needed to sell on the unfortunate fact of the maintenance requirement. Only this time, you weren't going to say a word. You were going to take your only chance of survival on bended knee."

"And then what?" I snapped, the words grating my throat. "I was supposed to forget I was ever cursed?"

She shrugged. "I'd hoped, after your life was saved, we could make it until tomorrow without you making any more fuss. I certainly didn't plan to gloat."

"And a year from now?" Her face was that of a mountain lion, focused and patient as it watched its prey. "Your choice would have been to quit as Head Magician or watch me fire you. Jude certainly will. Or have you been so full of spite that you didn't think that far ahead?"

One corner of her mouth twitched in warning. "Things certainly would have been smoother for me if you were made CEO—before all of this, I mean. But I never *needed* you." With a sigh, she rose from the desk and delicately placed the vial upright on its surface. "I haven't feared for my job for a while now. Not from you, not from Jude, and not from Oz."

She stepped out of the light cast by the desk lamp and disappeared like smoke. As my eyes adjusted to pick out the shape of her—going to the closet, punching in the code for the safe—so did my other senses. The hairs on my arms stood up as I felt the darkness behind me shift—there, on the loggia, through the open door. I couldn't make myself turn and look, but when I glimpsed that corner in the mirror, there was nothing there.

Mum returned with a white ring binder thick with pages and let it *thunk* onto the desk.

"So. You took the report from the safe, then," she said with only a hint of tension. "Where is it?"

I imagined lying, but what good would it do? "I burned it," I said. "In the bathtub."

"Did you show it to anyone?" She studied me, and the tight set of her shoulders eased. "No, of course you didn't. You came straight to me with your self-righteous accusations. Here."

She pushed the ring binder towards me and flipped open the cover. For a long while, I refused to look at it—I held my scornful gaze to hers and only dragged it down once I'd succeeded in irritating her.

The pages inside looked like a twelve-year-old's scrapbook. Printer paper warred with the torn-out pages of legal pads and spiral-bound notebooks, their ragged teeth bursting from the top and left-hand edges. Sheets in shades of white and yellow and in places pink. I flipped to a couple at random and found design specifications, some typed and printed, others in my mother's illegible scrawl. Suspicion rising, I kept going until I found the typed script of a programme in a language only Mythos's magicians knew.

"This is a spell," I said, disbelieving. "Except . . . you didn't want a record of it on the Mythos system."

"Not until it was ready to upload, no," she said as she sat back down. "No design documents, no development records. Every time I input a version of the code and it failed, I had to wipe the entire thing, make the changes by hand, and type it up again." She nodded to the binder, open on a page of code. "But it works now. Not only that, but it's ready to go. The upload was completed several months ago and the production was scheduled. If I'm not in the lab every day by nine o'clock to enter the password and kick it back twenty-four hours, it will trigger production." She crossed one leg over the other, languid and calm. "Think of it as a fail-safe."

I shivered. The world beyond the circle of lamplight was so dark it was as if there was nowhere to run, no one to warn.

"What does it do?" I whispered.

Her smile was small and soft, but it contained the oceans of her vanity. "*Immortality* turned out to be the key," she said. "Until now, every spell the company's ever produced has been powered by Martin Maddock's original source. But that wasn't enough to make *Immortality*. It needed to be fed more energy—needed blood." She looked up, her eyes cold and dark. "Just as Martin Maddock did when he claimed his power."

My response was automatic. "You don't know that." But the denial rang hollow. The words tasted empty. They were a fairy tale, the Maddock family's own, passed down generations to soothe and shape, to teach an unquestionable moral: that these were not ill-gotten gains.

"He gave a life for magic," said Mum, indifferent. "All I need to do to wield the same power is take one of my own."

It didn't make sense. She already wielded Martin Maddock's power; the evidence of it was strewn across the desk: the vials, the haphazardly bound spell. Mum had gotten a taste for bloodlust and now she thought she saw its possibilities everywhere. She'd gone mad. Then my eyes alighted on a single word on the page before me, and the world fell out from under me.

Replication.

"What do the Maddocks fear more than anything else?" she said in a singsong lilt as she saw me start to understand. "*Competition*. Your great-grandfather went to some lengths to keep power within the family. I alone can't dismantle the superstitious notion that the whole thing will come crumbling down if Mythos passes out of Maddock hands, but"—she threw up her hands as if in defeat—"privately, I seriously doubt old Martin was imaginative enough to do anything with his new-found power but sell it. Never mind. Because Dr. Claudia Cabot is now a permanent fixture of Mythos too. If any of you think about doing away with me—you, or Jude, or your children, or your children's children—this spell commands the source to replicate itself and gives control of the copy to me. I'll start my own company and decimate your value overnight. Gosh, perhaps if I'm feeling particularly sore about it, I'll make more copies and sell them on." She leaned forward, mad laughter in her eyes but her mouth a stern line. "I am the woman who conquered death. So long as I have magic, just *try* and compete with *me*."

"And the price?" I whispered, my throat dry. "The life?"

She twirled her hand in a dismissive gesture. "Whoever's closest when the spell starts. Most likely whichever trainee drew a manufacturing shift monitoring the hardware. It will appear as if they've had an accident. It's built into the spell."

Martin Maddock had given up his son for magic—had a tiny part of me believed the price of this spell would be *my* life? Yes, and yet somehow this was worse. Even with all my mother's callousness laid bare, I couldn't believe how she talked of handing down a death sentence to a random person—a trainee magician who almost certainly idolised her—as if it was an afterthought.

"Daddy tried to stop you, didn't he?" Even as I said it, the picture came into focus. This, more than anything, turned my stomach. "He didn't want his company's name on your criminal conspiracy. That's why you killed him."

Her head fell forward; in regret, I thought at first. But then her shoulders trembled. Her sigh became a wheeze that grew into a laugh. It was sharp-edged, unguardedly vicious.

"You hopeless girl. Do you think he gave two fucks what we had to do to sell eternal life for eight figures a dose? When I told him we couldn't get around this, he didn't blink. No, I had many a complaint with your father, but standing in the way of *Immortality* wasn't one of them." Her brittle humour vanished. "I didn't kill Oz. I only . . ."

For the first time, she seemed to shrink down in the chair, her face falling in guilt.

"You unplugged him," I finished bluntly. As if that didn't count.

Mum's head snapped up. "You think that was me? Don't be ridiculous."

But it had to have been her, didn't it? My mind tried to supply the evidence, tracking back through every way I'd been wrong—Charlotte creeping along the loggia; Fran, for reasons unfathomable. But before I got there, Mum spoke again, her tone at once wistful and bitter.

"It was an accident of his own making. He'd had this idea that incensed me, that we would be better off if *Immortality* wasn't announced publicly *at all*. This was Monday—*five days* before the party, he casually decided to change everything. Didn't even bother telling me why! He just called me to a meeting and said, it's going to be secret, invitation only. Given the maintenance requirement, it was a conspiracy anyway, so what difference did it make?" A muscle twitched in her jaw. Her eyes flashed with anger. "To me? All the difference in the fucking world. He was asking me to *hide* what I'd accomplished, to get no more recognition for solving *literal death* than a few hundred quiet handshakes from clients. He had a half-baked plan to get them to pinky promise to change their appearance and pass themselves off as their own descendants as necessary, and that was it, I better be off, he had a tee time in twenty."

She was spitting with every word by the end, her knuckles white on the arms of the chair.

"He could have bothered to tell me he'd developed some concerns about what vampires thought of the product," she said. "Now I think he meant it as a concession to appease them, something he'd offer the houses when they answered his last-minute invites and came to Fable this weekend. Yes, we were stepping on their power, but we'd do it quietly—the rest of the world didn't need to know." She huffed out a breath. "But Oscar Maddock doesn't explain himself, he simply does whatever Oscar Maddock wants. So he didn't *say* any of it, even when I accused him of just trying to tread on me. I was never small enough for your father, never happy to exist in his shadow. I told him I wouldn't go along with it, that either he announced *Immortality* or *I* would. And do you know what he did?"

"He fired you," I said. I knew because it's what I would have done, and maybe I was his daughter after all. It was cold comfort.

"He tried to," she said with a nod at the binder, all her anger at him suddenly spent. She sounded pensive. "When I explained to him about the spell . . . I can't describe to you, Teeny, the kind of enraged it made him. I'd never seen him like that. He was throwing things, upending furniture. Perhaps I should have been scared, but I was . . . fascinated. All he could think to do was rage, because I'd left him no other power." Her eyes were unfocused. Slowly, she cupped her hands like she was trying to catch rainwater. "I'd taken it all in my own hands, and as soon as I did, he wasn't the man I knew. He wasn't this . . . force, anymore." She let her hands fall into her lap. "He was just a sack of meat with high blood pressure."

The image broke my heart. My father—my untouchable, infallible hero—so distressed by his own impotence that he gave himself a stroke. I turned away from it, back to the even worse truth in my mother's story.

"I was told his assistant found him," I said tightly. "You left him there, didn't you?"

With achingly slow movements, she took up the vial and stared at its contents. "If it makes a difference, the doctors said the stroke was catastrophic. He would always have ended up how he did. But it's true that I didn't know that at the time." She had the nerve to look grieved as she turned to me. In barely a whisper, she said, "I never hoped for him to die. I only needed the chance to launch *Immortality* correctly, as I deserved, before he tried to take it from me with barely a thought. So I cleared up the evidence of his tantrum, let his assistant find him, and told everyone he was fine when I left."

Her grief was real, and I loathed it. I wanted to bleed it from her, keep it cupped to my heart where she couldn't snatch any of it.

But then something caught her attention beyond the dancing

curtain and the open loggia door. I stiffened. Mum cocked her head to listen, but when a moment had passed and the shadows held their shapes, she relaxed again.

"Who else knows that you did this to me?" I asked. "Does Mario?"

She snorted a laugh. "Of course not. Mario hates the Maddocks because he's decent and you're not, but the unfortunate trap of decency is he'd have protected you anyway. Hunter knows I wiped your memory," she added. "We'd agreed that evening that I would tell you and he would tell Jude, so he was expecting you to be in the loop by the party. I had to let him know what had happened, but I didn't trust him with the rest of it."

She had trusted him with enough that he hadn't given the game away, though. *Full-body paralysis. Docility. Suggestibility. Neurotoxin.* The words that jumped out of the design documents Hunter had smuggled away as leverage. She told me it was basic research, not what it looked like, and Hunter had told me nothing but the truth, minus any honesty. Yes, my mother was up to nefarious things in her lab. Yes, she was a psychopath. When I'd assumed his plan was a manipulation of the facts, I was right, only the truth wasn't about "basic research." These were the Oscar Maddock–sanctioned spells Mum was developing to help clients source blood.

I was dizzy. The air in my lungs felt too thin. I couldn't summon my anger, my righteous indignation. I tugged on every thread within me, searching for it, but the will I'd been stoking since the faerie's antidote had failed—to burn the world down—had evaporated, and I was empty. Mum's own rage and pain had sucked all the oxygen from the exchange and suffocated mine, even as the truth burned through her lies.

"Just be honest, why don't you?" I bit out. "I know why you did this, so just say it."

A crease appeared between her eyes. "Go on. Tell me why I did this."

"Revenge. I said you were a monster when you wanted to hear that you were a genius, and you couldn't bear it."

She encased the vial in her fist. "You know, I'm sure you and all your therapists have been working through the idea that you might have been an abortion, but when Oz and Gigi told me everything—the affair, the pregnancy, that they needed me to sign the divorce papers so they could get married right away—I never once contemplated getting rid of you. I hadn't wanted a baby, but I'd chosen to have one because it mattered to your father and his stupid fucking dynasty, and if Oscar didn't need either of us anymore, well, then, that was the first thing you and I had in common. I felt sorry for you—for both of us. And then when you were a girl and he was a boy, I don't know, it felt kind of vindicating. It was sort of . . . biblical, that we had been left at the wayside together. How accidentally sordid and embarrassing for Oscar that a daughter hadn't been enough for him."

"You weren't enough for him," I spat. "He loved me."

"Oh, he did." She was tapping the vial on the desk now, almost absentmindedly. "Not enough to raise you single-handedly. To hinder the work and the progress for *years,* for the thankless task of being a mother. You cannot comprehend how hard it is, how few fucks a child gives that you have your own wants and needs and desires, that you're anything other than a human *comforter.* And I don't blame *you*—of course you couldn't help it—but everyone else?" Her eyes widened until the grey was ringed with white. "He had my access to the lab blocked from six o'clock at night until eight in the morning. He didn't like that the nanny was giving you your bath or putting you to bed when he thought it should have been me. My own mother, a doctor twice over, would bring you to my office when *she* was supposed to be spending time with you, *to visit,* in the few short hours I was allowed to be my own person. Every single nanny who was paid to see to your needs and keep you happy was a passive-aggressive nuisance at the end of the phone every fucking hour of every fucking day. You got sick at school. You were whining for a treat. You wanted to say good night. When would I be there? What else could possibly matter? *What was wrong with me?* Motherhood is sacrifice, after sacrifice, after sacrifice.

"I gave up who I was for you. And when finally, despite it all, I scaled the mountain . . ." She held up the vial. There were tears in her eyes, and something desolate, lost. "You tried to destroy it. You spat on me, Teeny, like it was nothing."

"Not *nothing*—"

"Even when you knew how much it meant to me, that it was my life's work you were shitting on. I know what you think: despite everything, you don't think I've ever given you enough of me. But this time, you dealt the first blow, Valentina. This one's on you." Her lips pressed firmly together. Her eyes darkened like storm clouds. "I didn't do any of this to punish you—quite the opposite. I did it to put us back on an even keel. I did it so I could forgive you." She took a second vial out of the briefcase and held them both up. "We'll be taking the tonic in the ballroom just before midnight. If you can find it in yourself to stomach it—and I think you will—then you can join us. You and I will take the stage and lead a toast together."

The doses, mine and hers, went into her pocket for the big moment. Her hand came up to cup my cheek, her palm falling just as it had when she had hit me as I lay dazed on her bathroom floor. Then she crossed the room to put the briefcase in the safe, so her back was turned when the shadows stirred again.

"Really, Teeny, I've done you a favour. I've taken the choice away and you get to keep your conscience. Isn't that for the best?"

I didn't reply. She didn't need me to; I could hear in her voice that she thought her victory was complete.

Almost.

"Your father lied to you, by the way." She stood at the very edge of the circle of light thrown by the desk lamp so that her eyes glowed in her darkened face like a predator's in the forest. "He and I did strike a deal over the Head Magician job, but it was the other way around. He offered it to me in exchange for your stem cells." She moved farther into the dark as she retreated towards the door. "I would never have dreamed of leveraging that boy's life for my own gain. I would have signed off either way. For god's sake, Valentina, it was the right thing to do."

The shadows moved one last time as she left me there, clinging to the dark final hours of my mortal life.

24

There was a liquor cabinet in the office. I poured two fingers of something brown, which tasted of nothing as I threw it back. Nor did I taste the second two fingers. I had half a notion that someone was about to interrupt me, but when I slid down the wall, my knees tucked to my chest, and stared out the arched windows, I was alone. No more shadows. No one to tell me not to think my dangerous thoughts.

You'll get the choice I was never given: to live forever or to die.

To live or die; it was the only choice we ever made. Did we want to keep going or was it time to stop?

Despite what Mum believed, the upper hand was still to be claimed. I was warmed through to think of surprising her with my death. Mum so hated surprises, and what could spite a person more than choosing death over them getting their way? It was inspired—hilarious, actually. In the histories of the Maddocks, I would be the personality, the fun fact children remembered when they came home from the museum. *Valentina Maddock chose death over losing a fight with her mother. Iconic.*

But I could do more than die. The idea came to me like a storm breaking after a heat wave, so freeing I felt a smile stretch across my face.

I would refuse the tonic in front of everyone. I would humiliate her. What's more, I would destroy the launch. Announce in front of the event staff that we were all planning to drink human blood once we were immortal, and they would be rounded up and silenced forever; god, they would probably be drained and bottled. But if I just said no, the mess would not be so easily cleaned up. It would sow hesitancy among the clients; one offhand insinuation that the tonic wasn't safe, and Mythos would be doing damage control to recover their sales for months. Mum would likely be blamed for the entire thing, and if they couldn't force her out, they could probably make her life miserable.

If nothing else, it would really hurt her feelings.

I was breathing deeply as I made my way back to the ballroom. I was giddy, *excited* even. After everything, it turned out my mother couldn't do a thing to me. Not anymore. The same haunting strings of the band were a welcoming dirge. They played for me, the new villain of the night. The darkness and the dangerous flicker of candlelight were an omen only I understood; my heart turning to gold, a magic spell the likes of which no one here could replicate.

At the door of the ballroom, Jude swayed into my path, a glass of maroon wine dangling from his fingers. The matte black of his suit swallowed the light, but his shirt had the shine and colour of a new scar, pink and raw against his white skin. Whatever true wounds he was wearing were rippling shadows at the bottom of a deep, deep pool of alcohol.

"Listen. Petal—"

"Jude, I do not have the words to express how little I care about your stupid half-baked plot," I said. "Or your orgy."

He blinked slowly and tried to focus on my face. Then he decided to say the brilliant thing he had prepared anyway. "Just because you're so unfun."

"Okay."

I stepped around him, then turned back. "You can have the house," I said. "And the company. And you can throw Daddy the pretentious, shamanic beach funeral of your dreams. Slaughter a goat, dance under the full moon, burn him on a pyre, I don't care. But whatever you do with him, do it with me too. Keep us together."

"Wait. Where are you going?" he said, which I think was a drunken amalgam of every question he had.

"Don't let my mother throw my funeral. Or *come* to my funeral. In fact, definitely do the goat-slaughter thing for me too—she'll hate that.

Do you understand? I'm making you my next of kin or my executor or whatever. Hang on, let's get a witness. I want to write this down."

His hand closed tightly around my wrist before I could dart off to find someone. When I turned to look at him, something in his gaze had cleared. "What are you going to do?" he said. And then, lamely: ". . . Don't."

I know "don't kill yourself" isn't the most heartfelt expression of affection a person can make, but when it came to Jude and me, the bar was in hell. That's the only explanation for why my stomach twisted when he said it.

"It's done, petal," I said, my voice excessively bright. My grip tightened on the feeling I'd had only moments before, a sense of peace and victory.

The vertical line in the bridge of Jude's nose appeared as his brows came down. He looked the way he had aged seven, doing long division after he'd missed six months of school. I suppose impending doom changes a person, because I took pity.

"I'm cursed, I'm going to be dead at midnight, there's no cure," I said in a rush. "It was my mother, and I doubt you could prove it, but if you'd get a kick out of telling the police anyway, then go ahead. Maybe it'll cause her some problems."

I'd stopped sounding believable somewhere in the middle. Jude regarded me over the rim of his glass as he tipped wine down his throat like it was water.

"Your mother cursed you."

"Yes."

"Why?"

"To make me take *Immortality* tonight, but also because she's a succubus."

He snorted a laugh, and then schooled his face back into passivity when he remembered it was me who had spoken and that I was, as previously established, unfun.

"How long have you known about the blood?" I said.

Jude did a theatrical double take and looked around, but we were too far from anyone to be overheard. "We're not allowed to mention that."

"Who told you? It was Hunter, right?" He shook his head and took another swallow of wine. "What's the matter with you? Don't you *care?*"

He looked hurt, and deeply alarmed that I was still on the subject. The documents everyone had signed in their meetings swore them to silence, even among each other. That's why there'd been no risk of me learning something from somebody before Mum intended. And of course, who would want to be the first to allude to the murder pact they were all making?

Me, it turned out.

"What do you want to hear, petal?" said Jude. "Do you want the sound bites from the speech I got? That people die every day without it even benefiting anyone? They vacate their shitty, miserable lives and they're better for it? That it's natural to want to live? That there's nothing more human than chasing immortality? Shall I pretend like I lapped it all up and said, sure, one eternal life please? And it sounds disgusting, by the way. I'm a *vegan.*"

"Then why say yes?"

"After everything my life has cost, how do I say no?" He laughed and spread his arms wide. "I don't even like my life." The smile dropped off his face fast, and I think he tried to lean closer, but it was more of a sway. He was inches from my face, but I couldn't pull away. I was transfixed by his nihilism. He tapped an index finger against my temple. "I'll tell you what Hunter told me: sit with it. Let that little brain worm get its little worm jaws around a chunk of you, and soon whichever part of it makes you hate yourself the least will start sounding true. You'll start thinking, maybe if I live long enough, I'll understand why it mattered so much that I lived at all. You'll start thinking, how many years, how many centuries would I have to be here to make all the trouble my life has cost worth it? How many years before my parents' legacy is something other than selfishness and betrayal? How long will it take me to pay for what I took?" He curled his fingers into his shirt above his chest. *He* was what he'd taken; his life, his beating heart. "Once you've gone that far, it's easy. I don't even hate myself more than I did already."

Jude downed the rest of his wine, and a server he had probably asked to follow him around appeared from the shadows to furnish him with another glass. He blurred before my eyes as he threw back half the wine in one long swallow, and I remembered that I was drunk too. The candlelight had turned to flares of gold in the corners of my vision. The band sounded like they were playing underwater.

We had never talked about it, any of it. Aunt Georgia stealing her pregnant sister's husband. My own parents stealing my blood and bone. We had fought a proxy war, our arrows relentless and poison-tipped, but always aimed carefully to the left. I recognised Jude as a mirror, the monster in him the counterpart of my own. If I felt cheated, used, and undervalued, then Jude had to be smug, entitled, ungrateful. He wasn't *this*; he wasn't shame-filled and self-loathing.

As for a debt he felt he'd been shackled to—a debt owed to me? To the universe?—Jude's logic was flawed. For every year he lived and paid, he'd be taking more. More life, more blood. What he owed would only grow.

But he knew that, I think.

"Well, I'm not doing it," I said. "I can't."

"Doing what?"

"I already told you. I'm not taking the tonic."

It took his wine-soaked mind long moments to catch up, but when he did, he was gaping at me in disbelief. "Wait. You weren't kidding, were you? She's done something to you."

I wanted to drag him to a candelabra and show him, but Mum was across the ballroom. "My heart's going to turn to gold," I said around the lump in my throat. "Not long from now. She thought she could force me to take *Immortality* if I was dying, but I can't let her do that to me. So . . . I guess this is goodbye."

A laugh burst from my lips. I had thought I'd love saying that to him. We were so close to it now that Daddy was dead. We could have drifted out of each other's lives like we'd both always wanted. Instead, something was edging closer to snatch me away. I could feel it boring a hole in my back with eyes like coal.

"No." Jude shook his head. "We have to take the tonic."

"You do, maybe," I said, remembering Mum's words: everyone had to be complicit. For all Jude's rationalising, he might not have a choice.

He was swaying dangerously close again, threatening to take me with him if he fell. His eyes moved like he was trying to look into each of mine but couldn't focus. "*We* both do. You and me."

"What do you mean?"

He didn't answer right away, like he expected the pieces to fall into place. How he thought I could ever predict what he said next, I'll never know.

"I don't want to be immortal alone."

He looked into his wine; he was probably counting how many glasses had made him this honest. "Jesus, what a miserable fucking existence that would be. You probably didn't notice, but you and the succubus are the only family I have left. And you're so awful, but what am I supposed to do? I can't just . . . find people and love them. I've tried, and I can never believe in it, because people can just leave. And if they don't leave, they can die. We're not promised love from anyone, me even less than most—that's been made abundantly clear. And maybe I could have children, but you can't make people and force them to love you when they didn't even choose to be here. I'm not an idiot; I'm not going to hope for some future happy family like that'll fix me. Fuck, I'm drunk, I'm not making any sense. What I'm trying to say is, I know I can't have love, but I can have blood, right? I just—" He snatched my hand and forced it under the collar of his shirt, where he pressed it over his tattoo. "I just want to be tethered to *something*. And I don't want it to be her."

My fingers met the raised scar tissue where a venous access port had once carried my stem cells to his bloodstream, felt the bone beneath. We could inherit Maddock trillions, the Maddock name, but we both had Cabot bones, sharp and narrow. I stared at his hand pressed over mine, at the edges of the flowers inked beneath my palm. A tattoo over his port, another over the scar on my hip. I felt sick, the kind of sick

I'd been when I heard about Daddy's stroke, and so heavy I thought I might slump to the ground. I missed anger; if I couldn't summon it for my mother, surely I could summon it for Jude. The bane of my existence. The only thing I had.

We were only connected for a moment before he threw my hand off.

"And if any of that made it sound like I don't absolutely hate you, I do."

I couldn't hear this. I was supposed to be dead soon—the resolve had been so sweet, so empowering—and now Jude of all people was chipping away at it. "You don't need me," I said in protest. "You're depressed right now, but in a few weeks—"

"Do you even know why I wanted to stop you getting the company?" he cut in. "Why I've been so mean to you our entire lives?"

"Because you loathe me," I said, impatient.

"Yeah. I do." His glare was dark and cruel. "You cost me the thing I wanted most in the world, so I tried to pay it back." He said each of his next words slowly, forcefully, like they were supposed to mean something. "I have always been paying it back."

The thought of me having cost Jude a thing was so rich I laughed. "And what exactly have *I* cost *you*?"

"A sister."

The smile dropped from my face.

"You have no idea how my parents raised me to see you. The only thing either of them was ever sorry for in their whole fucking lives was that they couldn't pay you back. And you made it incredibly clear that I couldn't either."

Scrabbling for anything that felt like control of the conversation, I said, "What I meant to say about the transplant—"

"I'm not talking about the *fucking transplant,*" said Jude, eyes rolling so hard his whole head went round with them. "I'm talking about all of it. Your mother was pissed that I existed and so you were too. She infected you with all her bitterness and you ate it right up." He gestured to himself with his hands on his chest. "Meanwhile, all *I* hear is that I have to be patient with Valentina, she's from a broken home, be nice to her, Jude, even when she says she hates you, she's practically your twin, how *special*. Could *you* have done it? Would you have turned the other cheek? You don't get it. You would have been my hero if it wasn't for your fundamentally despicable character."

He giggled, entertained by his own scathing wit, then seemed to remember we were talking about my imminent demise. "But you're still, unfortunately, my only sister." He made a face. "And my only cousin. And if you're gone, and my parents are gone, and my best friend in the world is Roman fucking Astor—"

Jude's voice cracked and his eyes turned glassy. I flinched away from the risk of seeing him cry, but by some well-practised trick, his tears didn't fall. "Then I don't care about anything anymore."

"You're just mourning," I said weakly, but a truth was hammering its way through my denial, as ugly and real as all our scar tissue: that the wedge between us wasn't Daddy, or the transplant, or the complete family neither of us had. It was me. It had always been me. *I* could have been Jude's complete family and he could have been mine, but I'd cast him as the ultimate symbol of my abandonment and he'd given as good as he got in retribution.

But his best was only convincing to me because I was telling a different story, one in which Jude was the aggressor and I was only defending myself. In truth, the signs had always been there. The taste of his hatred, transmuted from a dozen other feelings he wished to bury. The way he sometimes seemed to forget to look at me like I was something he'd scraped off his shoe. It was a performance, just like my impression of Daddy. It was a skin to keep him from getting hurt by abandonment.

My abandonment.

The realisation hollowed me out and swept the ground from under me. My only recourse was to cling harder to what had felt right only minutes before.

"She is holding death over me to get her way," I said very slowly, breathing the word *death* when I couldn't get my throat to form the sound. "I can't let her."

"You're being ridiculous."

"I know."

"This isn't Shakespeare, Valentina." He'd slipped back into a comfortingly venomous tone, spoiled by the only use of my name I had ever heard from his lips. "The crowd aren't going to break into applause, you're just going to be dead. *Dead*."

"Stop saying that."

"Why? Because you hadn't thought that far ahead? Because you're hell-bent on punishing her? Be real."

I didn't say anything. The eyes of death on my back were scalding me, and he was right: I was afraid to look over my shoulder. It didn't matter. Whether I was thinking of the look on Mum's face when I turned down the tonic or what came after, the end result was the same.

"Alright, well, I'm doing it too."

I blinked stupidly as Jude downed a second glass of wine. "Doing what?"

"Dying. Tonight." He put a finger and thumb in his mouth and whistled for his server, who appeared with a tray.

"Jude—"

"Don't try to change my mind," he said, taking two glasses from the server and handing me neither. "If you don't have to be immortal with her, then neither do I."

He stood straighter. He was energised.

"Are you talking about suicide?"

"Aren't *you*?" He jabbed a wineglass in my direction, and a few drops of maroon liquid splattered on the marble. "You have a choice and you've made it. Don't I get one too?"

I was regretting letting the server walk off with the wine; four fingers of whiskey had worked their way through my system aggressively fast.

"I can't let you do this," I said weakly, aware that I had no argument he would hear and no way of physically stopping him. I would be dead when my heart turned to gold.

"I'm going to see if I can do it with drink," he said, coming up for air from his latest glass.

That was something of a comfort. Perhaps he would get too drunk to function or remember, then get his sense back when he sobered up. Maybe this was the drunken, grieving fancy of the self-pitying, over-dramatic boy he always was.

And maybe this was real.

Jude was stumbling away from me. He narrowly missed the corner of one of the pools as he walked into the centre of the ballroom, where he raised both glasses in the air and bellowed above the music: "To the first night of the rest of our lives!"

His friends screamed his toast in a drunken chorus and some of the dancers stopped to cheer him, but Jude locked eyes with my mother. Loathe to react, she watched him, bored, but I could see from the flicker of her eyes in my direction that she saw a glimmer of it too: the dark thing at Jude's back. The pit he'd been circling since my father's stroke.

Jude downed the last of another glass of wine and sent it to the floor, where it shattered to dust.

25

I left the ballroom and didn't stop.

The night was balmy, but my breath trembled as if my lungs were choking down needle-sharp air. It sounded like the unsteady shiver of the wind as it shook the forest. I chased that sound across the lawn until it drowned out the music and the lights of Fable were dulled by a sea of silver moonlight. Ribbons of cloud raced overhead. I was far more sober than I'd planned on being for the rest of my short life, but the thought of more alcohol made me sick. I wanted nothing but air; no thoughts, no pain, no ticking clock. I wanted to drown here.

Jude was right: I didn't win if the collateral was my life. Without the loping rhythm of the music driving my vindictiveness, that was suddenly obvious. I wasn't the untouchable fortress of a girl whose face I was wearing. I was helpless and afraid, a perpetual victim of my mother's will. I couldn't bear to let myself be used this way.

But neither could I bear to die. Forty otherwise decent people had found reasons to say yes to immortal life. Perhaps a different kernel of truth had sprouted in each of them, a key to a singular lock. For my father, I knew that he'd been powerless against the instinct to protect Jude and me, the children he had once almost lost in a canon of young death. My mother believed in a right to immortality, hers and ours, because she'd bested death with her genius; she'd earned it. And Jude had tricked himself into believing he had unsettled debts too costly to repay with his mortal years.

My choice wasn't the same as theirs. I didn't have the luxury of deciding that a long, full life wasn't enough. It was Jude's own refrain that had seeped into the cracks of my resolve: this was suicide, immediate and avoidable, and with consequences for more than just my mother. Did I have to live or kill Jude? It was his own decision if he wanted to follow me into oblivion, but I would have caused his death, like Mum was causing mine.

And what of the other reasons? Was the wrongness of it a given—so spectacular, so large that it didn't need acknowledging—or a thing that hadn't yet crossed my mind? In the heat of my fury, foiling my mother had been the stronger incentive. Vengeance had been my only goal. Now I wondered if I was even capable of taking a life to sustain my own, not once but routinely, forever. There was no involving the help, no one to obtain fresh blood for me, unless—and I'm ashamed of how quickly I turned the concern into a problem to be solved—we took turns. Jude and me. Roman too, since his grudging loyalty seemed to have bought him a part in the conspiracy. I could even ally with Charlotte under the circumstances, if she was to be let in. Mum had said there were new products in the works that would make it easy; easy meant quick, and quick meant less suffering. That was something.

But aside from the strength of my stomach, could I live with myself? I was so close to everything I had ever wanted, an imperviousness to harm that even Daddy had never achieved. The thought of him rent fissures in my heart. I had always been able to forgive him anything: the affair, the favouritism. Even the truth that *he* had struck the bargain that saw Mum claim Head Magician failed to land with the full weight of the blow—hadn't he only been treating with his ex-wife in the only language he believed she'd understand? And for the life of his son—how could I hate him for that?

I had betrayed myself. I knew every one of his offences against me, but I held myself at a distance from them, always one step removed from condemning him. One step removed from understanding who he really was. But this conspiracy of blood. I'd tried to cast him as a hero, but the instant Mum told me he hadn't blinked, I believed her. For what was not Oscar Maddock's for the taking? It was what I revered about him, what I wanted for myself. But I was trying to emulate a man I had never allowed myself to see clearly. He might not have been the architect of this horror, but it was still to his design. The real Oscar Maddock was ruthless. He had never slowed at a moral crossroads on the way to what he wanted.

He had blood in his teeth.

If I was to be anything like him, I needed to bury both my conscience and my fury and find a pitilessness to match my father's. There was no power to be had for those who wouldn't take it from another.

So perhaps there was no power for me.

I was bent double, heaving, when a twig cracked behind me. I'd known he would come. When Luc appeared at my shoulder, my first thought was that nothing mattered less. My second was that I could spend my final hour consumed by him and thinking of nothing at all. The wind whipped at his hair, obscuring his eyes.

"I'm sorry, Valentina. For what she did to you."

"How much did you hear?" He didn't answer. "You were already in the office when we arrived, weren't you? What were you doing?"

The open loggia door. The dark gathering in the corners of the room. Shadows that separated and folded back together, even when the mirror showed me there was no one there.

"I saw the briefcase arrive," said Luc. "I had a hunch that it contained the first vials of *Immortality*."

"And you were trying to steal it?"

"More or less. But it was never left alone like I hoped."

"That's a shame for you."

The moonlight carved a ghost of a smile. "I'm hoping I'll have another chance."

He was uncannily relaxed for someone confessing subterfuge, his hands in his pockets, weight on one leg. The topography of him emerged and vanished again as clouds raced across the moon.

"Did you know about the blood?"

He looked at the ground. "Knowing isn't the same as *knowing*. I'd seen no evidence. But I knew."

He had said this would be a choice; I just hadn't understood the one I was making. "How?"

"There's always a cost. People like your father always find someone to pay it."

"And me?" His brow creased in question. "Do you think we're alike, him and me?"

"Of course you are. Nobody made it to this party without being like him." The wind tugged at his words so that they came at me at an odd angle, disembodied. "But how alike you are is still up to you, Valentina. You have a choice. So what is it that you want?"

"I want to hear her screaming as I die, but"—hateful tears swelled then escaped down my cheeks—"I don't want to die. But I don't want to let her win. I would rather peel my own skin off than let her win."

"So it's revenge?" Luc's voice was soft, barely a whisper above the breeze. "Is that what you want?"

I shook my head. "I thought I was going to murder whoever had done this, but she's my mother."

His calm was still there, but it had taken on a harder edge, a focus, as he took something from his inside jacket pocket. "I'm not talking about killing her," he said as he held it out to me.

Despite the warmth of the breeze, I shivered. It was upon us now, the secret of Luc's that had become so unimportant to me in the shadow of everything else, which perhaps was not so unimportant after all.

It was his invitation. I turned it over, but there was nothing to tell me what it meant.

"Try holding it up to the moon," he said. "You might be able to see."

I did as he said. The moon was a faint light behind translucent ropes of cloud, but as they shifted, it shone through the thin places where ink had been meticulously removed. The ghosts of four dead words glowed white beneath the new ones: a name, impossible to decipher, and a demonym.

OF HOUSE THEBES.

I lowered the card and the etched letters disappeared, but the truth of them trembled through me.

"This invite was never for you."

"Not me specifically, but it was for my house. I'm sure Oscar would have agreed that our Maker had a right to send a representative in her place."

"Masquerading as someone he's not?" I snapped, my voice staccato with emotion. "Are you an Ancestor? Someone important?"

"No," he said, but it dangled like an incomplete sentence. *Not yet.*

"Is this how Mariah and Randolph knew you? Did you slaughter their kin?"

His face betrayed nothing. "Some of them."

"Ah." I thrust the invitation at him as I was taken back to our conversation with House Gothenburg. I'd felt like I was missing something, but the message had never been for me. "This afternoon in the library. Mariah and Randolph were snatching at their opportunity to tell Thebes they surrendered. They'd been trying to talk to you since yesterday morning when they approached us in the woods."

Luc's smile was half grimace. "Gothenburg have been trying to talk to us for much longer than that. They accepted your invitation knowing House Thebes would be here too, one way or another, and they'd get their audience. They came here contrite. And they didn't tell anyone that Randolph had seen someone sneaking around on Friday night because they believed it was me," said Luc. And why they had hesitated but eventually confessed. Luc's presence had been the permission they needed.

"Why did they leave?" I asked him again.

"Because I told them House Gothenburg could earn their atonement if they did." He shifted his weight, and I sensed the edge of something. "We don't owe each other loyalty." He gave me a meaningful look, and I knew he understood what the night before in the cave had been for me: nothing but an exploration of the limits of my fears, and the things they turned into when I brushed up against them. "But if our desires aligned again, could you and I be allies?"

I hesitated. The wind made ice-cold tracks of my drying tears. "What are you talking about?"

Luc took my hand. "Come with me."

We crossed the lawn back towards the house. Clouds continued to race overhead, sometimes occulting the moon, and in those intervals of darkness, shapes seemed to move at the edges of the gardens. In the spaces where security guards bearing torches should have walked, there was darkness and cracking branches, the rustle and scuff of gravel.

He led us around the house to the front door. There had been a pair of guards outside when I'd come from the ballroom; they were gone. Luc and I stood just inside the threshold and looked out at the night. The growing wind whipped the lines of cypress trees framing the drive and swept into the house, where it snuffed out candles and plunged the entrance hall into darkness.

"What are we doing?"

"Just wait."

He looked at me, assessing, the shadows deep in the hollows of his cheeks, his eyes empty sockets. Whatever leap Luc was about to make in trusting me, there would be no going back. Good. I was ready to do something we couldn't undo. I was hungry for carnage.

I wasn't disappointed.

For a long while, nothing happened. The strings from the ballroom fought with the moaning of the draught we had let in. Then the figures began filtering through the greenery towards us. It was difficult to put my finger on what was wrong about the way they moved. It was almost too graceful, both too slow and too fast. It was stillness, if stillness could walk. I took a step towards the door, mingled curiosity and horror tugging at me, but Luc wrapped a hand around my arm.

"Don't cross the threshold," he said.

When the vampires were all gathered in the driveway, they must have numbered fifty or more. Their ordinariness disturbed me. They'd all been people once: tall, short, fat, thin, light- and dark-skinned. People who wore glasses and bore scars, who'd been young and old. They were all those things still, in death. Normal, and yet here they were gathered in the drive of Fable, and none of the dozen security guards who patrolled the grounds had sounded the alarm. There was no one out there to see them anymore.

House Thebes had come to Fable.

"What are they doing here?" I sounded breathless, but whether it was from fear or something else, I could no longer tell.

"That depends."

"On what?"

"On you." Luc moved so he was standing in front of me. "On what you want to happen next."

In defence of what I did, he only told me some of it.

26

By the time I was alone, the open door and the blustering night had taken out every candle in the entrance hall but one. I twisted it free of its holder and held it close to the tip of my finger; close enough that its heat scalded, and its light revealed the tracery of gold. The gilding ran over every inch of my skin from my hand to my shoulder, where it disappeared under the sleeve of my T-shirt. I tugged the neckline down and found it again on my chest, where the pattern of veins was blossoming over my heart.

It would be moments now.

In the ballroom, the strings fell silent. Mum's words into a microphone rung clearly through the entrance hall, but a heavy stone tumbled inside me until I thought I would be sick, and they were nothing but noise. That was my cue.

"Ah! There she is," Mum said as I stepped into the ballroom.

As one, the guests turned their heads to look at me. From the far end of the room, I couldn't see their smiles, but I had the impression of teeth. Sharpened. Salivating.

"Valentina, come and join us."

It was like walking to the gallows. Someone had kept the candles burning in here despite the draught I'd let in, and flames shivered at the edges of my vision as I passed each cluster. I imagined them shrinking away from me as they caught the scent of death.

"As I was saying," Mum continued from the stage, "it has been our great delight to host you all at Fable. I don't think it's too soon to declare the weekend a spectacular success. I know that Oscar, whose recovery we continue to hope for"—here she paused, and I wondered if she was recalling that Daddy's murder remained unsolved—"would be thrilled to know that every one of you will be embracing *Immortality*."

She threw up her arms, and the guests broke into shouts of triumph and applause. They were rabid, their delight echoing off the ceiling like the baying of wild dogs. Heads turned to their neighbours, smiles trembling with relief. Each had made a leap, had spoken aloud a deplorable and blood-soaked desire, and been validated. No one here would judge them; they would only bury each other's wrongdoing with their own. I spotted Charlotte, as perplexed as she had been that first night by a frenzy she wasn't part of, but this time hunger shone in her eyes. *Immortality* was in her grasp now, but I doubted if she knew yet that it would cost her soul.

As I reached the midpoint of the ballroom, servers in black streamed in from either side, tangling me in their procession. Each of them held a small silver tray between both hands, bearing a single vial of red tonic with a name tag—my elbows almost toppled several of them as I fought my way through. Wearing fixed smiles, the servers wove through the crowd to their respective guests and stood before them to present the vials.

"Not just yet, please," said Mum to the crowd, a knowing in her voice. I could see it in all of them now, the compact—freshly made—glowing in their eyes as they looked into the faces of those ignorant staff and smiled. How soon after taking the tonic would the new immortals need to feed? The servers moved to line the walls of the ballroom and a beastly dread raked claws through my stomach. *Leave,* I wanted to scream. *Get as far away from here as you can.*

My mother summoned me forward with an impatient gesture, but it did nothing to hurry me, because that was the precise moment my heart seized. With a hand to my chest I stumbled, gasping.

"Valentina!"

The broken cry silenced the crowd. Enthusiasm turned to concern as they followed her line of sight. I took another step, sucking in air, the alien twinge in my chest receding. That wasn't it; it wasn't over, not yet. I was still here.

"Get my daughter. Bring her onstage," she barked. As a couple of the event staff came towards me, she shot a smile at the audience and forced a saleswoman's composure. "Valentina's going to join me for our toast. Please give her a hand."

The guests ate what they were fed, and cheering filled the ballroom. I was living in a play, or on a game show with cue cards for the audience. As I was steered onto the stage, I scanned their faces in search of Jude.

He was leaning against the wall, a little way from the audience and half hidden behind the folds of dark velvet hanging from the balcony above him. His cheek was to the stone, and one fist was clutching the front of his shirt as if he could hold himself up. He was gone, so drunk that he stared right through me, but he was clinging to some conviction. It was in the hard set of his features: the will to see his plan realised. The will to die.

Beside me, Mum was talking again, but her voice faded to nonsense sounds as another spasm gripped my heart, this one stronger than the last. My mind went blank, all thoughts turning to eels, too fast and slick to grasp. I was going to die.

"Mum," I gasped out, and still I recoiled from my own need. Still, I hated the hand that took the vials from her pocket, uncorked them, and placed one in my hand. Candlelight caught the uncanny movement of the liquid inside and made it dance.

"There'll be no spectacle," she was telling the crowd. "No change. Go ahead and claim your immortal lives." She raised her vial in a toast, rushed now, all ceremony abandoned.

Forty vials of *Immortality* were held aloft, but none caught the light like the one Mum held up on the stage, its pearlescent red contents shot through with shades of gold and amber. "To the first night of the rest of our lives."

You think you know who you are. You don't. Until the moment is upon you, you could be a martyr or a traitor to yourself, and no decision you'd come to, nothing you believed yourself to be makes a difference.

No change? I had already changed. I had been given a rare and merciless understanding, one which most are never cursed to learn. I was meeting myself in a moment of perfect crisis. Faced with it, nothing of my former self remained; not the ambition to emulate one parent nor the will to spite the other. I was empty of everything but animal terror, and the pain of a golden fist closing around my heart.

Immortality tasted like the finest champagne. As the first drop touched my lips, my fingers tightened around the vial, greedy, knowing. For a single heartbeat, I had chosen right. There was nothing to fear, no reason to hurt.

Then a mortal scream cut through my peace. Blood drenched my thoughts. My fingers slipped on the vial, and it had shattered at my feet before I knew I'd dropped it. Iridescent red liquid seeped across the stage. My life, studded with glass.

I looked up into my mother's face and saw only bemusement. For a beat, we only stared at each other; then she came back to herself and extended her arm to me, her own vial offered up.

The server behind her plucked it from her fingers.

"What are you doing?" she said weakly. She was so stunned that she did nothing as the woman calmly upturned the vial and tipped the eight-figure contents out onto the stage.

Panic seized her then, if not understanding, and she scoped around until her eyes landed on the event planner at the side of the stage.

"Another vial," she snapped at the helpless woman. "Take anybody's! Get her another vial *this instant*!"

The woman fumbled half-heartedly with her radio, but she wasn't even looking at it. Nor was she looking at us. She stared past the stage to the source of the screaming, which had swelled to a chorus.

A bubble of space had opened in the middle of the ballroom, and in it was a man. Someone from the kitchen, I realised, though at first I hadn't recognised his chef's whites beneath the ruby stains. They soaked one side of his smock, his sleeve, and the hand protruding from it. They were smeared onto his face and his hair, but the worst of it was at his neck. Blood still oozed from between his fingers even as he tried to hold it in his body, even as he leaned heavily to one side and his skin faded to grey and his eyes tried to roll to the back of his head. He shuffled closer, reaching out for help, until he passed out where he stood and fell, face first, into a pool. He landed with a smack and a small tidal wave of water, and floated there, immobile.

Behind him, silhouetted in the towering archway, was Luc. The sharpest of those gathered had seen enough, and they broke away towards the other exits. Others had the thought to down their dose of the tonic, but not a single Moth pulsed to signal the upload of a spell. Judging from their faces, they discovered from the taste something I had suspected from the dullness of the colour: their immortal lives had been swapped out for forgeries, the contents something that wasn't magical at all. The only genuine doses of *Immortality* had been the ones Mum had had in her pocket, earmarked for me and her. Gone.

Whatever chance the bolters believed they had died so very quickly. As one, the black-clad servers who lined the ballroom stepped forward to hem them in and block the exits. Others emerged on the balconies and from the shadowed doorways. I hadn't recognised their faces, swathed as they'd been in night. Not to mention I'd never been great at looking staff in the face.

Not one vampire anymore, but dozens.

Fable had rejected me when I'd tried to welcome Luc in, but the circumstances had changed, he'd said. My father was dead, and no one had inherited the house—but that didn't mean no one could let a vampire in. After all, the spirit of a bit of magic mattered more than the rule. He had a feeling. He wanted me to try it.

And I had. Why wouldn't I? The place was crawling with monsters already.

"*Security!*" Mum screamed at no one. Her hand was around my arm, nails digging in, but whether she was scared for me or knew that I'd done this, I didn't know. Her head snapped to the event planner by the stage again, but any command died on her lips. The woman was in the grip of a librarian-looking man, bespectacled and reedy. Needle-like canines protruded from his gums and hovered inches from her temple, and she was sobbing for her life.

We had moved past the futile screaming, and a whimpering, pregnant hush followed Luc as he approached the stage. When he passed into the candlelight, my first foolish thought was that someone had shot him in the chest. Blood stained his shirtfront and his hands and dripped onto the marble. A sharp streak of it glistened wet on the side of his neck, where he had wiped some away, but his face was unfanged and unbloodied. The expression, however, was one I'd never seen on him before. It was flawlessly cold. His eyes were steel, inanimate and emotionless. A messy sort of dread thrilled through me, turning me liquid and loose.

Mum pointed a shaking finger at him. "End this *now*! Or so help me god, I will fucking destroy you."

Some people had the idea to skirt around Luc and out into the entrance hall, which, to my surprise, worked for a time; the vampires let them go. Half a dozen guests believed they'd won their freedom before the screaming started up again from somewhere beyond the ballroom. I looked along the balconies and between the hangings. Yes, I had definitely let in more vampires than this.

"Dr. Cabot," said Luc calmly as he produced a handkerchief to wipe the blood from his hands. "Your security are all dead. The expensive *Shield* spells you all turn on when you're out among the rabble are all disabled and your phones have been destroyed. There are more than four dozen vampires inside Fable. You've already lost. This will go a lot more smoothly if you accept that."

A particularly blood-curdling scream rose from one of the adjoining rooms, and an echo of it shuddered through the guests.

"More smoothly for *you*," Luc amended.

"This is preposterous!" bellowed Eric Burton-Shaw, and everyone turned grateful eyes on him. Finally, someone important was complaining, and in wonderfully indignant tones. "How *dare* you treat us like this? I demand—"

A small vampire with a sleek chestnut bob kicked him behind the knee, and he went down hard. I winced to see an old man injured, even if he *had* made a pact to drink human blood.

The moment was the distraction Graham Crain needed to discover his own truest self, his perfect crisis reaction. And credit to him—he charged at Luc with an iron candelabra raised above him like a spear.

A black-clad figure came out of nowhere and barrelled into him. Luc never flinched as the man, vampire, and candelabra went crashing to the floor. The vampire landed on top, wrenched Graham's head up by the shirt collar, and smashed it into the floor. He drew teeth, exposed Graham's neck and—

He didn't bite him. It was more of a slicing, the clinical and swift end of an animal in an abattoir. Only when the blood was gushing loudly onto the marble did he put his face to the flow, as if he were drinking from a fountain. Athena made a noise as her fiancé twitched, just one in a cacophony of many as the frenzy began. Several people elected to simply pass out and were dragged into the shadows, from which emanated more wet, tearing noises. Zazie found herself backed against a wall, but as the vampire elongated her teeth and tilted them close to her victim's skin, the fear in Zazie's eyes melted away. A drugged serenity came over her as maw met flesh; she melted into the embrace. As if they could sense willing blood, two more vampires descended. Soon, Zazie lay supine, teeth in her neck, her wrist, her thigh, a look of bliss on her face as her eyes rolled to the back of her head and she shuddered a final time.

Charlotte would not go so gently. While most of the guests could think only to cower, run, or use their companions as human shields, Charlotte smashed two wineglasses against a wall and wielded the jagged stems. The cowering set were easy enough prey that this got her as far as the northern door, backing around the carnage, makeshift weapons brandished at arms' length. The closest she came to fighting for her life was when a vampire, pursuing a sprinting Roman Astor, came at her on a collision course. He was within inches of grasping a handful of Roman's collar when one of the ballroom's infinity pools appeared beneath his toe and he went crashing in. Roman careened to a halt, dripping wet, eyes locked with Charlotte's in a kind of mutual catatonia. Seconds passed, Roman's chance to shout a warning about the vampire at Charlotte's back stretching leisurely on. At first it seemed like shock, but slowly, the craven decision to school his face into impassivity settled over him. A sharp tug on Charlotte's hair, and she hit the ground. She seemed to be unconscious, stunned at least, when the vampire sunk teeth into her. I imagined Roman reassuring himself of her lack of suffering as he slipped around the feeding vampire and disappeared.

I watched it all with a kind of detached fascination. I had asked so few questions when Luc told me what he wanted me to do, wrapped up as I was in my own lust for vengeance and my imminent demise. They were putting an end to *Immortality,* he'd told me. Yes, some people might die. Yes, he could promise me Jude and Mum wouldn't come to harm. But the event staff? *Our* staff? I wish I could say I asked those questions. At the time, I didn't care about any of it. He could have told me everyone in that damn house would stain the marble with their blood, and I'd have let him at it.

Because if you hadn't already noticed, it was only my own blood I couldn't bear. Other people's was not such an issue.

"What do you want?" Mum was shouting over the carnage, apparently ready to cooperate. "What do you want?"

Luc gestured to some of his associates, and most of the remaining people were chased out of the ballroom. I spotted Hunter among them, sprinting as vampires took Mum and me from the stage.

"She stays," said Luc to the librarian with the captive event planner. "Bring the magicians."

As I stepped over an exsanguinated Eric Burton-Shaw—sweet man, bloodsucker—*the magicians* were produced from a side door. My freshest memory of Dr. Chandler and Dr. Yang—if not the most recent—was the pair of them in the bathroom at my mother's house, one with his hands bracing my head as I struggled and the other forcibly wiping my memories. So it gave me a jolt of pleasure to see them both bound and gagged, the former sobbing and moaning, the latter fighting and bloody, but with a broken nose instead of teeth marks. Their new Moths hovered by their shoulders; they'd been bribes, I realised. The magicians' silence had been bought with immortal lives of their own.

Chandler and Yang were forced to the floor in front of the stage. Beside them was Jude, half unconscious by his own hand and not sobering up with adrenaline. It was unclear if he had even noticed the violence. How much wine had he had? What else had he taken? Mum and the event planner joined them, and half a dozen vampires ringed the hostages. I was allowed to stand, which made me feel important even if it was the moment it became clear whose side I was on. Snot fell into the cavern of the event planner's mouth as it hung open. Dr. Yang was trying to murder me with his eyes, but such a look is deeply unthreatening from someone with a sock taped into their mouth.

My mother had no rage for me at all. Her eyes were hollow; her mouth trembled. It was disconcerting, and I feared I was about to discover she had yet another betrayal up her sleeve, before I remembered I was meant to be dying. My hand flew to my chest, over my still-beating heart. The painful spasms had ended.

I searched for a candelabra and found one still standing next to the stage. With my back to everyone, I wiggled a candle from its setting and exposed the skin over my sternum to the light.

No gold.

Moving the flame to below my sleeve garnered the same results. My murderous heart thudded in my ears as I traced the candlelight across my skin, moving down until a metallic gleam caught the light. The gilding was still there, I was still cursed, but somehow it had retreated to an inch or so above my elbow.

The *Immortality* tonic, spilled across the stage, was letting off a faint, shimmering mist as it evaporated.

"Dr. Cabot," said Luc. He stood over my mother, but as I turned, his gaze slid away from me like he had been watching. "I need you to tell me if anyone not in this room could replicate your formula for *Immortality*."

Mum's face slackened. "Replicate it?"

"Once it's destroyed."

She made a sound halfway between a whimper and a laugh. I watched the realisation creep, inch by inch, into her eyes. "It's my life's work."

"We will start killing your family and your colleagues," said Luc softly, "if you don't answer my questions. Could anyone else replicate your formula?"

While Mum tried to think of a way out, I tried to catch his eye. He had promised not to hurt Jude.

And now he wouldn't look at me. The first flutter of panic brushed up against my apathy.

"Dr. Cabot."

"No one," she said weakly, her shoulders dropping. "No one else knows how."

"I don't believe you."

"It was highly sensitive work. The three of us did it alone."

"You're lying."

"Fuck you."

Luc raised his eyebrows and scanned the hostages. He pointed at the event planner. "Let's start with her."

The woman was hauled, screaming, away from the others, and I realised she'd been kept back for this reason: to die. I'd been keeping my fear in a locked box in the corner of my mind, but another tumbler shifted into place as the vampires shoved her at Luc and she landed in his arms. He cracked his neck as his lips parted, and I looked away. I had found a tendril of sheer horror still free inside me, and it wouldn't let me look at Luc, the monster, as he held her, almost passionately, by the neck and sunk his teeth into her.

Her screaming cut off with a gasp, and in rushed every other sound of terror still echoing through the marble halls. Mum managed to limit herself to a single note of horrified shock. Dr. Chandler renewed moaning into his gag. Jude had rested his head against the stage and closed his eyes. He might have been sleeping.

Only when I heard the body thump to the floor did I dare to look. Luc was wiping the blood from his face. The event planner's dead eyes bored into mine accusingly.

"I'll ask you again," Luc said, breathless but once more unencumbered by fangs, "who else could replicate *Immortality?*"

"For god's sake, *no one.*"

I think I saw Luc's gaze hover over Jude before he turned to me. At his nod, one of them grabbed me by the back of the neck. There was just time for my vision to blacken at the edges—and not enough to remember Luc still couldn't bite me, or that he could hurt me in a thousand other ways—before Mum started screaming a mostly incoherent stream of pleas.

"I'll tell you, I'll tell you." She reached a hand beseechingly to Luc. "Fiona Farmer . . . Simon Paolini. Josh Robson. They helped in the early stages. They know how to make the tonic."

The vampire towering at my shoulder did not let go of my neck. Luc stared hard at my mother, then went to her colleagues and ripped the tape from their mouths. Both gagged as the socks came out.

"Is that true?" he asked them.

"Yes," gasped Dr. Chandler. "Yes. Yes."

Dr. Yang hesitated. Mum chanced an imploring glance at him, which Luc caught. He laughed softly.

"You're lying." He crooked a finger in my direction. "Bring her here."

I was propelled roughly into him. He turned his back on my mother as he sunk a hand into my hair, so that she might believe he'd drawn his teeth as he leaned close.

"Please! Please!" she cried in a voice I had never heard from her. It rent the atmosphere like a clap of thunder. "I lied. There's no one, please, I'm telling the truth."

Luc drew back. "Is she telling the truth?" he murmured.

"I think so," I gasped. "Jude needs a doctor."

"He'll be taken care of. I promise."

He released me.

"Alright, Dr. Cabot. I believe you. Do you believe *me* when I tell you, if you lie again, your daughter dies?"

"Yes," she replied through gritted teeth.

"Good. How many copies of the report are there, and where are they?"

She rubbed her brow with trembling fingers. "One is ash in my daughter's bathtub." Luc glanced my way, and I nodded that this was true. "I'm told Hunter Corcoran burned his yesterday. And a third in my office at the laboratory. That's it."

"And you hold the security override code for the Mythos laboratory. What is it?" She hesitated. Luc went on, voice soft as velvet. "Valentina will bleed to death before the police get here. And you know who she'll blame for it."

The gall of him. Never mind the accuracy.

Mum gave up the code.

Luc sent some of his associates to check for the ashes of the reports, and the ballroom enjoyed a moment of peace, the slaughter happening elsewhere a distant backing track. It was interrupted by a scuffle on one of the balconies, followed by a body being dropped into a pool. I couldn't see whose. The water that spread over the floor towards us was ribboned with blood. I skirted around it and knelt next to Jude. I shook his shoulder, and his head wobbled.

"Hey, petal."

He cracked an eye open. It seemed to land on everything else in the ballroom before he saw me. "It's almost time," he slurred.

"No, it's not. I'm not dying." I kept my voice to a whisper. Mum didn't deserve to know. "At least not right now. So you can sober up. This suicide pact I never agreed to is off, okay?"

"Nice try." He closed his eye again. "You can't stop this, petal. I took some pills too."

"Jude? How much did you take?"

He didn't hear me. He'd lost consciousness. The last of my family was going to fade away in the middle of a massacre for no good reason. I shot a look at Luc, who made a placating gesture. I didn't think he was lying to me—at this point, what reason could he have?—but an ominous feeling was settling in my bones.

"Why are you doing any of this?" Mum said wearily.

Luc cracked a smile that curdled swiftly into malice. "You really don't know?"

She shook her head. "We've done nothing to you."

"That's true enough," said Luc. He frowned, like a perplexing thought had just occurred to him. "Tell us then: How long do you think we should wait now that you've taken our magic as your own? How many races should we watch wither and all but die out as you grow more powerful, before we act? Ah, that's right." His voice was dangerously soft. "We're the last ones left."

"Oh, please." Mum sighed. I would have perished at her contemptuous tone, but Luc was unmoved. "You expect us to believe you're afraid of humans? That we're a threat to you?"

"No, Dr. Cabot, not humans," he chuckled. "The rich."

That gave her pause. I was also interested to hear where this was going.

"I imagine Martin Maddock told the witch who sold him her kind's secrets that he was no threat either, but what did he do? He convinced the world that what was stolen was worthless unless they bought it from *him*. He called their magic *crude*. Dangerous. They were driven out by the same people who had turned to them for centuries because of him."

"Stolen," Mum scoffed. "It was a trade. You said so yourself: she *sold* it to him."

"And you treated with House Gothenburg, but they had no right to do so either. If they had bothered to run their scheme to work with you past *us*, they would have been told what they were too young to know: that vampires have been putting down human attempts at immortality for millennia." He bent forward to meet my mother's eye, looming over her like a disapproving schoolmaster. "Did you really think, Dr. Cabot, that you were the first person to investigate vampire venom as the key to immortal life? The first to crack the code? You're only the latest in a long line of people who arrogantly believed they were entitled to more."

Something like heartbreak had cut through my mother's fear and anger and shaken her to her core. Not the first. Not special. She hadn't done what no one before her had managed; she'd done exactly as they had, and she'd fallen the same way too. I watched the realisation play out like the snuffing of a light behind her eyes, and I almost felt pity.

"And we've seen enough of your conquests," Luc went on. "The more you take, the more you think you have a right to take, and the more you want. You subjugate and exploit whomever you can profit from. And now you want to live forever, and you think you can use vampires to do it. You think you can mine us like a resource."

Mum was shaking her head. "We don't need a supply of venom to make the tonic; it was purely for research purposes. There's nothing more we need from vampires."

Luc crouched in front of her, and she shrunk back. "When you're immortal," he said, "and I'm immortal, and you're slaughtering people for their blood, and I'm slaughtering people for their blood, tell me: What will we be to each other? Allied? Quietly coexisting? Will the time come at last to exterminate the vampire race, or will you still fear me enough to let me be?" She didn't answer; perhaps, like me, she couldn't work out what Luc wanted her to say. He grinned. "We like your fear, Dr. Cabot. We like your reverence. We think we'll keep it."

A susurrus of laughter from House Thebes swam through the ballroom. Luc straightened.

"The likes of the Maddocks are satisfied with a hierarchy that sees those below them starve and suffer, as long as they believe they're at the top. But you've grown complacent. You think you've crafted this empire built on magic because no one could stop you. It's time you understood that *we* can."

Mum was shrinking down against the stage as her objections ran dry. For all of Luc's lead-up, this was nothing but predator meets prey, and he was right: we simply hadn't noticed that we were the lesser monsters.

"I confess I'm a little regretful that this has all fallen on you, Dr. Cabot. I would have liked to say all this to your ex-husband. I told him some of it, before I unplugged his life support. I doubt he heard me."

Her gaze snapped to me, wild and accusatory. It was too late for remorse, so I stared her down as if I'd been there.

As if I'd known.

"It sounds like your grievance is with me and Oscar, Mr. Sayle," said Mum. She nodded towards the massacred bodies, the ribbons of viscera. "You would punish all these people because he and I flew too close to the sun?"

Luc gave her an indulgent look. "It's not punishment any more than *Immortality* was your just reward. But you are one small vial away from being untouchable, and we can't allow it. There is a hierarchy to be maintained"—he grinned again, sharp-edged and malign—"and you people are too hungry."

One of Luc's runners returned positively seeped in blood and confirmed he'd found ashes in the garage wastebasket. I wondered who had died showing it to him. I wondered if it was Hunter.

"Good. Deal with those two." Luc nodded in the direction of the stage. Chandler and Yang were dragged away and quickly slaughtered. A vampire clutched the former in a bear hug, his face in the crease of Dr. Chandler's neck as he struggled and bled. I think the vampire was enjoying the man's death, his eyes closed, his faced relaxed in bliss. As soon as Dr. Chandler died, he dropped him to finish bleeding out on the floor. The vampire who killed Dr. Yang didn't even taste him. He nicked an artery in the same way Graham was killed—Graham, whose body still lay prone beside the fallen candelabra—and tossed him into a pool.

When I dragged my eyes away from the undulating surface of the water, below which Dr. Yang was almost done fighting the inevitable, Luc was looking at me like he wanted to say something. Again, a sickening sense of omen engulfed me.

"Uh, Sayle. Is this the kid?"

It was the librarian; he was leaning over Jude, his back to me. Stomach lurching, I came around his side. His cold, dead fingers were pressed to the pulse in Jude's neck.

"He's on his way out," he said.

Jude.

"Shit. Bring him here."

Wait.

The librarian and another vampire hauled Jude upright. Panic clouded my brain and stilled my tongue as I looked from them to Luc, who was shrugging out of his tuxedo jacket. Chestnut Bob produced a knife.

It was my mother who found the words. "What are you doing with him?"

I almost hissed at her. Like she gave a fuck.

"Luc—" I cut in. He gave me that look, the one that told me I didn't understand but he wanted me to. "What are you doing? You promised you wouldn't hurt him."

The vampires were stripping Jude of his jacket too, one supporting the weight of him and the other pulling his arms free.

"I promised you he'd be alright," he gently clarified.

"But—*Jude!*"

The commotion had roused him from total unconsciousness to semi-unconsciousness. His eyes were open but unfocused, and his peerless scowl descended. I tried to get to him, to get them off him—how had he made me this? The little shit, I hated him so much—but one of them caught me around the waist and lifted me off the ground with my own momentum.

I didn't understand. Even as they pulled his sleeve up, as Luc did the same to his own, I didn't understand. Then Luc's canines elongated, and he became a beast. The sight of him consumed me, and for a beat every other fear was shunted to the side. This was the being in whose hands I'd placed all our lives. This was the mouth I had let scorch my skin. I felt my knees give way, but the other vampire had me firmly in his grip.

"Please, Jude. *Fight.*"

But he refused. Something in the dazed and drunken way he looked at me was sorry, but that was all. He dragged his eyes to Luc, who now had him by the wrist, and his mouth curved into a smile for the vampire. "Bottoms up."

Luc was gentle as his teeth pierced Jude just below the elbow. I fought down bile as images of needles and tubes assaulted me, but Jude seemed not to feel it. His eyes were closed again, his head falling back on the shoulder of the vampire holding him, who grasped his jaw.

"Hey," he said, shaking Jude's head.

"*Stop that!*" I screamed. "Leave him alone! *Luc.*"

But Luc wasn't listening. Jude's blood glistened on his lips as he took the knife from the little woman. Without ceremony, he opened a vein in his own wrist. The other vampire still had Jude by the jaw and was trying futilely to wake him.

Time slowed as Luc put his bleeding wrist to Jude's mouth and I finally started to see.

They lowered him to the ground, where he lay without moving. His face was hidden from me by the vampire crouching between us—his Moth too, its light obscured. Luc knelt over him, his own blood dripping from his arm and speckling Jude's shirt. Minutes passed. The sounds of the massacre receded around me until all I could hear was my own ragged breathing. I stared at Jude's legs, one straight, the other bent at the knee and fallen askew. His bleeding arm was thrown carelessly to one side, his palm open, fingers curled in rest. He looked like Graham or Dr. Chandler or Eric Burton-Shaw, scattered, limbs akimbo across the ballroom, and only in noticing this did I understand.

I was about to realise Jude was dead. I could feel it coming; I could almost *see* the spectres of the vampires standing and moving away and his face appearing, pallid and lifeless on the bloodied ballroom floor. His Moth would be gone, winked out like all the others. They were whispering now, urgent things. I think the librarian said something about me, and Luc glanced over, then shook his head. No one was holding me back anymore, but I couldn't make myself take a step. I didn't want to see what I knew was over there.

And then Jude's whole body seized. He made a sound partway between gasping and retching as he drew in breath like he'd been drowning. All of a sudden, I was standing over him, watching him roll onto his side like the drunken idiot he was. Luc stood. The librarian swore in relief. Jude lapsed back into unconsciousness, but his eyes were moving behind his lids. Luc's blood shone on his lips, and disembodied shadows shivered across his body before disappearing. I peered closer; they were coming from within him. With each passing ripple of dark, the pattern of his veins showed black beneath his skin, and he shuddered.

His Moth had vanished forever. On his left cheek, I thought I glimpsed the scar I'd given him in Rio when we were children, risen like a ghost.

I turned to Luc. "You changed him," I said, the flatness of my words belying the blow of the betrayal.

"He was already dying."

I didn't know what I planned to do when I lunged at him. My fingernails caught him on the cheek and scratched, but that was all the damage I managed before the big vampire restrained me. I didn't even draw blood, just scored three marks from ear to clenched jaw.

"You lying shitbag," I spat, struggling against the hands on my arms.

"Valentina, you knew how all this would go," said Luc as Chestnut Bob bandaged his wrist. Any remorse he might have had about misleading me was behind him now. "If you heard me say Jude would live, it's only because that's what served you."

"I don't understand." I'd almost forgotten Mum was there until her voice broke through, and a new wave of rage engulfed me as she looked from Jude to Luc. All the wheedling and negotiating she had for me, for her precious *tonic*, and she'd watched them turn Jude without so much as a squeak. "Why would you do that?"

"He," said Luc, pointing at Jude, "is the new CEO of Mythos."

My mouth popped open in surprise. I think I might even have laughed, which was a relief; it turned out I was still capable of enjoying this.

My mother, by comparison, was about to expire.

"No," she said on a breath. "No, wait—"

"Dr. Cabot, here's what's going to happen." Luc came to me, taking something from his pocket as he did—his lighter, which he flicked open and held up to my skin. "Do you see this? Your handiwork has reversed itself by"—he shone the flame along my arm—"about a day, I'd say, with just a fraction of a dose of *Immortality*." He indicated the stage, where the tonic had evaporated entirely but left a pinkish stain. "Have you produced any more?"

She hesitated, and I could see her doing the calculations, seeking the most advantageous answer. Then her face crumpled, and she relented. "Yes. There's more."

"How many doses?" said Luc.

"Are you going to save her if I tell you?"

Luc flicked his lighter off. "That depends what you mean. I can keep her alive, but it's not a one-time agreement. I need a lot more co-operation from you, Dr. Cabot. Perhaps months of it. If at the end, I'm satisfied that you've done all I've asked, then as a gesture, Valentina can be the only person in the history of the world to live forever."

"You can't seriously mean to . . . to take the company this way," she said. Her shoulders straightened with a final show of confidence. "You'll fail."

"If you mean to warn me about your replication spell," said Luc, "then we both know you're going to give up the password when asked." I shivered as he brushed a thumb across my cheek and down my throat. Mum tried to murder me with a look, but Luc had learned this one from *her* mouth, not mine. "How many doses?"

It wouldn't work. She had already risked my death once, and for a petty revenge stunt. She wouldn't trade everything she had, everything she'd worked for her whole life, for me, the child she hadn't wanted.

But she and I were more complicated than that. She resented my existence and what it made her. She resented that I needed simple things and she'd failed to give them: sympathy, reassurance, a sense of safety in a world full of fear and pain. I think she'd always known that I didn't wish the transplant had never happened; I just wished it had been *different*. And she resented the things I never gave *her*: I wasn't grateful enough for the sacrifices I never asked for; I never made her the hero she imagined she might be to me.

But most of all, she resented that when they all told her I was more important than the work, they were right.

"One hundred doses."

At a gesture from Luc, Jude was hauled to his feet.

"Where?"

She rubbed a hand over her face. "At the lab. I was meant to check them myself after the party, before they went to secure storage."

"Don't let that frustrate you, Dr. Cabot," said Luc. "We can get into your storage facility as easily as we can get into your lab. Get up."

They marched us from the ballroom, Mum with a vampire clutching each arm, Jude being dragged between two of them and paddling his feet like a puppy dreaming of chasing a rabbit, me with Luc's hand on my elbow. The carnage had burned to the embers. There were no more screams for mercy or of terror, but someone was wailing loudly from the dining room. Everyone else was either dead or hiding. We stepped around streaks of blood and viscera, around bodies in every state but fair: dead, dying, wounded. Some of the latter tried to scramble to their feet and run, but the unencumbered members of our entourage caught and killed every single one. There were over a dozen survivors, I learned later—mainly staff—but Luc and his associates needed to leave no witnesses to our capture. In the story they wanted told, my mother and Jude were to have made a clean escape.

I, on the other hand, was dead.

They took us to the garage. It was emptier than it had been that morning; perhaps a third of the vehicles were gone. I wondered if some of the guests had managed to make it this far and escape. Luc stopped before my mother, who in the stark fluorescent light was the colour of chalk. She had vomited at some point; a smear of it was drying on her turtleneck.

As if in insult to her, one of Luc's lackeys was waiting with a fresh shirt, and he stripped out of the bloodstained one. A stain of pink clung to his chest where the caterer's blood had seeped through.

"We have a lot of work ahead of us, Dr. Cabot," he said as he buttoned the replacement. "But if you cooperate fully with selling the controlling share of Mythos to House Thebes and installing your nephew as CEO, you'll see Valentina again when this is over."

She and Jude were marched to one car, I another. It happened so fast that Luc and I were encased in a Mythos Blue glow before I realised that was our goodbye.

27

When the spell faded, we were in a hangar with ragged stone walls and bright fluorescent lights. At one end was a wall of glass facing a corridor of more rough stone. This was the landing bay of the Mythos laboratory, in the hollowed-out mountain of some unknown range. What looked like the missing guests' cars were already here. I peered up at the clusters of cameras mounted on poles across the hangar. Of course: House Thebes needed their pre-approved license plates to get through the first security measure.

"Leave the key on the dash," Luc told our driver.

A shell-shocked silence descended between Luc and I as the vampire got out.

"You killed my father," I said at last. "And left a copycat note. *Oscar Maddock has no heir?*"

"I had to come up with something—I was working on the fly." He ran a hand over his face, irritated—at himself, I thought, and his flawed improvisation. "I couldn't squander the opportunity to make it look like the same person and keep the suspicion off myself entirely. I knew it mattered to you to live up to your father's image. I thought I could plant the seed that what you wanted was yours to claim, that letting House Thebes in would be an act of power." He adjusted the collar of his shirt, buttoned the cuffs. "He didn't feel any pain." After a moment, he added: "He wasn't waking up, Valentina."

"Don't act like it was mercy," I spat. "You killed him so I could inherit Fable and let your little strike team into the house."

"Yes," Luc said, remorseless. "But that doesn't change the facts."

"How did you know it would work? How did you know Fable would recognise me and not Jude?"

"Because you told me your father hadn't written a will. The magic that keeps a vampire from crossing a threshold wouldn't simply fail because it didn't know who held the deed. If Oscar Maddock were to die, it would choose its own successor. I knew instantly it would be you." In his silence, I heard him measuring his words. "House Thebes might have only gotten the invitation to Fable on Monday, but we've been preparing for this opportunity for a long time."

The last of the air squeezed from my lungs. "You've been spying on us."

"Yes. We know everything about you, and Jude, just as we knew everything about your father, minus the missing will." Again, the imperfection in his plan seemed to pain him. "Jude could let a vampire into Fable because it was his childhood home. We believed that meant he'd be given the house in the will. As far as our plan, it was always supposed to be him. But you were too suspicious to let me get close to him. I thought you'd be a problem until you told me there was no legal successor. But there would be a spiritual one, and they would need to be just as hungry as their father. Just as ruthless. You had the power to let House Thebes into Fable because you decided you wanted to," he said.

Fable—mine. The victory was entirely hollow. "And Jude—"

"Is softer than you. I'm sure his soul is black enough, but he's too resigned to his own misery to see the possibilities in tonight's villainy." He shrugged; the dismissiveness stunned me. "You would've got between me and Jude, but your mother threw the two of us together for the weekend. You were the better mark. I did what I had to."

I was seized with the urge to score three claw marks down the other side of his face. A matching pair. "And would you have slept with Jude if you thought it would be him?"

Between the dim interior of the car and my own raging emotions, I was beyond being able to read the look he gave me. "You know I didn't need to sleep with you. What happened between us happened because we both wanted it to."

I recalled his words about eternity, how it had distilled him to nothing but his anger. Looking at him then, I marvelled at how I hadn't seen it in his eyes this entire time. It burned bright enough to scorch me to my core.

"If it's not a no, I'm taking it as a yes."

"I would have done whatever it took, but your own agenda made it a lot easier than I was expecting. When did you realise I turned off your father's life support? Because I noticed you weren't surprised when I said it was me." I stared at the back of the driver's seat and didn't answer. "When did it dawn on you that I had hidden my motives? Because you had none of these questions before you let a horde of vampires in to put down your guests."

"Finding out I'm to be a hostage so House Thebes can coerce my mother has put a downer on this for me. You've ruined it."

"You feel guilty."

"You used me." I felt the words work on my body like a poison. A wave of vertigo rushed over me then receded. "What do *I* have to feel guilty about?"

Luc didn't answer. Across the hangar, half a dozen people I took to be vampires were waiting by the doors to the lobby.

"The override code my mother gave up won't help you. The security measures inside this mountain are immense—your people won't get close enough to input it."

"They're already in."

I turned sharply. Luc nodded to the other cars, enough to hold far more than half a dozen of House Thebes's finest.

"Mythos's security here is four-fifths reliant on cameras and facial recognition. In other words, it protects only against living trespassers. My people walked right up to the security desk, and the system never even knew they were there." He looked at me steadily. "We barely did this. The real culprit is your own hubris."

"How long have you been planning this?"

"Decades," he said, proud and righteous.

I made a sound of disgust at the back of my throat. My fingers wrapped around the door handle.

"Wait." He reached out, but he didn't touch me. I could sense his hesitation before he said: "There's more you need to know."

No was the answer dying to burst from my chest. *No more.* But instead I sat back in my seat and waited.

"*Immortality* needs to be destroyed," he said.

"That was the point of all this, wasn't it?"

"All of it."

My heart gave a juddering beat, as if it sensed danger and was trying to escape its cage. Discovering I was to be a hostage, a victim of a wider plan Luc could pull off only because of me—not to mention what he'd done to Jude—had unleashed the feelings of betrayal I was attacking him with now. But only an hour ago, months of being leverage were months more than I thought I had left.

Now they were gone again. I was back to imminent death.

"You don't need to do this." The words came out in a whisper. "They can't reverse engineer a spell from someone's body."

I didn't know if what I said was true. Either way, Luc wasn't swayed.

"I'm sorry, Valentina."

"You're not."

"These decisions aren't just mine. It's out of my hands."

I pressed my fingers into my eyes. Had I slept at all this weekend? "What does any of it matter anymore?" I said, more to myself than to him. "Jude is undead and he's still going to be CEO over me. The little cretin doesn't even want it. My mother's a murderous harpy and my father is dead." I lowered my hands. "What was supposed to happen to *me* at the end of all this? If I hadn't been cursed, that is."

Luc looked at me pityingly. "A member of your family has helmed the company since it was founded."

"Only a descendent of Martin Maddock can control his magic."

"So said Martin Maddock," Luc said wryly. "Regardless, we decided that keeping a Maddock as CEO would make this look friendlier to the outside world. We'd chosen you, originally. You seemed the less conspicuous choice."

"But thanks to my mother, you couldn't bite me." He nodded. "Jude is a vampire. How do you presume to explain that?"

"We'll say he was the first to take the tonic, but it had some side effects. It's why your mother is stepping down and the product is being cancelled."

"And the massacre?"

Luc shrugged. "Not us. Nobody at Fable knew who I really was aside from you. Common vampires attacked the party and the lab, and the sale to House Thebes is part of a deal in which we also take care of the perpetrators. It's not as if you could do it yourselves." He paused. "I really hoped you and I would save your life this weekend. I mean it."

"To what end?" I scoffed. "It seems you have no use for me and I could only stand in your way."

"I honestly don't know what the end result would have been. Perhaps I would have been ordered to kill you." For a moment, Luc looked out at the hangar, long fingers pensively tapping the armrest. "I want to offer you another option."

"I'm assuming it's truly awful, so no thank you."

He laughed miserably and reached into his jacket. When his hand emerged, in it was a slim black case of the kind that might contain a bracelet or watch. Luc held it in his lap, turning it slowly as he spoke.

"I meant what I said before. You're not that different from your father, though you might think you are. You agonised and you chafed when you found out what you had to do to live, and then perhaps you told yourself the chafing made you a good person. That you'd hurt and kill to survive, but as long as you felt bad about it then it wasn't who you were, it was just a thing you were doing. You could hold it away from yourself, maybe not think about it at all. But you were critically wrong. All that matters is what you do."

"You *kill people*, you condescending bat."

"I am a soulless blight upon this earth. But I'm not a hypocrite. If the doing is what matters, then I'm obligated to give you credit for helping me, regardless of your reasons. So, I'm offering you what you want—a chance to go on existing. You can't be saved, Valentina. Not your life, and not your soul." He held out the case equidistant between us, an invitation to take it. "But you require neither to be like me."

The case felt cold; I don't know if I imagined that. Inside were two things, both fastened against the velvet interior. One was a vial, the contents the dark red of blood. The other was a syringe, the substance inside clear and unknowable.

"I can't give you the immortality you thought you were getting," said Luc. "You're going to die. But you don't have to leave." He pointed to the syringe. "This first. Anywhere on the body, but you need to hit a vein."

The world tilted. I squeezed my arms close to my body.

"Then drink this. All of it. You'll want something else to chase it down."

"I think I might be sick." Saliva flooded my mouth. I drew several deep breaths before the feeling went away. "Why?"

"You should know," he said, nodding at the case. "It's lonely. If my kind lack human compassion, it's not a side effect of our curse, but a thing that happens over time. When I was newly turned, I would choose blood I didn't like the look of. So many do, and we all end up going mad with hunger for a time. Killing someone who can make you laugh, who could be a friend if you'd let them—it's difficult. But the harder you try to avoid it—the more you allow people their humanity—the more every lowlife in every bar starts to look flush with life. Barely born, innocent. If any kill hurts, they all have to, and so we try to smother that part of ourselves." He grimaced. "It's not a slow death. If it's ever really complete, I'm not there yet. So, it's lonely, Valentina.

"And I've tried to make it less so. For a long time I was seeking something hopeless. I didn't outgrow the things I'd wanted as a human man: someone with a kind heart, compassion, warmth. But I can't have someone like that. This curse eats away at you until there's barely anything of the good person left. I would need to love a damned one. Or find company in one, at least. If you choose this, I'd like you to come and find me."

"Are you proposing?"

"I wouldn't dare."

"Good, because you're already about a million miles over the line."

He nodded soberly. "Then I apologise. I only wanted you to know that if you decide to use that, you'll have an ally on the other side."

A part of me wanted to throw the accursed case back in his face, but instead, my fingers tightened around it possessively. "What's going to happen to Jude?"

"He's safe. I promise."

I shook my head. "You're going to use him. But he won't help you."

"What Jude is going through isn't easy. But not long from now, he's going to realise his priorities have changed. His survival instincts are going to get stronger. They need to, for someone to make it through the transition. Their first kill." He looked at the case again. "He'll still know you. And you would both be of House Thebes. You'd still be family."

I didn't want to think about it. I tucked the case into the pocket of my leggings, and we got out of the car. An anaemic-looking vampire with bright red hair to his shoulders approached, two more of them at his back.

"We found something you might want to see," he said to Luc.

As we followed them out of the hangar, Luc pitched his voice low and said, "Stay near me. Remember you're not needed any more. They expect you to be killed, sooner or later."

The lobby was a capacious hollow of raw stone and glossy white. Above, a glass-fronted mezzanine housed the client-facing offices, where consultations for bespoke spells took place. Past them and behind a wall of security gates, an escalator led down. I averted my eyes from the prone body of a receptionist near the front desk as we descended, though he was undoubtedly only a taste of what was to come. The Mythos laboratory operated twenty-four hours a day, partly to cater to clients the world over and partly to obscure its true time zone. There would be other victims in this vampire-riddled mountain.

The laboratory level was less mountain chic. We alighted in a bright white corridor, blue linoleum underfoot. No signs pointed us anywhere or reminded us of protocol; the walls were endless stretches of sterile white, but the vampires had already learned their way around. We were led to the production floor, a double-height room overlooked by an oblong of windows, its clinical sheen blemished with smears of brownish red. Sterile fluorescent light washed its way into every corner, rendering the room dimensionless and unreal. Counters, conveyor rollers, and sleek, unknowable machinery formed rows, in between which four junior magicians lay dead where they'd fallen. A partly finished batch of tonics—*Umbrella*, read the handwritten scrawl on a scrap of tape affixed to a ring binder—was gathered messily at one end of the production line. Someone's hip-hop playlist was still coming through a speaker hooked up to their phone.

Ten or so more vampires were standing around a glass-fronted booth at one end of the production floor, and it was this Luc's comrades wished him to see. They made a space for us as we joined them and peered inside.

There was nothing recognisably magic about its contents whatsoever. All that occupied the booth was a chair, a desktop computer on a counter, and something that looked like an old-fashioned modem or external hard drive, black and slim. A strip along the front glowed a familiar blue, the light wavering and uncannily bright. A laminated sign tacked above the machine read: *Strictly NO food or drink in the control booth*. Next to it, a second read: *Do not touch the source under ANY circumstances! Refer all issues to Dr. Cabot (extension 2800)*.

"Is that it," someone said; almost a question, but their fragile curiosity was throttled at the end by sadness.

That was it. Not a black hole in a vacuum chamber, or a blinding, twinkling light, or even a witch kept comatose so she could bleed into a beaker as needed. It wasn't found three days' walk into the deepest, darkest forest, or down the wrong path at a fork in the road, or at the end of seven circles walked counterclockwise around a mound. Instead, it was something that had once been wondrous, turned by the touch of human hands into another bit of tech. Into a product.

I was the first to step away from the glass, unsettled by a vague feeling of shame.

"Let's get this done," said Luc, the quiet, flat words cutting through a silence I could feel in my lungs.

A second glass booth on the opposite end of the floor enclosed a wall of shelves, some stocked with newly completed spells. The door to the booth was open, a bloody palm print on the biometric lock speaking to a magician's coerced compliance before they died. Luc's people had already retrieved what they came for; on a counter near the storage booth, their contents a translucent red, were five racks of *Immortality* vials.

That was it: five cases of twenty vials each. Billions' worth of Mythos property. The product of a lifetime's worth of obsessive striving.

The redheaded vampire lifted a case above his head, the whites of his eyes showing in his manic glee. "Bye, bye," he said, and sent the case to the floor with a crash. Some of the others whooped and laughed; Luc brought it to a ruthless end.

"Enough," he ordered, his tone brooking no challenge. "You were told how to dispose of it."

As the vampires scrambled to organise themselves, I looked down at the spent vials. Red-toned magic had splattered across the linoleum as the vials had shattered.

One hadn't. It had rolled under a counter and out of sight. I made a sound of disgust and crouched to pull broken glass out of my shoe.

The approved destruction of the tonic involved mixing it with hydrofluoric acid in a plastic bucket, the fate of which I couldn't guess at. I don't think it mattered; the acid would do the job. Luc left two vampires to the work and ordered that everyone else sweep the rest of the mountain. Any work related to *Immortality* had to be found and disposed of.

Luc and I stood in one of the corridors overlooking the production floor and watched vials of *Immortality* being uncorked and added to the tub. Whatever adrenaline I'd had left in my veins had burned away, and my exhaustion felt like I was floating at the base of a colossal wave as it began to crest above me. I didn't know the time, or what happened next, but here we were as Luc got what he'd wanted, and it felt like the end had come.

"Did you know that's all it was?" he asked me after a time. "A box hooked up to a computer?"

I'd been wondering that myself. I had a memory of the production floor, one in which it was vaster and I smaller. To hold my father's hand, I had to reach up past my shoulder; his other hand grasped Jude's. I didn't remember the "source," but was that because it hadn't been shown to me? Or had my young mind overlaid my confusion with something I could understand? Because what my family had accomplished was supposed to be wondrous, a miracle. It was supposed to be the greatest feat in the history of humanity.

"I think I must have chosen to forget," I said weakly.

Luc made no reply to that. A minute later, his phone buzzed in his hand. Our eyes met, and I thought he meant to say something—an apology or a confession; something honest—so I pivoted to face him. But after a moment he said only: "Stay here."

He turned down an adjacent corridor. I could see him through two layers of glass, phone to his ear, still watching the production floor below. Long minutes passed. The sounds of the vampires turning the whole place over—filing cabinets opened with crowbars, locks forced, glass broken—grew distant as they moved through the building. Below, the last of the *Immortality* was poured into the bucket and carried from the room. Luc's phone call went on. And on.

I doubt myself. I doubt the memory of Luc staring down at the empty production floor, never shifting his focus to glance my way. I doubt the belief that he never moved his lips to speak for the entirety of the call, certain I must have filled in this detail later, when I was trying to convince myself he knew what I would do, that he let it happen. I tell myself that perhaps I wasn't in his field of vision; that when I took a step, and then another, and Luc turned his back on the mouth of the corridor, it was a coincidence and not permission. I tell myself that when he asked our driver to leave the key on the dashboard, he wasn't thinking of me.

I slipped past him without a backwards glance, certain that at any moment the illusion that the snare had loosened would vanish. The lab was crawling with vampires, any one of whom might sooner kill me than return me to Luc, but it was too late to fear anything. If one of them caught me sprinting for my life, then I had tried my hardest, and so I ran.

I'd tried to map the lab level in my mind, but my shaky counting of doors passed and turns taken burned up like the air in my lungs as I flew through the corridors. If I only kept moving in the direction we'd come, eventually I would recognise something. It was a fragile hope, but my flight felt like a dream, one in which my fears lay behind me, and something gauzy and ephemeral waited ahead.

Every third or fourth turn was a dead end, every corridor a narrowing tunnel of white and blue—anonymous, identical. As my anxiety ratcheted up, the sounds of activity elsewhere in the mountain chased me, creeping ever closer, always behind. At last, a noise like wheels or dragging. Something large. I gasped with relief as I realised what it was: the escalators, just out of view at the end of the corridor.

But voices were approaching the next corner. I doubled back and ducked through an open doorway, where I pressed myself into the dark and peered down the corridor. Three vampires, their uncanny movements stirring an instinctive fear that convinced me, for a heartbeat, that they were coming this way. Instead, they vanished towards the escalators, their voices echoing as they rose into the lobby.

My hope shrivelled. I couldn't go up there. Even if the vampires continued up a level, or into one of the corridors coming off the lobby, I couldn't step out onto that vast open floor. There would be nowhere to hide. But there had to be other avenues that led to the hangar—how were pallets of products taken up there?

There was no hope back the way I'd come; I would only run into the vampires combing their way through the lab from the production floor. Instead, I retraced my steps to the previous junction then headed the opposite way, hoping I could approach the sector from behind and come across an exit before I got there.

The longer I searched, the less air seemed to reach my lungs, and the more the mountain pressed down on me. A smothering warmth coated my skin. I imagined a colossal being watching me from above, a rat in a maze with no exit, scrabbling desperately for the thin shreds of her life. I pushed open yet another door leading to what I assumed would be a dead end and found myself in a corridor slightly grimier than the others, its walls a decaying cream. And down one side, bins. Bins had to be disposed of, and the only way in and out of the mountain was the hangar.

Heart in my throat, I turned the corner to find an industrial elevator and, next to it, the door to a stairwell. I had no courage left to attempt patient stealth or to delay the truth of what I'd find at the top. I pounded up the metal steps and flew through the first set of doors at the top.

Ancient strip lights hummed to life. Dumpsters, and in place of the clinical white of the laboratory level, a concrete floor and the bare stone interior of the mountain. A sweet odour of rot filled the room; a suggestion of stickiness. At the far end was a ventilated service door that opened with a push bar, a clean white light emanating from between the ventilation slats.

The hangar. My knees almost gave way. With a hand braced against the stone, I hauled myself towards the service door and peered through the slats. We had arrived in an SUV, indistinguishable from the fifty to sixty others in the hangar—the fleet that shuttled Mythos's staff to and from the mountain, plus the vehicles stolen from Fable's garage. From my imprecise memory of parking, there were half a dozen cars it could have been, and only one with a key on the dashboard.

And the hangar wasn't empty. My stomach dropped out of me as one black-clad conspirator, then a second, appeared between the vehicles near the doors to the lobby. They moved without purpose, faces scanning the space. Guards. Either Luc hadn't planned for my "escape" at all, or these two had missed their orders to be searching the mountain.

Either way, I was on my own.

I sunk into a crouch and gave myself the length of one full breath to panic. As my lungs compressed, I pushed the bar handle as gently as I could. At any moment, a vampire could look my way and there'd be nothing I could do. Haste was my only friend, so when the door was opened just wide enough for me to slip through I did, still keeping low, and pushed it gently closed behind me.

I half ran, half crawled towards the cars, unable to bring myself to look up or locate the pair on guard. Only when I was shielded by the bumper of the nearest SUV did I peer under the car. The vampires were pacing slowly, still near the doors. I hadn't been seen.

Always in a crouch, I wove a path through the vehicles, peering into each SUV when the coast was clear. With each empty dash, my hope took on water, its hull cracking and the weight pulling me down. Maybe I was in the wrong part of the hangar. Maybe I was looking for one of the dozens upon dozens of other SUVS scattered throughout.

Then, like magic, I found it.

The driver's door opened with a soft click, but in a cavern of stone, the gentlest sound echoed. I felt the guards' attention turn my way before I saw them—two heads snapping to find me.

"Hey!"

The bellow rattled my bones. As the vampires started running, I climbed into the car and slammed the door shut. For one mindless moment, I didn't believe I knew how to start the car or send it anywhere. But that was panic talking, and I did not have moments to spare. The vampires were coming, so I pressed the button for the engine, and the car roared to life. The display winked on. Another second more, and they would be on me. I punched a random destination from the recently used list, and in a flash of blue, I was gone.

Epilogue

When the police arrived at Fable, the vampires were already gone. It was Fran who eventually summoned help. Shut up as she was in her soundproof apartment, the massacre escaped her notice and she the massacre's, until—suitcase packed and tears stifled—she emerged to leave for her brother's. The security guard she stumbled across on the way to her car would have put paid to her plan, of course, even if he'd been alive, because nobody had been allowed to leave. In the end, Fran never had to.

My mother and Jude were the only survivors who could speak to Luc's motive or shed light on who had betrayed us. Neither ever did. The incident was described in a statement signed by them both as an "act of terror," the maleficent will of a singular cult figure and his following. He was not connected to the noble vampire houses, who uniformly condemned him, House Thebes and House Gothenburg included.

Claudia Cabot, incapacitated by grief at the loss of her daughter and ruined by the failures of her *Immortality* tonic when administered to her nephew, became a recluse. Two months after the incident, a representative for Jude announced that his aunt had handed the reins of the company to him; he was accepting the role of CEO, just as Luc had said he would. In a move that stunned the world, he also sold his controlling share of Mythos to House Thebes. Magic belonged to the magical once more. I don't think much is asked of Jude in his new role. He's spotted sometimes, strolling a beach in Iceland under a stormy sky, or watching the stars from a rooftop in some far-off city. Still taking long vacations but going out less. Roman is no longer at his side, but I'm sure he's found a way to survive yet again.

Shortly after my mother retired, the news broke that she had taken her own life. I'd been anticipating the end of her usefulness for some time, and amidst my complicated grief, I've come to believe that it was justice. Perhaps that's hypocritical of the girl who had the tonic to her lips. At the time, I'd been fighting to survive with bloody, broken nails. But what did eternity look like for me now? Did it last longer than ten days, when I either fed on someone or perished? Would it end in a jail cell, me opening my own veins with nails and teeth in rabid hunger? Immortality was no longer a matter of conscience but one of opportunity. Without magic, without power, what it took to survive was simply insurmountable.

I'd thought I'd been so very far from power, when really the tips of my fingers were brushing the ceiling. The same had been true of all of us. When it came to the reasons we accepted the cost of our immortal lives, I had imagined existential truths and tiny lies; enticing kernels of self-deception. But the reasons were simpler and all the same: we did it because we could. Money made us different from other people and that was all there was to it. If any among us believed the rest of humanity was lesser than, or that our fortunes were owed to us for our virtues, that was incidental. Eternity was for sale, so we bought it.

The choice didn't feel so simple in the aftermath. On a roadside in the middle of nowhere, a day after the massacre, I held a lighter to my skin and traced the veins of gold all the way to my sternum. The single drop of *Immortality* hadn't stopped the spread, only set it back, and now the curse was advancing on my heart a second time. With the unstoppered vial in my hand, I waited until the first spasm racked my heart, until I was forced to dive one way or the other out of death's path. To the right, swallow down the whole vial and claim immortality. To the left, wet my lips with another drop, live a little longer, and never have the full dose to save me.

Four months have passed, and I am still cursed to die. I have bought myself the time to come to terms with that. Less than a third of the vial remains; I estimate I have five or six weeks left.

Which is fine. I don't want this life. At first, the novelty of it was something. I was fuelled by a series of simple and essential tasks, each a thing I'd never done before. Trade a multimillion *Swift*-enabled SUV for anything with wheels (find the shadiest person you can to take it off your hands, because criminals don't talk). Pawn all the jewellery you have with you—a pair of small diamond studs, a gold bracelet, two gold rings. Drive a thousand miles to an anonymous city and rent the cheapest studio apartment. Get a desperate pizza place to hire you as a delivery driver for cash in hand, then prove you can be reliable. Dye your hair a colour Valentina Maddock would sooner kill herself than wear: mousy brown, my natural shade. I still get told I look like her, only with a blunter nose and squarer jaw. My Moth is stuck on *Incognito*. No one ever really suspects.

There were other things I'd never done before. Buy clothes from a thrift shop. Use a public library to access the internet. Eat unclaimed pizza three meals a day. Shiver at night.

When desolation confronts me with why I'm living like this, I remind myself of Luc's trap. I could have escaped the lab and gone straight to the police or the press. I could have confessed what really happened at Fable. They would have given me back my life and my name—minus my parents and with blood staining the marble, but perhaps I could have lived. At the very least, I'd have died in comfort.

But vampires are cruel, even to their own. Come the next ritual culling, none could have earned more cruelty and harmed House Thebes more than the one who'd told Valentina Maddock everything and then let her escape; who let their secrets unravel, and with them a conspiracy decades in the making. I didn't care about Luc, but cullings razed lineages in their entirety. If he died, Jude went with him.

And by blood or bone, Jude's life was mine to save.

If Luc had meant to let me go, it was with the knowledge that I could never do a thing to incriminate House Thebes, and that included being alive. But there was a path still open to me, and it would not be an easy one to walk if Valentina Maddock came back from the dead. As the days pass, I wonder if I had a second purpose in choosing this hard and anonymous life; if, after all, my fear of leaving this world was still stronger than any good I could claim.

And I am so afraid.

But I don't think I'm alone. When the first frost sweeps into town, I come back to my apartment—where black mould blossoms around the window frame and the electric hums maddeningly—and a package is waiting for me on the welcome mat. I assume it's for a neighbour, until I am standing over it and staring down at my name—my real name. Dizziness washes over me, a dozen almost-realities—theft, unwanted questions, the media—paling beside the solid truth that somebody knows I'm here. With a glance behind me, I bundle the package inside.

It's a winter coat, down-filled and waterproof, five times the protection of the thin, synthetic puffer with the fraying stitches that I'd been hesitating over at the thrift store. I don't sleep that night, despite being warm for the first time since summer.

A paranoia sets in, so strong and constant it becomes a physical sickness. I ache from tensing, feel faint from shortness of breath, begin to decay with the exhaustion of readiness. I am haunted. A creak on the stair, followed by a silence as hot as held breath. A figure across the street whose reflection I can't find in the glass when I stop under the awning of a hardware store in the rain—gone when I turn around. The single window in my apartment looks out on a concrete block wall, grey in the daylight and Mythos Blue at night, when a streetlight casts a comforting, moon-tinged glow. Cats and rats and stacks of rubbish from the Chinese restaurant downstairs tell me a story in shadow puppets. Only when someone walks past the alley does true darkness fall, a moment's worth and then gone again.

The first time someone stops there, holding back the light for long minutes, I lie still on the couch that becomes a bed and stare at the darkened ceiling. I am a child again, kept safe from the dark and the things that lurk there only by self-paralysis. I've grown good at it since the coat arrived. The depleted vial of *Immortality,* tucked in the dresser drawer, is a smoking gun sizzling in my awareness. After what feels like hours, blue light slides across the wall and leaks in through the window. There is no sound.

For three consecutive nights, there is a visitor in the alley. On the fourth, the anticipation is the pain, and my breathing eases only when his shadow descends. On the fifth night, I'm sitting on the couch, my blankets still piled on the arm, when it happens. I get up and go to the window.

He's a silhouette, backlit and featureless, but yes, he's watching; his head is tilted towards the window. The glowing tip of a cigarette flares, and smoke blurs his edges. Despite it all, dread doesn't come. All I feel is less alone.

And so we fall into a routine. I get home from work in the small hours, grease-stained and another sunset closer to the end. I shower and wash my hair if I have any shampoo. I let a single drop of *Immortality* hit my tongue, then check the gilding has receded with a lighter. When I crawl into bed, I am clutching a slim, black case retrieved from the same drawer in which I keep the tonic, and I hold it in a fist under my pillow. I'm exhausted—in body, in spirit—but nothing can compel me to sleep until darkness falls and the vampire comes.

Acknowledgements

I started this book in May 2022 and spent the rest of that year writing it wrong. In January 2023, I began again from scratch with something that contained the seed of what it could be, buried deep in only adequate soil. For eighteen months, I came back to that version to tend and prune and graft until, at last, I could see what I'd grown. It was harder than I'd thought writing a book could be. Most days, I had only the faintest grasp of what I was doing and why. I clung instead to an email from my agent, sent back when I'd pitched her the idea, which said, in all caps, OH MY GOD. YOU HAVE TO WRITE THIS BOOK. So thank you first to Zoë Plant, for your enthusiasm, your patience, and your uncanny ability to see where I'm headed even when I can't. You're the best cheerleader and advocate an author could ask for.

Thank you to my US agent, Jenny Bent—your expertise has been life-changing—Victoria Cappello, and the entire TBA team, including my foreign rights agent Emma Lagarde, Martha Perotto-Wills, and Aminah Amjad.

To my editors: Thank you, thank you, thank you, Julia Elliott. I'm blown away by the amount of thoughtful attention you gave to every question and crossroads. This book is twice what it was when it landed on your desk. To Calah Singleton, whose opening line the day we met was 'I love you', I want you to know how often your enthusiasm for my work warms my heart. I love you too! Thank you also to Natasha Bardon for your passionate advocacy.

The William Morrow village: Isabella Ogbolumani, Brian Moore, Nancy Singer, Lisa Glover, Marie Rossi, Erin Merlo, Emily Fisher, Jessica Williams, Emily Krump, Jennifer Hart, Emily Dansky, Beatrice Jason, and Liate Stehlik. Thank you to my copyeditor Kathleen Cook, and Zach Meyer for your beautiful cover illustration.

The HarperVoyager village: Chloe Gough, Sam Willis, Catherine Perks, Toby James, Emily Chan, Bec Gillies, Maud Davies, and Robyn Watts.

My own village: Mum, Dad, Sam, Ellie, Paolo, James. Sue, Kevin, and Lorna. My friends and family, all of you, who have listened, politely baffled, as I explain rounds of edits and years still to wait until publication. You are too many to name. Not to mention the community of fellow authors who have commiserated and celebrated, exchanged notes and experiences, schemed and shared. I am grateful for all of you.

And finally, Jack. I know I haven't dedicated a book to you yet, but they're actually all for you. Don't make a big thing of it.

About the Author

Hannah Mathewson is the author of two YA fantasy novels, *Witherward* and *Wayward*. She was born in Cambridge and graduated from the University of East Anglia with a BA in film and television. She lives in Oxfordshire. *The Age of Blood and Magic* is her adult debut.